QUAKE CHASER...

Suddenly, the landscape churned around Vallon. The map became a seething mass of tormented earth, of landscape rising and falling in waves, of earth exploding upwards. Steam and geysers blew up houses and cities. The force threw her back in her chair. An attack. It had to be.

Vallon grabbed for the change but it was impossible to grasp. Too large, too powerful, and from too many directions at once. That didn't make sense—

[Hold the cities and towns. Form a barrier.] She screamed at the L.A. and New York desk agents and felt them add their strength to the fight, but something dark rose out of the east.

It slammed into her like a tsunami into a sandcastle. Seared cinnamon and burned almond and pomegranate assaulted her nose, and suddenly she was drowned in caustic Change. She floundered for purchase, fought for her feet, but the Change lifted her up and tossed her.

She slammed into her body and into the back of the desk's chair. The desk wavered above the map and the air stank of ozone so thick it hurt to breathe as she hauled herself forward and over her console. The entire map vibrated with shock waves. Her head filled with agent voices demanding to know what was going on.

"Shut up. Just shut up. I'm working on it."

No blasted Change was going to stop Vallon Drake from what needed to be done. She -reached- back into the earth and sped eastward again, prepared to do battle.

BOOKS BY THE AUTHOR

***The Cartographer Universe* series:**
The Warden of Power

The Cartographer's Daughter

Afterburn
Aftershock
Aftermath

Terra Incognita
Terra Infirma
Terra Nueva

Also by the Author
Mutable Things
Emberstone
Ice Dragon

Written as Karen L. McKee
Ashes and Light
Shades of Moonlight
Judas Kiss
Second Spring
A Different Nightmusic

AFTERSHOCK

Karen L. Abrahamson

Contains a coupon for a free download of the e-book version.

Dedicated to the Seattle/Vancouver Big Book crew who always
provide a compass.

This world is but canvas to our imaginations.
Henry David Thoreau, Civil Disobedience (1849)

CHAPTER 1 —THE DRAGONFLY DESK

The dragonfly desk hung in the ozone-scented air of the main American Geological Survey map room, its elongated, movable stanchion joining the bulbous desk to the floor like the seat in a carnival Octopus ride. Unlike the Octopus ride, there was no carnival atmosphere, no lights, no families, no laughter—only silence that hummed in Vallon Drake's ears. The desk's motor, however, hummed up through the metal seat that she sat in, and directly into her spine as if the damned chair vibrated her bones apart at the cellular level. As if she were falling apart when she had just put herself back together enough to come back to work.

She'd thought she'd be coming home to family.

Instead it was like entering an enemy camp.

And that was enough of that kind of thinking. Even if being on the desk was the most thankless, difficult job at American Geological Survey headquarters. The desk only emphasized the empty, hollow feeling that seemed to grow like a cancer in her chest. She toggled the controls and the desk swooped low, out over the infernal map pit in the center of the room. Heated metal tinged the air and she pulled her cardigan a little tighter around her neck, because apparently she'd forgotten just how cool it could get up close to the ceiling, with the incessant air conditioning blowing down past the fluorescent lights. It might be August outside, but in here she needed a parka. Or a turtleneck, at least. Darned engineers who'd designed the map hadn't thought about the people who had to work with it. Instead, they used the air conditioning to manage the map's heat buildup that could quickly turn the room into a sauna.

The map room was an empty, cavernous affair, now that the AGS agents' peripheral desks had been relocated into a separate room in the AGS building. The floor around the map pit seemed perilously empty and the high ceiling seemed to echo with the lost voices of AGS agents.

Or their ghosts. With all the deaths, there had to be ghosts floating around. Of course, if she were a ghost, hanging around the AGS map room was about the last thing she'd do. Unless she'd decided to come back and terrorize the AGS's new management.

Actually, that might be fun, given that they already saw her as a problem child, even after she'd almost died saving their asses during her last little adventure.

The map lay below her, a blue-green-brown marvel of modern technology. Its surface was a fine membrane of cells that had the tensile strength to hold up a person and the delicacy to form whatever landscape the desk might happen to be looking at. It also was sensitive enough to the living landscape that the desk agent could see imminent Change as it simmered beneath the surface. Right now it held a Pacific-Northwest-from-space kind of view that included Washington, Oregon, Idaho, and half of British Columbia, too.

She sat back in her chair. Strange. Usually the desk kept its observations south of the forty ninth parallel. Her fingers flicked to the computer keys to bring the map back to American coordinates, but a flicker on the Canadian part of the map stopped her. Something was happening along the coastline of British Columbia. The map features trembled as they always did when under the influence of significant Change. She stopped. It wasn't really her business, but darn it, Change shouldn't be happening anywhere, and this massive a Change couldn't just be an accident that came out of someone's dreams.

In fact, it would take more Gift than most AGS agents possessed. That size of change, and maybe it could be....

A low, warm flush ran through her body. Xavier? Was it him? Was he here? The records of Xavier de Varga said he had often entered the U.S. from Canada. Could it be the mysterious stranger who had terrified her at first, but who had proved to be her more-than-friend had actually returned? Damn man hadn't shown his face since the Murdoch thing was over, and she'd been left hanging the last four months, waiting.

Well, I see you, Mister. And I'm coming for you.

She stabbed the coordinates and the map readjusted, the fine membrane shivering in a series of small waves that stilled into a view of a long Canadian fiord and a harbor—or the harbor it was becoming. She -reached- and her awareness slipped over the intervening landscape, and the ozone-and-ether stink of Change soured her nose. The map landscape shimmered as if the nanites that worked in the map couldn't decide whether to be the trees that still stood there, or the metal tanks and pipelines that flickered into existence along the waterfront. The essence of the trees flowed out of the pine and spruce and became the metal pipes that cut back through trees that wisped away like smoke, and around the town eastward, the landscape reshaped. The Change had a metallic under taste of copper, not the scent of incense she knew as Xavier.

So it wasn't him.

She almost pulled back, disappointed, but something about the place was familiar. It had been in the news. The town had to be Kitimat, and the pipeline that crawled across the shifting landscape had to be the Northern Gateway project that planned to have oil supertankers ply the western Canadian coastline on their way to China. The Canadian government must have gotten tired of all the protests and decided to simply put the pipeline and harbor in place. There'd been talk of doing something similar in the Midwest with the Keystone XL pipeline, but Gleason had refused, citing the AGS mandate and the secret U.S. legislation to maintain the landscape. But once the Canadian changes were in place long enough, the population would simply accept that they had always been there and the change would be fixed. Until then, though, there were going to be some pretty tired Canadian Gifted holding this change in place.

She sat back, shaking her head. The Gift wasn't meant to be used like that; otherwise, there'd be no solid world to hold onto. The AGS's total mandate was to hold America secure against just such attempts to Change the landscape to one party's advantage. Heck, if terrorists ever got hold of the Gift, they could wreak havoc without an agency like the AGS to intervene.

She touched the computer console to bring the view back to Washington and Oregon. The new map wavered in the eastern sector as if it couldn't quite find its form. Odd.

She -reached- into the map to steady it, but something interfered, like different wavelengths clashing.

That made no sense. The map was a closed environment except for its sensory connections to the landscape.

She -reached- further, her hands flying over the computer console. There were no plans for large Gifted activities in Washington that she'd been briefed on. A whiff of ozone and lightning tanged the air, and that shouldn't be there, either. Something was happening. Her finger hovered above the radio call-button that would send an alert to all field agents.

Which was where she should be, instead of cooped up in this damned desk.

Where was the change? Nothing in Seattle, though small ripples ran through the map like water over ice. Nothing in Yakima or Wenatchee. She touched a button and the map expanded her viewpoint. Not the neck of Idaho, either, or Montana, though the ripples in the landscape were worse there. They became more intense the farther east she went, and the map shimmied dizzyingly below her.

What the hell was going on?

Vallon yanked her gaze back from the map and felt the earth's slight tremor like a deeper shiver up her spine. Whatever it was, it was hellishly big to be outside Washington and Oregon and still so clearly felt. Change on a large scale and—

The room jerked. Jerked again and then settled into a steady shudder that set Vallon's teeth rattling. Not huge, probably most people wouldn't even feel it, but here on the desk and above the map, the vibrations cut through her concentration.

Quake, and a big one. *Where?*

Her fingers flew over the keyboard as she broadened her search. Yellowstone wasn't coming alive, thank God. The San Andreas hadn't unzipped—the California Station would have been all over that. She -reached- out through the earth, past where the Yellowstone doomsday volcano still slumbered.

[*Where?*] She sent to the desk agents in L.A. and New York, the two main stations to Seattle's headquarters. Instant awareness flooded into her, one chalky mint and the other salted like seaweed. Halston and Yamamoto. In both those locations were maps similar to hers, except they lacked the capacity to go farther afield than the continental US.

[*There.*] Halston and Yamamoto fed her readings and she triangulated through the growing vibrations.

She followed the station lines toward their point of intersection, seeking, reaching. What was the source? What was happening?

Suddenly, the landscape churned around her. The map became a seething mass of tormented earth, of landscape rising and falling in waves, of earth exploding upwards. Steam and geysers blew up houses and cities. The force threw her back in her chair. An attack. It had to be.

Her hand slammed down on the large red emergency button on the left of the desk and she -reached- for the earth, for the tormented soil, for the houses, the towns, the cities that were wisping away. She would not let it happen. This was American soil, and she and the AGS were here to make sure shit like this didn't happen.

She grabbed for the change but it was impossible to grasp. Too large, too powerful, and from too many directions at once. *That didn't make sense—*

[*Hold the cities and towns. Form a barrier.*] She screamed at the L.A. and New York desk agents and felt them add their strength to the fight, but something dark rose out of the east. She stopped, trying to comprehend what she saw. A wave of Change. It grew as it neared.

Large, so large her brain could not comprehend it. It made her want to cover her head and run. Instead she reached out for it, would break it apart.

It slammed into her like a tsunami into a sandcastle. Seared cinnamon and burned almond and pomegranate assaulted her nose, and suddenly she was drowned in caustic Change. She floundered for purchase, fought for her feet, but the Change lifted her up and tossed her.

She slammed into her body and into the back of the desk's chair. The desk wavered above the map and the air stank of ozone so thick it hurt to breathe as she hauled herself forward and over her console. The entire map vibrated with shock waves. Her head filled with agent voices demanding to know what was going on.

"Shut up. Just shut up. I'm working on it."

No blasted Change was going to stop Vallon Drake from what needed to be done. She -reached- back into the earth and sped eastward again, prepared to do battle.

The Coastal Range and the Rockies wisped away one moment and thrust up taller the next. Denver fell and grew larger than it had ever been. She sped across the great plains, now an inland ocean, now not, the stink of ozone so powerful she could barely breathe. There! There another wave crashed outwards toward her and she drew on the earth's rose-scented ley lines to feed into the landscape and hold it against Change. The new wave came on, eating away the landscape, wiping away everything, and leaving disaster in its wake. She held where she was as the wave grew. As it devoured everything and seemed to reach to the heavens as it met her. But she was not allowing it to go any further. The western landscape would hold with her. It would. She linked with the ley lines that ran like veins through the earth, but here, in the plains, they ran deep so that they pulsed like a lost lover's remembered heartbeat. Much harder to feed her strength from something so difficult to access.

The wave crashed down like a mountain. Power and Change crisped her innards. A churning sea drowned her in overpowering fermented pomegranate, almond, and cinnamon. Who? Who would do such a thing? The power ripped her loose from the ley lines. She tumbled across the landscape. The Change seared like acid and then—was gone—disappeared as if it had never been except for a faint whiff of almonds.

Vallon gasped and slumped back into her body, the reek of cinnamon and almonds filling a huge burned-out place inside her. The map undulated as if some leviathan moved under the surface. But the ripples ceased and the map returned to normal. The room was normal, but so cold she might never be warm again, and the stink of ozone and ether were so thick her stomach churned. She fought to steady her breath and the hollow, empty feeling.

"What the hell was that, Drake?"

"What's going on?"

"The whole flipping city winked out for a moment."

"Vallon?"

"Vallon?"

"Vallon?"

Voices clamored in her headset.

"Just be quiet a moment. I'm trying to think," she muttered and tried to slow her heart's thunderous racing. What had just happened? So hard to think with the fluorescent light stabbing her eyes, and she wanted to stuff her hands in her ears to stop the noise. She yanked the headset off her head and dropped it on the seat beside her, her body throbbing with all the sensitivities that came with afterburn.

"Drake! Drake, get the damned desk down here, right now!"

The deep voice thundered into her poor injured brain. Chief Gleason never did have much sympathy for agents, even when they were suffering from afterburn. Correction, Deputy Chief, since the new management stepped in, though it didn't seem to have affected his attitude.

"Drake? Do you hear me?"

She stirred in the desk and managed a nod, though movement sent fierce red bolts of pain right into her brain. She slid her hand across the curved console because she didn't think she could lift it, touched the down button, then sagged back in her chair and kept her eyes shut against the vertigo that came as the desk swooped across the map and settled against its floor mooring. She didn't move. It felt like her innards might just fall out of her eyes, or what was left of her could just disappear into the chasm of emptiness inside her. Shadows shifted around her—probably agents who had responded to her hitting the emergency button, but she couldn't be sure.

A hand fell on her arm and she almost cried out at the surge of heat and awareness that came from the Gifted touch.

"Damn it all to hell, Drake! Warn a man when you've got afterburn. Gloves! I need gloves here." And then someone had her by the shoulders and half-lifted her out of the desk console and stood her on unsteady feet. "Here. Drink this."

A cold, mint-scented bottle was thrust into her hand. She stood there wavering, trying to understand how this had happened *when she hadn't done anything. She hadn't had a chance.*

"Would you drink the inhibitor before you fall down?" The growl of Gleason's voice cut through her questions. She brought the bottle to her mouth and let the cool, cool liquid pour down her throat. It would help for a short time. Hopefully give her enough time to give her report before she collapsed.

Cool poured into the raging heat in her limbs. It filled her up like water, slowly working towards her head. She staggered back a step as the cold completed washing over her and opened her eyes just a slit.

Wrinkled blue suit, white shirt, and striped tie that hung too loose on a bony frame in front of her. Not like the usually neat and tidy Gleason at all. She followed the tie upwards to its neat oxford knot, and then higher, past the wrinkled neck to the cadaverous face that peered down at her through intense dark eyes over a roman nose that seemed to inhabit most of his face. His bald head reflected the fluorescent lights and his body radiated the scent of squeaky clean. Of course, all that intensity meant she probably wasn't going to be able to find a corner, curl up, and either die or sleep.

"Report, Drake."

Oh, yeah. So much for concern for her. That was Gleason.

"Something happened, Sir. Change. Eastward. I had to triangulate using L.A. and New York." She felt everyone around her still. "That's not the worst of it, Sir. It was huge. Massive."

"We felt it."

Of course they would have. Anyone with the Gift would. She paused to gather her thoughts, but the clack of crisp footfalls on the map room's tile floors made her want to curl up with her hands over her head. Her sensitivity to light and sound had never been this bad before. What the heck was wrong with her?

"Gleason. What is going on here? Report."

Her heart sank. Just what she didn't need. It was bad enough having to deal with Gleason, but he at least understood what it meant to be Gifted and knew the horrible debilitation of afterburn. But this was the new Chief, Amundson, and his oh-so-perfect white-blonde hair and pale eyes and his school-perfect diction. He was the new boy in town and he was all about pissing contests to see who had the biggest one. He also didn't give sweet 'f'-all about the Gift or how it worked, given he didn't have a lick of Gifted blood in his Teutonic body. The sick taste of bile rose up her throat. She turned away, back to the desk to steady herself, and keep her head down. Let Gleason deal with him. Just let her go home. Better still, let her find Xavier and deal with the afterburn in the most pleasurable of ways.

"Well?" Amundson demanded.

She felt his gaze on her and how he stiffened when he recognized her. Yup, there was no love lost between her and the new Chief, ever since she'd eluded him during the Murdoch affair.

"It seems our Agent Drake had to deal with an earthquake. As you can tell, it has hit her quite hard."

What the…? No simple earthquake would do this to her. Not to *her*. What was Gleason thinking?

She opened her eyes in time to see Gleason's bony six-foot-four frame step between her and Wolf Amundson and then ease the new AGS Chief away.

Gleason lowered his head down to Amundson's slightly shorter blonde one. "This is her *first day* back to work. If I'd known she was still so weak, I would not have allowed her to return; and I certainly wouldn't have put her on the desk."

"*You* would not have allowed it?"

Gleason seemed to freeze. There was a hole in the murmurs of the agents in the room, and then Gleason inhaled and looked at the other man. "I know you wanted all agents back to work, but I am still in charge of administrative matters such as illness leaves."

It was like watching two tectonic plates grind against each other, or the posturing of sumo wrestlers. For a moment Vallon's mind played with placing sumo wrestling attire on the two men. She stifled a giggle— damned inhibitor actually did exactly the opposite and loosened the bonds she placed on her tongue.

"For now," Amundson allowed. "I want a full report on my desk before the day's out." His solid frame almost vibrated with the need to knock down his adversary. His pale blue gaze locked on Vallon and she had to look away from the hate. "Immediately. Before she goes home."

"Of course." Gleason nodded, his bald head looking almost too big for his shoulders. He stood there, hunch shouldered, until Amundson stalked to the lone office that gave onto the map room and closed the door behind him.

The door clicked shut and Vallon's knees gave way.

CHAPTER 2 — NO SERVICE

Gleason caught her arm just before her knees hit the floor. The Chief was faster than he looked for a big man, but even through his gloved hands his touch sent heat pouring into her and right down to her core. Heat the inhibitor couldn't reach, and Lord, she wanted a man right here and now. A low moan escaped her. The inhibitor was good enough to dull the edge of afterburn, but not enough to stop the effect of direct contact; and oh, God, she wanted contact. Full frontal, missionary, doggy style, whatever.

Xavier, where are you?

She reached for Gleason and he shoved her hand away.

"Damn it, Drake. Get a hold of yourself."

He shoved her back against the desk and she stood there trying to slow her breathing and her racing heart. Gleason was about the furthest thing from her type, but this afterburn was as bad as any she'd had. She fought the lust down, swallowed back bile, and pushed herself upright. The air was a mélange, fragrant with the rich scents of the agents: cut grass, sage, cherry, wet dog, and mornings. Too much, too many. Her knees went weak again.

She fought the nausea and looked back at Gleason. Nodded. "I'm fine, Chief. Really."

"Good." He gave a perfunctory nod. "Dean. On the desk." He nodded in the direction of the clean shaven agent who, in Vallon's sensitive state, positively reeked of jasmine. "You. Come with me."

He motioned her to follow but, thank God, didn't touch her. She followed, stretching to keep up with his long, lurching stride. Gleason glanced back at her. "And I am not your Chief. Not any longer."

His voice was like rough sandpaper over her skin. She swallowed. Nodded.

"That's better. What the hell's going on, Drake? You're pale as a ghost." He held the door from the map room open for her.

"I wish I knew, Sir." *Sir.* It felt so strange in her mouth. Almost like perfume, and that wasn't right, but then neither was the sensation that her brain stood on the edge of a cliff and her Dayton boot-clad feet were about a thousand miles beneath her. The long hall that they stepped into seemed to undulate around her and she staggered against the wall. She closed her eyes a moment until the movement stopped.

When she opened them again, Gleason was looking at her, his hoary eyebrows bristling close together. If she didn't know him better, she'd almost think he was concerned.

"Better?" he asked.

She went to nod, but thought better of it. "I can manage." She pushed herself away from the wall and started down the hall again. "We going to Landon?"

"Yes."

She set her sights on a doorway halfway down the hall that bisected the long, low bunker that was the AGS headquarters, but when she reached it, Gleason motioned her away and led her down to the far end of the building, where in the past there had been a small office with bunk beds for itinerant agents and a cleaner's alcove. He stopped her at the alcove, and the overpowering scent of new paint and old ammonia came from the small, brightly lit room. A computer and battered desk now took most of the space, but couldn't disguise the drain in the cracked tile floor.

"Landon?" She blinked. It didn't make sense. It just wasn't real, because Landon Snow was a creature of dimly lit rooms with strange concoctions brewing on Bunsen burners that emitted even stranger smells. He was a creature of shelves full of old tomes and walls plastered with ancient line drawings of mandalas, hermaphrodites, and snakes swallowing their own tails. He did *not* sit blinking under harsh fluorescent lights, his white lab coat replaced with a suit that made his diminutive frame look even more like a child playing dressed up.

But it was him. His faint almond and baby-fresh scent warred with the ammonia. Thinning white hair exposed pink scalp, and his pale pink-blue eyes were watery behind thick spectacles that he usually never wore. He swung around from his computer screen, his chair squeaking, and neatly touched a button so the screen went dark as he smiled up at her.

"Vallon! What a pleasant surprise. Come in. Come in."

He motioned to a scarred wooden chair in front of the desk and she collapsed into it. But a surprise? They'd spoken only last week and she'd said she'd come see him. She'd planned to, after her shift was over. Of course he *hadn't* mentioned that he wasn't in his lab anymore. *That* was the surprise.

"Landon, what happened?"

He looked so little and misplaced, like an insect in a bottle.

He glanced up at Gleason and something seemed to pass between them as the room tilted precariously around her. She closed her eyes and grabbed the chair arms, and the chair squeaked again; and suddenly a second mint-scented bottle was thrust against her hand.

"What the hell happened to *you*?" Landon asked.

"She was on the desk and punched the alarm. I need to know what happened and I need a report for Amundson."

Said as if they were two different things. She closed her eyes and drank the inhibitor down, even though two hits of the stuff were going to leave her in a bad way when they wore off. She needed to be able to think, and without the inhibitor that seemed beyond her at the moment. The inhibitor might not allow her to prevaricate her way out of a bad situation, but it would give her a chance to report. The cool of the liquid left her shivering, but it was better than the debilitating afterburn fever.

When she opened her eyes, she found the two men looking at her. "I'm okay. That helped. A little. Thanks."

Both of them seemed to relax. Landon's smile showed small precise teeth through his pale lips. He might be an odd-looking little man, but he had always been there for her and had stepped in as her guardian when her father went missing all those years ago.

"You're sure, Pigeon? Because at this moment you're paler than I've ever seen you, and that is going some." He looked over his glasses at her as if to say she could come clean with him, given what they'd been through together.

She scrubbed her face. The trouble was, Landon wasn't her father and he wasn't Xavier, either. He could never fill the hole her father left and he could never do for her what Xavier could. The sweet, low throb between her legs became pain everywhere else. "I feel like I've been scraped off a windshield. God, what was that thing?"

Gleason made a chopping motion and nodded at Landon.

"You certain? It'll get picked up," Landon said.

Gleason nodded again and Landon pulled open a drawer and touched something inside. A vibration seemed to fill the air between them and hum in her bones.

"That should do it," Landon said. His lips curved at the question on her face. "A little something so we can talk without Amundson's goons listening in. Things have changed since you went off work, Pigeon. Not the least of which is the Chief's and my new circumstances." He motioned around him.

And she hadn't known. Hadn't a clue as she convalesced at home, even though she'd known Landon was now living in a condo in Seattle, when all her life he'd lived in an apartment on the AGS grounds. According to Landon when he'd visited her during the summer, his suite and another that had been reserved for returning agents had both been taken over by Amundson's newly contracted-out IT section and a security detail—a bunch of big, burly guys—both from some company named Loadstone.

Gleason checked out the hall and then returned. "I feel like a damned kid trying to hide something from his parents." His grim gaze slipped to Vallon. "Report, agent." He started pacing behind her, though the size of Landon's office allowed only two strides.

She closed her eyes and tried to get her thoughts straight, but regardless of the inhibitor, it was all a bit of a muddle. Images bled into each other and came apart like milk curdling in coffee.

"It all happened so fast. I was checking something out on the map." No need to tell them it was something across the border and that Canadian Gifted were going to be hellishly depleted keeping that pipeline and harbor in place for a while. "I'd just pulled back when I felt something."

She reported how she had used L.A. and New York to triangulate and how the quake that wasn't a quake had hit. "It was a huge wave of Change, so big I couldn't stand against it. But when it was all over, I don't think it had changed anything. I mean, how weird is that?"

She looked up at them, rubbing her temples. The sweats had started. Small beads formed on her forehead and the backs of her hands.

Gleason and Landon looked at each other as if they could read each other's minds and… "Would you mind letting me in on whatever has you two so concerned?"

"Where was the quake centered, Drake?"

"The epicenter?" She stopped. She *had* triangulated, but she hadn't really had time to notice in the frantic attempt to stop the Change. She closed her eyes and thought back to the map pit and the connection to the L.A. and New York substations. An image of the continental United States formed in her mind. If she ran her internal transit line straight from here towards the point of origin and took the information from New York and L.A. and did the same… She did the math, and the results left the hollow place inside looming large.

"Oh, crap." If she'd looked pale before, she must look like the dead now, because this was bad. Very bad—and a bout of shakes ran through her. "New Madrid."

The name hung in the air and Gleason sat down hard on Landon's desk. "New Madrid? Christ."

The three of them looked at each other, each clearly reflecting on what was known. New Madrid had been the epicenter of the largest series of quakes in American history. In 1812, quakes and aftershocks ranging right up to 8.2 on the Richter Scale had been generated by the geological formations in the Mississippi Valley. The quake had sent church bells ringing as far away as Boston and New York. It would have caused untold loss of life, except that in 1812 there were just a few settlers and log cabins and Indians in the area. Survivors had told stories of the earth rolling like water and then exploding in mud and sand geysers. Entire plateaus had risen or fallen. Lakes had formed or been drained, and for a time the direction of the Mississippi River had changed.

"Fuck. New Madrid." Gleason resumed pacing, then stopped. "You're sure it was Change?"

Landon rolled his eyes. "This is Vallon, Gregor. If anyone would know Change, she would."

Gleason went back to his quick one-two pace-and-turn so that Vallon had to turn away or get dizzy watching. "Are you thinking that someone's trying to break the New Madrid fault loose again?"

"Could be," Landon said. "But where was New Madrid station?"

Gleason swung around. "Of course. " He turned to Vallon. "Where were they? They must have sent warning? Have tried to stop this thing?"

"New Madrid station." As a substation, it didn't have the same staffing levels as New York or L.A. and certainly didn't have the high-tech maps that those stations shared with Seattle headquarters, but the substation agents should have been helping. They at least should have sent warning. She closed her eyes trying to remember, but there was nothing. The sense of the L.A. desk agent with her scent of chalky mint, the seaweed scent of the New York agent, but beyond that, nothing.

She shook her head. "They weren't there."

She -reached- out for them, doing something she shouldn't be able to do unless she was on the desk with the map in front of her, and ranged east across the plains to the curved oxbows of the Mississippi Valley and New Madrid substation, set there to monitor the myriad fractures of the earth's crust that were the New Madrid fault zone. But instead of the warm presence of a desk agent, there was—

—*cold and a sense of screaming.*

She jerked back and shuddered, and the hollow place pulsed larger inside her. She felt like crying—and not just for the agents of New Madrid station. She was just *so alone,* and the hollowness wasn't something she could push away anymore.

"They're not there." It came out in a whisper.

"Nonsense." Gleason said. "There are three agents assigned to New Madrid. They have to be there."

She shook her head and wished she hadn't, because her brain had started to feel like it sloshed in her skull. "They're not. But if you like, I'll check."

She reached for the phone, but Landon had it before her. He dialed as if he had every station's number memorized, and she could hear the dial tone turn into the distant trill of a ring tone. When a voice answered, for a moment she thought she was wrong. Then Landon set the phone down so they could all listen to the tiny, mechanical voice as it repeated its message.

"The number you have reached is not in service. Please check your number and try again. The number you have reached is not in service."

CHAPTER 3 — LICORICE AND SPICE

The mechanical operator's voice drilled doom into Gregor Gleason's skull. This couldn't be happening. Not this. Not now. All his years leading the AGS to be ready for just this type of threat, and it happened now, when he and the AGS were the most vulnerable and the least able to respond. He stopped behind his exhausted agent in the cramped space that was all that was left of his chief researcher's—Landon's—office and scrubbed his face.

The woman was trouble and had been since she was a girl. The day her father had brought her to the AGS it could have blown the lid off of everything Gleason had so carefully worked for, except he'd managed to keep the lid on things, hadn't he? And he could do it now, too, even though after two doses of inhibitor she was still like a brilliant flame of heat that every cell of his being wanted to avoid. This close, the powerful pull of her afterburn was like a heavy sexual musk that awoke parts of him that he had long trained into submission. He clamped down on his controls.

"Assessment?" he asked, taking control of the situation, even though he had a sinking feeling he knew what was going on. Landon drummed his precisely manicured fingertips on the desk and Drake closed her eyes as if she were close to passing out. Not that she would. The woman was a constant source of surprises: some, like her strength, a positive. It was her attitude that had always resisted adjustment. It was in her files right back to the AGS Academy, as if the rules didn't apply to her because she was different. How different, he just couldn't say.

"Foreign?" Landon asked. Gleason's strange little friend and ally was about the best researcher and analyst the AGS could hope to get. Although Gifted enough to recognize the Gift in others, he showed none of the talent for Change that other Gifted had. Instead, right from the beginning of the AGS, Landon had been in charge of research and development. The inhibitor was his creation. So were a lot of other things. "Intelligence assessment suggests that if organizations like Al Qaeda had access to the Gift, places like New Madrid would be their target."

Both of them looked at Drake, who seemed to have shrunken in on herself, until she took a huge breath and straightened. She blinked once, twice, as if she were sorting through something. She shook her head slowly.

"I don't think so. I didn't get any sense of foreign."

Landon sniffed. "And what does foreign feel like, Pigeon? Perhaps it doesn't feel like anything at all."

"No." She looked adamant. "No, if they were foreign, I'd know. I think."

A guess, then, but Vallon Drake's guesses had a history of being right, right back to when she was a schoolgirl. Still....

"A foreign government? America has many enemies, and if not enemies, at least those who wouldn't cry at our destruction." A massive quake in New Madrid would wreak havoc on everything. Transportation routes cut off. Infrastructure and the American heartland devastated. It could make 9/11 look like a walk in the park and devastate our economy.

"And the world's population wouldn't recognize it as Change or an attack," Landon said.

"Something like that would be enough of a destructive shock it *would* enter the collective consciousness—like the Indian Ocean Christmas tsunami. That alone could hold the destruction in place. People would accept news of the destruction. They would see it as America under fire by the environment—as payback for our capitalism." Or imperialism, some would say.

"America reaping what we've sown," Drake said almost dreamily. The inhibitor was entering the second stage, where it became harder to think.

"We need to decide a course of action and move," he said and started pacing again. "If not foreign, then who? Who else would do this?"

"Rebecca Murdoch tried," Drake said, her nut-brown eyes gone almost grey against the dark circles under them, her skin even paler, and even her honey-blonde hair had gone limp. She looked thin, too, as if she hadn't eaten well during her convalescence.

"One of ours?" he asked. Could she really suggest such a thing? He looked to Landon for confirmation.

The little man nodded and then nodded at Drake. *Let her go,* he was saying. *Listen to what she said,* because Drake often picked up on things others tended to miss.

"All those files," she murmured, her voice far away.

"What files, Pigeon?" Landon leaned over the desk, his voice soft but almost eager.

She swallowed. "The files you gave me during the Murdoch case. All those disappeared agents we thought someone killed. But what if they didn't all die, like Simon? Rebecca Murdoch said something like that. She suggested my father might have disappeared on his own."

When she looked up at him, there was a light like a faint hope in the sea of pain in her eyes. Her father, who had been part of the beginning of the AGS and who had been the first to disappear, lost during a Change that had taken the house she had grown up in.

"You're talking about rogue AGS agents." Something he'd always suspected could happen, ever since the *Gild the Lily* plans had been articulated so long ago—and thankfully been kiboshed. Or so he'd thought. But Francis Drake, Vallon's father, had been a chief proponent of the plan to use the Gift to advance the Gifted. He'd believed that the Gift was an evolutionary advantage, so why not use it. His position had led to a schism between Drake and the first head of the AGS. And now Vallon Drake was suggesting that agents were doing exactly what the AGS had tried to contain so many years before.

A pain bloomed near his heart and bled out through his chest. Acid reflux again. That was all it was. He reached into his pocket for one of his pills, but stopped himself. Appearing vulnerable was not anything he could stand for. Not now. Not ever. "That's worst-case scenario. Homeland Security won't stand for rogue agents. They'll shut us down as the source. It could mean the end of the AGS."

And he wasn't prepared to go there, for oh, so many reasons.

Landon nodded. Drake just looked at him through weary eyes.

"What else could it be?" he asked, seeking options.

Landon looked thoughtful, then he nodded at Drake. "Maybe Vallon could shed a little light on that."

Gleason turned to her and she suddenly jerked alert and upright in her chair as if all the exhaustion were feigned. "No." She shook her head. "It wouldn't happen."

"You tell him, or I will, Pigeon. You know how this works. Eventually you have to come clean."

Even under Landon's unrelenting gaze, she kept shaking her head. Eventually she dropped her head in her hands and massaged her temples until finally she slumped in her chair. Her jaw was stiff with reluctance.

"Gregor, you may not recall my theory about the Gift and the bell curve. I sent you a report on it years ago," Landon said.

"Refresh my memory." Though Gleason remembered the report quite vividly.

Landon nodded and cradled his hands on his desk. "A bell curve, if you recall, is like the spread of grades one expects in an average classroom. You will have people who fail a test, and you will have people who get 100% right, but most students will fall some place in the middle." He demonstrated by drawing an upside down U with long ends to either end of the curved body of the letter. "I have always thought that we have a bell curve of the Gift in the population. On the one end, we have people with absolutely no Gift. The vast majority of the population has various amounts of Gift that allow their dreams to sometimes make Changes, which the AGS handily undoes. On the other downward slope are those with enough Gift to cause purposeful Change. AGS agents as an example. I used to surmise that we were the outliers. But over the past few years, I've wondered just how far the line of the bell curve goes. Mathematically, theory says that the line for outliers of the Gift could go on forever, with the Gift being larger and larger the farther you go. Think about that. Think what it could mean."

Gleason thought, and he didn't like the sick feeling it added to his heartburn. Which option was worse? Rogue agents, or the possibility Landon's theory was right?

"You're suggesting these hypothetical outliers could be responsible for what happened today?"

Landon shook his head. "Not hypothetical. I believe Vallon has made contact with one of them."

§

Vallon has made contact.

The words kept running through Vallon's head as she guided her Subaru WRX 265 homeward towards Seattle's Fremont Bridge. The fresh salt air poured in the open window, tinged with the scent of car exhaust and marine diesel from the yacht clubs along the shore of Lake Union. The fumes burned her skin like sandpaper. The steep, treed flank of Queen Anne Hill placed a shadow over the road that was like the shadow over her heart. The low-slung black car purred around her, but even her aviator Ray-Ban sunglasses didn't keep out the needle to her brain from the sun's glare.

Vallon has made contact.

She still couldn't believe that Landon had told. He'd said it was their secret.

And the truth was, he was wrong. She might have met Xavier. She might even love him, but she was totally alone now, just like she'd been alone all her life. Her father, for all he had been there when she was younger, had never really had time for her. The AGS had demanded his attention. Landon had taken over after the horrible day when her father and her house had disappeared, but mostly he'd been there to deal with the problems she got into at the AGS Academy where she boarded. And Xavier. Xavier had apparently only used her to relieve their afterburn, even if he had called her sweet names like *Bela Menina*. But he'd been lost in the battle with Rebecca Murdoch. Or he'd left. She didn't know, anymore, which she hoped had happened. All she knew was that even thinking about Xavier was like ripping her heart out. She'd loved him more than any man, even though she'd hardly known him, and he was gone.

Vallon swallowed back the memory of his ragged dark hair and smoldering gaze. At first his hawkish features had made her think him the enemy, but then for some reason he'd helped her, and the connection between them had flared as brilliant as Xavier's Gifted presence. They'd made love and somehow, through that, he'd shown her a connection to the earth and each other so profound that just thinking of it almost brought her to tears. More painful was the fact that she hadn't seen him since the battle with Rebecca Murdoch. She'd thought he'd left her a sign that he still lived and would be back, but after four months, the hope had faded. If the sign had said he lived, it had also been a goodbye statement.

Just like every other man she'd ever had in her life.

But others like Xavier could be behind the new Madrid Change.

He'd said he was an observer and Guardian, and that implied he worked for someone. There were enough someones in the world who would like to see America hurting. That had been the point of Landon and Gleason's discussion. That and the fact that Amundson could not be allowed to know of the possible involvement of Gifted in the New Madrid quake, nor of the possible presence of other, more powerful Gifted. Amundson had no love for the Gifted. He resented the fact that they had something he could never fully control. Knowledge of other Gifted beyond the American Geological Survey could lead to rash decisions that would undoubtedly be bad for the AGS and its agents.

She cruised over the Freemont Bridge.

"Hello, Troll." She gave her ritual greeting to the troll sculpture that actually dwelt beneath the nearby Aurora Bridge, but if there was anywhere a troll would live, it would be under this one. And then the streets tilted up the hill, past small boutiques and trendy eateries in refurbished brick and wood heritage buildings where the artsy residents of Fremont strolled and dined. Her stomach rebelled as the wind carried warring scents of boutique coffee, Mexican peppers, and the spices of Southeast Asia.

The turn into the quiet residential area where she lived left her suddenly unable to breathe. She slammed on the brakes and sat there shaking. What if her house was gone when she turned the corner, just like when she'd been a child? What would she think and feel and do this time?

All the talk of rogue agents and thoughts of Xavier had brought up too many old memories. But her house couldn't have disappeared like her father's house had. It wouldn't. She wasn't a child coming home from school and discovering that everything she knew and loved was gone. If something like that had happened now, she, or her replacement, would have felt it when on the desk. Her house was there. It had to be.

But she cautiously urged the car forward again and around the corner until—there it was, with its Japanese maple tree with its deep red leaves, and the overgrown rhododendron up against the simple brown-painted two-story house. She exhaled and found a parking spot two blocks up.

The suburban white noise of lawn mowers and wind in the trees and distant traffic was a welcome replacement for the car engine. She inhaled the fresh green scent of gardens and moist soil, but the scents seemed to clot in her lungs and the shiver of bamboo in the nearest house's yard was a flay against her skin. Deep purple petunias bruised the neighboring house's freshly painted front porch and she closed her eyes against the nausea.

All the fear and confusion she'd felt at the AGS this morning hit her in a bolt of pain again, because while Landon and Gleason were plotting how to deal with the situation without Amundson's knowledge, her brain had been limping along its own paths. Because what if it wasn't Xavier and the others? What if Dad and the other disappeared Gifted were involved? He wouldn't do that, would he? He wouldn't have abandoned her! He wouldn't attack his own country! Rebecca Murdoch, the disillusioned ex-AGS agent who had tried to destroy Seattle—and the AGS with it—had only been trying to hurt her when she'd said what she'd said. It had been a close thing, and it had only been Xavier who had defeated Rebecca and disappeared in the process—if that were truly what had happened. It had left Vallon to deal with the volcano Rebecca had shifted under Seattle—thankfully successfully, with the help of Landon and Rebecca Murdoch's daughter, Fi.

Her father hadn't had a lot of time for her, but he'd loved her. He had. There were the camping trips, just the two of them. On those occasions, they'd spent time in the mountains and he'd sat her down on stone and made her sit there until she could feel the rock's vibration. *The heartbeat of the earth,* he'd said. *It beats in all of us,* he'd said. *It beats in you,* and he'd touched her over her heart and smiled.

"He was a busy man. A great man, devoted to his country," she whispered. Because the memories of things done together were like shiny, bright pennies sprinkled in her palm. She could count the memories of doing things with her father too easily. He'd given her hugs when he came home from a business trip. *When she went looking for him and found him— usually in his home office.* It was never the other way around. He never came to her school. Not even to her bedroom, when it had been right down the hall.

No. He loved her. A child knew when she was loved. He wouldn't leave her to become her enemy. They were all they had in the world—each other. Hadn't he told her that often enough? *I'm all you've got, baby. I'm it.* It was true, given her mother had died in childbirth.

Xavier had been wrong when he theorized that the lost AGS agents had actually left of their own choice, disillusioned with the AGS and the fact that they weren't used to heal some of the great wounds to the American psyche, like the explosion at the Alfred P. Murray Federal

Building and Hurricane Katrina. Not to mention 9/11.They could have raised the New Orleans levees. Heck, they could have replaced the twin towers. She knew what disillusionment felt like. That still didn't mean that you'd do something like cause a quake that could devastate your country. It didn't. Her father wasn't like that.

He wasn't.

So if it wasn't her father, then something else was happening. She just needed to figure out what. And if her father was involved somehow—or Xavier—if it was one of them, he—they—would have a good reason. She would need to understand and then convince them they were wrong.

She swallowed back the taste of metal and ran her fingers through her hair, then slid out of the car and stretched. It didn't unwrap the kinks in her muscles, nor the fatigue in her eyes, but it eased the throbbing in her head a little. A quick, habitual scan of the neighborhood before trudging downhill towards the house. Still no black suburban—Xavier's favorite car.

There was, however, a too-familiar plain brown sedan at the curb in front of her house.

Vallon stopped and peered inside. Police radio discreetly under the dash, a litter of old fast-food wrappers on the floor. She closed her eyes. Not that. Please. Not now.

She turned and looked up at the house. Plain two story. Six lichen-green painted steps up to the red painted front door. The deep green of the rhododendron at the corner, all the old blooms plucked off. A bed of red geraniums along the foundation, the newly cut lawn—all Fi's, her roommate's, doing. After her years with her mother, Rebecca Murdoch, gardening was part of Fi's 'therapy' to be normal after too many years of being about the farthest thing from normal she could get.

Vallon let herself in the front picket gate and girded herself as she limped up the cracked sidewalk. The breeze burned her face and her too-sensitive skin. She so didn't need this, least of all now, when her whole body vibrated with the need for release and the inhibitor faded, leaving her skin flushed with the afterburn heat. Her only hope was that Fi would help her—unless she really was going to give up on Xavier.

Like he'd given up on her? Because then she could take advantage of other options.

Maybe it *was* fortuitous that the good detective was here.

No. That was not happening again. It was not.

She fished in her pocket for her house keys, but the red door swung open before she could use them. The far-too-sexy form of Detective Jason Bryson filled the doorway, his arms filled with a bundle of black-and-white fur—Maggie, her cat. His rolled-up shirt sleeves revealed strong, muscled forearms that made her mouth go dry. Oh, mama, sexy wasn't half of it.

"Vallon, hi." He said, looking down at her from his six-foot-two height, his smooth café au lait skin like magnetic north and she was the magnet. That skin would be warm over hard-body muscle that contained enough power to serve her purposes more than nicely. Though he wore suit trousers and the crisp white shirt and tie, she knew far too well the light dusting of rough hair on his broad chest, and how that hair led a path down his chest and right to his—

Stop that!

Breathless, she yanked her gaze back from following her thoughts and found his espresso gaze searching her face. His licorice and spice scent got up her nose and her knees went weak at the same time as the rest of her body sprang to attention. *Detective Jason Bryson would serve very nicely, thank you very much.*

She slipped past him, careful not to touch him because that just might shove all her cautions to the wind. He closed the door behind her and she faced him in her living room. Unfortunately, the usually calming deep blues and burgundies of her couch and oriental carpet didn't seem to do their job. He stood too near. His scent was too clear. She stepped back and the ancient hardwood floor clumped under her boots.

"What the hell are you doing here?"

My God, her hands were shaking with temptation. She crossed her arms to hide the telltale signs of her arousal and grabbed hold of the fact he was in her house.

"I—I was in the area and just dropped by. Fi let me in. I was just feeding Maggie." A half-smile as he ran his palm down the little vixen's black-and-white back, and if anything she snuggled into his arms just like she never did with Vallon. When Jason paused in his pats, Maggie nudged him with her little pink nose. A total traitor.

And enough already. One step and she relieved him of Maggie and set the cat on the floor. Maggie mewed once, in protest, then flicked her tail at them and scooted for the kitchen. Vallon followed. An open can of cat food waited on the old Formica counter next to the sink. Sunlight through the antique glass bottles Vallon had on shelves over the kitchen sink window sent rainbow colors flooding over the yellow kitchen walls. The light played on the locked door to the basement that gave off of the kitchen and she froze. Had he noticed? Had she left the door locked?

Maggie threaded through Vallon's ankles mewing plaintively.

"See? She was hungry," Jason said, relaxed and easy.

Okay. So maybe he hadn't been snooping. Vallon just arched her brow at him. "I see a chubby little cat taking advantage of your gullibility. She was fed this morning. She has her crunchies. She'll get more wet food tonight and that's it. She's on a diet."

"I thought she wasn't fat."

"She's not, because I watch her waistline."

"I thought you said she was just big boned." Jason smiled and approached too close and she held up a shaking hand to stop him.

Even from three feet away, she felt his heat on her hypersensitive skin. It had been a bad idea to come into the kitchen. They'd done the nasty here before. The room positively vibrated with their past friction. They could do it again; it would be just that easy. But easy wasn't what she wanted right now. *Xavier, damn it! Where are you?*

"What do you want, Jason? Where's Fi? I don't have time for you to be all cute and circumspect today. I've got things I need to take care of." Her toe went rat-a-tat-tat on the floor.

It would be so easy to grab him, so easy to plaster herself on him and rip off both their clothes. She'd hike herself up on the kitchen counter and spread her legs wide and let him do to her what he'd done before and oh, God, the way he would move in her. The way she would feel and the release. She'd be able to think, to deal, to figure things out.

But Xavier. And things with Detective Jason Bryson were complicated enough, given he was the only unGifted she'd ever met who recognized Change, and remembered the use of the Gift.

He stepped up and caught her arms and his touch sent a bolt of lightning through her so bright it left her half-blind. And then she *was* pressed against that magnificent hard body, her hands on those broad shoulders, her nails running down his arms, her lips on his. His heat burned through her and her mouth slipped down to his neck, was blocked by the stupid, in-the-way, too-uptight tie. Xavier never wore a tie—at least not that she'd seen.

She froze.

Jason's hands slipped from her hair to her breasts and found the hard nubbin of her nipples. His hot mouth trailed down her neck and stretched the neck of her blouse to get at her bare shoulder.

A shudder ran from the top of her head right down to her toes, and reverberated in her core like a never-ending echo.

She wanted this. She wanted him. She wanted that scene on the counter again. Oh, God.

She yanked back and crossed her arms across her chest. He wasn't hawk-faced and scented of deserts. He wasn't mysterious and steeped in secrets. His touch didn't take her to places she'd never been before—to oneness.

He wasn't Xavier.

"What's the matter, babe?"

She slid away from the counter and put the kitchen table between them, then pulled her blouse and cardigan and bra back into place. "I'm not your '*babe*' and that shouldn't have happened. It's not going to happen."

Jason only shrugged. "Not what I came for, but you and I—we're pretty damned good." He smiled, revealing good even teeth, just like Jason was a good even guy. He didn't deserve to be used just to relieve her afterburn. She'd done that before and she refused to keep leading the guy on.

"*We* are not pretty good because there is no 'we'." Damn, her heart just wouldn't slow down and she *wanted him*. Badly. Jason Bryson was available and why did she always go after the guys who weren't? "I think you should leave, Jason."

"But…."

"Go. Just go." She ran her fingers through her hair and straightened her sweater. She was shaking, damn it. The afterburn made her clothes painful, because she was meant to fuck something after she'd used the Gift. At least that was what Xavier had said, though in far less crass words. He had made it sound like a religious experience. '*All Gift comes from the earth, Bela Menina. So you make offering to her through the act of procreation, just as you need her power to create, no?*'

With Xavier, it wasn't just a fuck. It was something far more, and the way he'd touched her, the way he'd looked at her with such tenderness. Surely that wasn't a lie. Surely he couldn't have just decided to leave her.

But her father had. And he was *supposed* to love her, too.

For a moment the room spun around her, but she caught herself and marched back to the living room. She yanked open the front door. "I'd like you to leave, Jason. Now."

He'd followed her into the living room, Maggie scooting around his ankles and mewing like he was the only person in the world she could trust to feed her. What was it about Jason and females?

"Vallon, I'm sorry about that. Really. But it wasn't just me...."

As if she didn't know it. Every part of her wanted to grab hold of Jason Bryson, but she was. Not. Doing. That.

She motioned to the door once more. "Go."

He grabbed the suit jacket he'd carefully folded on the back of a chair and went to the door, stopped when he came even with her. "This isn't over, Vallon. There's something...." he stepped out onto the porch and turned back to her. "We need to talk."

She shut the door on him.

CHAPTER 4 – ROSEWATER CASTLES

"Stupid. Idiot."

Jason slammed his palm against his steering wheel and glanced up at the small brown house with the red door. The car's familiar stink of old food and human sweat oozed from the upholstery, but failed to act like a balm. How the hell he found himself out here, he could barely explain even to himself. How the hell did he plan to get Vallon to do what he wanted now? He'd had it all incredibly well planned when he arrived.

It all made no sense, and yet it did. Six months ago he'd been on the job and trying to act normal while everything inside him was coming apart. Cheryl was dead, and even after these past few years, he still wasn't over it. Stuck, was how his partner described it, but he didn't think that was it. There just hadn't been any reason to carry on. Then he'd met Vallon and suddenly the world he knew exploded around him. Sure, she'd been a suspect, but then he'd broken all the rules and there'd been the most incredible sex. For the first time in years he hadn't had nightmares of losing Cheryl. Then Vallon had dumped him like a hot potato to go off with Mr. Tall, Dark, and Mysterious, Xavier de Varga, and all sorts of crazy shit had started happening. The kiss-off had thrown him right back into his funk, but then he'd seen what Vallon could *do,* and during his long convalescence in the hospital, he'd realized that changed everything.

So he'd come to her today expecting Vallon to still be off on sick leave, but then Vallon hadn't been there. And then he'd decided to stay and wait for her, even though she was hours away from being off shift. And then she'd come sauntering in that red door with an oozing hip-shot sensuality that almost had him undressing right there, even though that wasn't why he'd come. Damn it, he was a fool *and* an idiot. Good thing Maggie had caught her attention and not the way his body reacted. And then in the kitchen....

He slammed his palm against the steering wheel once more. "You wanted to talk to her, damn it. Not screw her, because she isn't the one you want. She isn't the one you dream about. Remember, idiot?"

But he hadn't screwed her—not that he hadn't wanted to. But thoughts of Cheryl had held her back from a repeat of the first time he'd been in her house. And that time had about blown his head off.

He rolled the driver's side window down for some cool fresh air and his cell phone squawked on the seat beside him. He picked up. "Bryson."

"Where you at, Slick?" His partner's voice drilled into his ear. Big voice to fit the big red-headed personage of Detective Clint Blacklock. The two of them had worked together for years. Clint and his wife, Carol, were the family Jason had lost, or never had.

"Why? There a problem?"

A beat too long on the phone and Jason realized he'd told too much by answering a question with a question. "I'm headed in. I guess I got carried away. It's great weather for cruising around."

"Uh huh. Well, cruise your butt around down to pier seven. We got ourselves a floater." Then another beat. "I'm really hoping you're not where I think you are, Slick. That woman's got bad news written all over her tight little ass." Then he hung up.

Jason listened to the dead air for a minute and then set the phone down and keyed on the car. Because Clint was right. Chasing Vallon Drake had nearly ruined an investigation. It had also nearly cost Jason his job.

He pulled out from the curb and around the couple of corners onto Fremont and headed south towards Seattle's industrial waterfront, but regardless of Clint's warnings, he knew he'd be back. The trouble was that Vallon Drake carried answers to so many questions he had.

Most of all, she might be the answer to his prayers.

§

Gregor Gleason held the thin sheaf of papers and inhaled to steady himself before he knocked on Amundson's door. The map room was uncommonly cold this afternoon and more so after the heat that had radiated off of Vallon Drake this morning. The gentle whir of the duty desk console as it swung across the map, the low hum of the map itself, and the quiet murmur of the desk agent all said things were normal, the map showing hot spots of Gift activity in the Pacific Northwest and the desk agent dispatching agents to deal with them. All as it should be. All as it should have been this morning.

All at risk of being lost, given what had happened, and the worst part of it was that the AGS slumbered unaware because he dared not let his agents and thus Amundson know.

The knot in his gut tightened. All his years as AGS Chief he'd known this day would eventually come. How could it not, with the Gift springing up seemingly spontaneously in the population? Landon's genealogical research into the AGS agent's family trees had started as a means to predict just such things, so that the AGS could either recruit or deal with such occurrences. But people like Amundson would see the presence of Gifted in the general population as a threat to American security. It would place the whole AGS on the list of suspected insurgents because people like Amundson didn't trust what they could not fully understand and control. So the first order of business was keep Amundson in the dark about what was happening.

He knocked once on the door of his old office, then stepped inside without waiting for an answer. Amundson might be the de facto law around here, but Gleason was still the man in charge of the work. He was trusting that to get him through this.

"Here's Drake's report as requested." He slid the thin sheaf of papers onto his desk—no, Amundson's desk. The only comfort was that the blonde man might be tall, but he still looked diminished and uncomfortable in the chair that had been specially built for Gleason's frame. Served the bastard right for not letting the chair follow Gleason down to his new office. He turned to leave.

"Hold on. Have a seat while I go through this." Amundson's voice was smooth, slick even. It hid the jagged fangs of the man.

Gleason stifled a sigh and sat.

Perhaps it was the fact he sat on the wrong side of the desk, but the office felt smaller than it ever had. Or maybe it was the way Wolf Amundson had plastered the plain cream walls with pictures. They were photos, mostly. Amundson glad-handing with various politicians and movie stars. As if that was supposed to show how important he was. Interesting. Very interesting in fact, for a man who dressed like a shark and had eyes as pale as the predator with whom he shared his first name. Was Amundson's need for external validation something Gleason could use?

The blonde man swiftly scanned through the papers, then raised his icy gaze to Gregor. "So? What isn't in here?"

Christ. Did he know?

Gleason shook his head. "Nothing. I had Landon go over it with her. It was a quake—a big one, but for some reason there was limited damage. We should thank God for that."

Amundson's gaze glittered. His pale hair swept straight back from his high forehead. With his fair skin, the only coloring he seemed to have was the wet pink of his gums when he spoke. His silk suit rustled as he shifted in his seat.

"What brought on the quake?"

Gleason shrugged. "No one understands how the New Madrid fault zone works. That's the problem. There've been theories about the continental plate impacts and others concerning local ground water hydraulics, but the bottom line is no one knows. Ever since the 1812 quake, there've been concerns about something similar occurring, but no one has really pushed seismic preparation until the past twenty years. Given nothing has happened, there are some who say the fault zone is stable now." He shrugged again.

"So you're telling me there's nothing to worry about."

Gleason met Amundson's gaze and braced himself to lie. "That's right. Just a quake. And if that's all your questions, I'm going to get back to my work." He heaved himself up out of the uncomfortably small chair and turned for the door. "One more thing. Drake was sorely shaken up by this whole experience. I'm concerned she's returned from her sick leave before she was ready. I recommended to H.R. that she be placed on long-term disability until such time as she's deemed fit for work by our assessors. I just thought you'd want to know."

He managed a thin smile and then stepped out the door, closing it firmly behind him, before he started to breathe again. He'd done it. Step one of his plan to flush out and deal with the rogue Gifted.

§

Vallon shut the door on Jason and fell back against it, the shadows of the burgundy and deep blue living room enveloping her. Usually the room relaxed her, but she could still flipping feel Jason's heat through the wood, and every temptation was to open the door and call him back. Get it over with.

She yanked her hand off the door knob and returned to the kitchen. Maggie mewed plaintively and wound herself around Vallon's ankles.

"You are not going to be fed until dinner time. So give it up, you little traitor."

Maggie gave a flirty kiss-off with her tail and scooted out her cat door as if to tell Vallon what she really thought of her as an owner. It left the room cool and empty, or it would have except for the way her skin burned. All the strength she'd found to pull herself from Jason seemed to drain right down her body through the soles of her feet to the ground. She grabbed hold of the counter to stop the swaying and ran a cold drink of water from the sink.

It didn't begin to cut the afterburn heat. There really was only one sanctioned way to deal with it, but that way was lost to her as long as she was determined to be faithful to Xavier. Sure, sleep would help. It could keep her going for a while, could keep her sane. But not forever.

That left only the *unsanctioned* methods. Along with the inhibitor, Landon had developed pills that could help with the symptoms—also for a while. The trouble was that the cumulative side effects of afterburn left too long could leave an agent with the mind and self-control of a five year old, according to the test results she'd hacked on Landon's computer. So the pills were definitely not a preferred option, but she had to do something because there was no way she was going to be able to figure out anything about New Madrid in this condition.

So that left Fi. The daughter of rogue agent Rebecca Murdoch and one-time Seattle homeless street person, Fi was now on the long road to recovery from years of abuse at the hands of her mother. She also seemed to have a talent for diffusing afterburn that had never been seen before.

From upstairs came the muffled sound of music and singing that Vallon hadn't even noticed when confronted by Jason. A chair scraped across the floor in Vallon's spare bedroom. Surely to God, Fi would help her after everything Vallon had done for her.

She headed upstairs and the music got louder—a pounding Nine Inch Nails tune with rasping vocals that drilled right into Vallon's head. She clung to the stair rail to steady herself. An acrid scent hit her as she topped the stairs and the hallway telescoped away from her. She closed her eyes. Paint? Was that paint? What the hell was Fi doing with paint when Vallon had just painted the room less than eight months ago when she'd redecorated the room in creams and whites?

The door to the guest room—now Fi's room—was open to the hall and spilled bright sunlight onto the hallway's matted brown plush carpet. The pounding music and the paint stink laced pressure around Vallon's brain and squeezed. She grabbed the door frame to steady herself and peered inside. Closed her eyes against the nail-spike headache and tried again.

Fi was dancing little Snoopy-dog dance steps, her blonde hair cut short in a pixy cut to get rid of her previous dreads, her long, thin arms and legs exposed by a pair of paint-splattered cut-offs and one of Vallon's t-shirts with the sleeves ripped off. She held a paint brush and swayed and dabbed the walls in time to the music. Not exactly how you were supposed to do the job, but for the first time since Vallon had reunited with her old friend, Fi looked truly happy.

Unfortunately, it was at the expense of her guest room.

In the center of the room stood a sheet-draped heap of bed, dresser, and side table. Just how Fi had moved it all was a good question. A chair nabbed from the kitchen stood near the wall and obviously had been used so Fi could reach the high spots. The window and baseboards and ceiling had been taped with blue, but it was the paint job that turned Vallon's stomach.

Acid green paint covered two and a half walls and she winced at the violence of the color. The fourth wall was a purple so dark it verged on black. She swallowed back bile as Fi caught sight of her.

"Vallon! Hi! What do you think? Isn't it wonderful!" Fi almost sang the words as she twirled towards her—actually twirled with her paintbrush and sent a light spray of green around the room and the protective sheet over the furniture. A light damp spray hit Vallon's face. Acid green dotted her cardigan and blouse.

She frowned. "Whoa there, Miss Paintbrush. You're dangerous."

Fi looked from the brush to the spray of green on Vallon's clothes. "Oops. Sorry. Sometimes I just get so excited." She bent down and fished the iPad and docking station Vallon had bought her out from under the drop cloth and turned the music down.

Her wide-set blue eyes blazed with excitement and her pale skin held the light tan of the summer months complete with green freckles across her nose and a purple smear along her fine jawbone.

"So," Vallon fought to find words. She ran her hands through her hair. "What's going on here?" Fi was still vulnerable from her years with her mother.

Fi set her paint brush down on the edge of the paint can. "Well. I got up this morning and I was thinking about what you said about this being my home now." She sighed and scratched at her shorn head. "I know you said this room was mine, but it didn't *feel* like mine. So I decided to do something about it. That's right, isn't it—if you don't like something you do something about it? Isn't that what you said?"

Uncertainty threatened Fi's flicker of a bright smile. They were far too infrequent. Rebecca Murdoch had almost destroyed the mind of the girl who had been Vallon's best friend in school. But acid green and purple…?

Vallon went for noncommittal. "Where'd you get the paint?"

"Well, after I decided, I was so excited I ran right out to the paint store in Freemont. The clerk helped me pick out the colors. She said they're really in fashion. I was going to go with all purple—I think it might be my favorite color—but the clerk suggested it might be too dark by itself." She turned and looked critically at the purple wall. "I like it, but she was probably right. Isn't it wonderful!?"

She spread her arms wide and spun.

"Wonderful," Vallon said, but Fi must have caught Vallon's dismay. She stopped dead in her tracks and the smile disappeared as if it never existed.

"You don't like it." Her lips quivered and her eyes started to fill. "Oh, God, I'm so sorry, Vallon. I'm such a fool thinking I could do this. It's your house and I've ruined it." Her breath hitched. A single tear started trailing down her cheek.

"No! It's great." Vallon couldn't stand to see her friend cry. She focused on the purple, because it at least didn't eat into her brain like the acid green. "Fi. It's good. In fact, it's great that you did what you like. It *is* your room. You're free to make it what you want." Just please keep the door closed because while I've got afterburn it might blow up my brain.

Fi looked at her uncertainly, the tears poised to fall, and she looked so tragic, so vulnerable, Vallon stepped into hug her.

And was almost blasted across the room. Fi ripped away and fell back against the covered furniture, her eyes wide.

Vallon staggered back to the doorway and grabbed the doorframe. "Sorry. Sorry. Sorry." Fi's Gift might be messed up from all her mother's abuse of it, but it set the afterburn blazing like a furnace.

The room spun around her and it felt like her skin had singed off wherever she'd touched Fi. Stupid, stupid. She knew better than to touch any Gifted in her condition.

"Vallon? Are you okay?" Fi's soft words cut through the fireworks blinding Vallon's brain.

She kept her eyes closed and waited for the world to steady and the pyrotechnics to stop. When she opened her eyes, Fi's Gifted presence glowed like a bonfire in the middle of the room, a far cry from the muddled mess it had been when they'd been reunited. Unfortunately, it still had far too many dark streaks running within it, even though Vallon had been trying to help heal Fi over the summer.

Vallon looked away to the window, and the neighborhood beyond had been transformed into the flickering candles of trees and the sparks of birds in the sky. Beneath the gleaming carpet of grass flowed the deep currents of the ley lines that ran so close to the surface here in Seattle. She blinked and it took everything she had to drop back into her normal sight again. When she looked back at Fi, her friend was studying her.

"You've got it bad."

"As a matter of fact, I do." Damn it, her voice was actually shaking.

Fi turned her back and began to fuss with her paint tins. "I need to finish before this paint dries. I don't want streaks in the paint, now do I?" Almost as if she'd shut Vallon out and no longer remembered her presence. Fi picked up a roller and rolled it through paint, then, too heavily laden, she began sluicing more acid green on the last unfinished wall.

"Fi, please. I need your help."

Fi started to hum as she kept rolling the paint.

Vallon straightened and stepped back into the room. "Fi. Please."

The paint roller stopped and Fi's shoulders seemed to hunch.

"Fi, you saw. You felt. Something happened at work. It left me like this." She wanted to touch Fi, to make her look, but common sense and afterburn held her back.

"You've got ways of dealing. You always did back at school…." Fi knelt down and rolled the roller back and forth in the paint again.

Back in the AGS Academy, Vallon had been a sexually active kid. All of them had been when they were experimenting with their Gift, and Vallon more than most. Heck, the activity of the kids had been to the point where Vallon swore they probably kept contraceptives in the water.

"But I can't, Fi." Or wouldn't, if she could get around it somehow.

Fi glared up at her. "Why?"

Exhaustion threatened to crumple her legs. Vallon half leaned, half sat on the paint-spattered heap of furniture.

"You know why. Xavier. I—I'm trying to be… " What? Faithful? Most of her life that word hadn't even been part of her vocabulary. But Xavier. She closed her eyes because just thinking of him brought a flush of heat through her. She wanted him so bad. Wanted his scent of incense and cedar of Lebanon and the mysterious sense of deserts she got from him. Wanted his strong arms around her and his body moving with hers. In her.

She shuddered as she almost came, wrapped her arms around herself, and looked at Fi. "I can't be unfaithful to Xavier and he's not here. I need *your* help Fi. Like you helped me before."

Fi shimmied her head 'no'. "I don't want to."

She had to make Fi understand. To help.

"Fi, please. Xavier's important. I think I love him."

Fi's head snapped around, her face in a feral little scowl. "You're lying. You never love anyone."

The words cut deep and Vallon slipped down to crouch beside her friend. "That's not true. I love you, Fi, for one. We've been BFFs since we were kids."

Fi hunched her shoulders, the bangs of her pixie cut sheltering her face.

"I thought I'd die when your mom pulled you from the Academy and when you never wrote back to my letters—I swear it was the hardest year of my life until I finally convinced myself you weren't ever coming back. And now all these years later we found each other—or you found me—and I still love you, Fi, as my best friend. But I've never loved a man before—that's true. At least, I've never felt like I can't breathe as long as I don't know where he is. Please, Fi, help me. I don't want to ruin something precious before it has a chance to really get started. I don't want to lose him because of something I might do."

Her legs ached. Her skin burned and the deep places inside her throbbed with the need to be filled. She wanted to grab Fi by the shoulders and shake her, make her help, but Fi had been through too much already in her life.

"I don't want you to hurt, but I'm scared." Fi's voice wasn't much more than a young child's plaintive whisper.

"Scared? What are you scared of?"

Fi's shoulders hunched lower and she hugged herself as if she was freezing. All the advances Fi had made over the past few months seemed to slip away as Fi started rocking.

"I don't want you to be like my mom. Mommy. Mother." Her voice had gone sing-song.

Vallon sat back on her heels. "That's not going to happen, Fi. Ever."

Gingerly she caught Fi's t-shirted shoulders and fought back the pain. She turned Fi towards her. "Have I ever done anything to hurt you? Have I ever forced you?"

Fi's gaze skittered away like a frightened kitten. Then she swallowed. "Mom didn't at first, either."

"Well, I'm not your mother, now am I? And we've done those little experiments through the summer and haven't they worked?" Actually, Fi had seemed a little bit better after each session, the flame of her gift less clouded.

The pale blonde head nodded.

"Then how about we give it a whirl now, when it will really help me out?" Vallon held her breath, because when Fi was in this state all bets were off as far as how she'd respond. Fi's mother had truly screwed with her daughter's mind.

Slowly she nodded. She held out her hands, but still wouldn't look at Vallon.

"Not here." Vallon stood up and swayed as the blood rushed to her feet. She sure as heck didn't want to stay in this hot mess of a room any longer than she had to. "Come on. You've been asking about the basement. We'll do it there."

Downstairs she unlocked the basement door and flicked on the light to expose a flight of wooden stairs that led down to an unfinished concrete basement. She led Fi down, their footfall hollow and echoing, as if the space was larger than it should be.

The basement was the reason Vallon had rented the house so cheaply and the sole reason she had wanted it so badly. Walled and floored with concrete, a crack in the foundation that would send most renters running had spread down one wall and across the floor. That crack was what had attracted Vallon, for though during the rainy season the cracks glistened with water, most of the time they ran with the ley-line power that ran so close to the earth's surface here in Seattle. That power filled the room with a faint scent of rosewater and lavender and anise.

She'd always figured that the presence of the power so close to the surface was why there were so many more Gifted in this part of the country. With the rental house, she'd taken advantage of the cracks and built herself a little workshop. Behind the stairs and the low half-wall that separated the furnace from the rest of the open basement space, she had set up a series of drying racks that now held ewe's skin stretched and drying into vellum, one of the key tools of an AGS agent. To the left of the stairs along the wall she'd built a workbench where she experimented with inks and where she cut her vellum into paper-sized chunks—totally outside of anything AGS sanctioned. Against the wall that faced the base of the stairs sat her practice pit—what looked like an overlarge sandbox, the sand gleaming whitely under the single bare bulb that hung in the center of the ceiling.

Vallon went to the workbench and pulled out the lone stool and motioned for Fi to have a seat. Fi just hugged herself as she scanned the room.

"What is this place?"

Vallon shrugged. "My workroom. At least that's how I think of it. The AGS expects us to just do our job and not think about how we do it. I don't work like that. I want to understand, and most of all I want to understand just what I can do. So I work on stuff down here and I practice."

Practice, Fi mouthed as if the word was dangerous. Then she shivered. "I don't like it down here. My skin itches."

The power, Vallon knew, because at the moment just being in the presence of the gleaming cracks in the floor made her skin feel like it was on fire. She rubbed her hands together and almost expected them to burst into flame. "Okay. Just relax and let's do this thing."

Fi climbed on the stool and Vallon caught her hands, bracing herself against the surge of Fi's Gifted flame. Black, smoky streaks marred what should be the clear golden glow of Fi's aura. But it *was* better than it had been when Fi first found Vallon. Then it had been like a dark, clouded glass. Part of the clarity might be that Fi was living better and not on the streets, and part was undoubtedly that Fi's mother was no longer treating her daughter like just another street person to feed off of, but part of it also seemed to have improved each time Fi and Vallon had cycled the Gift.

"Why do we have to do this here? Why can't we do this upstairs or outside, even. We could go in the backyard. It's sunny there." Fi's voice had taken on the injured tone of a school-aged child.

Vallon shoved her hair back from her face and bent down to look at Fi eye to eye. "We're here because I feel so bad and because we're closer to those." She motioned to the cracks in the foundation. "It's easier to access the power."

Fi's soft gaze hardened and she suddenly she looked about a thousand years old and weary beyond years. "That's the problem. It's too easy. It was too easy for her, too."

Vallon flinched—a little. "I'm not your mother, Fi. Now come on, let's do this. Okay?"

Fi's stiff shoulders finally slumped and she nodded. "Please don't get like her, Vallon. Please."

"Ain't gonna happen." Vallon caught hold of Fi's hands at the same time as she -reached- into the earth through the cracked foundation. Heat surged into her from the earth up through the floor through her feet and flushed up through her body. Power, scented of rosewater and—strange— the faint scent of almonds filled her nose and made her muscles restless. Her calves cramped. Her stomach clenched. The afterburn was worse than she'd thought, and that made no sense at all, because she'd never had time to do much against the quake. She hadn't had the chance to. And yet she felt like she'd just battled Rebecca Murdoch.

She swallowed and sent the influx of power surging through her left hand and her connection to Fi. Fi went rigid and her fine blonde hair lifted away from her skull. Her eyes clamped shut, her eyelids trembled and shook. The power slammed back into Vallon through her other hand and she let it go, back into the ground. She broke the connection with Fi and stood there trembling.

Only grabbing the workbench kept Vallon from falling. "This isn't working," she said.

Fi avoided Vallon's gaze. "There was always some use before. With my mom, she was using power some way. You were saving Seattle. You were playing around with garden beds outside during the summer." She sounded bitter and not a little accusatory.

Vallon chose not to notice. "So you think I should be using the Gift in some way." Vallon turned back to the workbench and fished in the cupboard above the bench for a piece of vellum and a fountain pen filled with ink she'd made from the numerous baggies of ground lapis and onyx and herbs and copper sulfide.

Fi's eyes widened. "You're not supposed to have stuff like that."

Trust Fi to remember those rules from school. "Well, when there's people taking out agents, I think it's better to be prepared. Okay? I'm not hurting anyone. So let's do this." She placed Fi's hands on her wrists and -reached- for the power again. *Please let this work.*

Rosewater scent and heat seared across her skin from the powerful ley line that ran just under the foundation. She siphoned power up and held it within her like a trumpet player might hold air. Then she began to draw, sending power like a river into Fi through one hand and accepting power back through the other to flow into the vellum, into the earth.

The sand in the overlarge sandbox stirred.

A castle, ramparts, a single tall tower, all made of stone. She sketched it down. There would be fields around it for the peasants to grow food and notches at the top for men at arms to stand guard. Inside would be kitchens and stables and tapestry-draped rooms for the Lord and Lady of the manor. Atop the tall tower flowed a standard of a black crow on a green field. Her pen flew over the vellum, the black ink sinking deep into the specially prepared paper and the power flowed like flames: in through one hand, out to Fi, and then back in like molten silk.

And then she was done, the reek of ozone and roses fading. The drawing complete, stark blue-black lines on cream. Her body cooled, and her muscles eased into relaxation she hadn't felt since the quake.

She sighed in relief and raised a smile to Fi. "It worked." No harm, no foul.

But Fi ripped her hands away and one flew to her mouth. Her blue eyes went wide with horror.

"What have you done?" She knocked over the stool as she stumbled back.

"What? What's the matter?" Vallon followed Fi's finger to the miniature castle standing in the center of the sandbox.

It stood five feet tall and just as she'd imagined, fashioned of well-set gray stone and mortar. Small green fields of corn and wheat stood around it, the thick wooden castle gate stood closed and the green and black standard hung limp in the unmoving basement air.

"It's okay, Fi. It's just something I made. It'll fade away in a couple of days. They always do."

Fi shook her head and edged towards the stairs. "Something moved. I saw something move."

She was like a kid with a bogeyman under the bed. "There's nothing there, Fi. Really." She bent down to show her.

And a hail of tiny red darts rained down on her hand as she reached up to touch the ramparts.

CHAPTER 5 — LOST AND FOUND

Two months earlier: Venice

The old, black stone of what had once been a Venetian palace radiated cold and damp that ate into Xavier de Varga's bare torso and bones. He sat, manacled to a backless metal chair bolted down in the room's center. A barred metal door stood in one wall and Xavier had no doubt it was locked and guarded both with a Cartos guard, but also with wards against Cartos meddling. Not that anyone would come for him. His father certainly wouldn't. The only one who might was half a world away and totally unaware of whether he had lived or died. He had intended it that way, because he could not leave Vallon Drake without hope. Not when her very existence was a constant source of hope to him.

He opened eyes swollen from the latest interrogation. A single candle set into a niche in the wall generated the barest breath of light that glimmered in the moisture flowing from the walls. The constant *drip-drip-drip* was a reminder of the way the small locked room was no longer above the water level of the Venetian lagoon. The only reason the space was not filled with filthy water was because the Council deigned to keep it that way—and him alive.

So far.

His head hung loose on his shoulders in a vain attempt at slumber, but the pain radiating from his shoulders twisted back behind him these past— how many days?—made sleep impossible. So did the other dripping sound and the too warm trickle down his too cold arm as his lifeblood trickled away, drop by precious drop, from the catheter they had inserted into his forearm.

It was the Cartos approximation of the cascading sand of an egg-timer, but this was played with the true source of life. Without all his blood, his power was compromised. Without any of his blood, he was dead. The choice, according to Leticia, the jail keeper, was his. He just had to make up his mind; the Council waited.

He was aware of Leticia's arrival a good five minutes before the locks thumped and ratcheted back into the wall with a grinding wail reminiscent of nightmares. Then the ancient metal door swung open and the blaze of battery-driven electric lights poured in, momentarily dazing him. Then Leticia's slim form materialized out of the light.

Black leather skin-tight pants seemed to go on forever from high-heeled black boots to a blouse so painfully white he had to look away. *Click, click, click* and long fingernails raked the side of his face. He yanked his head away and peered up from under his lank forelock of hair. Her pale face was framed by chignoned black hair and the blouse's collar of frothed lace.

"So, *caramia*." She spoke with a thick eastern European accent, the sibilant 's' transformed to a cross between a 't' and a 'z'. "Do you have any words you would like me to take to the Council? Perhaps these last hours have changed your decision to stand by your transgressions?"

"I have done nothing wrong. Nothing to compromise the Council." It came out in a groan and even he could hear his adamancy fading with each drop of blood. Had he compromised everything? All because of a woman?

"*Tsk, tsk, tsk.* You hurt me with your lies, *Cara*, almost as much as it hurts me to leave you in this place, no?" She brought her face down next to his, so his lungs filled with the rich gardenia scent of her, florid as she was sensual. "Aah, *Cara*, can she be as wonderful as we were together? Do you remember the nights in Marrakesh, our bodies doused in sweat and spices so that each pleasure burned like flame? Surely such as this one is not worth your life."

He would not look at her, nor respond, for she'd twist his words somehow. Leticia was good at twisting words. As good as she was at contorting her body into every pleasure-giving position, and at confusing the minds of those she worked upon.

The long talons of her right hand came up and tapped his cheek and were then replaced by a gentle pat as she stood and walked behind him. All the hair rose on the back of his neck, for to not know what she was doing was far worse than to see what she had prepared for him.

The crack of the whip came a split second before the lash licked his flesh and his world reduced to staggering pain that cut right through him. He bit back any sound for he would not give her that satisfaction. Another lash followed too swiftly by another and Leticia's small, excited grunts as she swung the leather cat of nine tails. Finally she stopped and Xavier slumped forward, too weak to groan at the pain in his shoulders. The warm trickle of blood down his back weakened him further.

Leticia came around his other side and squatted wide-legged in front of him, grabbed his jaw one-handed, and dragged his face up to her. "You see, *Cara*. See how to do this makes me cry?"

A single crystal tear trailed down her cheek and his gaze was trapped following it.

"Does this other one cry for you, Xavier? I think not. You cannot have the years together as we do. Now tell us who she is, that we may deal with her. We need you out there, *Cara*. Not locked in some pit one Council decision from drowning."

The single candle's light caught in her gaze and revealed a hint of urgency and that was not like his old paramour Leticia at any time he had known. Pleasure and pain were all the same to her—sensations to be explored and exploited and enjoyed. Once, in the jaded years of his youth, he had thought as much himself, and they had been special together. But no longer. It was many years since Leticia or any woman had brought him to the sublime presence of Pangea.

Until Vallon. He jerked his gaze away from Leticia, afraid she might read the name in his gaze. Not that Cartos could read each other's minds, but sometimes they could gain impressions from each other. He would not place Vallon at risk. It was why he had left in the first place. If he left, and reported that all was as it should be in Seattle, there would be no reason for the Council to investigate. Unfortunately, his intervention with the Murdoch woman *had* gained the Council's attention when the use of power was picked up by their monitors.

And so he was here.

But Leticia's urgency told him something. Something was wrong and they needed something from him. It was a source of hope as she stood up and walked to the door.

"Think of your predicament, *Cara*. The Council is tolerant, but not of actions that will place us all at risk. With each moment your blood flows and your power diminishes, just as your importance to the Council fades.

Soon there will be no reason to hold back the water, and this portion of the palace will be returned to the lagoon."

The door slammed shut and the locks groaned into place. Xavier straightened in the open-backed chair and flexed his muscles against the torn flesh. So. Leticia might be the finest interrogator of the Council, but this was a time when her own feelings undermined her desire. For it had allowed him to read her, as well. There was something the Council wanted of him. Something they needed desperately enough that they were prepared to forego the punishment usually meted out to those Cartos who broke the most basic law of their people: secrecy.

He -reached- down for the earth's power, but the blood depletion made it like a thirsty man reaching for a water mirage. So stay still in this dripping hole in the earth, conserve strength and consider what he could promise that might appease them.

As long as it did not cost Vallon her life.

§

Vallon tripped and fell backwards onto the cold basement concrete. Fi screamed, turned, and was gone up the stairs, her departure setting the bare light bulb swinging wildly on its electric cord. The door at the top of the stairs slammed shut behind her leaving Vallon to pick herself up and figure out what the heck was going on.

At least the afterburn wasn't pounding in her brain. She could think again, but the hollow place in her chest felt as deep as the Marianas Trench, and the pressure of the depth made it hard to get enough air even though she was breathing.

The faint scent of ozone teared her eyes as she cautiously approached the miniature castle. She hadn't imagined it. Tiny brown barbs were stuck in the back of her hand and she had a sudden unreasonable need to giggle. Was she *Gulliver*? Impossible. But a flicker of movement along the ramparts sent her mouth dry and her stomach plummeted.

Just what the hell had she done? She'd made things before in her sandbox. Heck, that was why it was here. But those things were houses and landscapes. Never living things. And never—ever—anything like this—a whole frigging town.

She righted the stool and settled onto it, trying to figure out what to do. The basement ticked around her and the air cooled. From upstairs came Fi's angry movements in the kitchen and the ring of the front door bell. Whoever the heck it was, she didn't want to talk to them. If it was Jason, she'd kick his delectable ass right off her porch.

Fi's footsteps went to answer and Vallon looked back at the castle. Tiny men were now visible on the ramparts. A shiver went up her back and her stomach did a slow roll. She'd created life, or something like it, and it felt very wrong. Use the power to wipe them away? It would reawaken afterburn, but only in a small way. She could deal with that. She -reached- for the power, but something stopped her.

These little creatures were alive. To destroy the castle—and them—would be like murdering.

The door to the basement jerked open. "Vallon! You've got company." Fi's voice, almost taunting.

"I don't want to see anyone."

"Well, he's in the front room now, so you have to." The basement door slammed—again.

He? Vallon closed her eyes. What the hell was she doing? She couldn't leave this thing—these things—in her basement. They shouldn't exist at all. But to wipe them away was to use power again and that would be clear to any Gifted nearby. She -reached- and the glow of a Gifted filled her living room, and not just any Gifted. Gregor Gleason.

Fuck. She hadn't expected him so soon. Better to just let the castle and its occupants fade away as all of her creations usually did, than risk him noticing her use of power. The easy way out. Sighing, she climbed off the stool and trudged up the stairs.

§

Landon Snow sat at the desk he'd been given in possibly the worst office in the world. No door, when he preferred privacy. Too bright lights that hurt his eyes, and the stink of old cleaning fluid that—when he'd protested to Amundson—he'd been told shouldn't bother him 'given he preferred to surround himself with chemical concoctions.' It was true that he had always filled his lab with decoctions, but Wolf Amundson had no idea what they were for and what they might do.

Or perhaps he did. The man was no fool, regardless of his less-than-good decision to try to take over an organization of Gifted when he had no Gift himself. It left him at a total disadvantage because he would never know if a Change had been made. He had to depend on the loyalties of the agents, or those he could coerce, and from what Landon had seen, he'd been working hard on coercion once he had Gleason and Landon 'quarantined' away from AGS staff. 'To continue their work without distraction', Amundson had said, when the new office situation was clearly his retribution.

Landon tapped a pale, manicured fingertip on his computer keyboard. Do this or not?

He'd been thinking about this ever since Gleason dragged Vallon into his office, with the afterburn positively sizzling in her veins. The one good thing was that she hadn't asked him to help her deal with her condition, because he would have had to say no and that could have raised suspicions. It was painful to see her in such distress, but the process of cycling gave the people involved too much access to each other's minds. At least that was what he had experienced. He could not take that chance, because he carried too many secrets in his head. Like this file directory.

It seemed to taunt him from the computer monitor. Everything he knew was there, and ready for destruction if he was prepared to take a chance. When Homeland Security took over the AGS, it had happened so suddenly Landon had barely been able to save his precious genealogical files onto a flash drive. He had the information at home, for private continuation of his work, but the circumstances had prevented him from deleting the files on the AGS mainframe. He'd tried initially, but all files had been frozen—the transition from AGS to Homeland Security computer systems, he'd been told. Then he'd been hesitant to try anything for fear that the H.S. overseers would be monitoring everything that happened. So he's waited and bided his time, hoping that they would reduce their surveillance as time passed and nothing happened.

It needed to be done; the files contained the data from the AGS's secret breeding program. After all, how else could they expect to nurture Gifted of sufficient power to protect the United States from foreign interference? The Gift they sought was too rarified even here in Seattle, where at least some level of Gift existed in almost all of the population. It was why AGS headquarters was here and it was why they had the largest contingent of agents on American soil. The population of lesser Gifted were forever causing small changes that AGS agents undid. Vallon rightly described the night vision of the city in the map room as looking like a pot at slow boil.

The trouble was that it was likely Amundson's new IT gurus had the mainframe set up to prevent purging. At the very least, there would likely be alarms that would immediately draw attention to the files under attack, and they could not afford to have Amundson and Homeland Security discover what they'd been doing—or discover Landon's private little project. Wolf Amundson had all the signs of a zealot patriot. Sure, he wanted the power of controlling the AGS, because he at least understood the significance of the Gifted power, and Amundson was nothing if not about the power. But there was a downside to this. If Amundson ever realized how little power he actually had over the Gifted, he was likely to see them as a threat.

That possibility boded ill for every Gifted. If the general population got wind of the Gifted's existence, worldwide purging could make the holocaust look like a garden party.

So trust that enough time had passed and attempt to delete the files, given everything that was happening, or simply leave them? This morning, on his way into work, he'd made the decision to leave them, but the quake in New Madrid had made him rethink it. More so since he'd opened the directory of files. His gaze once more scanned the list of dates of last modification, and his heart raced a little faster.

He took a deep cleansing breath and hoped like hell that his efforts worked to subvert any spyware that Amundson's pet IT gurus had put in place. This was no time to get excited. No time to go off, as Gleason would say, 'half-cocked.' No this was a time for careful inspection to determine exactly what damage had been done.

The dates of last opening of his breeding program files all showed within the last four months—months when he had studiously stayed away from the files. So someone else was accessing them. He ran his cursor over each file, hoping whoever it was would be identified. Only a series of numbers came up, which made the cubbyhole they'd placed him in go even colder. That meant that someone unknown knew what they'd been doing. He could only figure it was Amundson or someone who worked for him. The entire computer system had been handed over to the same IT company that managed the rest of the systems in Homeland Security.

Okay. So the breeding files were compromised. That damage was done. It meant families were in possible danger and that meant he might have to get out warnings. He jabbed his finger at the keyboard and brought up another directory, one that contained mundane payroll files —the safest location he could think of to bury his password-protected genealogical files.

Because knowledge was power. He'd always known it. Knowledge allowed him to wield power in the AGS, even though the Creator had failed to give him the ability to use the Gift he was born with. This particular power would allow him to track back the family trees of the AGS agents in order to find possible links to other Gifted in the world, or, if he was truly fastidious in his research, to potential families that might be part of those outlier Gifted he'd always hypothesized.

He scrolled down through the financial folders, opened the correct one and then scrolled down for the right file and clicked 'delete'. His monitor flickered and went dark for a second before coming back up to the top of the file folder contents.

Nothing happened.

He frowned. Usually a menu prompt came up asking if he was sure he wanted to delete. He scrolled down from the top again.

Did it again and his heart beat a little faster and the idiot suit he was forced to wear instead of a lab coat seemed to constrict and make him even hotter. He loosened his tie and closed out the folder and checked that he had opened the correct one, because the fact that the delete process hadn't worked normally was setting off every one of his oh-so-heightened alarm bells. It was more like pressing delete had set in motion another process.

He had opened the correct folder. And the sub file folder had been there a moment ago, refusing to be deleted.

A bead of sweat caught on his pale lashes and stung his eye as he reopened the financial folder and ran through its contents again.

There was no question. This time his secret genealogical charts and the other top secret files were gone. The trouble was that he no longer believed that they'd truly been deleted. He also no longer believed his anti-spyware was effective.

CHAPTER 6 — SIGNS OF THE PAST

She was sick, or at least that was what Gregor Gleason had said. Still so weak from her efforts to save Seattle that she was relieved of duty—and here she was three days, three airplane rides, and three hours later, with the hot Missouri air blowing in the rental car window, while Fi slumbered beside her. She could almost believe Gleason's lie the way heat made the sweat pour down her chest and bead her forehead and the way she just wanted to turn this flipping car around and head back to St. Louis. The radio had broken just outside the airport and the air conditioning had died an hour out from St. Louis on the way to New Madrid. She should have turned around then and headed right back to Seattle.

Instead, she was driving through a landscape of dusty strip malls with too many boarded up stores, and service stations where the pumps were closed. In between stretched miles and miles of fields so flat she almost understood the terror of agoraphobia. Just how did these people live with so much flat? How the heck did they ever have a sense of direction without mountains and ocean to orient them east and west?

The wind carried the scent of dry heat and tinder-dry vegetation, and the fields were a faded checkerboard of drought-stunted crops—cotton, corn, and soybean from what she'd read in her research on Missouri. Few trees, though here and there a small copse blessed a bit of the landscape with shade. Wind picked up the dry soil and coiled it upwards in small dust devils. Baby tornados, and this was tornado alley, and the small towns she'd passed looked exactly like the kinds of places that the news showed reduced to kindling wood. Not exactly a good place to be. Not any place she'd ever want to live. It made her think of dust bowls and the old pictures of the dirty-thirties.

A low moan beside her and Fi stirred. Her face was flushed from the heat and her lips were slightly cracked. Strands of her blonde hair were plastered against her cheek, the rest blowing straight up in the wind from her open window. She wore cut-offs and a sleeveless t-shirt—a much more fitting wardrobe than Vallon's jeans and short-sleeved t-shirt and Daytons, her usual attire on days off.

And she was on days off, at least to the rest of the world. A vacation that Gregor Gleason had urged her to go on, because someone had to determine what was happening or not happening in New Madrid. Even though Gleason had made ongoing attempts to contact the Missouri substation, no one had answered. Amundson, well, he didn't even realize it was gone.

Fi yawned and stretched. "Are we there yet?"

Vallon rolled her eyes. "And just how many times are you going to ask me that? We'll get there when we get there."

Fi rubbed her eyes and grinned. "Yeah, but how often do I get to bug you like this? It used to drive my mom crazy when I'd ask her again and again."

Vallon shivered a little. "I'm not your mom."

Fi looked out the window and shook her head. "Yeah, but you're dragging me to the back of beyond anyway. She did that, too."

And so not the same thing. Rebecca Murdoch hadn't given a damn about her daughter and had used her unmercifully along with a whole batch of partially Gifted. "We are on a vacation like I told you," Vallon said primly."I could have gone alone, but I thought you'd like an adventure." And Fi provided a bit of cover for Vallon's mission, too, in case Amundson or the person causing the quakes was looking.

"But you told me this would be interesting—the Mississippi river and southern hospitality and all that. That maybe we'd swing south to New Orleans?" Fi pushed herself upright and scanned the landscape. "Why would anyone go on vacation here?" She motioned to the unending flat and Vallon could really agree with her, but....

"We're going to New Madrid, remember? That's our starting point. I've been curious about the place ever since I was in school. I mean, think, Fi. This is the site of the largest earthquake ever recorded in the continental United States. It could have wiped out everything if it had happened today."

"So we're going to some dusty old museums? Friggin' marvelous."

She thumped back in her seat and crossed her arms and jeezus-god, the woman was pouting. Actually pouting, and that was the hard thing with Fi—one minute you could almost share a joke and have a conversation like an adult and the next minute you were dealing with a petulant child. The only good thing was that since Fi had helped her with the afterburn there had been a noticeable improvement. She *was* adult more often.

Of course, the downside of that little misadventure was the fact that the castle and its occupants were still in the basement when Vallon and Fi left for SeaTac Airport. She'd left the basement door locked with a newly installed lock and the neighbor with only a front door key to feed Maggie. Unless the small beings decided to venture up her basement stairs, everything should be fine and the castle gone when she got home, because nothing she'd ever created lasted longer than five days. Next time she'd be a damn sight more careful what she imagined as she sketched on her vellum.

"Vallon, what's that?" Fi pointed out the window. "See there? See how the soil is so different? Is that a crop circle?"

Vallon eased off on the gas and allowed her gaze to follow Fi's pointing finger. In the middle of a field of stunted corn, the regular dark earth was marred with a circular marking of glistening white. She almost drove off the road even though it was straight as a ruler. And then they were past and continuing on to New Madrid, the white circle lost behind them.

"Not a crop circle. I think it's the remains of one of the sand geysers from during the quake. Remember? The personal accounts of the quake talk about geysers of sand and water blowing up through the earth. They happened all over closer to the epicenter. We must be getting close. Cool, right?"

Fi glanced at her with something like resentment, but then turned back to her window. "I remember the school lessons, Vallon. I'm not stupid. And yes, it's kinda cool to see it."

Okay, so maybe Fi was more adult than she thought. "So that's what we're looking for on this trip: the kinda cool stuff. Okay? You'll be okay with that?"

Fi looked unimpressed. "It's not Disneyland or Universal Studio."

"Sure. But it doesn't cost as much, either."

The crossed arms again. Another resentful look. This was going to be one hell of a trip if Fi was going to be like this the whole time. Vallon sighed and pressed back in her seat to ease her driving leg. Sweat trickled uncomfortably down between her breasts and the steering wheel was sticky under her hands. Necessary evils in order to get to New Madrid. That was what she had to keep telling herself, because she had to find out who was behind this. Not just because of the devastation another New Madrid quake would mean to her country, but because the perpetrator might lead her to Xavier or her father.

§

The hot September Seattle sun beamed through the unmarked car's windshield where Jason tried not to sweat as he slouched low in the driver's seat and sipped the last of his cup of coffee. Damned car should be designed so the aircon worked even when the engine wasn't on. Through the open window, the steady sounds of traffic on Fremont Avenue and the low comforting hum of a landscaper's lawnmowers were white noise that, with the heat, made sleep almost inevitable.

Except he might see Vallon.

Hell, planned to see Vallon, because why else was he sitting here sweating his ass off?

Her house sat amid the dark green foliage of rhododendron, shadowed by evergreens in the neighbor's yards. The bright red geraniums along the foundation looked dusty and wilted in the hot sun. Almost as if no one had watered them. Vallon and Fi must have gotten up and headed out early today, but something about the house didn't sit right. It was like chalk squeaking on a chalk board, and yet he couldn't quite put his finger on what caused the hunch in his shoulders. Maybe the way the front room curtains were drawn: she usually kept them open during the day. Maybe the way the windows on the second floor were all closed even in this heat. Most of the houses had second floor windows open even though people were away for the day—homeowner decisions that made the B and E rates go sky-high in the summer. Vallon's place, though, didn't just look secure. It looked closed up. No newspaper on the stoop and the mailman had walked right past the door.

So what's your excuse for being here, Slick?

He could almost imagine the car's sway as Clint's big ex-footballer frame came up from behind and slid into the car beside him. Clint would grin and then go serious. *You've got a problem, man.*

"Yeah, I've got a problem, and her name is Vallon Drake. But it's not what you're thinking, Clint, ol' buddy, ol' pal. Oh no, it ain't. And you wouldn't believe it if I told you."

Because how did he explain the things he'd experienced to someone who'd never seen it? How a house could melt around you. Hell, how you could melt like some atomic bomb was tearing away your flesh. It had happened. He'd been there. And it hadn't surprised Vallon or Xavier de Varga at all, but it had surprised them that *he* had remembered it happening.

And he'd remembered other things too, like how Vallon had fought to hold him together. Like how on a September day after Cheryl had died he'd gone to visit her grave, desperately wanting her to be alive. He hadn't been able to find her grave. Later, after he'd come to grips with his panicked devastation, the grave had been exactly where it should be. Almost as if his desires had momentarily erased Cheryl's grave. Meeting Vallon had let him see that the world around him was much more malleable than he'd ever believed. Much more than a police force ever accepted.

And if the impossible was possible, then why not other things as well? Maybe, just maybe, he could enlist Vallon's help to bring back Cheryl. Because life hadn't been the same since she died. First there was the stunned disbelief that had taken him through the first year. Then had come the depression that grayed his days-weeks-months. Hell, years, until he'd stumbled into an old concrete parking lot on a call and met Vallon Drake. When he thought about it now, his attraction to her had been because something about her reminded him of Cheryl, even though she was nothing like Cheryl physically. Maybe it was the quiet power Vallon exuded. And maybe, just maybe, she actually had the power to do what he wanted.

He just had to convince her that she could. That she should at least try. But first he needed to talk to her, and that had proved more of a problem than he'd expected.

Movement in the street brought him upright from a daydream of how Cheryl would look at him when he held her again. A woman wearing bright red sandals and one of those weird Asian-pajama inspired suits, in black, with the Chinese buttoned jacket and the shapeless baggie trousers hurried out of her yard and down the street to Vallon's house. She had short, geometrically coiffed hair in what couldn't possibly be a natural red and let herself in through Vallon's gate.

She didn't look like the type to be borrowing a cup of sugar.

At the door she fumbled with a key and Jason's knees popped as he fumbled out of the car and stretched. He sauntered up to Vallon's front gate.

"Excuse me," he called and the woman looked up. The oriental suit seemed to drink in the sunlight, and why would anyone wear black on such a soul-sucking hot day? "I've been waiting for Vallon. I don't think she's home yet." He grinned and tried to look friendly as he let himself in through the gate.

The woman didn't volunteer anything, just stepped down a step to meet him and looked up and down the street as if she was hoping someone else was around to see their meeting.

"I'm Jason Bryson." He stuck out his hand. "Detective Jason Bryson, actually." He fished in his pocket for his wallet and flopped it open to his badge.

The woman studied it a second and seemed to relax a little. "What can I do for you, Detective? I'm in a bit of a hurry here." She jingled the keys she held and Jason had to stop himself from staring at them.

"I'm looking for Vallon. She and I are old friends. I wanted to talk to her about—a case I'm working on. She's been helping me out."

The woman shook her head. "Well, I'm afraid you've missed her. She's gone on vacation for a few days. I guess her boss thought she'd returned to work too early or something. That old injury to her lungs was still acting up. Anyway, she and Fi headed out on an adventure back east and…." She stopped and cocked her head at him. "Maybe you could help me out. I agreed to feed Maggie, but I've just been called out of town for a meeting. I was just going to put a heap of food on the floor and hope for the best, but if you know Vallon, maybe you could help me out. Could you fill in for me? I hate to leave Maggie with no one."

Such a hopeful expression filled her face that Jason had to stop himself from grinning. Maybe things were going to go his way for once. "I can take care of Miss Maggie. I had the little Vixen at my place a while back. When'll Vallon be back?"

"She said about a week, but I'll be back in two days. I can take over then, okay?" She barely waited for his nod before she handed him the keys and shoved past him. "You're a lifesaver. Thank you." She shoved through the gate and jogged down the sidewalk to her place, and with a little wave climbed in a BMW that matched her sandals and was gone down the street.

Jason looked down at the key ring in his hand. One key on a simple round key chain with a rabbit's foot attached. It had almost been too easy. He turned to the red door and slid the key in the lock, *because, Clint, I'm here to help Vallon out. Feed her cat. Check her windows. Then get the hell out. That was all.* He was helping out a friend.

The lock turned easily—too easily, almost as if this was preordained—and the door swung open to release the reek of new paint and the deeper rose scent of Vallon and her secrets. He closed his eyes and stepped inside.

§

Maybe it was the metallic multi-million-dollar nanotech fluid in the sink hole of a map in the next room, or maybe it was the leftover chemical-and-flame miasma from the evil gnome's—Snow's—work room, or maybe it was just the general untidiness of the whole damn place, but the AGS bunker hadn't smelled right from the minute Wolf stepped through the door. And instead of becoming a gradual 'white noise' of the nose, the stink continued to burn in his nostrils and left him with a constant low-level headache that just wouldn't let go. It was as if the low-slung bunker on its evergreen-covered campus conspired against Homeland Security's takeover.

And that could not be allowed to happen, because Homeland Security had to ensure the AGS did not pose a danger to America, because the security of America was everything.

America was his home and the source of his power, and he had no intention of seeing that power eroded. Thus he had ordered the gnome's lab shut down and anything of value confiscated. He'd kept the little albino around, but only because he, like the other staff of the AGS, was too dangerous to let go. He'd immediately taken measures to ensure the AGS assets were preserved against any possible tampering because ex-Chief Gregor Gleason and his pet gnome could not be trusted, and he'd begun the slow process of recruiting from within the AGS agents.

But it was very slow, because how did he ever know if these men and women could be trusted? They were Gifted, and from what he understood of their power, they were the most potentially dangerous population allowed to exist in these United States.

He inhaled and opened his eyes. His office was small—too small, and not what he was used to as Seattle's Homeland Security Station Chief. His main office sat in downtown Seattle, where the rest of his trusted staff hung their hats—men and women with the skills he needed that he had contracted for through Loadstone. At his office he had a million-dollar view of Elliott Bay and the Olympic Mountain range beyond. Here he had—nothing. Four walls, one shuttered window that looked out on that unnatural map and infernal desk. Inside, a few photos he'd brought as company and Gregor Gleason's desk and chair that were too damn big and left Wolf almost feeling like a child pretending he was his father.

But he would not change the desk or chair. No, there was a point to be made by *not* changing them. A symbolic point to be made. He had assumed the throne of the AGS, and the agents and Gleason had best deal with it or he would deal with them.

His special cell phone drilled in his jacket pocket and he fished it out. AGS business and yet not, that was what he'd allocated this phone for. A direct line to his Loadstone allies. He touched the screen.

"Amundson."

A brief hum and snap as security measures came into play. Then: "Sharp, here. We've got something for you. We're not exactly sure what it means, but we've been reviewing the Little Man's files like you asked. Near as we can tell, they indicate some kind of breeding program was going on."

Wolf sat up. Sharp controlled the research resources at Loadstone. Their research section was made up of the very best that money and the best of facilities could lure away from Government and academia. It contained some of the best minds in the country and was solely concerned with the security of America. Sharp wouldn't be calling unless there was something Wolf needed to know.

"Breeding? Of what?" He tugged a pad of paper towards him, but stopped himself from doodling. Anything written revealed too much of oneself.

A pause at the end of the line as if Wolf wasn't getting it, then Sharp came back on. "The agents. Your agents."

"What? What are you talking about?" Because that made absolutely no sense at all.

"I'm saying that most of the younger ones are the product of a breeding program. If you look at the records like my team has been doing, there's been selective breeding for most of them for the past twenty years or so. Virtually all the students at the Academy are the children of liaisons specifically arranged through the AGS."

Wolf sank back in his chair, considering. There was only one reason they would do something like that. "They were trying to breed for the Gift."

"That'd be my reading of it," Sharp said.

"Have you found anything on that little project I gave you? It may be more important than ever, given this news."

Sharp was silent again and for a moment Wolf had second thoughts about the man. Sharp was exactly that: Young, dark-haired and ferret-faced, and driven to excel. That was the trait he could most admire, but the way Sharp's gaze always shifted and was hard to pin down suddenly seemed unsettling. Like now, it was like he was considering how much information to give.

"It was good that you pointed us at the Snow files. He seems to have been their chief researcher and there were almost forty years of files to review, but we're getting somewhere; and yes, we seem to have come across some promising avenues for further research, but it means we'll likely be looking for some live subjects to test our findings on. Think of it as Gift reduction testing."

Wolf let that sink in. "You've found something."

"I'd rather not get your hopes up until we're sure."

He spread his hands out over the desk. Long fingers, manicured nails. Immaculate. "And I'd rather not lose an agent."

"I really don't care where you get the subject from. Having one would make the work go much faster."

The chair squeaked under Amundson as he leaned back.

"I'll have to think on it." Because an agent gone to Loadstone was an agent lost for good. Send one of his recruited agents? Or someone else? Clearly someone else was preferable. "I'll get back to you later with a name."

More silence on the phone.

"Is there something else?"

A sigh and: "Actually, yes. Something happened a few days ago. You know we've been keeping tabs on Little Man's reach into the files. Well, four days ago, our clone of his computer showed him going strange places. Financial files. Not exactly places he should be going. So we watched a little closer and he led us right to a file. We grabbed it when he tried to delete it and have been studying it since. In addition to the breeding program, Snow seems to have been obsessed with genealogy. He had files on everyone traced back a few hundred years. Lord knows how many years it took to do it."

"A hobby?" He asked it, but he couldn't believe that was the case. Landon Snow might be an evil little man, but everything he did, he did for a reason. Snow had no place in the new AGS, but he was too dangerous to let go and just as dangerous to keep.

He could almost hear Sharp shake his head. "We don't think so. Not when he tried to delete them. They show family trees with linkages all over the world."

Another pause, and for some reason a cold chill ran up Wolf's back.

Then: "It even sounds crazy to me, but it looks sort of like he's trying to trace where your agent's talents came from."

CHAPTER 7 – IMPRESSIONS

The exit to New Madrid lifted Fi and Vallon up and over the so-straight-it-was-painful highway so that small copses of trees showed leafy heads above the buildings. The air blew humid here, so close to the Mississippi, and Vallon swore she could almost feel the power that had caused the quake. Well, not really, because she wasn't touching the earth or -reaching-, but she could imagine feeling the heated power across her skin, because Xavier or her father might be here—she might feel them. Yeah, it was taking everything she'd denied was possible in Seattle and saying it *might* actually be true. She hadn't shared the idea with anyone, because what if Xavier *was* here, or her father *was* alive?

She wasn't sure which one she wanted most. Her father so she could understand why he'd left her; he had to have a good reason. Or Xavier who she thought-hoped-prayed loved her.

The view northeastward across the sun-scorched buildings and fields showed the sun-browned straight line of a raised earth levee, so floods from the Mississippi were also a regular problem.

"Nice place to live. Tornado alley and Mississippi floods. Add that to the drought they've been having and there just isn't a lot to recommend this place, is there?" she said as the road sloped down again into an area of used car lots and mechanic shops and boarded up buildings. Definitely not in Seattle anymore. Hell, definitely not in the United States of America anymore. But it was. Middle America on economic life support. In Seattle you didn't see it quite so much.

"You're the one who made us come here. I'm still voting for Disneyland. Or Hawaii." Fi sat back with her arms crossed, her scent of anise and mint tinged with sweat.

"We're here. I'm not about to leave without at least looking around for a few days, so get over it." She was going to look around even though her clothes were soaked with sweat and the humidity in the air said they wouldn't be drying off anytime soon. She glanced at Fi. "You agreed to come for the adventure, remember?"

She was going to give herself time to arrive and look around and *to find them*. A quake like that, there had to be signs of the person or persons who caused it. "Besides, it looks quiet and I'm not anywhere the AGS can find me. That'll be a nice change."

Fi radiated her doubts, but the New Madrid landscape would do Fi good, if only to have something new to complain about. They turned onto Main Street and passed a small shopping mall that looked boarded-up empty—not too auspicious—then Vallon came to their turn. She slowed the Camry down.

"I'm thinking it's early enough in the day we should take a drive before we check in. You up for that?" And she could see if Xavier or her father just happened to be walking down the street.

Fi pushed her hands through her hair and shrugged. "Sure. I'm having so much fun anyway."

To heck with her. Vallon kept driving. Small shops, a narrow sidewalk. Green lawn and a copse of trees on the right hand side that parted to expose a grand house of yellow and white that almost screamed *Gone With the Wind's* Tara. Well, maybe not quite that grand, but a far cry from the dirt-poor-looking houses she'd seen so far. She stepped on the brake and cruised past. A small sign said '*A.B. Hunter Sr. Mansion (1910)*'.

"How's that for not Seattle?"

Fi craned around to follow the house as they passed. "Not bad. Not bad at all." She turned around, her eyes suddenly brighter and slightly less resentful. "Okay, I rethink my assessment of this adventure. Will there be more like that?"

"The hell if I know. We'll come back and see about a tour. There's a tourist bureau somewhere in this town to tell us the sights to see. I read about it. We'll go in and see them and scope it all out."

She aimed the car down the narrow street. It was like stepping into the 1960s or so with the beat-up trucks and men walking the sidewalk in western hats and ball caps. A few women wore cut-offs and capris, but there were others in faded flowered dresses that just didn't fit with the world outside. The marquee of a venerable old brick theatre called the *Dixie* advertised a production of *Guys and Dolls* by the local theater group.

Unfortunately, there were no tall dark strangers in flowing trench coats—or fathers, either. At least not hers.

On her right, across from the Dixie, was a diner called Randy's, with a blinking 'open' sign. A small hardware store on the left. A small shop selling clothing. Not much more and not much open this late in the afternoon. Ahead on the left was a mechanic's shop, and across the street a brick building with white trim with a circumspect white sign that said '*New Madrid Historical Museum.*' Beside it lay another levee that must run beside the river, because the scent of mud and water was strong and the air so heavy it seemed to slick her skin. Standing in front of the museum— surprise, surprise—was a grubby man in filthy trousers and jacket holding up a sign that said '*The End of the World is at Hand.*'. As they drove past she caught the stink of unwashed human body.

"Would you look at that?" Vallon said.

"I thought homeless people were only in the cities," Fi said.

"Apparently not." And that was troubling, given this *was* America. And more troubling that she could scent a person like that, but not Xavier.

"So we'll check out the museum tomorrow okay?" And hopefully avoid the homeless guy. It was kind of odd that she felt so determined *not* to see him again, but something about him just creeped her out. But the museum people might have some good insights into the town and could probably comment on whether there were new people in town who might be the source of the power that caused the quake. That would give her a place to start looking.

She shivered a little as she guided the car up onto the levee, and for the first time since leaving St. Louis, the Mississippi River came into view. It was broad here, mud-brown and lazy below the steep-sided levee, and made her think of Samuel Clemens and Tom Sawyer and his raft. The water ran southward in a coiled oxbow curve, and a tug strained upriver, hauling a series of three silver, curve-topped barges. Not something she expected to see, given how low the water looked.

Across the water a thick band of trees lined the river, so she could almost imagine an adventurous kid in a straw hat on a raft and a white paddle wheeler swooping upriver. It was how this side of the river must have looked back at the time of the New Madrid quake, but now, along the water's edge, white sandbars reflected the harsh sunlight. South of the town, a huge, tree-covered island seemed to float like a green-sailed ship on the river. With the water this low, it was hard to believe that just a few years ago flood waters had required the Army Corp of Engineers to breach the levees to try to ease the flooding northward of here. The result had been the inundation of thousands of acres of New Madrid farmland, not to mention people's houses being under Mississippi water.

On this side of the river, the levee area had been turned into a park with green lawn now parched brown in the sun, a wooden pier that stretched out over mud, but which must have once sat out over water, and a paved walkway that followed the levee along the town's waterfront. Stunted trees stood in pots and a parking lot provided access to a now-empty boat launch. Nothing like Seattle's busy waterfront, where people regularly walked their dogs and jogged.

"Not exactly Disneyland," Fi said, her arms crossed again.

She was right. A hot, rancid breeze came off the mud flats, and on the river side of the levee, the grass was tall and dry and dead looking and rattled like small bones even in the heavy humidity. Back from the river levee, the small town seemed to droop along its narrow streets. Even the leaves of the trees seemed to curl in on themselves against the burning sunlight. Small clapboard bungalows huddled in parched lawns and chain link fences. The few trees seemed to offer little shade, and along with a water tower stood a tornado warning siren. Yup. Definitely a disaster town waiting to happen. As if New Madrid hadn't had its fair share already.

"Well, it is different than Seattle—or any place I've been before." She tried to keep her voice positive, because she *had* dragged Fi into this.

"That's because no one in their right mind would choose to live here. I mean, shoot, Vallon, I just got my job and you asked me to take time away for this? The backyard at home looks lots better."

Vallon had to admit she was right. "Tell you what. We'll spend a few days here and check the place out, and if it doesn't impress us, we'll head home. or south" Because in a few days she should be able to tell what had happened to New Madrid Station and who or what was responsible, or at least be able to assess whether the answer was here at all. Then she could pass the information back to Gleason and let him determine what needed to be done. Then she could take her holiday.

She grinned at Fi, but her friend's eyes had narrowed. "You dragged me all this way for just a few days?"

Instead of answering, Vallon eased the car out of the empty parking lot and back down onto Water Street, which paralleled the levee. "Let's keep looking around."

According to Google Maps, the address for the geological research center that was the front for New Madrid Station was a few blocks east of Main Street on a street called Kings Highway. She'd just cruise past and take a look at the place. She casually turned onto Kings Highway when she saw the sign and slowed. It didn't look like any place for a government installation. Small houses painted white, brown, or sunburn red sat scattered on brown lawns with drooping trees for company. Mobile homes were scattered among them like refugees from tornado-ravaged trailer parks. Children's plastic toys, truck canopies, and old cars littered side lawns, and crows and flocks of brown-headed cowbirds perched on the power lines or pecked at lawns. Not where you'd expect to see a low concrete government bunker, at all, but the station was supposed to sit on this street just two blocks back from the water. She drove four blocks before she stopped the car.

There was no sign of the station. Small homes lined the street except for one larger place. She turned the car around.

"Where are we going? I thought we were headed to the guesthouse."

"We are. We will. I just want to check something out first."

Fi was silent a minute, as Vallon guided the car back two blocks and stopped in front of a large southern mansion that, with its lawns and outbuildings, took up almost an entire city block. The house was white with green shutters and stood two stories high with a lovely columned portico around the front door. An American flag hung limply from a standard to the left of the door, and rich green lawns spread out like skirts from its foundation. All the hair on the back of Vallon's neck stood on end.

She glanced at the desiccated lawns and faded paint of the houses across the street and then back at the big house's green lawn. Gee, which thing didn't fit? It was like the house and its property had new, moist skin laid over it, untouched by the sun and the cloying humid air. She dropped the car in park and went to open the door. This could be it. Xavier or her father.

"Why are we stopped?" Fi's eyes were narrowed and her mouth was pursed. "What's going on? Vallon, what aren't you telling me?"

"The house looks interesting. I thought I'd stretch my legs a moment." Because the darned house sat on the only stretch of the block that could have matched the New Madrid station address.

Not wanting to deflect anymore questions, she climbed out in a hurry, leaving a suspicious Fi behind. Across the roof of the car, huge old oak trees artfully framed the house and flowering trees stood along the curving driveway. A small white sign with black lettering proclaimed "*The Kochtitsky house, build in 1880,*" which made no sense at all given everything about the place screamed brand new. Strange, unless….

She trailed around the car and studied the unnaturally green lawn and the small white sign, then -reached- as she headed for the driveway and the house's front door. She stepped from the gravel verge of the street and up onto the barely scuffed driveway concrete.

Cinnamon and pomegranate-scented power ran up her legs and slammed into her like a freight train and tore her away. Her feet were a million miles below her. The stench of burning cinnamon seared her nose. Pomegranate clogged her throat and she couldn't breathe, couldn't hear except for a hum that came from deep in the earth. Couldn't feel except for her knees crumbling, and the earth lay far below her but coming up fast.

She fell.

Then everything went black.

§

The powerful scent of new paint hit Jason as he stepped inside Vallon's. He stood there a moment, just inhaling, just feeling her house around him almost as if it was a surrogate for her presence and her secret power and what it could mean to him. Vallon Drake was a force of nature. Hell, Vallon Drake could *control* nature, and he had a sneaking suspicion one Xavier de Varga could as well. Which meant there were probably others like her, too.

Now *there* was something to think about: a cadre of people who could change the world around them. What the hell had they changed already, was what he'd like to know, and why hadn't anyone noticed and done something about it?

Were they a secret society? A government conspiracy? Vallon's boss had had official-looking papers that claimed her agency was part of Homeland Security. But in all his years as a cop, there'd never been even a hint of something like that. Government top secret stuff, maybe. Hmm.

Did that mean he should think twice before following through on the crazy idea that had come to him when he met the neighbor with the key? Because maybe he could find how Vallon did what she did. Maybe then he could help himself and not have to involve Vallon. Or maybe at least he could find something to both prove that he wasn't crazy as a fucking loon and that she actually could help him.

He closed his eyes and inhaled, and caught a brief hint of her scent of roses. This time it didn't spike his arousal. This time, being in her house and all, it made him feel powerful.

"You are one sick puppy," he murmured, but opened his eyes and followed the gleam of sunlight through the open archway into the kitchen. The room was silent, dust motes dancing in the golden beam of sunlight through the window's old, wavy glass over the sink. The old linoleum turned almost honey colored in the warm light.

Start here? He'd looked through a few of the cupboards the other day when he was supposedly feeding Maggie. There'd only been the usual canned soups and vegetables, the jars and bags of spices, the canisters of flour, sugar, and rice. Nice and predictably normal. So normal he could doubt everything he believed. Clint would say he was out of his mind, but then, he had been for a very long time, since Cheryl's illness and death set his own slow-motion death under way. Because that's what it was, wasn't it? His mind burning away like candle wax in the heat of his grief. And his longing. The world was so damned lonely and had been ever since he was the kid of an air force pilot, dragged from base to base. He'd learned to be a loner so well that having a partner on the police force was even a stretch.

But not with Cheryl. Cheryl had fit into his life like some perfect part of him that he'd never known he missed. Cheryl with her thick auburn hair and flirty hazel eyes. Cheryl and her curves had thrown him a curve ball, because that was how they'd met. She'd been the friend of one of the civilian members from Seattle P.D., come out to a precinct softball match. Jason had been pitching against her team, but the way her t-shirt had pressed over her breasts and the way she'd looked so damn serious, he'd actually sent one right down the middle and she hit the darn ball right out of the park. Afterwards, she'd come up to him and accused him of throwing the game. They'd ended up spending the afternoon together and the rest of her life until the cancer took her. But now he was alone again and Vallon Drake might have the means to give him Cheryl back.

He turned from the kitchen and went up the stairs. He'd been up here before. He knew where her bedroom was. *And just what the heck are you doing, Slick? Cops don't do this!*

At the top of the stairs, Jason shook himself like a dog and scrubbed his face. He had to do this, no matter what Clint said. No matter that Clint was right. There was nothing more important in the world than getting Cheryl back. He pushed off like a man leaping into freefall and stumbled down the dimly lit corridor.

The stench of paint came from what had once been the guest room. He peeked in and winced at the designer wall colors and pulled the door shut behind him. Vallon wouldn't leave anything of importance there. Which left her bedroom and the small office he'd noticed last time he was here.

The office had the blinds closed with sunlight leaking around their corners. Bookshelves filled one wall with fiction titles and cupboards lined the lower wall behind a desk with a silent computer, but the space, with its dusty paper scent, gave him the sense of disuse. A desk that clean was either just there for show or the owner did their work elsewhere. Then again, that could be camouflage.

He gave the office a once over. Fiction ranging from *Game of Thrones* to *To Kill a Mockingbird* and everything in between. Cupboards filled with neat boxes of office supplies—unopened. He sat down in the wheeled desk chair. The bottom desk drawer held tax files and files of household receipts. The top drawer held the usual assortment of pencils. Not even a telling scrap of paper.

"Come on Vallon. This is your home. Just where do you keep your secrets?"

Evidently not here. He turned the desk chair to face the computer and turned it on. It came up password protected, so he thought a moment and typed *Maggie*. He was in. But he didn't figure Vallon for lazy; in fact, she was about the least lazy person he knew. A password that easy was unlikely to protect anything she really wanted to keep secret. Still....

There were few programs on the computer. E-mail. A financial tracking system and a word processing system. The internet.

Not exactly a computer enthusiast then. He opened the word processing system, but the most recent files were a few months old and looked like letters to her employer requesting a return to work. Just like Vallon. She'd been injured in her race to stop the destruction of Seattle, but she'd still tried to get back to work before she was really ready.

He closed that system down and opened her e-mail. Virtually nothing was there—even the deleted folder cleaned out—except a few e-mails to work and something from a travel agent. He clicked on it. *This is confirmation of your payment for your travel arrangements. Please print off and retain for your files.* It was followed up by a little personal message: *'hope you enjoy the east.'*

He scrolled down but there was nothing more. Just an outbound date and that was all. Now just where would leather-jacketed, Dayton-boot-sporting Vallon go on holiday by choice? He gave a quick once-over to her financial records, but there was nothing much beyond rent, grocery, and gas bills except for a payment to a local abattoir. Now that was strange, but there was no memo to explain the bill for a few hundred dollars.

He shut the computer down and went into her bedroom. Cream walls, white duvet on the bed, white painted furniture, three weird empty picture framcs over the bed. Sunlight streamed in the gauzy curtain over the window. He went to the closet and started there. Clothing—mostly jeans and sweaters, one low cut black dress that he'd bet she'd used to seduce a man or six. All released her faint scent of roses. Not exactly a clothes horse, unlike Cheryl. The floor was cluttered with running shoes, an old pair of Daytons, a pair of fuzzy pink slippers that surprised him. On the shelf above were a few boxes of shoes and that was all.

Damn it, this was the woman's home. There should be something about her—some clue of who she was and how she did what she did.

The top of the dresser held a gold-painted bowl filled with smooth stones that looked like they'd been collected by her. He fingered the cool stones, some with weird holes in them. A hair brush. A bowl with a pair of fine gold hoop earrings. "Damn it, Vallon. Work with me here."

Because it was beginning to feel like she was locking him out just as well as she'd turfed him out of her house the other day, and he was not going to stand for it. He yanked open the top drawer and almost spilled the entire contents on the floor. Caught it and rifled through the silken underwear and lacy bras that spoke of a much sexier woman than one her clothes bespoke. But then, he knew that, didn't he. He'd had the pleasure of a little Vallon time. The scent of roses was heady enough it could almost arouse him. So what, he was becoming a fucking deviant now, as well as a freakin' break-in artist?

He slammed the drawer shut and pulled the next one open. T-shirts and nothing else. The next drawer was sweaters. One he recognized from his interrogation of her: soft cashmere. He plunged his hands beneath and ran them over the drawer bottom. His hand bumped against something and he dug it out.

Cigar box. Old. Antique, even, but with colored crepe paper pasted over it so it was a mottled mess of red, yellow, green, and blue like a child would make. Almost pretty, and worn to cardboard in the corners from fingers opening it. A treasure box. He'd know one anywhere, had had one as a kid that had held one treasure from each place he'd lived to help him remember. As an adult he'd looked at that pathetic bunch of memory scraps and thrown them out. His was a life that he had barely lived, barely remembered until Cheryl came into it. What was important enough to Vallon that she held onto hers?

He flipped the lid open. A photo lay on the top of a man and a girl. The man, tall and square-jawed and good looking, but with eyes that seemed to look right through the camera. He smiled, but his mouth looked uncomfortable. He wore a grey suit and one well-manicured hand rested on the girl's shoulder. Vallon, at about age eight. It had to be. Same blonde hair, though a trifle lighter. Same intense brown gaze, but she had an electric smile that leapt right off the page and made him smile in answer.

But the man… Her father? It didn't look like it would be fun growing up with a father like that. He set the photo down on the dresser and rifled through the rest of the box's contents. An old school graduation ring with the initials AGSA set around a pale blue stone. Concert ticket stubs. An old cat collar. A couple of agates. A broken pen. That was it.

"Not much of a memory box, Vallon. Does it say about you what mine said about me?" A momentary bit of sorrow clogged his chest, but he pushed it away, replaced the photo in the box and the box under the sweaters, then slid the drawer shut. He stretched his back out and looked around the room, suddenly feeling intensely wrong for being here.

See what you're becoming, Slick? Everything you profess to hate. Clint's voice buzzed like a fly in his head and Jason wiped a slick of sweat off his forehead. It might be true, but he had to be here, didn't he? Didn't he?

For Cheryl he did.

"Fuck!" He slammed out of the room, holding his head in his hands. Just what was he thinking? He was violating everything he'd sworn to uphold when he became a cop. Didn't that mean anything anymore?

Apparently not. When he'd staggered down the stairs, he found himself facing the kitchen again, the sunlight illuminating the door to the one place he hadn't looked before. The basement. He strode through the dusty sunlight and grabbed the door knob.

It didn't turn.

He tried it again, the knob jiggling under his hand, the sun warm on his back and the scent of Vallon's roses so rich it filled his head. He let it go and stepped back to lean against the counter. Locked. Excitement surged up his body with the same almost-sexual heat that he felt when he caught the metaphorical scent of the perpetrator in an investigation. This had to be the place. It had to contain the answers. He hauled the key the neighbor had given him out of his pocket and returned to the door to try it, but it wouldn't even fit in the lock.

Okay, you've got a problem, Bryson. Now solve it. Prove you've learned something after all these years as a detective.

He chewed his lip as he considered the door. It was in the house, so it was obviously a place Vallon wanted secure even from her roommate and most definitely from anyone caring for her cat. But because it was in her house she'd want easy access, too. Keep the key to the door on her personal key ring? Possibly, but probably not, because the ring that carried keys for car and house would be too bulky to keep in her pocket in the house. Which meant either that she kept the key on her all the time, like on a chain around her neck—but he'd undressed Ms. Vallon Drake before and she hadn't worn anything like that—or that the key was around here somewhere, handy to the door whenever she wanted to go downstairs.

He yanked out the kitchen drawers seeking the junk drawer that graced every kitchen, found it, and pawed through take out restaurant menus, cork screws, scotch tape containers, and packages of batteries. No keys. Not one.

Frustrated, he leaned on the counter and looked out the sunny window. The backyard was filled with light reflected green by the neighbor's cedar and pine trees and the rich rhododendron bush that sat just under the kitchen window. Small birds fluttered around a bird feeder, and a hummingbird feeder hung just outside the window. The sunlight caught in the hummingbird feeder glass and caused strange reflections as the feeder spun slowly in the outside breeze. The sunlight was warm on his hands and caught in the colored glass of the antique bottles she had displayed on small glass shelves.

Pretty enough. On the middle shelf in the midst of the glass bottles stood a pottery jam pot with a design of an apple tree and orchard ladder on its side. His gaze came to a stop there.

That was it. He plucked the pot off of the shelf and something rattled inside. When he turned it over, a single key tumbled out into his palm. Remind him to do a better job if he ever wanted to keep something a secret.

When he tried it in the basement door lock, there was a soft click and the basement door swung open.

CHAPTER 8 —THE SCENT UNKNOWN

Screaming. Distance and a gut-wrenching fall. A roar, a blast of power, and tumbling through space. Through darkness—no—through many colors, all colors, and the stink of cinnamon and pomegranate and—was that almond? It burned around her, burned up her nose, on her skin and yet she'd lost her body, was part of everything, and everything was coming apart.

Power tore her away, tore pieces of her away. She writhed in agony, fighting to hold onto herself as power splintered her apart into slivers, shattered her further and further and who was she, what was she, why was she here?

"Vallon!"

A scream. A cry she should recognize. But the power sent her away, sent her floating like microscopic dandelion seeds in a tornado, and she should be doing something. Should be fighting back, preserving what and who she was. Who was she? A vision of her father rose up to greet her.

"Vallon! Vallon Drake, don't you dare do this to me. You dragged me here."

Hands on her shoulders. Hands? Shoulders? Hands drag her across the ground and drop her—hard—and—

—everything went silent. Rough concrete under her cheek, the scent of hot pavement up her nose, and sun heat beat at her back, but it was still better than wherever she'd been. *Where was that?* Where was she? *Who* was she? She groaned as all the tiny flayed pieces of her flesh coalesced into one painful person, and rolled over. A shadow blocked the sun on her face.

"VallonohVallonyou'realivealivealive."

Vallon. That was right. *She* was Vallon. Vallon Drake. And this was Fi crouched above her, rocking, her hair wild, her eyes wide and desperate with tears. "alivealivealivealivealive." Her voice faded off.

"What the hell was that?" Vallon said and tried to push herself up on her elbows, trying to peel back the image of a man from her sight. She ended up flat on her back. She lay there, panting, inhaling the warmed-grass, hot-earth scent, the memory of cinnamon and pomegranate and almond burning. She winced. The almond went with the man.

Fi's fingers clutched Vallon's arm like a child's and a small sob escaped her. Vallon caught her hand. "It's okay, Fi. I'm okay. Really. I haven't left you."

This time she managed to sit up with a groan. "I feel like I've been run over by a truck." And then torn apart by dogs and run over again. The man was her father.

Fi threw her arms around her and then pulled back.

"Vallon? What happened?" Her breath hitched with horror as she wiped at her bare arms as if getting rid of bugs.

Afterburn pulsed through Vallon's body. Her head throbbed with each heartbeat. Oh, God, no. Not that. But the sweet, sexy ache down deep and low in her body wouldn't be denied. Her gaze snapped to the white house, dappled with leaf shadows, and the sunlit driveway leading to it. Just what the hell *had* happened?

She scrambled up using the car for balance and stood there studying the Kochtitsky House. The little white sign seemed to taunt her as she stepped up to the edge of the driveway.

"I just stepped on the driveway. It must have been the heat and too much sun." A lie, and a stupid one, but maybe it would fly. She wasn't going to think about the fact that she might have brought Fi into danger.

Try stepping down on the concrete again? As weak as the felt, she didn't think she could withstand another attack like that. Not when her brain already felt like it was melting out her ears.

"How'd I get back here?" She nodded towards where she'd come to next to the car.

Fi backhanded her tears away and crossed her arms. "I dragged you. It was awful. There you were, marching towards the house, and then you suddenly went down like someone axed you. You didn't even make a sound. I got out of the car as fast as I could and I yelled for help, but nobody came. So I grabbed your shoulders and dragged you back towards the car. I was going to get you inside somehow and take you to a doctor. If I could find one." Her sneakered toe tapped the pavement. "So just what's going on, Vallon? You've got afterburn. What'd you do?"

Vallon shook her head. "Nothing. I just stepped up onto the pavement like you said."

Fi grabbed her arm and held on when Vallon tried to pull away.

"You're lying." Fi shook her head and backed away. "You've got afterburn and now you'll expect me to help you again."

It was way too close to the truth, because wasn't that the main reason she'd brought Fi with her? It wasn't very nice when she thought about it—not nice at all. Bring her friend for a handy-dandy fix-me-up whenever things got bad.

"But I didn't do anything. I didn't." And that was the strangest thing of all, but it was just like the quake. Vallon studied the innocent white house that right now looked anything but innocent. "I stepped down on the driveway and it was like I stepped on a mental landmine. It nearly tore me apart. If I used the Gift, and I don't remember doing it, it was to protect myself." From her father? Her head throbbed and she winced. "Apparently, I didn't do that good a job at it, either."

But Fi shook her head. "I walked on the driveway to get you and I didn't feel anything."

So Fi didn't believe her, and the fact that Fi hadn't felt anything made no sense at all. An attack like Vallon had felt should have ripped Fi apart. She had the Gift, though it was damaged by her mother's abuse.

Vallon's knees started to give and she yanked the passenger door open and sank onto the damp seat. The world undulated slowly around her, or it felt that way. Fi looked down at her.

"No way are you driving." She went around the car and climbed behind the wheel. It took everything Vallon had to swing her feet inside. Damn it, she was shaking and she felt like her skin had been hollowed out and set to burning. The blinding pain in her head now beat like a couple of Taiko drummers playing.

"Give me the keys," Fi said.

Vallon obeyed and closed her eyes.

"This isn't something I like to do, you know? Mom would get in a bad way and ask me to drive. I thought that was over."

Vallon opened one eye to peek at her friend. She looked straight ahead as if she were afraid to make eye contact.

"I'm not your mother, Fi. I'm not. I didn't do anything. I don't know why I'm like this." She held out a hand that jerked with palsy. "Afterburn doesn't happen like this."

Fi didn't answer. She just turned the key and started the engine.

"Maybe it does," Fi said finally, and dropped the car in gear and pulled away from the curb. Vallon watched the house through the side mirror. A stirring of second floor curtains made her think someone was there. Perhaps it was the someone who had attacked her. Attacked her! It made no sense. No one knew she was coming here except Gleason, and possibly Landon, and neither of them would want to attack her and neither would want her heavy in the painful grip of afterburn. Neither would Xavier.

She closed her eyes against the sun's glare and inhaled the fug of heated Mississippi River air. The image in her head was too real.

That left her father.

§

Francis Drake—not the famous British adventurer and pirate, but the former AGS agent and Vallon Drake's father—had been one of the founders of the AGS. He had also been the very first to go missing, according to his personnel files—something Wolf had checked after Sharp sent the genealogical files.

The man had been brilliant. A strategist who had helped sculpt the mandate of the AGS—but looking at the old performance assessments, his beliefs had not exactly meshed with the supposedly benign direction the AGS had eventually approved. No, he had been something Amundson could admire, a man ruthless as his namesake, with a more radical vision that hadn't quite fit in an organization focused on removing change and smoothing over the impact of change on the population. Francis Drake had been a man of action and one given to too-well conceived delusions of grandeur. The file contained a few terse memos telling Drake categorically that his proposed plans for taking discreet action to build the power of the AGS were *not* to move forward.

Wolf looked up from reviewing the file for the third time. And looked back at the genealogical chart on the screen. The white gnome's secret research had been enlightening, to say the least. Yes, it had been interesting to track the breeding program and to note the relationships of the Gifted and what lines seemed to lead to the highest test scores at the Academy. Not that he approved of the fathering of children by different men on different women, but this research went further. From giving him a sense of the amoral sexual behavior of the AGS agents, the charts provided a sprawling portrait, not only of the potential danger to the population of the world by these strangely powerful creatures, but also of the extent of the danger.

His stomach did a little flip-flop and he leaned back, ignoring the protests of the overlarge chair. The photo-adorned office walls just seemed too constricted, and it was suddenly hard to breathe the recycled air of the AGS bunker. He shoved the chair back and found himself pacing the small space in front of the desk.

Gleason had probably been happy when he found out about the extent of people with the Gift in the general population. Sure, according to the reports it hadn't developed enough in most people to give them any controllable skill, but it was there. And growing. That was the scariest thing. And Gleason had probably plotted with the gnome just how to use this knowledge to overthrow and enslave all the normal people like Amundson. He probably laughed at Amundson behind his back. He and the gnome. Hell, they all probably did—Amundson, the stupid normal. *Normal.* The way the term was used in the files, it was almost looked down upon.

Because according to the genealogical charts, not only were there Gifted out there, there were likely whole families of them. Whole families of American citizens who needed to be put on a watch list as potential enemies of their country. Whole foreign families who could pose a threat to the stability of the world order. Families that, if they fell in with organizations like Al Qaeda, could use the power of the Gifted for terrorism.

Another round of pacing, trying to determine how to stop the coming apocalypse. Where to begin?

Gleason.

§

There was light at the bottom of the basement stairs, and Jason stood in the kitchen doorway breathing in the scent of must and standing water and something acrid and—was that wood smoke? Why leave a light on if you were going away for a holiday? It didn't reek like a marijuana grow op. It smelled of—spices. Pepper, cinnamon, nutmeg, like an Indian spiced tea, and that made no sense at all. Even more strange was the fact that someone—Vallon, presumably—had tacked a stiff leather strip along the bottom of the door into the kitchen, almost as if afraid of something going in or coming out under the door. Just what was that about?

He really had no business snooping here, but he started down the stairs anyway, his feet clumping hollowly until he reached a spot where he could peer down around the kitchen floor joists to what was below.

A single large room filled the space under the house with a half wall that set off the furnace from most of the rest of the room. No grow-op. Instead, wood racks had something that looked like skins stretched almost translucent and gleaming whitely. He looked away, feeling slightly sick even though they clearly weren't human. Who dried animal skins in their basement? Just what kind of animals were they and what kind of person was Vallon? He thought of Maggie and immediately rejected the idea, because the thought of Vallon with a sharp knife skinning out her cat was just too sick to be believed.

He dragged his gaze away to the rest of the basement. There had to be a reason for the skins, just like Vallon Drake had a reason for everything she did. The trouble was, until you understood just who and what she was, you couldn't comprehend the reason.

The house's foundation was cracked and the cracks in the floor gleamed of oily moisture. A dollhouse, skillfully crafted to look like a castle, stood against one wall. He'd have never figured Vallon for a dollhouse gal. A work bench, a cupboard. Supplies to build the dollhouse? He thumped the rest of the way down the stairs and crossed to the workbench. Nothing sat on the top except what looked like a well-used mortar and pestle. Odd, unless she was using them for the spices he smelled. He pulled open the two cupboard doors. Just plain 'odd'.

A stack of greasy-looking yellowed paper that was oily to the touch. He glanced over his shoulder. Yeah, it was the same color as the skins on the stretching frames. He scrubbed his fingers on his jeans and considered what else the cupboard held. Small screw-capped glass jars that looked remarkably like ink wells. Baggies of dried plant matter that wasn't marijuana or magic mushrooms, as well as bags of what looked like powders of different colors. He opened one of faded green, dampened a finger with his tongue and stuck a finger in. Sniffed. Coppery scent. He spilled some in the palm of hand, spat on it and it turned darker green. One of the bottles held a color that was a similar.

She was frigging making ink and paper, and he harkened back to another case that had involved Vallon and a sketch that had seemed to show an archway that didn't exist.

In a corner of the cupboard was a folded piece of the oily paper. What was it called again? He sought for the word. Vellum. It was vellum, like monks used to make and use in the middle ages. He unfolded it and turned to the castle. The sketch on the paper was the castle he was looking at, except the main gates were open.

So she made the castle and then sketched it? Or she sketched the castle and then made it? Given what he knew of Vallon's skills, either could be the case, but… the field of corn around the base of the castle seemed to be moving and there wasn't any breeze in the basement at all.

The little hairs on the back of his neck all stood at attention and his detective antennae went on alert. He crouched down to see better. There. Those were corn stalks, and since when had model crop fields ever looked so real? He knelt down next to the tower and parted the stalks—

A tiny woman looked up at him and screamed.

A hail of darts exploded from the castle ramparts and found his face.

He stumbled—back and back and back until he came up against the basement's half wall.

His heart beat a tattoo in his chest, and he had to remind himself to breathe as a cluster of tiny beings fled from the cornfield into the castle and the miniature gate slammed closed.

What could Vallon Drake do?

He had his answer.

CHAPTER 9 —PERMUTATIONS

The man who reeked of pomegranate and fear stood at attention across the boardroom table, his face encased in the shadow caused by the too-brilliant sun through the window and the overripe capitol dome lifting over Washington's tree-lined streets. Francis Drake yanked his gaze back from the view of the city that always left him immensely jaded and slightly aroused, to the man's half-hidden face, and tried to compute the implications of his tightly-wrought messenger's news.

"I don't understand how this could happen," he said, keeping his voice even. "The trap was specifically set to catch any Gifted of the specified power." He pressed his fingers onto the gleaming tabletop and held his gaze on the other man's ascetic face. "Perhaps you can explain it to me?"

The cords of Evan Carragio's neck were as tight as Old Glory lanyards. He shook his shaggy, dark head like a dog trying to shake a flea loose. "If I understood it, I'd be telling you what we did about it. As it is, she walked."

Francis studied the smooth tabletop. Smooth except for his onyx-colored coffee cup. Smooth as he would contain himself, even when his blood frothed and fumed in his veins. "But it was carefully planned. I saw to that. I knew Gleason would send her. She's his wild card that the AGS can't contain. Her modus operandi is to skulk around until she discovers Changes. That was why they were there, for God's sake. Like a damned road map to lead her to us. And you come here to tell me that you and the others couldn't make it work?"

His voice had risen and he picked up the cup, drank once, and set the damn thing down hard enough it sloshed black coffee in a slick over the gleaming surface. He drew in a long breath to steady himself. "I'm sorry. It's just—this has taken a long time to set in motion—for all the pieces to be in place."

"We've all waited," Evan said and sighed. He hauled out a chair and settled across the table from Francis as if he were an old friend. Perhaps he was—at least he was an old business associate, one of the chosen ones who had left the AGS because he believed in Francis's vision of a better world, and a better place for the Gifted. But he had *not* invested everything in this particular affair. He had moved a family to safety on some South Pacific tropical island. Cliché, to say the least, but Evan never had been particularly imaginative.

Francis swallowed back his frustration—and the irritation that Carragio assumed he was Francis's equal—and framed his question. "So tell me. How did it happen?"

He avoided the offending coffee cup and poured a glass of water from a pitcher beaded with cold that had sat on a sideboard. He shoved it towards Carragio, then poured another for himself. He watched Carragio drink deeply but didn't drink himself.

Carragio was a slim man with a casual Dean Martin slouch and not a whit of Martin's charm. He had a weak chin and a soft man's watering eyes, which totally belied his talent for the Gift, and a set of febrile hands that always gave away his emotions. He wore tan khakis and a robin's egg blue polo shirt under a dark blue wind breaker that stank of sweat. The man never did know how to dress, nor how to show respect. At least he nodded his appreciation for the water, but he settled in his chair, leaning back as if he belonged here and not in the pissant Midwest town Francis had found him in thirty years ago.

The light sheen of sweat across Carragio's brow and the way the man kept his hands hidden under the table confirmed Francis's suspicion. This had been a screw up and Carragio knew it. The others in his little cabal knew they were taking their lives in their hands to report their failure, and so they'd chosen Carragio as Francis's oldest associate—and perhaps the most expendable of any of them.

"It went down like this. She came into town and we spotted her, the same car she'd picked up at the St. Louis airport. She didn't head for her guesthouse; she decided to take a spin around the town and seemed primed to just walk right in to us, just as we'd planned. Except not. She didn't come alone. She had a friend with her and when the surge took her down, the friend dragged her off the current before we could respond. It all happened so fast and then she was gone, heading over to her guesthouse. We weren't sure what to do. That was when I decided to come to you. Let you know how things went down and so on."

"And so on." The words twisted in his craw. He wanted to twist them up and tie them around Carragio's neck or, better still, stuff them down his useless throat and let him strangle on them. Instead, he stood up and smoothed the folds of his grey trousers and jacket. "I appreciate you bringing the news to me in person. We'll deal with this. Too much depends on it. And now I need time to think." Because this changed everything.

He rounded the table and patted Carragio's shoulder, then went to the window to stare out at the dome that represented so much to so many, and yet was something that must be brought down if people like him were to stand a chance at surviving. Years ago they'd all been young fools to expose their Gifted talents to the unGifted. In their dewy-eyed youth, they'd thought they could help uphold what that dome represented, but really all they'd done was become tools of the corruption and targets for anyone seeking a pogrom that the 'normals' could rally behind.

"Francis, there's one more thing. I almost forgot."

Francis swung around. Carragio stood in the doorway. "What is it?"

"Someone else came to New Madrid. Our old friend, Landon Snow."

For a moment Francis felt the room tremble under him as he met Carragio's watery gaze. Then the other man turned and left, the door clicking softly behind him. Francis went to bar in the corner and poured himself three fingers of twenty-year-old Macallan, inhaled the acrid perfume, and knocked it back to revel in the cleansing burn as it went down his throat. The sweet, amber oak scent was a damn sight better than sickening pomegranate. A man's drink. A hard drink. He had no time for Carragio's softness because this was *his* time. This was the time when all his years of careful work came to fruition and he would *not* allow the failings of others to ruin it for him.

At times like this, under the brutal mid-day light, the capitol dome and the shifting ceiling of green that parted the brownstone and the alabaster monuments of the city were reminiscent of Rome and what it must have been like before the fall—the failing beauty overlaid with a crumbling façade of false invincibility. A façade he had every intention of breaking apart to protect his kind.

A crisp knock came at the door.

"Come," he called.

The door pushed open and a man, wattle-necked and hawk-nosed as a carrion bird and dressed all in black on this glorious September day, hunched inside. Not what Francis had expected, though he should have.

"So? What's the news? Are things progressing?"Ray Fitzsimmons, Director of Homeland Security, stepped inside and closed the door carefully behind him, then paused for a single beat. "By the look on your face and the drink in your hand, I'd say not."

His silk suit rustled as he crossed the room and sank into the chair Francis had vacated, a pointed reminder that Fitzsimmons *owned* the Homeland Security building in central Washington. His small, heavily-lidded eyes gleamed up at Francis and, hunched as he was in his expensive silk suit, and with his long nose, he no longer looked like a bird of prey. He was a pterodactyl: ancient, predatory, and in Fitzsimmons case, fighting against extinction. His heavy brow rose. "So?"

Francis set his scotch down. He was not about to lose his edge when sparring with this partner.

"Apparently it did not go as planned. She had help. Someone who got her out and away from the intended pick-up point."

"AGS? Because I can deal with that."

"Apparently not. A friend, Carragio says. An AGS agent should have just fallen victim to the same pulse as Vallon. That suggests something odd is going on."

Fitzsimmons's eyes glittered and his head bobbed on his shoulders as his lips thinned. "Then I suppose you have a problem, my friend. Something you should deal with instead of enjoying the stocked bar of a Washington office. Correct? Our backers grow more impatient with every day it takes to do this."

No good would come of showing the twist of anger in his gut, so Francis went back to the window. "After all these years, a few more months won't make a difference. Not to do it right."

Yes, there was power in this city still, but it no longer came from the people voted into that big white dome or the house on Pennsylvania Avenue. Now it came from the lobby groups and the huge corporations that bankrolled the parties. The elected officials just hadn't yet realized that all their best people had left—lured away by the riches offered by the global corporations, leaving bare husks of a severely indebted government infrastructure behind.

When the end came—and it would—when the same corporations that had gouged government with their lucrative contracts came back demanding to be paid everything they were owed—the government of the United States of America would discover it had nothing to fight back with.

Francis's little project would just help the process along.

"You know them. They've invested on my recommendation. I won't have you stringing them along."

Francis turned back to the prehistoric predator, because Ray Fitzsimmons was an antique from another time when bureaucrats wielded power. Fitzsimmons still managed to hold on because of his strong links to Loadstone, the IT and Security Company that had grown to a multinational superstar because it provided security to corporations and governments in war-torn locales. Fitzsimmons had been Francis's entry point to those powerbrokers and their partners, and a believer in the talents of the Gifted. It had been his awareness of the AGS and the Gifted skills that had made it possible for Francis to approach him with the plans for *Gild the Lily*—to use Gifted talents in a way that the AGS's mandate would not allow.

"Has it not gone as planned up until now?" he asked Fitzsimmons. "We caused the quake to get their attention, and like the predictable man he is, Gleason went behind your man's back and sent someone to investigate. Of course it was the girl—my daughter. She is the one who works most at the edge of acceptable practice. She is the one most constrained by their policy and practice, just as I was."

"Yes. Yes. You lured your daughter so you would have access to her power. Bring her into the fold and all that. But when will the project be ready to move forward? The Board of Directors wants to know."

Francis looked back to the city and shook his head. The idiots who backed him had no idea what they were in for. Because really, this whole thing was simply a staged maneuver to get the attention of something much greater than anything this city held. He wished for another drink as his mind whirled through all the permutations of what could go wrong and how he would address each problem. "Tell them Thursday."

Five days hence.

§

Two weeks previous:

The moist air of Venice's curving Grand Canal seeped in through the window of the ancient palace. If not for the breeze off the lagoon, the air would be fetid, but that was one of Pangea's wonders, that she would keep this sinking city like a lotus upon the waves. From outside also came the whine of boat engines and the calls of people, both on the boats and on the bridges, so that from where Xavier sat it was almost an assault upon the senses after so long in that subterranean room.

The place where he sat was actually hallway, tall with arched ceilings replete with murals that conveyed the story of the meeting of Creation and Pangea and the birth of the earth's people, all painted wondrously and now faded to the sepia tones of the Italian Masters. The marble floor gleamed as did the sideboard across from him, with its tall vase shaped like a fish, with its cascading display of white lilies, hydrangea, and perfumed jasmine.

He leaned back against the wall behind his backless, club-footed bench and rubbed his forearm. The bandage itched under his crisply ironed black shirt, as did the wounds on his back, but the itching was a sign of healing and his kind healed relatively quickly, though not quickly enough for his purposes.

If he were healed, he would be away from this place of old men and women who helped to hold up a sinking city because it had been their home for generations. By remaining here, it was like they had set down roots into the sinking city and so had trapped themselves in archaic ways of being that were often not relevant in the modern world. He knew that now. Had suspected it when they refused to make contact as the Gifted began to arise amongst the general population.

The voices in the next room were muffled and dull—controlled, just like everything about the Council. Controlled and contrived until there was no spontaneous life in the world. Once he hadn't thought so. Once he had thought these men and women the keepers of everything important in the world. Now that they had given him the choice of the name of the woman he loved or his life, his opinion had changed. So had his loyalties.

Through the door beside him came the sharp sound of heels on marble. Then the door pushed open and Leticia stepped out. Today she had traded in her sleek leather for something softer that belied her nature. A simple silk cream sheath fell from her shoulders and clung to every curve. The silk rippled as she breathed, creating an image of a trembling virginal woman, something Leticia was many years from being. She wore her hair up in a chignon that allowed stray curls to play along her nape and brow and she was lovely enough to bring back old memories of their times together.

Not now. He stood, his muscles reveling in their freedom from the chair. Leticia had been his love long ago in the springtime of his life, when she was still a girl unspoiled by her long life.

"So, beloved." She placed a cool palm upon his chest. "They have agreed to hear your request, but I cannot help but think this is a fool's game you play. Give me the name and be done with it. It will be over and the pain will eventually pass." She curved her crimson lips.

"The name is mine to give or keep. I will do nothing to compromise her safety."

Leticia studied him with night-dark eyes. Then she shook her head. "Then you are a bigger fool than I thought. This is our life, our very existence you play with." She nodded at the door. "Go on, try your bargain and see what they say."

He half-bowed to her and straightened, then stepped proudly through the door into the Council Chamber, for he was none other than Xavier de Varga.

The murky, Venice air followed him into the Chamber, two ornately carved wooden windows allowing in the background noise of the canal and letting out the incense coiling up towards the ceiling from braziers in each corner of the large room. Once it might have seen balls and other soirees that included the very best personages of Venice, including the Doge. Now the broad expanse of black marble floor was empty and meant to symbolize that though Cartos kind might be diminished, they still were strong within a broader non-Cartos world.

The Council sat in a half circle of ornately carved chairs, each with its side table that held water glass, cell phone, and tablet. Each chair was carved to represent the lands that the Council lord was responsible for—Italy, Portugal, Northern Europe including the British Isles, North Africa and the Middle East, India and China and the lands of Southeast Asia. The new worlds of the Americas and Australia were not represented, for they had no indigenous Cartos population. In fact, since the rise of the Gift amongst the general population, few Cartos travelled there at all. Except a very few agents who had the talent to travel unseen and go unnoticed. It required gifts rare even amongst his people, like the talent to transmute.

"My Lords and Ladies," Xavier said and went to one knee as was expected. He bowed his head before them. Let them see him as a man humbled and brought to heel.

He felt their study like the flick of a feather duster across his skin. They attempted to read his essence. Well, let them. Let them see his pain that his people were afraid for their safety. Let them see how he mourned his place within their society. Let them see everything except his determination to return to Vallon.

"Arise, Xavier de Varga. We will not have one of such parentage grovel at our feet," said Hector Gonzales, the current spokesperson for the Council.

Xavier stood to face him. Hector was a slight man, with a horseman's straight back, though his years on the Council had stooped his shoulders somewhat. His dark hair had lightened to grey, though he was only a few years older than Xavier, and his face that had always carried a smile now carried careful neutrality, which was not a good sign. He came from Cordoba, not too distant from the lands Xavier's family had held in Southern Portugal. Once he would have sat at the Council meetings in immaculate suit and tie, but that had changed, apparently. He wore draped cream trousers and a loose tunic that was far too informal given the seriousness of this meeting. But then, perhaps it was not serious to Hector. Once they had been friends and had traded each other fine Andalusian and Lusitanian horses, but that was long ago and his gaze no longer showed the signs of friendship. Hector might be the current voice for the Council, but he was also its youngest member and thus subject to all the whims of his elders.

Xavier nodded his greeting. "It is good to be amongst my kind again."

He made a point of meeting Hector's gaze and then attempting to meet each Council member's gaze in turn. Voda, the representative from South Asia met his gaze and nodded, her dark sweep of hair around her shoulders like a shroud. But the others, pale Wark with his iceberg gaze from northern Europe, Aziz from the Middle East whose scent of coriander permeated the chamber, Polo from Italia and the Balkans in her sleek black dress and stiletto heels even at sixty years, tiny Norvanaphum from Southeast Asia with her cherub lips and her unforgiving gaze, and Chan of China who wore traditional Chinese silks and would not meet Xavier's eyes. Worst of all was Carlos de Varga, tall, straight and enough alike to Xavier to give the uncomfortable sense that this man was Xavier's future. Two years Xavier's elder, his brother-in-all-ways-except-spirit, Carlos followed the Council without question, while Xavier—did not.

Only two he might count as friends among them, and one of them was Hector. His brother—well, things had not been so well between them for years since Leticia changed her preferences from Xavier to Carlos. So there was no certain favor there.

"It is a sore thing, indeed, to have a de Varga before us on such serious charges," Hector began. "To expose our existence to one of the so-called Gifted of the New World." He tsked. "We understand that the situation arose out of concern that the use of Gifted power might expose our existence anyway. We have debated long on this excuse and have come to the conclusion that it is not enough. Such exposure would have focused on the Gifted, not our older race, but now the Gifted know we exist. They will not stop their search for us and their people have already disrupted our lives enough, that we must keep ourselves masked at all times to avoid their detection."

"And you out-and-out told them!" said Wark, his neck veins bulging. "Do you know the challenges this may mean? And if word of this gets beyond the Gifted? Do you wish the purges of old to return?"

Hector waved Wark to silence, then turned back to Xavier. "As I said, it is a serious charge, made more serious by your refusal to tell us who knows this thing so that we can fix the situation."

He could not deny it. The Council's combined gazes were a weight on his shoulders, their Cartos presence like stinging whips as they sent small surges of blue-gold power at him. In his weakened condition, it was all he could do to hold against them. But he squared his stance and did not falter. Let them bring him to his knees, but he would not give up the one name that meant something to him.

"At least he does not lie," Voda said, her voice resonant as the ancient string instruments she was well known for playing. "He has not from the beginning. We must give him that."

He inclined his head in her direction and took a deep breath. "That is the truth, for you would learn of this thing soon enough. But you may bleed me dry and still I will not betray the one I protect. So I present to you your choice. You may kill me for my crime, or you may let me go free and I will avoid all further contact. The woman in question already believes I may be dead. We can let her believe this and then she will have no reason to seek further."

He refused to be afraid, whatever their decision. During his long hours in the subterranean chamber under Leticia's careful care, he had thought long and hard about his bargaining position and could identify only one thing that might save him.

He shrugged. "Audacious, I know, but there are so few of us with the skills I possess—but if the skill to move from place to place is easily replaced, then I accept my fate."

For a moment the Council seemed stunned by his bargain.

"Kill him, I say," said Wark. "His example will be a good one to all. This is no time to bend the rules simply because some of our kind have throwback skills."

"And that would seem to be a wrongheaded decision," Voda replied with a shake of her gleaming head. She poured herself a sweating glass of water and drank. "That type of thinking would see us no longer foster our healers or even the longevity of our species. To execute Xavier would be akin to a horse breeder slaughtering one of his finest studs because he dumped his rider." She sent a humorous glance his way as if to see if he appreciated her simile.

He gently bowed his head.

Hector held up his hands. "We will hold our dialogue in private. De Varga, you will await our decision in the anteroom under Leticia's guard."

It seemed cool in the anteroom after the intense scrutiny of the Chamber. Leticia paced the length of the hallway, her high heels clicking. When she returned to him she frowned.

"You think you can get away with anything. You think you are above us all simply because of your talents. Well, you are not unique, you know. You could have done far more for your kind by producing others like you, but you prefer to be alone, wandering the world like some Lazarus."

He leaned back against the wall, suddenly exhausted and not caring at the pain the pressure on his flayed flesh brought. "I know, Leticia. I am a bastard because I would not love you. I am worse than a bastard because I would not sire a child on you, and I am thrice a bastard because I was not jealous when you married Carlos. I know both you and Carlos can transmute, but neither of you share my temperament. I do not prefer the power plays of Council politics. I am a man who prefers to deal with specific people and problems."

She glared at him and whirled away, then stomped back to him. "I say you are a throwback in the worst of ways—your temperament is akin to those Cartos who refused to listen to the edicts millennia ago. You are a danger, Xavier de Varga. A danger that I will see removed, if I can."

He smiled mildly up at her. "I see. Then you have controlled my brother's vote, have you? And perhaps a few others as well? Hector? Wark?"

The dark gleam in her gaze said he had the right of it. Leticia might not sit on the Council, but with her body, she had gathered power nonetheless.

So he knew what the verdict would be. *Ah, Bela, would that we might be together again.* And the longing cut his chest like a knife and almost doubled him over. To never see her again. To never stroke her silken flesh or see her smile or hear her maddeningly stubborn, wonderful ideas again. To never again reach the nirvana of union with her.

Life would have far less meaning than it had now. He would wither away into as soulless a creature as Leticia if he were not with her. He had felt himself going that way before he discovered his Bela early in her time as an AGS agent. He had seen her and been captivated and had secretly watched her ever since.

The opening of the Council doors brought him out of his remembrance of her flow of blonde hair and the long, tigress stride he so admired. Voda stood there, which could be either bad or good.

"Xavier," she said with the faintest of smiles on her lips; then she nodded at Leticia. "You should come as well."

She led them inside and Leticia closed the door behind them as Voda reclaimed her seat.

Hector rose. "Xavier de Varga, step forward please to receive the Council's justice."

He kept his head high, his shoulders back as he readied himself to hear his fate. He stepped into the arc of the circle of chairs and once more felt the weight of their Cartos consideration. He would not bow before it.

"Xavier de Varga, after the full and careful consideration of this Council, it is our decision that you shall be released to carry out your duties to Cartos kind. You are to not to set foot in the New World again—there are tasks enough here to keep you busy. And to ensure you abide by these rules you will be joined with a partner who shares your talents, but who perhaps has greater loyalty to our ways."

He stiffened. This was not what he wanted. He was not someone who worked with a partner and never had been.

Hector must have seen his hesitation. "Do not question this decision, Xavier. It is the only reason you are still alive."

Xavier swallowed back his frustration and his anger. He never should have returned after the Seattle venture, but he had tried to do the right thing. "Then who is this paragon I am to partner with?"

His voice sounded as angry as he felt, but there was no masking it.

"Leticia Arbos de Varga. You will leave your work as interrogator. You will become his conscience and his partner."

§

The scent of water-rich soil at *Miss Elizabeth's Guest House* seemed oddly out of place with the sun beating down on the landscape, but here on the blessedly shaded front porch of the two-story house, the geraniums and impatiens cascaded over the edge of the planters set along the white-painted porch railings. Two white wicker chairs with floral cushions beckoned and Vallon could imagine sitting there sipping iced tea or a mint julep, whatever the hell that was. She braced her hand on the door frame and stabbed the brass-encased doorbell. From inside came the faint strains of Dolly Parton's *Nine to Five*.

Oh yeah, definitely not Seattle. Even with the sprinkler's help, the front lawn was as sun baked around the edges as the lawns of the other houses, but in this area of New Madrid, the homes were larger and showed a higher level of care in the neat lawns, the paved driveways, and the more expensively painted houses than had been evident in the area around New Madrid Station. Correction: the place where New Madrid Station once stood.

She closed her eyes, trying to fight back the panic. Here she was again, barely able to stand, the hot and cold flushes of the afterburn running through her and her brain hurting so it was almost impossible to think and she *hadn't done anything!* How the hell did you get afterburn in a situation like that? Her heart still beat so hard in her chest that she was sure anyone would spot it.

"Damn it! Isn't anyone home?"

She stabbed the doorbell again. Again.

"Shh, Vallon. It'll be all right." Fi hovered right behind her and that was worst of all, because Fi knew how bad off she was, and yet she hadn't offered to help. In fact, she'd been silent as hell the entire painful ride over here from the so-called Kochtitsky House.

Through the ride, each throb of the afterburn had ached with the question of what the hell that had been and why and how her father had been involved—if he was. Was the bolt a remnant of the change they'd wrought on the AGS station? A new kind of Gift? An attack on any Gifted who came near, or an attack on her? The permutations made her dizzy. The fact that her father might be involved had soured her stomach until she'd had to ask Fi to stop the car so she could retch into a ditch. Whatever had changed the AGS station and caused the quake had been powerful. And where were the three AGS agents?

Damn it, the agents! She'd been so taken aback by the sense of her father that she hadn't even tried to look for them. Through the afterburn haze she tried to -reach- but only succeeded in shifting her vision to a watery view of streaking colors and not much else. She wasn't going to tell much at all like that.

She fell back into herself and sagged against the doorway as footsteps *clippity-clip-clipped* down a tiled hallway inside the house. The door opened, releasing a blast of mint-scented frigid air, and a woman stood there—blonde hair coiled up in a chignon, white blouse and turquoise skirt and high-heeled turquoise mules on her feet that, taken altogether, had her looking like an escapee from the 1960s.

"Why, you must be Vallon Drake," the woman said in a soft southern accent, her blue eyes crackling with sharp intelligence. "I'm sorry to keep you waiting. I was baking bread in the summer kitchen at the back of the house. It took me a moment to get my apron off and my greetin' face on." She smiled, exposing perfect white teeth.

And she didn't seem to have a hair out of place, or an ounce of flour down her perfectly ironed skirt. She looked like a flipping Barbie doll aged to almost forty.

"We're here about the rooms," Fi said over Vallon's shoulder, because Vallon still hadn't found the strength to speak. It took enough effort just to understand what she was seeing, because standing in the dimness of the stairs behind the woman was an apparition out of an old Colonel Saunders commercial. A man clad in a white linen suit complete with black string tie, his white hair brushed back from his face with some kind of pomade that couldn't mask his baby-fresh scent or the flare of Gifted. A man whose pale features and strange eyes were even stranger in the getup.

A man who shouldn't be here.

Landon.

CHAPTER 10 – FINDING

Vallon Drake didn't look like the answer to anyone's prayers at the moment. His poor pigeon faced his new friend, Elizabeth Ducharme, as if someone could push her over with a feather. Her eyes were huge and dark and her flesh pale enough it told him as much as the afterburn radiating off her. She leaned heavily against the door frame as her friend, Fi, spoke over her. *Now just what have you gotten into, pigeon?*

A little flush of excitement ran through Landon as he swished down the stairs in his extravagant white suit. Hide in plain sight had always been his motto. Maybe whatever had happened to Vallon was proof that his long-awaited dream was finally coming to pass and he could get what he wanted. In the meantime he caught Elizabeth Ducharme's hand.

"Lizzy dear, poor Vallon looks as if she's about to fall down. Why don't I give you a hand and show the two ladies to the parlor while you bring us all a glass of that wonderful lemonade of yours."

Elizabeth Ducharme, the owner and hostess of *Miss Elizabeth's Guest House,* stopped her chatter at the two women and looked down at Landon. "Why, thank you, Mr. Snow. I do appreciate your kindness." She turned back to Vallon and her friend. "Come in, please. Come right on in."

She gracefully motioned them past her and Fi stepped inside. Vallon more rolled around the doorframe and followed the wall with her shoulder until she leaned on the vaguely oriental floral wallpaper. Almost as if she didn't think she could stand.

If something had happened to her, it certainly didn't fit with what he'd seen when he did a survey of the town. New Madrid was pretty much the kind of place that anyone with dreams of anything greater than living in a town that perpetually looked like the set of a natural disaster movie had long ago abandoned. It left behind the kind of folks who stuck to themselves and who weren't about to make trouble.

Unless perhaps she'd come in contact with her Xavier, but that would leave her with less afterburn and probably a cat-that-ate-the-canary smile. Which was too bad, given everything that was happening.

Landon had bugged out of Seattle with just a quick phone call to Gleason, because seeing his genealogy file virtually disappear before his eyes suggested Amundson's agents would be after him sooner rather than later. If Vallon's mysterious Gifted paramour would at least show his face, it would make the rigors of hiding out in this rather desolate town at least bearable. To actually have the chance to ask questions of one of the outliers… what he might learn.

He waved Elizabeth back towards the kitchen and her footsteps faded *clippity-clippity* back into the depths of the house. He'd come to New Madrid by flying into Memphis and then driving up to New Madrid. He'd arrived two days ago and found Elizabeth Ducharme a most congenial hostess. They had hit it off well from the start.

He looked up at Vallon's pale face. The acrid scent of ozone and ashes overlaid her musky rose scent.

"Pigeon? What's happened to you?" He went to grab her arm to steady her, then held back because contact with an agent in afterburn was never a pleasant experience. With an agent who had it as bad as Vallon—well, he wasn't taking a chance. "The parlor's this way. The first room. Can you make it?"

"Of course I can." She shot him a look of impatience. "Just show me a place to sit down."

Still bitchy, at least. That was a good sign. Bitchy came long before the debilitating later stages of afterburn. He hooked his head to indicate that she should follow him and padded in his patent moccasins into the guesthouse's main room.

"Holy cow," Fi said as she entered, though Vallon said nothing. Her gaze just swept the place in a practiced, agent's assessment.

"Amazing, isn't it? Like inhabiting a peacock aviary that a fox has just gutted," he said, ignoring the image of carnage he'd just described. He settled on a faux Queen Ann chair with a chintz pattern of muted purple and blue feathers. A similar patterned fabric covered a couch that backed onto a dining room at the rear of the house, while an overstuffed chair had a pattern of peacock tail feathers in full display. The walls had peacock wallpaper, and a tall vase over a white stone fireplace held an arrangement of white peacock plumes, lamp shades had feather tassels, and knitted throws with feather fringes hung over the backs of the chairs. On the walls of both parlor and dining room were naturalist paintings of herons and cardinals and bluebirds, and in the front window, saved from direct sun by a gauzy white curtain, stood a floor-to-ceiling bird cage occupied by five canaries that struck up a song as soon as Vallon entered. She limped to the overstuffed chair and collapsed into it. Fi perched on the couch.

"I think she likes birds, don't you think, Vallon?" Fi asked.

His Pigeon had her head back, eyes closed. "The room smells like bird shit."

A small giggle came from the dining room and Vallon's eyes flashed open, guarded, dangerous even, in her hyper sensitive state. "Who's there?"

No one showed themselves, though Landon recognized the voice.

Then her face got confused. "There is someone there, isn't there?" Strain filled her voice and her gaze slid to Landon at first for reassurance, then: "And you? What the hell are you doing here?"

Mutable. Confused. Not exactly a good sign.

Another giggle and a tiny, blonde-haired, pixy-person sprang up from behind the couch. "You said 'hell.' And 'shit.' You'll get in trouble if Mama hears."

"Vallon, this is Farrah Ducharme, Lizzy—Elizabeth's daughter. Farrah, this is Vallon Drake, a friend of mine. I hope she can be your friend, too."

Farrah came around the couch, straightening a frilly purple skirt and a pink top with a purple Dora the Explorer cartoon on the front. She came up to Landon smelling of baby powder and sugar candy, but her uncertain blue-grey gaze never left Vallon.

"Hello. Are you sick?"

"Farrah! That is not what one says to a guest!" Lizzy *clippity-clipped* into the room, her bright smile momentarily obscured by a disapproving frown, as she carried a tray of five glasses and a pitcher of lemonade that was frosting in the air conditioning. She set the tray down on the table amidst the rattle of ice cubes, frowned a reprimand at her daughter with her hands on her hips, and then settled herself smoothly at the far end of the couch from Fi. She filled the tall glasses and the light scent of lemon filled the air with freshness.

Then Lizzy smiled brightly. "I'm so sorry for my daughter's outburst." She pulled Farrah onto the couch beside her. "Now, young lady, what did we say about how to greet guests?"

Farrah sighed and stood up again. She came around the parlor table and up to Vallon and held out her hand. "Pleased to meet you, Miss Drake."

Her tone said she wasn't pleased at all, but Vallon accepted her hand and shook, then quickly pulled her hand away. "Pleased to meet you, too, but call me Vallon."

But Farrah looked at Vallon curiously and rubbed her palm on her skirt, then she dutifully went to Fi and repeated the process, but after they'd shaken hands she kept looking at Fi. "You have the same color hair as me and mama."

"Yes. I do." Fi nodded.

Farrah swung around to look at Vallon. "She has hair the color of honey and she feels like honey, too. She makes my hand all sticky." She rubbed her palm on her skirt again and made a face that wasn't exactly favorable.

But her comment was interesting. Perhaps a comment on Vallon having sweaty palms after her long drive, or something more? Landon sat forward and -reached- for the child because she should not be able to sense anything off Vallon unless she was Gifted. But the girl carried no more of the Gifted flare than her mother and most of the American population. Stranger and stranger. He sat back and found Vallon looking at him, hunger blazing in her gone-black afterburn gaze.

"So, Miss Drake, Miss Murdoch, we are very pleased you have chosen New Madrid for your holiday. What brings you to our fair town?" Lizzy Ducharme sipped her lemonade, somehow avoiding placing pale pink lipstick prints on the chill glass. Vallon roused herself to gulp her drink down. She kept looking at the child, who had crept back in beside her mother.

"Just an interest in this part of the country, actually," Vallon said. "My father's great-grandfather was in the Civil War, and his records say he was in the Battle of Island Number Ten. I thought maybe I could learn something about the battle and maybe about the famous New Madrid earthquake." She shrugged. "Tourist stuff. You must see it a lot."

Lizzy's gaze did a dive to her hands. "Of course. You've come to the right place for both of those things. Farrah, why don't you tell Miss Drake about the New Madrid Earthquake? You remember. Your kindergarten teacher talked all about it."

Farrah shook her head and buried her face in her mother's shoulder.

"I'd really like to hear about it," Vallon said. Somehow she'd pulled herself together to engage the little girl, but he wanted—no—needed, to get her alone and find out what had happened to her.

He lifted his lemonade and the chill liquid sent a trail of lemon ice down his throat to join the excited flutter that had started as soon as he saw Vallon. She watched him sip and then downed her own glass as if it wasn't even cool. The afterburn must burn that hot. But the little girl barely peeked at her. Vallon sank back in her chair as if even that effort had exhausted her. Her eyes were fever bright and her scent of roses so overpoweringly raw even an unGifted should scent it.

"Ms. Ducharme, I think friend Vallon has had a long drive. Perhaps it would be wise to let her go to her room and have a rest while Ms. Murdoch checks them both in?"

Vallon gave him a grateful look.

Elizabeth Ducharme's hand fluttered to her mouth. "I am so sorry. I forget myself. It's just so nice to have folks come to visit from the outside. Farrah, honey, would you be a dear and go into the kitchen and get the keys and the papers I left on the kitchen table for Miss Drake and Miss Murdoch? Mr. Snow, if you would be so kind as to assist Miss Drake upstairs to the room across from yours, I'll be right up with Miss Murdoch."

She was suddenly up and fussing with lemonade glasses and throws on the furniture. Landon waited for Vallon to stand and led her to the carpeted stairs. "You look absolutely fagged, Pigeon. As if you've fought a war."

She looked up at him warily as she followed him up the stairs. "Not surprising. It's what I feel like."

Her knuckles were white on the stair railing and that wasn't the girl who loved to go for a run every morning, or the agent who had faced down Rebecca Murdoch and rescued a police detective from sulfuric acid. Upstairs he led her down a white-painted hall lined with family photos, to one of two open doors that let in the bright Missouri sunshine. He entered the first room to reveal a four-poster double bed covered in a print of carnation-red flowers, and plain wood furniture that had the sheen of recently being dusted and oiled. A vase of fresh daisies and carnations stood on the doily-draped dresser, a door gave off into what must be a private bathroom. A single window covered with gauze curtains let in the bright blue reflections from the swimming pool in the backyard.

Vallon stopped in the doorway.

"Problem, pigeon?"

Her throat worked, but she didn't move. Only her eyes turned to him. "It's just nicer than I expected from what I've seen of the town."

She stepped inside, barely made it to the bed before her legs gave. She sagged on top, covering her eyes with her forearm.

"What happened, pigeon? You weren't this bad in Seattle after the attack, and Gregor said you'd recovered when he last saw you."

Her mouth worked as if she chewed her words. Then a huge sigh racked through her. "I found him," she said.

§

A cell phone's ring drilled into Jason's head as he sat halfway up Vallon Drake's basement stairs. The glare of the single bare light bulb on the ceiling placed stark shadows over the cracked concrete floor and the oily moisture in the cracks. One of those shadows was of a castle, and therefore the castle couldn't be a figment of his imagination. It couldn't. But the fact it was real.…

It left him almost breathless, left his legs unable to stand. After all his hopes and the fears that he really was going crazy because of what he suspected about Vallon, this proved he wasn't. She *could* do the things he'd suspected. She *could* 'create' things. And if she could do a castle and miniature people like those he'd seen locking themselves in the castle and that he still caught glimpses of in the tower window and along the ramparts, well then, then she could do a woman. Cheryl, with her soft waves of auburn hair and her hazel eyes that had always let him see into her soul. Cheryl, who had left a hole in his soul when she died.

He blinked back tears as the phone drilled again. Jeezus. The damn thing just wasn't going to let up. He fished the infernal device out of his pocket and checked the caller I.D. Clint. Fuck. But not surprising. He took a deep breath to steady himself and touched the phone on.

"Bryson."

"Dammitalltohell, Slick! I've been calling you for hours. Where you at, man?"

Where indeed. Jason's gaze grazed the floor joists that were even with where he sat, the bare bulb, the scene down below where wood smoke lazily rose into the air above the castle, and was tempted to tell Clint exactly where he was and what he was looking at, but Clint wouldn't get the joke at all. Nope, ol' buddy Clint was likely to have the boys in white coats here in short order if Jason told.

"Out. Around. I must have been in one of those cell blank spots."

There was silence a moment. "Would that be because the carrier didn't provide coverage, or because you just blanked out?"

It was tempting to just hang up the phone. He'd been sitting silently on the stairs waiting to see if the castle gate would open again and the people return to their farming. Because they were farming. Vallon Drake had an entire Lilliputian town in her basement. He sighed when he heard Clint take a gulp of coffee at the other end of the phone.

"Does it really matter? You already figure you know where I am."

"Wrong, Slick. I *know* where you are. I had them check your twenty on GPS an hour ago. I've been phoning ever since." Clint wasn't exactly successful in masking his disapproval.

Jason took the phone away from his ear. An hour? The phone had been ringing on and off for an hour? How long had he been sitting here, anyway? He checked his diver's watch and yanked himself upright. Holy hell, he'd been here what? Five, no, six hours.

"Fuck. Fuck me. Clint, buddy. I'll be right in, okay. I lost track of time. I was checking on Vallon's cat. She's away. That's Vallon, not the cat." He stabbed the call off, stood, and almost fell because his legs had fallen asleep. Had he really sat there all this time? Painful pins and needles filled his feet and calves as he stumbled up and out to the kitchen. He left the basement light on and stood there a moment. Yes, that was the scent of wood smoke on the air. Not his imagination. The building, the people truly were there even though standing in this normal-looking kitchen it was hard to believe what existed down those stairs.

Mrreow?

Maggie's querulous meow said it was time for her dinner. She rubbed up against his legs, sniffed the air, and darted into the open basement door.

"Shit!" She was gone, fat little black-and-white hindquarters making a dash down the stairs. Now wouldn't that wreak havoc with the Lilliputians.

He thundered after her and caught her up just as she stared up at the castle, her tail bristling. A low growl came from her throat and she struggled in his arms. A claw swipe at his throat and he dropped her and she scooted up the stairs at a run, her tail like a black-and-white flag. The soft *flap-flap* of the cat door upstairs said she was gone outside again.

What the hell had gotten into her?

But something had spooked her, but good. He turned back to the castle. It looked the same, except—almost like it was in soft focus or something. He blinked and rubbed his eyes, but it was still there like a haze. Hmm.

Something was happening. The air smelled funny, too. Almost like an electrical fire. He glanced up at the light bulb wiring, but there was no sign of anything wrong, and time was ticking, and he needed to get Maggie fed and at least put in an appearance in the office, or someone's head was going to roll and it would rightly be his. He took the stairs two at a time and closed and locked the basement carefully behind him. Then he pocketed the key, slopped cat food onto a plate, and rushed out the front door into late afternoon sunshine.

The sweet scent of cedar and cut lawn met his nose. From a few houses over came the drone of a lawnmower. Someone retired, probably, or a landscape company. He closed the picket gate behind him and strode for his car when he caught movement up the street. The gardener probably, but something made him stop and turn.

The door opened on a black SUV, shoved in amongst the small foreign cars parked along the street like a Great Dane amidst Chihuahuas. A man stepped out, clad in all black trousers and rugby shirt, shoulder length black hair pushed back behind his ears, and a set of dark aviator sunglasses masking his eyes. Despite the lack of a long trench coat, the man still exuded that fatal combination of mystery and power—the kind that always seemed so attractive to women. Even from this distance he could tell who it was.

Xavier de Varga closed the SUV's door and started towards Jason.

CHAPTER 11 — A MURDER OF CROWS

Even though she felt like hell, Vallon couldn't keep the twisted excitement from her voice, because maybe, just maybe, she was finally going to get to meet her father. She uncovered her eyes, and in a beam of sunlight through the gauze-covered window, Landon gripped the edge of her dresser near the vase of daisies like he might faint. This, even though she hadn't said who she thought she'd found. Landon's baby-fresh scent seemed to fill the room and the oversweet scent just increased her headache and the alternating chill and heat that beat through her chest and arms.

"Just who did you find, pigeon?" He tried to sound casual, but for the first time ever, she could hear the effort. He settled in the lone chair by the window. "What happened today?"

How was she supposed to say this? Because she wasn't about to give everything away, not even to Landon.

"Why are you here? You always told me you don't do field work." The way the muscles in his neck worked, there was clearly something there, but Landon just pressed his pale lips together.

She pushed herself up on her elbows. "Looks like we're at a bit of an impasse here. I'm not telling you anything until I understand why you're here."

Maybe she was just being paranoid and bitchy—afterburn could do that, but really—why had Gregor Gleason sent his right hand? To check up on her? If that were the case, she was tempted to just pack up and head home. Except for possibly finding her father. Why she suddenly thought he was here, she couldn't say, except it just seemed so plausible.

Landon's gaze clashed with hers, but she held steady until finally the little man looked away. And that was a first, too, and so was the fact that Landon looked older: more sunken in the cheeks, and his white hair actually had begun to yellow. How old was Landon, anyway? He'd been around as long as she could remember.

"All right, pigeon. Let's just say things were not going well at home. Amundson has no love for any of us, and for Gleason and me least of all. I tried to destroy some old research files, but unfortunately, even with my precautions, Amundson's IT section discovered it."

The light through the window placed a slight halo through his slicked-back hair, but she had a hard time thinking of Landon as anything other than a creature of shadows. He'd always been her friend and confidant, but he was holding back on her now. "What kind of research?"

His lips pruned a moment. "Research into the Gift. Why we have it. Why others don't."

The way he studied his hands and sucked in his cheeks told her he still wasn't telling her everything, but she wasn't sure what more to ask. "So, what? Gleason thought you were better here helping me?"

He looked up at her then. "No. I told Gleason that coming here was better than waiting for Amundson to have me arrested for tampering with United States intelligence information."

"Fuck. You mean that prig could be sending men after you here?" The afterburn stabbed through her skull as she jerked up to sitting. She collapsed back, eyes clamped shut to hold her brain in. "Damn it, Landon," she groaned. "Do you know what you've done?"

"Unfortunately, yes."

"You could be exposing all of us. If Amundson gets involved, it won't be about who's created the New Madrid quake, it'll be about all of us. He'll tar all Gifted with the same brush." She squinted at him and saw a little surprise and a fair amount of admiration cross his face.

"Well done, pigeon. That is my assessment, as well."

"Then why come here? I can see leaving the AGS and Seattle. Hell, we've all thought about it since Amundson took over. I know I have. But coming here just compromises my investigation."

He pursed his lips again and glanced out the window. The bright light showed dark circles under his pale eyes and a tracery of lines across his face that she'd never noticed before.

"I thought I might be of assistance to you."

"And what? That that might save your ass?"

Landon did his customary shrug that made him look even more like a kid in his father's suit. "Perhaps. Perhaps not. Either way, I will not be so easy to catch for Amundson's men. I do have contingencies, pigeon."

Contingencies. Trust Landon to always have them. Like a Chinese puzzle box, he was just as hard to fathom. She finally nodded.

He gazed at her over templed fingers. "So. May we move on in our discussion? Perhaps to what you discovered in whatever event happened to you?"

The way Landon almost seemed to press himself into his chair, it was like he was holding himself in check. This was a bit of knowledge dearly important to him. Why, was the question.

The damned afterburn pulsed through her veins like acid and she truly just wanted to curl up and die. It wasn't what she needed to be doing. She needed to be up and pursuing her investigation, but in this condition she wasn't going to be good for anything. She rolled on her side to look at Landon. "I need your help, Landon. I need you to help me with the afterburn the way you and Fi helped me in Seattle."

His eyes widened a little, his lips tight and almost translucent over his teeth. "Is this extortion, pigeon? You will not share your investigation findings unless I do this and that for you?"

She wasn't sure how to answer. "I'm in pain here, Landon. I need help."

"There are ways of dealing with afterburn. You've used them yourself for years."

Oh, God, the pain made it so hard to think with reason. She pressed clenched fists into her ears. "I can't. I just can't. Xavier…" A shudder ran through her so hard and fast she tasted blood where her teeth caught her tongue. Regardless of the afterburn's heat, she was cold. So cold she didn't know if she'd ever get warm.

The rustle of fabric and a painful movement of air across her skin said Landon was moving. "Perhaps it would be better if we continued this conversation later. Perhaps we should go for a walk after you've had a chance to sleep. That will at least take the edge off so you can think."

And then he was gone, leaving her with the gnawing question as to why he would not help her. The door clicked shut behind him, leaving her there to curl into a prawn and claw the carnation-covered duvet up and over her. She clenched her eyes shut and tried to push away the fear that came with the darkness. Distant screams and falling and the overwhelming scent of almonds. Her father.

§

She woke to an amber light through the window and the sound of voices from downstairs. Sweat soaked her hair and clothing and the duvet that she'd long since pushed off her body. For the moment, the cool air of the house seemed to have cooled her, but she felt tender all over, like a human-sized bruise. Every part of her complained when she moved.

She rolled over and hunched on the side of the bed. Sometime or other someone had come into her room and removed her boots. They sat neatly by the dresser. Her suitcase stood on a rack beside the door. The Ducharme woman, possibly, but it could have been Fi. Landon had left with a finality that said he wasn't coming back until she was prepared to talk to him. She wasn't sure if she was, even now. If he was prepared to watch her suffer, why should she do anything for him?

A soft knock came at the door. Vallon ran her fingers through her matted hair. She had to look like hell, given how she felt. "Who is it?" she croaked, her throat parched for water.

"If you want to go for that walk, we should go now. Dinner is in an hour." Landon's voice came through the door.

Did she really want to go for a walk with him? She sighed. What was going on that he refused to help her and she refused to tell him what she knew? He'd always been her sounding board and he'd always helped her. So just what was happening between them?

"Give me five." She stood up and wobbled and had to sit down again. Best make that ten. She stank of old sweat and her skin and t-shirt were sticky. She stripped off her clothes and stepped into the shower in the closet-sized bathroom, then toweled off and pulled out a clean t-shirt and the one pair of shorts she'd brought with her. Her hair she yanked back in a ponytail. Then she slipped her feet into sketchers and ran out the door feeling, if not better, at least not like she'd be better off putting a gun to her head.

Landon checked his watch at the bottom of the stairs and silently opened the front door. Outside it was like walking into a wall of water, the humidity was so high. "My God. And people live here? By choice?"

The lowering sun glazed the trees, barren yards, and low slung houses golden. A murder of crows passed overhead seeking their evening rookery, their wings dark commas against the sky. In the southeast, gold-tinged cumulonimbus clouds were trying to develop the towering hammerhead top that spoke of storms and possibly tornados. There was no breeze, and nothing moved.

"A butterfly wing would cause more of a breeze," she said as Landon stepped down off the porch and to his car, a small blue Prius rental. "Where's Fi?"

"Cleaning up for dinner, as far as I know," he said.

"But I thought we were going for a walk."

He just opened the door. "We are. Drive first, though. We'll be back in time for dinner."

Hesitating, she climbed in beside him. His faint almonds and baby's breath scent cut through the rental car smell. Landon remained silent, maybe angry at her attitude, maybe thinking about something else.

"I'm sorry we got off on the wrong foot earlier," she said hoping it would get him talking and she might understand.

He backed out of the driveway and headed towards town. "I shouldn't have pushed. You were in a bad way. A bottle of inhibitor would have been more helpful than Lizzy's lemonade. I just didn't happen to have any in my back pocket, and it would have looked rather odd to our hostess."

"You had inhibitor and you didn't give me some?" Not that she liked the deadening feeling it left her with, but it was a damn sight better than feeling like dying. She looked at him. "I thought you were my friend. You saw how bad off I was. Why wouldn't you help me?"

"As your friend, I also know how much you hate taking inhibitor." He pulled the car to the side of the road in front of a boarded up shop and turned to her. "Vallon, what is going on? Right now it feels like you don't trust me."

She closed her eyes and shook her head. "Why should I? I don't understand you—me—us. Something set off this afterburn and then suddenly you turn up. It's like my brain's connected the two events and won't see the illogic of it."

"Pigeon, I came to help you."

"Well then help me!" She turned to him and held out her hands, begging him to take them, to help her cycle the afterburn and give her relief.

And that was it. That was the problem. She looked at his familiar face pinked by the setting sun, the watery blue eyes that had seen so much of her growing up. "You see. That's why I don't trust you. A friend would help. You were there in Seattle. You could help me now."

Landon looked away and found something to study outside the car. A crow hopped across a lawn to where a sprinkler rescued a bed of flowers from the drought. The bird stood under the water and fluttered its wings. They turned bronze in the sunlight and beautiful even in this godforsaken landscape.

"Pigeon, I don't think that's a good idea. I did not appreciate the way it made me feel—as if I was stretched and not totally in control of myself. Why not ask Fiona?" he asked, his voice quiet in the car.

"You think I haven't? She'd afraid of the process. Afraid of me turning into her mother—as if that would ever happen. Rebecca Murdoch was addicted to the power."

"Are you so sure, pigeon? It could be she was addicted to what came after—to the very process you are trying to get Fiona to do for you." He shook his head. "No. I do not feel that me helping you is a good idea at all."

She came half out of her seat to turn to him. "The way you feel! You should try this, Landon. You should try afterburn eating through you like snakes on fire. You should try not being able to put two thoughts together. You should try barely being able to find your feet to stand and having the whole world go unsteady around you. But then you can't feel it, because you're not Gifted like I am. So maybe the reason you don't want to help me is because you're jealous. Yeah. That sounds about right. Make pigeon pay so you don't feel like such a failure!" It was out of her mouth before she had time to even consider what she said.

A barely perceptible shrug was all the reaction Landon showed. "Perhaps you are right. I don't know. But it is still my choice, pigeon. I do not wish to experience it again."

He eased the little car forward and she slumped back in her seat. The conversation was over, she could tell. Landon had a way of stiffening his jaw when he no longer wished to engage in a conversation, and his jaw was practically locked right now. Close of subject. She'd find another way to deal. If all else was lost, there had to be a decent man in this town. Hell, even an indecent one would do.

Landon cruised down main street, then turned onto a street called Mill and soon was driving amongst the small bungalows she'd seen this afternoon. A few children played in a dusty yard. A mongrel leapt at a chain-link backyard fence when they passed, and the barking followed them down the street. Ahead, like an oasis, lay the newly minted green grass of the Kochtitsky House lawn and the glowing white façade of the house itself. Landon barely slowed down as he passed, but his brows rose. He went around the block and headed back towards the center of town. Then he wound through side streets and found one that crossed the levee east of town and headed out into farmland, following a levee that must cut off a large swath of farmland. He drove for a few minutes and then pulled over, turned off the car, and opened the door. The silence of the evening was still better than the strained silence of the car. Vallon climbed out.

The sun had lowered until it rested on the horizon and the browns and greens of daytime had gone grey at the edges. The humid air smelled of dust and old mud and grass so dry it would break if you stepped on it. Across the road, a two-story house and a group of dusty farm buildings hunkered down amid stubbled cornfields for the night. Behind her, the ridge of the levee lay covered with sun-browned tall grass. Landon came around the car and silently climbed the levee, leaving her to follow. At the top she could see out onto the shadowed landscape beyond the levee.

It was a darker side of the world. Treetops flanked the other side of the levee, the leaves tossing from the mass of crows roosting in the branches. Their croaks and calls filled the silence and she could almost feel the wind of their wings as more birds flew in from elsewhere.

Beyond the narrow line of trees lay a meandering water channel and then more fields.

"They're on the wrong side," she said and glanced at Landon. "The fields, I mean. On the wrong side of the levee."

"Well that's their problem, now isn't it, pigeon? They knew they were outside this levee when they bought the land. Maybe not this generation, but their ancestors did when they bought the very fertile land so cheap. They knew that when the river's flooding endangered towns upriver, they were in the spillway." He looked at her and she was pretty sure he was trying to say it was a lot like the Gift and afterburn. You used the power and you paid the price.

"I didn't do anything, Landon. That's what's got me so pissed. I just stepped up on that driveway. I mean, you saw. The house and lawn stands out like a skin graft, a scab over where the substation should be."

"It was not natural, yes." He stepped up beside her, his diminutive form barely coming up to her shoulder. "Tell me what happened."

"That's just it. I really don't know. When we got into town I did my usual tour. When I saw the house, I stepped down on the driveway pavement just past the curb, and it was like the whole world exploded around me." She stopped, trying to puzzle it out. "No. It was more like something geysered up around me. It was like acid, Landon. It ripped me apart and…." She ran her hands up over her face. It was so hard to remember, to get clear what she'd felt when it was a memory every part of her wanted to forget. "There was screaming, and I wasn't sure if it was me or someone else. I've never experienced anything like it. But the one thing I remember better than anything else was the scent. Cinnamon and pomegranate, and I swear there was a hint of almonds. When the screaming stopped it almost took my breath away, because for some reason it reminded me of him so much."

Damn it, her throat was closing up almost as if she'd start crying, and after all these years she was *not* going to do that.

"You were screaming?" Landon's white suit seemed to glow as the sun fell and the dusk gathered around them. For a moment she had to think.

"I don't think I was. Fi said I just—crumpled. She didn't say anything about screaming."

"So where did it come from, I wonder?" Landon mused, looking at her. "You said 'him', pigeon. Who is him?" he asked softly.

The heat seemed to run out of the world as the light faded. She turned away from him and the flat landscape ran away forever. Standing on this levee, it was hard to believe mountains even existed, just like it was hard to believe what she was going to say.

"It was my father, Landon. I'd know his scent anywhere." She felt like a little girl. The little girl who had run away from the academy so many times to go home to the place that wasn't there anymore. The low-slung ranch house was gone, replaced by a heritage-blue two-story house. She felt like the little girl Landon had picked up so many times and whom he'd comforted when she cried.

She looked at him and realized her eyes were filled with tears, like blood welling up in a reopened wound. "I didn't imagine it, Landon. I didn't."

His eyes were sad, almost disappointed, but unlike the old days when he'd given her a hug, he just stood there. The afterburn, probably. She understood, but part of her was still that little girl, still wanted human contact and comfort.

"I don't disbelieve you, pigeon. I just thought it might be, oh, your mysterious friend."

"You believe Dad could be alive?" After all those years of denying it, he was finally going to admit the possibility.

"I've always believed all those deaths were too convenient. The agents we lost were too skilled to be caught in the accidents that killed them. And of course, there were no bodies—until Simon Lamrey. And your father was one of the most skilled of them. And other things." He shook his head and kicked at the long stalks of grass with his moccasins. Small seeds leapt free in the last of the sun's glow. The crow-filled trees on the eastern side of the levee and the distant fields were lost in gloom. The birds chortled together.

"What other things?"

Landon chewed his lip and turned to her. "It is not a pretty picture, pigeon. Not one I wanted to paint for you of Francis Drake."

Everything went silent around them. Her stomach tightened into a knot and her skin turned to gooseflesh. "Just tell me, Landon. I'm a big girl."

But she wasn't sure she was.

Landon nodded slightly. "Remember *Gild the Lily*, pigeon?"

"Using agents as weapons. I remember."

Landon wouldn't meet her gaze. "It was more than that. It was using the Gift to benefit the Gifted. There were some who said that the Gift was the next step in nature's survival of the fittest, as if we were an evolutionary leap forward. *Gild the Lily* suggested we should just take what we wanted because we have the power to do it."

"You mean take from the unGifted?" She felt sick to her stomach. She could imagine what it would be. Worse than a blood bath, it would be the wisping away of people the Gifted didn't like in the worst kind of 'disappeared.' The removal of houses that would be replaced by places the Gifted lived. And people would never know as long as the Gifted had the power to hold the change in place until the 'normals' accepted it into their world view.

She felt Landon's gaze on her face. She didn't like his pity, and the memory of almonds almost made her ill.

"What does this have to do with my father?" But she knew. She could see it in his eyes and the way he looked at her as if she might break at the words. Because she remembered the pitiless expression her father could get. Once she had thought he reserved it for her when she disappointed him. "Just get it over with, would you? Damn it, spit it out!"

"He was the architect, Vallon. He wrote the whole thing."

The sun had fallen. The deep blue of the sky went black, and the stink of ozone suddenly overwhelmed the scent of dust and sour, standing water. The huge flock of crows rose into the air in a cloud of rough cries as the levee suddenly jerked and began to shake under her.

CHAPTER 12 – XAVIER

The late afternoon breeze off Elliott Bay tangled Xavier de Varga's hair so that he looked even more dangerous than usual. He strode down the sidewalk toward Jason, with an overt physicality that was intended to threaten. The hard expression on his face, coupled with his hooked nose, spoke of anger and retribution and the fact he had probably seen too much of the world. At least too much of the darker side of it. That was something they had in common. He was a tall man, too, so when he strode up to Jason, they were eye to eye. He had a soft, heated, dry scent about him that seemed out of place in Seattle's damp air.

"Bryson. I did not expect to see you here." De Varga's voice carried a slight accent Jason couldn't quite place: Southern European or Spanish or something, but educated in some place like Britain, or Canada, perhaps.

"I could say the same. I thought you were supposed to be dead."

The dark man shrugged, but his black eyes glittered with anything but casualness. "What is the saying of your Samuel Clemens? *Word of my demise has been greatly exaggerated?* Business called me away. I am back now."

Jason didn't like him. Didn't like the fact the man had returned just when he had a chance to get Vallon where he wanted her. But that was what Xavier de Varga did, wasn't it? He stuck his nose where it wasn't wanted. He'd walked into Vallon's world and taken over just when Jason had realized what he had in Vallon, and she had thrown him over for Xavier so fast it was indecent. As a matter of fact, he *really* didn't like the guy.

"Vallon is well?" the foreigner asked.

"She's just hunky dory. No thanks to you." *Let that stick in your craw, asshole.* Jason crossed his arms as Xavier's gaze flickered to the house. Like Vallon, his eyes did that weird out-of-focus thing that made them look like they almost glowed.

"She is not here." His gaze turned back to Jason, remote, almost as if Jason was an afterthought. "Where is she?"

"That'd be for me to know and…." Jason stopped himself, lest he sound like an idiot kid, but this guy just pushed every button he had with his tall mysterious looks and the fact that the information available on him in the systems was, at best, lacking. Xavier de Varga, a Portuguese national, was a geological consultant for some esoteric, Venice-based firm called *CartosNationele.* For some unspecified reason, he had floated into Vallon's sphere during the murder investigation of her last partner. He'd also been around during all the weird-ass goings on and, given the way Vallon looked at the guy, it was clear something had happened between them. "She's gone. Holidays, apparently."

"And you take care of her cat." The slight curve of the man's sensual lips made Jason feel like he was Vallon's servant—just as it was probably intended to.

"I helped her out because no one else was available. More'n some do." He ground the words out and de Varga stiffened. Good.

Jason turned to his car. Let the bugger stew in his own juices until Vallon returned.

"Thank you."

The words surprised Jason enough he swung back to the man. The air seemed to crackle around de Varga and his whole body suddenly seemed to radiate need.

"What was that?" Jason asked.

"Thank you. For caring for her when I could not."

Fuck. Just what he needed was for the guy to be decent. He just nodded and turned back to the car again.

"Where is she?"

He turned back to the foreigner again and crossed his arms. "Am I detecting a little desperation here? Jeezus man, you've been gone for months. You ever think Vallon might have moved on?"

It was an asshole thing to say, but it got the reaction he wanted. The dark man stiffened, and if anything, his normally olive skin paled.

"That may be," he said. His voice was cool and his gaze did that little glimmer thing again that made Jason feel like a wind had just cut though him. He shivered, suddenly cold even though the angled sun was still warm on his face. "I still need to talk to her about business."

The way he said it was like he expected Jason to just accept it. "So is this going to be another fun adventure like the last one? Maybe try to get her killed again?" And himself. He'd come closer to dying than anyone should.

"There are things happening."

So he didn't deny it. Jason shook his head and keyed his car door open. "Sorry. I can't help you."

De Varga took two long strides and his hand fell on Jason's shoulder before he could open the door and a jolt like electricity went through him. He spun around, knocking de Varga's hand aside, his hand going for his gun. The air smelled of licorice and cedar.

"Be careful, de Varga. I could run you in for assaulting a police officer." And frankly, as pissed as he was at his whole life circumstance, not much would give him greater pleasure.

"It is important that I see her. Where has she gone?"

Maybe there was a possibility here. Maybe he could use the man. He studied de Varga's expression. Yes, this just might work. "East is what I know, but I could find out for you. For a price."

"A price? The price of what?"

Fish or cut bait time, Bryson. He could hear Clint's voice. *You are one sick puppy, Slick.* Say it now or it would probably never get said. "I find you Vallon's location. You help me get my wife back."

§

The air swirled around Vallon as the levee lurched under her feet. Landon stumbled and fell to his knees amid the dusty weeds, and the dusk filled with rumbling, the beat of wings, and the screeching cries of the rising crows. The stink of cinnamon- and pomegranate- and licorice-power filled her nose, and deep in the earth, power built and forced its way upwards. *Towards her!*

The grass underfoot began to wisp away like candle smoke.

"Come on!" She grabbed Landon's hand, ignoring the pain of their touch, dragged him upright, and plunged down the side of the levee, long grass whipping her legs as she slipped, slid, sat down, and slid on her ass down to the road and the Prius. Overhead the sky was blue-black and in the west the sunset placed an angry red welt across the horizon as if the west burned. The fiery glow caught on the towering clouds building. Storms coming. Rain would be a good thing. The things that came with the rain would not be.

Landon fumbled the car keys out of his pocket as the rumbling grew to a roar. The little car's edges began to soften, smoke lifted from the engine hood, from the roof, from the windshield. He beeped the car doors open.

"Get in. Get in," she shouted. The car door was soft as butter under her fingers around the edges. She slammed the car door behind her and Landon buttoned the car on and tromped on the accelerator. Go-go-go, before you turn to dust. The damn Prius took its own sweet time and the ground vibrated under them.

Then the car got going and the vibration—stopped. What the—.

"Landon, pull over."

He shook his head. His hair was all askew, his white suit covered in dust and clinging grass seeds.

She placed her hand on his on the steering wheel and let the afterburn shock him. The car jerked to a halt, still on the pavement, and she released him. He hung his head, still clutching the steering wheel. The silence filled with the sound of his rapid breathing.

"I have told you not to touch me when you are in such a condition, have I not?"

"I'm sorry. I had to get you to stop somehow." She opened the car door and stepped out. The fire glow was fading in the west and the sky had turned ink-black overhead, the familiar stars somehow strange and new. A momentary vertigo struck as, against the darkness, wings swooped and wheeled and gradually settled beyond the levee again. It was over. The quake had ended, leaving barely a hint of licorice on the heavy Mississippi River air. Nothing moved except mosquitoes that buzzed near her ear. She inhaled to steady herself and -reached- into the soil.

The landforms of New Madrid and the Mississippi Basin were different than those under Seattle. Fractured stone and bedrock made up the earth's crust like a packed cup of granola, the tenuous stability caused by the pressure of the earth's tectonic plates from either side. Unlike Seattle, where the ley lines ran so close to the earth's surface one leaked into her basement, here they ran deep under the soil so their rose scent should be almost imperceptible.

Except it wasn't.

The scent, coupled with the licorice and ozone stench of power, still hovered on the air even as the night breeze tugged it away. There had been power here, brought up to the surface, and coiled around the licorice-scent were hints of cinnamon and pomegranate and definitely almonds.

She turned back the way they'd come and the scent came clearer. The power had been localized.

She walked further back towards where they'd been and heard Landon get out of the car behind her. He knew better than to interrupt her concentration as she sought the extent of the power surge. She stepped down on soil and felt the fizzle of old Change under her feet. Here was the edge of the Change that had been wrought. Not twenty feet ahead were the deep tire marks in the dusty verge of the road left by the Prius as Landon tried to get them away from the force.

She glanced up to the top of the levee. The path was there and the thick stench of ozone and licorice almost made her skin crawl. The Change had been localized all right. Localized right under them.

It couldn't be a coincidence. A leaden feeling filled her stomach, but she pushed it away. She was not afraid of whoever did this, even if it seemed they'd aimed for her.

But if it's your father?

She ripped her thoughts from that direction and spun around to retreat to Landon, but something in the air… A soft breeze blew in her face and tasted of cinnamon and pomegranate….

She stopped and inhaled, tilting her head back to capture the scent. Yes. They were there, ahead somewhere—the people who had tried to do this.

The darkened country highway was lit only by the long lines of the Prius's headlights on the pavement and the red glow of the tail lights, but far down the road a neon sign flashed yellow-blue-red, yellow-blue-red. They were there, if she could just get there fast enough.

She jogged back to the car. "What is that?" she asked Landon when she reached the car and pointed down the road.

"No idea," he said. "What did you find, pigeon?"

She shook her head. "Get in. Whoever caused the quake is there."

His pale brows rose, but he slid behind the wheel and touched the power button. The unnaturally silent car slid down the darkened two-lane highway like a lozenge down a gullet, the neon glow growing in front of them.

The Flooded Duck glowed the neon sign, a relic from another time when neon was a kitschy art form. This one had a cute rubber-ducky-type character paddling along while blue water rose over its head. Then the duck and water disappeared to flash red letters into the darkness from the roof of a low slung building that had to be a roadhouse.

It sat in the midst of a gravel parking lot, empty fields stretching back from a wire fence into darkness. The building was rough clapboard with a tin roof, and though it had arched windows, they were painted black. A bevy of pickups and battered cars bellied up around it like suckling pigs. Vallon rolled down her window and the dull thud of music flooded in.

"Pull in," she said.

Landon did and she stepped out of the car. The presence of power and Gifted flooded up through her feet. She bent down to look at Landon. "I'll just be right back. Park over there, would you?" She nodded at an empty spot at the edge of the parking lot.

"You're sure you don't want me to come in with you?" His face was more anxious than he usually showed. Because he wasn't used to field work? Or had he figured out what she wasn't saying: that the Change had been targeted on them?

"Positive. Stay here and keep the car running." She stopped herself. The damn car had turned off just because they were stationary. "At least keep the key in the ignition."

She patted the roof of the car and turned toward the road house.

A single solid-looking wooden door stood at the top of three wooden steps. Her sneakered feet crunched across the gravel and she looked down at her attire. Shorts and a light t-shirt, for God's sakes. Not exactly how she'd dress normally to face an enemy, but she'd work with what she had. The roadhouse door swung open and spilled loud hillbilly rock, and a man and two tight-jean-and-halter-top-clad women came out onto the stairs. The threesome leaned together like a three-legged stool as they tottered down the stairs and towards her. A comment and some not too muffled laughter rose as they passed her. Okay, so she wasn't dressed for this, but too bad.

She climbed the stairs and stepped into the wall of music. The door slammed shut behind her and the afterburn flared and staggered her back against the door.

Too many people. Thick clouds of cigarette smoke that defied every city bylaw, but such bylaws probably didn't exist in back-of-beyond

Missouri. The stench of beer and greasy French fries and chicken from the kitchens, the heat of sweat off the dance floor, and the sexual scent of too many men and women in heat. It touched off her skin like a flame on starter fluid and she was the kindling underneath. She fought to steady her breathing, to focus on why she was here.

A little dancing, a little beer, a quick fuck, and all would be right with the world. There were enough down-home country boys here who could probably do the job just fine. She felt the damp flush run over her skin. Felt the dampness in her panties. She clamped her eyes shut and shook herself—until a hand fell on her arm.

"You all right, pretty lady?"

Her eyes flashed open and she jerked away from the heat that travelled directly from his grip right down to her groin.

Tall. Broad shouldered, wearing a t-shirt with the sleeves torn off to expose tanned, corded muscled arms, a USMC tattoo on his left shoulder. Shaggy blonde hair covered his ears and fell over his tanned forehead so she just wanted to run her fingers back through it. Bright blue eyes and a wide mouth grinned sexily. He tilted a brow at her and her mouth went dry.

"You okay?" he asked. "You looked a little sick there fer a moment."

The soft southern drawl was honey over her skin and, whoa mama, she could be more than okay with this hunk. She swallowed and tore herself away from his too-attractive gaze.

"I'm fine, thanks. I'm looking for someone." Because she *did not* want to encourage this guy, who was just a trifle too yummy in her condition. She had a job to do. But her hands were shaking.

She stepped past him into the press of sweating people, her feet crunching in sour-smelling sawdust and crushed peanut shells. The air ran electric fingers over her skin as she -reached-, because there was at least one Gifted here. In the corner a band pounded out something about a black-eyed lady in a blackened room and all the lovin' things they would do to her there. Oh yeah. The grind of the music hit her low down in the belly. A little bump and grind would be so nice, but the damned sensation made it hard to think.

The room was ablaze with the shimmering candles that regular folk showed in Gifted sight. But these candles shifted and moved like a spreading flame across the dance floor and caught in shoals up against the dimly visible bar.

"Come on, babe. You're ruining my reputation here. Have at least one drink. Ya look parched."

Blonde guy again, with his hand on her arm that jerked her out of the sight just when she'd caught the bright flame of a Gifted somewhere there—near a corridor that led to the washrooms.

"I don't need a drink, thanks." She pulled away and heard a chorus of laughter from behind her. She glanced up at the guy. Amazingly good looking in a down-home kinda way. And she was throwing him to his friends' derision. "Listen, I'm sorry, okay. Maybe some other time."

She spun around and left him, slipping back into Gifted sight again. There. Through the smoky walls of the corridor flamed the bright aura of a Gifted. She plunged into the shifting crowd, dodging her way around tables, apologizing as she knocked people aside. The dance floor was a seething mass of people stomping on a scarred wooden floor to a wailing chorus about a cheating heart. She needed to reach that corridor, and this was the fastest way. She shoved in among them, elbows out and ignoring the shouts of protest. Someone tried to grab her waist and do-si-do her around. She ripped loose and fell into someone who groped her butt. She almost turned around and punched him. Almost had the blonde-haired stranger right there on the dance floor, where the air pulsed with pounding like her heart and was slick and hot and heavy with sex.

She ripped herself away and came up panting on the far side of the dancers. The way her body pulsed, she was tempted to just grab the first guy she saw. Too bad Mr. Blondie wasn't here. A quicky in the washroom maybe.

She shuddered. She had a job to do and she'd made a decision to stay faithful to Xavier, no matter what it cost her. Right at the moment it was costing a hell of a lot. She was flipping shaking like a leaf in strong wind.

She slipped into Gifted sight again and the Gifted figure had reached the end of the corridor, was disappearing out into the parking lot. Hands on the walls for balance, she hobbled down the hallway after him or her.

Men's washroom, women's washroom, each with too-cute signs of cowboy and cowgirl ducks. Another door that must lead into the kitchen. A door at the end of the corridor with a red exit sign overhead. She hurried towards it, and plunged out into the night-dark parking lot.

Five stairs led down to the rear of the road house. Three tall trash bins huddled up beside the building. More trucks and cars were parked here, and beyond them were a wire fence and the flatness of a stubbled cornfield.

Where was the Gifted? She -reached- once more, and small flickers of light in the sky spoke of bats overhead. In the field were the sparks of rodents and the flicker of a coyote or dog. She panned the parking lot, and there! A truck engine started and she leapt down the stairs, ducked around the garbage bins, trucks, and cars, and reached the end of the building just as a dark pickup hauled ass backing out of a parking space. She ran for it, reached the road through the parking lot just as the truck roared for the highway. It sped past her so fast she stumbled back while trying to catch a glimpse of the license plate.

That was when strong arms came around her.

CHAPTER 13 —THE HEAT OF LEAVING

The strong forearms around Vallon sent the afterburn raging. Heat surged through her, igniting her even though the night was cool. Vallon elbowed their owner. Stomped down on a booted foot and gravel, and spun, fists up and prepared to fight. Blondie stood there, almost doubled over and nursing one foot. The neon yellow-blue-red reflected on his hair and placed deep shadows on his handsome face. The scent of man sweat and a too-floral aftershave pulled every part of her to attention.

"What the hell was that for?" he demanded.

"Why the hell are you following me?" Because he *was* following her, and with her suspicions about the quake being targeted, she wasn't taking anything for granted. Not even though this guy showed no Gift at all.

"You looked like a lady in distress. The way you snuck through that dance floor like a hot knife through butter, I thought maybe it was a lovers' spat, and those can get nasty. I came out here to make sure no one got hurt. Like you. Good thing, too. He nearly ran you down." He lifted his chin at the disappearing taillights headed north on the highway. "That him? Your ex?"

"Something like that." All the adrenaline was ratting through her body, and left her pulse jumping and the afterburn surging and this was a good-looking boy toy in front of her, and my God it was hard to breath in this humidity, even though the night was cooler than the day. It was quiet out here after the blaring music inside, even though the base of the band's amps seemed to pound at her right from the ground, and they were alone and no one would ever really need to know it had happened. She teetered one step towards him.

Teetered another and he caught her arms and all the reservations she clung to went up in a burst of flames that seared through her. She had her arms around him, her lips on his, was tugging his shirt out of the top of his jeans, had her hands up on the rock-hard belly under his shirt as he held her away from him.

"What the hell's happening?"

"What'd'you think's happening?" She shoved him back against a truck and pulled her t-shirt over her head. "I'm Vallon. What's your name, handsome?"

"Fuck." He swallowed. "Toby. Toby Watts."

"So nice to meet you, Toby Watts." He didn't protest when she shoved his shirt up and pressed her flesh against his.

His hands came down and cupped her ass and hauled her into him as his mouth ravaged hers and then down her shoulder, yanked her bra strap down and found her nipple. A cry of pleasure escaped her. Yes. This was the way it should be. It had to be. Too much afterburn and she would explode. She couldn't function. This was the only way, and didn't lead to accidents like that in her basement.

His hand slipped into her shorts and his fingers slipped down the crack of her ass to her moistness.

"You want this, don't you?"

"Fuck, yes," she moaned. "Let's do it."

She fumbled his jeans open and shoved her shorts down and then he had her up against a truck fender and she was guiding him inside and then oh-God-she was doing it as he thrust inside her. Again. Again. And she'd forgotten even protection and oh-God *what was she doing?*

But her hips matched his rhythm. Her nails found his back, then slipped down to his ass to make sure he went harder, deeper. She threw her head back and moaned as he found her deep places, as the tension inside her increased like a fault line ready to give way. Building. Building. Slick body on body and he thrust one more time and his head went back and he shouted into the darkness, his body pulsed inside her. Again. Again. And then he slumped over her as her insides rippled as she came. She hung there, limp, between him and the cold fender, his sweat and floral scent almost enough to turn her stomach.

What had she done? This wasn't her man. Hell, she barely knew his name—Toby something—and he sure as hell wasn't Xavier. And she'd promised—at least to herself—that she'd be faithful to him. Her breath caught in her chest and it was worse than the afterburn. Shame was like that.

She shoved him off of her. Hit him with her fists when he tried to caress her. Pulled her panties and shorts on, straightened her bra, and reclaimed her t-shirt from the ground and tugged it on. She stank of him. Stank of their sex. Stank of everything she hated about afterburn and what it led to. She'd tried to accept it all those years—at school, on the job. It had been fun at first, the power over the boys and over men. The ability to get any man she wanted. That ended when she met Xavier. It wasn't just the release of afterburn she wanted. She wanted the connection to everything Xavier had shown her. The connection to her heart.

"Vallon? What's happening?" Landon's voice came out of the darkness and she stumbled towards it, leaving Blondie struggling to get his clothes back on.

She found him standing beside the Prius. Had he seen? The appraising way he looked at her said probably and she felt her face color. Thank God for nighttime and the yellow-blue-red neon. That might hide some of it. She ran her fingers through her hair.

"There was a Gifted here. He took off when he realized I was after him. That was his truck that went flying out of here."

"Aah. I thought I heard something in the parking lot."

Very possible given the moans and Blondie's shout. "I didn't hear anything. I was just checking around for evidence. And so on."

Something she should have done instead of fucking her brains out. But at least she could think now. At least think more clearly than she had before.

His pale lips curved faintly. "And so on. I'm glad to see you're recovering from your travails today."

He just turned from her and slid into the car, leaving her to compose herself. Stupid. He could always tell when an agent was suffering from afterburn and when they weren't. He'd know what happened just like any Gifted would. She climbed into the car beside him and crossed her arms over her chest as he turned the car on, then drove out of the parking lot.

"An interesting night, pigeon. Did you meet anyone interesting in the bar?"

"Oh shut up. This doesn't change anything about the way I feel about Xavier."

In the dashboard lights, the blasted man had the gall to smile.

§

First things first. An invigorating ocean wind whipped at Wolf Amundson's suit jacket as he stood outside the condo apartment building in Seattle's downtown, and for a moment he didn't miss Florida anymore. Sunlight and wind and temperate air were much more to his temperament than the florid heat of South Florida. The salt air and sunlight seemed to fuel his blood flow. He hadn't realized just how that hutch of an office at the AGS was sucking the life out of him. It wasn't like him to huddle in a room and just review papers. He liked to get out with his men. Like now. It was like being given back his life after being seriously ill.

The sunlight was bright through the trees along the street and spot lit the glass front of the tower and the humvees his men had double-parked along the street. In the building lobby, a business-like looking security guard sat at a desk and peered back suspiciously at Amundson and his men. Time to go in. Time to do what he should have done right at the start, and cut the head off the two-headed snake of the AGS. He'd start with Landon Snow.

He glanced over his shoulder at Page, the huge, shaven-headed, ham-fisted H.S. agent who had done three tours of duty in Iraq with Loadstone before coming back to the states and being assigned to Homeland Security. The man had been with him every step of the way from Florida to this point in his career and Amundson was not about to let an important asset like Page go unrewarded. He'd already been promoted to Assistance Chief of Seattle Station in the wake of the successful takeover of the AGS. Now it was time for the man to demonstrate his loyalty.

"Let's do this," Amundson said.

Page pursed his mouth and touched the radio in his ear. He frowned. "You sure, boss? I've had phone calls placed to Snow's home for the past fifty minutes. No one is answering."

"He should be there. Gleason said he talked to him this morning."

Page cocked a sandy brow and nodded, but the doubt was clear in his eyes.

Had Gleason lied? A little frisson of uncertainty quickly transformed into certainty. He'd have Gleason's hide for this. He would. He plunged through the doors, into the lobby and the scent of lilies from a huge, twisted-wood and floral arrangement on a central table. He flashed his badge at the security guard, a big man with graying hair who had all the signs of being a retired cop.

"Wolf Amundson, Homeland Security. We've an interest in your tenant, Landon Snow."

The guard nodded. All the suspicion had fled and been replaced by the eagerness so often displayed by the wanna-be cops when they met the real thing. Come to think of it, a lot of cops showed the same thing when they met H.S. agents.

He shook his head. "I'm afraid Mr. Snow isn't here. Sir." Definitely ex-cop. The 'Sir' came with the training.

Wolf glanced at Page. So he was right—again—but the 'Sir' said he'd likely get whatever he needed out of the guard. "Where has he gone and when do you expect him back."

The guard scratched his forehead. "That's the trouble. He said he was going away for a few days, but he didn't say where he was going or give a return date. Sorry, Sir."

Damnation. He wanted the man in custody. He wanted to know what he knew and what he—they—the Gifted—planned. His fingers tapped his pant leg for a moment. "We need to see the apartment."

Ex-cop hesitated a moment.

"This is a matter of national security. Now move, man."

Ex-cop fumbled for keys. "I'll ride up with you."

Typical, but he wasn't going to argue. He let the guard lead him, Page, and three agents to a bank of elevators and they rode up fifteen floors to a long hallway, complete with more flowers on a mirrored side table. Tasteful pale gold wallpaper covered the walls and a thick russet carpet muffled their footsteps. Just how did a government agent afford a place like this?

The question increased when the guard used an electronic key on the lock and the door swung open on a panoramic corner view of Elliot Bay, Puget Sound, and the Olympic Mountains to the west, and Pioneer Square, the stadiums, and Mount Rainier to the south. He stepped inside.

Twelve-foot ceilings made the main greatroom space feel vast. Dark hardwood floors and dark wood surfaces were counterpoint to the white leather and chrome furniture set tastefully in the living room space, and the pristine steel appliances in the open-concept kitchen. A large abstract oil painting of what looked like a northwest rainforest hung on a huge expanse of wall. Landon Snow might be the enemy, but he was obviously also a fastidious man of good taste. A hallway cut off to the left following the angle of the exterior wall. It meant the other rooms would enjoy the same kind of expensive view.

Page glanced around the apartment and whistled softly. He motioned for the three other agents with them to check the place out. "What does a place like this run on the market?"

Ex-cop shrugged. "A mill, now, at least. Maybe a little less when they were built five years ago."

Page threw a glance at Amundson. "Pay grade's a little better at the AGS, is it?"

How the hell had Snow afforded this—unless he had a little business on the side? Better and better. The white gnome was making it easier and easier to justify what he intended to do.

"Sir. The place is clear." Trent, the slim, black leader of the three agents returned to the great room. He was a totally unimposing looking man except for the way his shaved-bald head was reminiscent of the shape of Egyptian pharaohs, but in a fight he was a lethal blur. He also came by way of Loadstone, but then most of the best ones did. "But I think you better come see this."

Amundson and Page followed him down the hall, doorways giving onto a bedroom and an office with panoramic views, until they came to a door at the far end of the hall that gave into a room on the other side of the hallway. Trent flipped on a set of lights to expose a white clad room equipped with brushed steel tables, chrome fridge, and what looked like medical equipment. Frowning, Amundson stepped inside. The place looked scrubbed clean, but a faint odor of antiseptic and something like rotting plant matter still lingered on the air.

"What is it?" he asked.

Trent pursed his lips. "Something medical, for sure. Research, maybe." He went to one of the banks of cupboards and pulled them open. Empty. Checked around the room. "Looks like whatever it was, it's been cleared out."

"Like he knew we'd be coming."

"Sir." Trent stood beside a table at the side of the room. He motioned to what looked like an envelope on the top. "Sir, this was here. It's addressed to you."

§

The only thing worse than the stink of burned coffee was the taste of the stuff. Jason shoved his offending coffee cup across his desk and closed his eyes to calm himself. He didn't need coffee. He was awake. As a matter of fact, he was more awake than he'd ever been in his life, except perhaps when he'd been with Cheryl.

He now knew for certain that Vallon was the answer, and if not her, then Xavier de Varga. He could not believe his fortune at the man showing up. Maybe, just maybe, he could use the information about Vallon's whereabouts to trade for the little piece of magic—yes, it was magic—he needed to bring Cheryl back.

The computer keys rattled under his fingers as he typed in the request for the airline companies. Vallon had to have flown. He'd already had airport police locate her car parked in one of the long-term parking lots that abounded around SeaTac. The lot owner had produced paperwork that said she had flown out to San Francisco, which would be a good holiday destination, but just didn't feel right. Vallon Drake wasn't the kind of person to take a holiday. He knew. He couldn't remember taking a holiday since Cheryl died. Something ate at Vallon in the same way.

So he searched the airline database for flights out of San Francisco, an immense job given he had no idea where she was going other than the 'east' the red-shoed woman and the travel agent's e-mail had said. That meant the continental United States, and he really should have just gone and rousted Vallon's travel agent, but he didn't want to take the chance on Vallon hearing about him asking about her, and there were too many times people on vacation came up against a change in itinerary that required contact with their agent.

"So, Slick, just what does an airline query have to do with that floater down at the harbor?"

Damn it. Clint had come up behind him, so quietly he hadn't heard. Or else he'd been so lost in his daydreams of Cheryl he'd missed the sound. He swung around in his chair and looked up at the redheaded bear of a man. Clint had the shoulders of a linebacker and the belly of someone who liked too much beer. He'd be an obese mountain of a man if his wife, Carol, didn't keep forcing him to eat salads instead of the meat and potatoes and gravy he preferred. So Clint ate rabbit food, because there wasn't anything he wouldn't do for Carol and his kids.

It should make him understand how driven Jason was, but right now Clint's blue eyes were like brittle blue gems. Not sympathetic at all.

"Not a damn thing. I was just killing time waiting for the coroner to call." He bluffed his way past Clint's glare. The big man finally shook his head and went around Jason's desk to his own. He slumped in his chair.

"We gotta have a serious talk, Slick. This has gone on too long. I'm not covering your ass anymore."

Jason glanced back at the query and stabbed 'send.' "I never asked you to cover for me."

"Then why the hell're you hanging around the Drake woman again? We haven't got a case involving her. You've got no excuse."

Jason rifled through papers he had on his desk. "What I do on my personal time is just that: personal."

Clint ran his fingers through his hair and leaned on his desk. "Don't you get it, Slick? I'm your friend here. I'm trying to stop you from self destructing. Since you met this woman, you've gone all strange. You're out at all hours. You're never here when you should be. Hell, I've taken on three cases alone this past week because you weren't here to go on the call with me and I couldn't reach you. Look at yourself, Jason. You look like you haven't slept in a week. Hell, you smell like you haven't showered in two. What am I supposed to do, Slick? You won't talk to me. I'm tempted to talk to the department psychologist."

Jason stiffened and slowly looked back at Clint. The man had been there for him through it all—Cheryl's prolonged illness and her death. The strange case of an AGS agent's murder that had brought him into contact with Vallon Drake and the subsequent fallout. The man had always been his friend. His wife had been like a sister through all the bad times. Hell, he and Cheryl had been godparents to Clint and Carol's two girls.

But Clint wasn't looking any too friendly at the moment. Clint's gaze itched like wool on fever-inflamed skin and he was too hot. Had started to sweat and couldn't quite fill his lungs.

He stood up struggling to loosen his shirt collar. "You know what? I'm really sorry I've caused you so much trouble."

"Whatchu doing, Slick? Think before ya act, why doncha?" Clint being all good ol' boy friendly. "Don't go off half-cocked and shoot yourself in the foot." Clint was looking like he might stand, and Jason was so flipping tired of all this shit of trying to keep his act together when everything in his life had come unmoored with Cheryl's death.

He shuffled his papers into a pile and was thankful he'd thought to have the answer to his queries sent to his private department e-mail that he could access at home. "Clint, I appreciate your concern, but at this moment this is what I gotta do."

"Bu...."

Jason held up his hand. "Really. Don't try to stop me. And don't ask why. What I do is none of your fucking business."

And then he was out the office door, Clint's gaze on his back, and a whole world and a hell of a lot of clean air and possibilities before him.

CHAPTER 14 — TALENT

Xavier would understand. He would.

Vallon's foot vibrated under the table as Elizabeth Ducharme bustled around bringing serving dishes into the bird-covered dining room. Paisley bird wallpaper covered the walls, and the canaries in the front room window chirped and sang in counterpoint to the conversation around the brightly lit table. Landon was holding forth with Elizabeth, regaling her with his knowledge of the Battle of Island Number Ten (who knew Landon was such a Civil War buff?). Little Farrah, with her hair in pigtails, sat tossing her head and had engaged Fi with some or other tale of time with her grandparents on a trip from New Madrid to a circus that came to a neighboring town.

The smell of chicken fried steak, mashed potatoes, and corn, and the heavy scent of gravy, about made her stomach heave and for a moment she wondered whether she was pregnant. Could you have such a reaction so quickly when an egg was fertilized? It would be just her luck. One screwup and look what happens. *Ha ha, Vallon. Nice pun.*

Or it was just the guilt making her stomach feel like an uneasy ocean?

It just happened this once, God damn it. It's not going to happen again, so get over it.

"You okay, Vallon? You look like you ate something bad." Fi stopped herself with fingers over her mouth, her eyes wide as she looked up at their hostess, who had just come in carrying a basket of steaming fresh biscuits. "Sorry. I didn't mean this food. This food's great." She hurriedly took a bite and gave a little moan of delight.

"Nothing I ate," Vallon managed a mumble. "I think I'm just tired."

But she could feel Landon's and Fi's gazes shift to her like too-bright searchlights and she knew Landon, at least, was reading her; and damn it, the way he was looking at her, it was like he was waiting for her to explode or something.

She ignored him and looked up at Elizabeth Ducharme, looming fresh as some amazing cooking genie as she settled herself at the head of the table. "Elizabeth, I'm so sorry after you've gone to the trouble to make all this wonderful food, but would you mind if I excuse myself? I think this whole long day of travel in the heat has simply been too much for me."

Elizabeth gave her a compassionate smile as the rest of the dinner table went silent. "Of course, Vallon. I wouldn't have it any other way. This house is a place to rest and refuel."

"Mommy, is Miss Drake sick?" Farrah asked. She turned a worried little face up to Vallon.

"No, honey. Not really *sick* sick," Vallon managed as she pushed back her chair. "I'm just tired. I guess all that driving makes me not feel very good."

Farrah cocked her head, blonde pigtails bouncing and blue eyes sparkling. "Travelling for a long time isn't any fun, is it? Not even when there's a circus at the other end." She leaned towards Vallon. "When I did it, I felt really sick in my tummy, but grandma made me have a nap and I felt better afterwards."

Vallon couldn't help but smile at the helpful grown-up advice of the little girl. "Then that is exactly what I'll do. I'll go upstairs and have a sleep and hopefully I'll feel better tomorrow." She caught Fi's eye. "So tomorrow, how about we do a little of that sightseeing we'd talked about? I'm really sorry all this happened. I hope you had a relaxing time at the pool."

Fi shrugged noncommittally. "It was fine. As for tomorrow, *I've* got nothing planned."

So Fi was still miffed. Vallon managed a smile once more at Farrah and took her leave.

A shower and a change into thin cotton pajamas and she sprawled, damp and still sweating, on the crimson flowered bedspread. *Xavier, where are you?*

Would you quit acting like a lovesick puppy and get on with the investigation?

Restlessness forced her up off the bed and to the window. The turquoise light from the pool reflected up into her eyes and obscured the stars. No stars and a featureless landscape, and how was anyone supposed to get her bearings? Across the fence lay baseball diamonds—flat—and beyond them a levee and beyond would be more flat. In this part of the world, she could almost believe the ancient stories of travelling to the edge of the earth and falling off.

A soft knock at the door turned her around.

"Miss Drake?" Farrah's small voice.

She padded over to the door and opened it. Farrah stood there, scented of baby shampoo and bath suds, her small, well-scrubbed face beaming up at her, dressed in a Hello Kitty night shirt with frills around the bottom. Her mother lurked just down the hall, a small proud smile on her face.

Oh, God, what now?

"Ms. Drake?" Little piping voice.

"Yes? What is it?"

Farrah glanced uncertainly back at her mother, and for a moment Vallon was small again, a kid of no more than five or six, standing in front of an office door, knocking, and having the terrifying visage of her father opening the door and using exactly the same words she had just used. She shivered.

"Call me Vallon, okay?" She took a deep breath and managed to find a smile.

Farrah nodded and timidly held out a small rag dolly. "When I'm not feeling good, Maggie always makes me feel better. Maybe she can help you, too."

Vallon looked at the gift, stitched face worn almost threadbare, hair matted from too much careful nuzzling. Obviously a treasure that this little child was prepared to share. She knelt down, her insides feeling strangely mushy. When was the last time someone gifted her like this? When was the last time she gifted someone? The realization left her feeling shaky. She accepted Maggie and cradled her in her arms. "Thank you. I think she *will* help me. Maybe I'm not feeling good because I miss my Maggie. I have a very special cat and her name is Maggie, too."

Farrah's blue eye widened. "You do?"

Vallon nodded. "Yes. And I had to leave her behind. She was very sad. I was, too."

Farrah stepped up and gave her a warm, little girl-and-baby-shampoo-scented hug that about melted Vallon's heart. When it was over she stood up and briefly met Elizabeth Ducharme's gaze. Then she looked back at Farrah. "Thank you very much. I'll take just as good a care of your Maggie as I do of mine."

"She's very special," Farrah said, nodding solemnly.

"I can see that, sweetie," Vallon said hugging the doll to her chest. "She's just what I needed."

"What color is your cat?" Farrah asked, clearly ready to enter a long conversation.

"Farrah, darling, I think Ms. Drake wants to go back to bed. You should be in bed, too."

"Night then!" And Farrah turned with a little flirty wave of her fingers and scooted down the hall to her mother, who took her down the stairs and to wherever the family lived.

Vallon returned to her bed and set the doll on her bedside table and lay down again in the darkness. Sleep wouldn't come. Too many emotions tangled inside her. How could her father have left her when he loved her?

The same way you were able to fuck that other man when you say you love Xavier?

Didn't she love Xavier? Didn't her father love her? That memory of him in the doorway could almost make her question it. His look had always been so cold, so uncaring, as if he barely recognized her and she was a nuisance he would be happy to be rid of. Of course, that could just be a childish misinterpretation. The man was probably incredibly busy and she had just caught him at the wrong time. He'd sent her back to her au pair without even looking at her. He'd just shut the door in her face that time.

There had been other times, too. And all the missed school recitals and sports days when she was in public school.

The air conditioning was suddenly too cool and the room too empty. Thinking about her father had always made her feel sad at his loss, but thinking about all the times her father hadn't been there for her, just made the loss greater—as if she had just lost the illusion that he'd loved her. No wonder he'd been able to leave her. Maybe there was something truly unlovable about her.

She fumbled the bed covers over her and curled on her side, but the loneliness she felt was almost overwhelming. The little doll slumped on the bedside table. She snagged it with one hand and felt stupid as she hugged the little figure into her chest. Farrah's comforting scent came off of it and she closed her eyes.

And went seeking.

Night lay across the landscape and the stars banded the sky, the North Star she used to set her course like an ancient mariner or the nineteenth century surveyors who had subdivided the continent. Broad expanse of night-grey checkerboard fields, the breadbasket of America, the broad stubble of the prairies like the mangy back of a ill-treated dog, and the broken lands of the badlands and southern canyons all spread before her. To the north, the brooding cataclysm-to-be of Yellowstone National Park and the nascent super volcano. Westward, mountains in rank upon rank upon rank, folded by geological pressure as the Pacific tectonic plate crushed into North American, breaking the rocky earth's crust and thrusting peaks up towards the stars.

She balanced on a peak, snow under her bare feet, the broken folds of mountain valleys and icy tarns in darkness below her. The scent of glacial waters on the air and a cold wind blew around her, blew through her, emptying her out, and she was impossibly cold. So cold no one should be able to move. But she had to find Xavier. Xavier could make her warm and could help her re-experience the bliss of the connection to all this.

But Xavier was gone, like her father, and perhaps dead.

She -reached- and spread herself wide as the world, until the cells and molecules of her being were lost amid the millions-billions-uncountable number of molecules that made up the earth. Where, Xavier? Where? Are you buried under the Seattle waterfront? Have you abandoned me to go back to the deserts and sand that scent your skin, to the vast silent places that seem to run in your eyes and your heart until you touch me?

The pain welled up, ran through the distant parts of her being and she sent it out into the world, her searching, her desire, the loneliness she had always contained. Far away, in the east, the sun sent a halo of rays above the horizon. The night was almost done and Xavier was nowhere to be found.

In exhaustion she fell back into herself, the breadth of the world rushing away from her as she collapsed into a bed with a child-scented doll pressed into her cheek and her tear-dampened pillow. Could she be wrong about her father? Could the event at the Kochtitsky house and the quake on the levee be something other than an attack? Could it be that it was an attempt to get her attention? An attempt to reach out to her after all these years? That could explain things. All her muscles tightened. *Small bird call from beyond the border of slumber. The sounds of water running in pipes and people stirring. Life.*

And from somewhere beyond in the night-bound world came a single word in a voice precious beyond belief. "Vallon."

She opened her eyes and didn't know if it was part of her dreams or an answer to them.

§

"That is the most foolish thing I have ever heard come out of your mouth, pigeon!" Landon positively bristled as he padded across his bedroom. He turned back to glance at her, looking strangely elfin with his sharp features under his tousled white hair and his pink skin flushed as he tugged the string tie closed over his Colonel Saunders' suit. "And that is saying something."

Vallon sat in the tub chair under the bedroom window covered with its gingham curtain. The room was decorated in gingham, as if in homage to an earlier time in America when gingham was almost the flag of 'down-home.' Blue gingham bedspread that regimented Landon had neatly made, even though Elizabeth Ducharme was prepared to do it. His clothing neatly hung in the closet or, she presumed, folded in the drawers of the gingham-draped dresser, so unlike how she continued to dig through her suitcase for the clothes she wore. The wrinkles in her t-shirt were proof of it. The room smelled of Landon's baby-fresh scent, as if he'd sprinkled himself with talcum powder.

"And I think you're wrong. The whole thing could be a set-up to get my attention." And maybe—just maybe—her father was finally looking for her. She'd known this was going to happen—that Landon wouldn't believe it. He was a skeptic about so many things. "Think about it. It was my first day back at the AGS and I'm on the desk. There's a massive quake that draws all of our attention to New Madrid and there's the scent of my father. No one else would have picked that up. So I come here and the first thing that happens when I blow into town is something knocks me right out. What if they'd planned it that way so they could pick me up, and the only thing that stopped them was having Fi there? She got me away before they could collect me."

He was looking at her through her reflection in the dresser mirror, and had paused with his silver-handled hairbrush in his hand. The brush was some humdinger of a fashion statement. She'd never actually allowed herself to think of Landon as foppish, but in the string tie and suit and brushing his hair with such a brush, she had to revise her opinion.

"Are you listening to yourself?" he said. "You sound like a little child imagining a dead parent will be alive if only she can wish hard enough on a blue star. You're not Pinocchio, pigeon. You're already a real woman, and even if your father were alive, I don't think you'd want to meet him."

She frowned, every muscle gone rigid. "Who's not listening? You're not looking at the evidence, Landon. Everything points to him knowing just where I'd be and when. Aside from the terrifying thought that he's having me watched, that means we have an 'in' into his organization. We need to reach out to him. He's my father. And I'm proposing to use that relationship to get inside whatever operation is causing the quakes."

"No. You're not. You're acting like a lost little girl who's hoping to find her father and then all will be right with the world. Isn't that right, pigeon?" He glared at her, stripping the brush through his hair but never taking his gaze from her.

"Landon! Why are you working against me? My plan is about the only one we've got right now. I—I can let it be known that I'm not happy at the AGS. Maybe he'll come looking for me then, instead of attacking. I'll get inside and then I'll be able to stop them."

He snorted—he actually snorted—and turned around to cross his arms over his chest. "Are you happy at the AGS, pigeon? I don't think you need to waste your effort creating a story. You've done that quite nicely already."

She looked down at her hand, picking at a loose thread in the bottom of her shorts. "Just how do you expect me to respond to that?" She shook her head. He was wrong about her plan even if he was maybe right about her. "I'll take your concerns under advisement." And stood and left.

§

Resigned.

Wolf Amundson stepped out of the blue Buick sedan into yet another sunny Seattle morning, this time in Fremont, but his mind still dwelt on an apartment in downtown Seattle.

The blasted white gnome had disappeared and had had the gall to leave a note behind in his emptied-out apartment for Amundson to find. He'd resigned from the AGS effective immediately, and attached to the necessary paperwork had been a terse note to Amundson telling him not to come looking. Taunting him, really. Apparently the little cretin thought he had ways of dealing with any agents Wolf might send after him.

Wolf hiked his summer-weight Brooks Brothers suit jacket straight on his shoulders. One needed to look properly authoritarian when one was about to place an agent under arrest, especially in a place like this. On a Saturday morning in daylight, the neighborhood on the Freemont hillside was totally different than the last time he'd been here, when night and rain had blanketed the city and the neighborhood had slumbered. Now seagulls soared on the blue sky and the air smelled of salt water, turned earth, and cut grass. The area was alive with the sounds of lawnmowers and people talking in their gardens. The fools who lived in these houses went along in their busy little lives, unaware that the woman who lived in their midst had the ability to wipe them right off of the earth if she so chose. If they'd known the truth, they'd run screaming. If they'd known the truth, they'd demand what he was about to do, even though Vallon Drake had come back into the fold after apparently going rogue earlier.

And Landon Snow had helped her during her time on the run.

The absolute gall of Snow's escape set Amundson's blood boiling. No one walked away from him until he damned well said they could, and least of all some effete Gifted. He would not have Gifted running around unmonitored. But he had ways of getting the little man back, even if a night of his Homeland Security agents searching the AGS computer systems and combing airline databases had yielded no sign of the little man's movements at all. That left an uneasy sickness in the pit of his stomach, and that was totally unacceptable, as well.

The good thing was that the little man—his nemesis, he now realized—had a weakness for the girl, Drake. It had been evident from the first, how he protected her; and Moore, Amundson's pet agent who had once been Gleason's Executive Assistant, had confirmed it. Snow had been Drake's guardian after her father disappeared. That meant he likely cared for her.

Page's huge shadow darkened the sidewalk in front of Wolf as the H.S. agent came up beside him. The sunlight seemed to glow on his shaven pate and his bull neck seemed too large for the pristine suit collar and broad shoulders that strained against his suit. "So?" Page said.

"We're invited in. At least that's the plan. We ask her what she knows about Landon's disappearance. We play it like we don't know what's happened to him. Like we're worried about him."

"Got it," Page said and scanned the house and street. "Nice neighborhood."

Wolf sniffed. "A bunch of wanna-be bohemians." He nodded at the wind chimes hung in a stand of bamboo across the street and shook his head at terra cotta faces hung on the front porch of a house beside Vallon's. Not people to be readily trusted, that was certain.

The front gate squeaked as he pushed the slatted affair open and went up the walk to the door. Page was on his heels, keeping an eye on the street. You never knew what would happen with people who were the country's enemies. He rang the doorbell, ignoring the sound of a car engine and the soft *thunk* of a car door.

No sound of movement inside the house. The curtains were drawn, too, now that he really looked at the house. Of course, Drake hadn't been well last time he saw her. She could be sleeping. He stabbed the bell again and heard its melodic dual tone through the red front door.

Still nothing.

"Boss," Page said. "I think you need to see this."

Wolf turned around as a man came through the front gate and a taxi pulled away down the street. The man was oddly familiar. Tall, dark, with the kind of chiseled good looks women often found attractive. He had the broad shoulders of an athlete and moved like someone trained to know his body. And like someone who carried a weapon and was aware of the need to access it quickly. Law enforcement of some kind. The shorn length of his hair suggested police. Local, most likely.

"Can I help you?" the man said. His voice was deep and authoritative. He strode up the short path and stood below Wolf at the porch, jingling a set of keys in his hand.

"We're looking for Vallon Drake." Wolf made a decision about how to play it. He stuck out his hand. "Wolf Amundson, AGS Chief and Vallon's boss. I came to check up on her given she'd been off on sick leave."

The newcomer accepted his hand, but his gaze shifted between Wolf and Page. "I know who you are. We've met before, one night in this house. Jason Bryson. I'm a friend of Vallon's."

The name rang a bell, but he couldn't for the life of him remember the meeting, and yet… he had a vague recollection of an old-fashioned kitchen and this man. That couldn't be right. His memory was excellent. But… "You were in Seattle. The tunnels." And was one of the people who'd helped Vallon escape when Wolf was sure she was a rogue agent. He also looked different than back then, his dark gaze now more haunted and his face gaunt. If Wolf were a gambling man, he would lay money on something not being quite right with Jason Bryson. "Seattle P.D., if I recall." He frowned. "And a friend of Clint Blacklock, if my memory serves me right."

"Partner. Clint's my partner." But there was a slight edge that suggested something wasn't quite what he'd said. Something about the man—the way his gaze kept flickering to the door was almost like a junky eyeing his next fix. "So… Vallon's not here. She went on a holiday with her friend, Fi. I'm taking care of her cat."

He must have seen the way Wolf and Page glanced at each other.

"You're not here just to check on Vallon, are you?" A slight gleam had come into Bryson's eyes.

A friend of Vallon's was likely to help her and block anything that might harm her. "Actually, we're looking for another agent. Landon Snow. Do you know him?"

Bryson chewed the inside of his cheek for a moment. "He's the little guy, right? Albino? Sure. He wheeled Vallon around to see me a few times when we were both in the hospital. What about him?"

"That, I am afraid, is American Geological Survey and Homeland Security business."

"Classified, you mean." Bryson looked at the house and back at Wolf. There were calculations running through the police officer's expression. And was that excitement? "Because of the things she does. Can do."

All the alarms in Wolf's head jangled, but he held himself still and simply glanced at Page.

"Classified. Yes." But by the look in the man's eyes he knew far more than an agent who might be privy to classified information. "Has Agent Drake spoken to you about her work?"

Bryson snorted. "Hell, no. But I've been around, remember. The Murdoch thing. The volcano in the city." His lifted his chin towards the downtown.

The claxons screamed in Wolf's head because no one should remember the volcano. He didn't, and he'd been there. He'd just read the AGS files and had to take it on the word of Gleason and the other Gifted that it had happened. But this man did remember, or said he did, if he could be believed. There was only one way that could be. His mouth went dry. Bryson could be one of those unknown Gifted hinted at in Snow's files.

"So you share Agent Drake's Gifts, do you?"

Bryson crossed his arms over his chest and Wolf could feel his study. Finally he shook his head. "Nope. Not at all. But I notice things, if you get my meaning. Things maybe you don't." His gaze narrowed and then he nodded as if to himself. "Listen, I've got a proposition for you. I've been trying to catch up to Vallon myself to have a little conversation about a project I'm interested in. Maybe we can help each other."

Stranger and stranger. Normally he would simply give a police officer the brush off. They could not move in the rarified realm the Homeland Security trod. A police officer was simply a foot soldier to be called in when additional bodies were needed. Stranger still was the fact that he, Wolf Amundson, bothered to talk to this man, but there was something about him.

"What did you have in mind?"

"Well… I did a little research. I found out where Vallon went. Maybe we could work together and you could arrange for Vallon and me to have our little conversation."

"Mr. Bryson, please don't take offence, but if Seattle P.D. can locate Agent Drake, I'm sure Homeland Security can do the same if we believe it important." He nodded at Page and the two of them went to step past the police officer back to their car.

"Wait!"

Bryson caught Wolf's arm and he froze. Looked down at the strong fingers surrounding his bicep and wrinkling his suit and was ready to nod at Page to take the man down.

"Listen. Sorry." Bryson released his arm but was bouncing on the balls of his feet, his gaze skittering from Wolf to Page and back again, sweat beading around his hairline. "I was around Vallon long enough to know she can do things. The fact I saw and remembered it seemed to surprise the hell out of her. She said I shouldn't be able to. I thought that just might be of interest to you and that maybe we could trade. I give you Vallon's whereabouts and I can tell you if she tries to—use her talents. In return all I ask is for some private time with her."

A dicey decision to be sure, but if this man could really do what he said, it could be an answer to a prayer. With his help they could track the changes and not be dependent upon the less-reliable Gifted. There might even be ways this man could help identify Gifted. It could be his secret weapon against the whole aberrant population.

"You propose something entirely out of the norm, Detective Bryson. I will need to think about your offer. Perhaps you could come with us to our office?" And then be available for testing himself.

This time Bryson backed away. "I don't think so. This is a one-time offer: today. Right now. I just thought you might be interested." He shrugged and turned back to the house, and pulled out a ring with lone key. "Good luck in locating Snow and Vallon."

The man made a show of unlocking the door while Wolf's brain spun through all the permutations. Could what Drake had told Bryson be true? Could this man be unGifted but still have the ability to remember the Change? Someone with that kind of talent would mean Wolf wouldn't be dependent upon Gleason anymore for information on what was changed. It would be a game changer.

Page was already going for the car, but Wolf stopped him with a look. Wolf walked back to the bottom of the stairs and looked up at Bryson. "I hope you have some idea who you're dealing with. I won't take it lightly if you are interfering in an internal investigation."

Bryson's brows rose and Wolf realized he'd probably given away more than he wanted by saying the attempt to locate Snow was anything more than a desire to locate a missing agent. Then Bryson smiled and he stuck out his hand. "Deal?"

Wolf accepted.

CHAPTER 15 — MISSISSIPPI MEETINGS

The sun was already preheating the day to oven temperatures by the time Vallon and Fi headed out the door of Elizabeth Ducharme's guesthouse. They'd eaten a breakfast of fruit and toast, after much protest from Elizabeth Ducharme that she should be cooking them something and much questioning from Farrah about the cat named Maggie. It had actually been a joy talking about something normal after the argument with Landon. He'd sat there like a frigging evil lawn ornament at the breakfast table and she'd left him with his trusty laptop to do research on the Flooded Duck Roadhouse while Vallon took Fi out to 'sightsee' while she tried to do some follow-up on the Kochtitsky house.

The temperature inside of the Camry was already to baking as they drove down Main Street. Through the open car window there was barely a hint of nighttime moisture, though the huge A.B. Hunter Mansion that they'd seen the day before still had sprinklers running. Vallon was glad she'd chosen her clothing more carefully this morning and that she wasn't wearing her usual jeans, t-shirt, and Dayton boots. Instead she was wearing her tan shorts, a light blue blouse, and a pair of athletic sandals.

She looked over at Fi, who wore a yellow sundress that she must have bought from her paycheck when Vallon had her back turned. "You look good," Vallon said. It was another small sign her friend was healing.

"I'm really glad we're getting some time together. I was kinda pissed you didn't ask me to go on the walk last night with Landon."

Vallon glanced at her. "I'm so sorry. If I'd known, you could have come." Of course it wouldn't have been a good idea given what had happened, but Fi didn't have to know that. "Landon told me you were swimming so I didn't even ask."

Fi just crossed her arms over her chest.

Along Main Street, the small shops were just opening and a few pickup trucks nosed the curb, but otherwise the street looked abandoned this early in the day. A few crows hopped along the pavement, but fluttered up to the telephone wires when Vallon and Fi drove past. As they neared the river, the humidity rose like a leaden weight on their shoulders.

"It doesn't look any better than yesterday," Fi said. She didn't look happy.

"Come on. Give it a chance. The air's cooler this early." Barely. "We'll go see the museum and then go see some sights." And in the meantime she could do some searching of another kind.

She drove past the brick museum and up onto the levee, and the panorama of the Mississippi stretched before them. The car parked, they got out and wandered down onto the pier some prior town council had, according to the signage, seen fit to build as a viewing platform over the river.

This morning a soft mist rose off the water and the moisture in the air softened the view into watercolors. It would be a bitch to get a good survey reading in such conditions, but it was beautiful nonetheless.

"You can almost imagine what it must have looked like before people came," Fi said dreamily as she leaned on the wooden railing. "Trees like those ones across the river running down to the water everywhere."

"There wouldn't be a levee. We'd probably be standing in water— or on mangrove roots or something."

Fi shrugged and grinned. "So our feet would get wet. That could be fun."

"You are one odd duck, Fi Murdoch. Anyone ever tell you that?"

Fi's gaze flashed to her. "You, maybe?" A quick smile, but then she was gone back to the river. She frowned into the early morning angled sunlight. "Look!"

Astonishment filled her face as she straightened and pointed. Vallon followed her finger, and far down the river a white apparition came churning towards them. A riverboat. A paddle wheeler. Like a stately grand dame, the apparition swept through the mist. Then the low throb of diesel engines reached them, along with the rush and thrum of water against a wooden hull.

"Oh. My. God." The two of them stood side by side, watching as the white boat swept closer, past the southern island. Strains of *Dixie* floated across the water as the boat came even with them. The American flag flew proudly from multiple standards along the sides of the top deck, but the confederate flag flew just as proudly from her stern as tourists stood at the four deck rails. It was as beautiful as a wedding cake. It was beyond anything she'd imagined. It was a confection of a lost past that tightened Vallon's chest and made her feel like crying. Fi started waving madly. Vallon looked at her, then threw caution to the wind and whooped and joined her, leaping up and down like an idiot madwoman, and people on the boat waved back. Someone rang a ship's bell in greeting and then the boat was past, coursing northward, its huge paddlewheel churning the muddy waters, smoke streaming out of its filigree-topped double smokestacks. It left an empty feeling in Vallon's chest as Fi swung around and grabbed her in a hug.

"Did you see?" she squealed, caught Vallon's hands and started dancing. "Wasn't it fucking-A marvelous? Could we go on ride do you think?"

"I don't see why not if we can find out where it docks and get tickets."

Fi ran back to the railing and watched the boat out of sight. Every part of her vibrated as if she'd be out in the water swimming after the paddle wheeler given any encouragement.

Vallon walked up beside her. "Now aren't you glad we came?"

"If we can go on a boat like that, yeah."

Her blue eyes were bright, the morning breeze tugged her hair prettily around her face, and she seemed almost normal. Vallon's friend finally whole. Then her face suddenly changed and her shoulders hunched. She shifted behind Vallon as if hiding from something.

"Fi? What is it?"

She shook her head and hunched a little lower, her eyes locked on something behind Vallon and her hand suddenly clutching Vallon's so hard it was painful. Vallon went to look behind her and Fi's fingernails dug into her palm.

"Don't look. Don't look. Don't look." The momentary look of normalcy was gone, leaving the wild-eyed Fi of the Seattle streets behind.

"How am I going to know what to do if I don't look?"

Fi shivered and shook her head, but Vallon eased her hand free and turned.

To be confronted by the filthy homeless man they'd spotted yesterday, standing all of five feet from them. Even with the breeze off the river, the stink of piss and unwashed clothing was an assault to Vallon's senses. The man's hair was a greasy mat of grey-brown that fell from high temples around his face. Oddly, it was only ear length and someone who had so clearly been on the street long enough to get that filthy should have hair down to his shoulders at least. Piercing blue eyes peered out between sunburned folds of flesh and the man seemed to stare right into the rising sun as he faced them. He wore a dirt-caked brown suit and what might once have been good leather shoes, dirt-caked now, and he carried what looked like a hand-painted yellow sign with black lettering. When he saw that he had their attention he held up the sign. *The end of the world is at hand.*

Okay. She'd dealt with homeless people before. Crazy ones, too. The trick was to make them know you really listened to them. Most of the time they were lost souls and just needed someone to care about them. Look at how well Fi was doing with a stable place to live and good food. *And the occasional turn cycling power for Vallon.*

She shook herself and stepped forward to meet him, keeping him away from Fi. "Can I help you?"

The strangely brittle blue gaze settled on her face. It flickered a moment, and for an instant she could have sworn she saw recognition. She looked at him closely. Something about him *was* familiar.

"Do I know you?"

"The end of the world is at hand the end of the world is at hand the end of the world is at hand...."

Damn it, the voice was familiar, too, even though it sounded as parched as some of those corn fields they'd passed in central Missouri.

"The world's just fine, Mister. I should know. I work for the American Geological Survey." Not the US Geological Survey, but people could be excused not knowing the difference.

"The end of the world is at hand the end of the world is at hand the end of the world is at hand...." His clawed hand came up and made as if to touch her, then fell back to his side. His mouth worked as if it took everything he had and he still couldn't find the words.

"What's wrong?" She stepped up to him. Something was seriously wrong with this man.

"Vallon, don't."

Fi's warning came too little, too late, as the man's hand grabbed her wrist so hard she knew it would leave marks. "Vallon," he said, his gaze clear for an instant.

Fi screamed and then the world blew away.

§

The laptop screen glared back at Landon. At least it would have glared if it had been human. Such were the emotions behind the carefully worded message on the screen in front of him from Wolf Amundson. The Chief of the AGS had obviously figured that anyone of Landon's talents would have the means to continue to monitor his e-mail wherever he was.

He sat in a comfortably cushioned wicker chair on the trellis-covered deck behind Elizabeth Ducharme's house, the pool alive with lazy turquoise ripples, the barely-there breeze rustling the potted palm leaves. The rattan furniture with its pale green and white oleander-patterned cushions was quite comfortable and the cup of iced tea on the table beside him was eminently passable. If one could ignore the scent of muddy river water, one could almost think they were in some more acceptable place in the tropics.

Landon scanned the message again and shook his head. The man had actually thought that sending it would have some impact. Like accusations of being a traitor to his country and endangering state secrets were going to bring him back. Wolf Amundson was a fool of the first order, even if he was a patriot—and even that was questionable. No, Wolf Amundson was and always had been out to build his own empire, and controlling the AGS was part of that empire building. The problem was that he—an unGifted—could no more control something he did not understand than a small child could control the wind. The best he could do was stand back and let it pass over and by him.

The one worrisome piece was that Landon had not heard from Gleason. The man who would always be his Chief knew just as well as Landon what they were up against. But Gleason had been determined to stay behind and hold the crumbling AGS together, first and foremost to ensure that the US did have a response to any attack against American soil, and second to be available should Wolf Amundson do what they all hoped he would and show himself as the hopeless incompetent he would be at managing the AGS.

Landon had been sending messages to a secret e-mail account since arriving in New Madrid. The fact that Gleason hadn't responded filled him with dread. Had Gleason been arrested because Landon had jumped ship? Had the account been compromised so Gleason dared not use it?

It was a chance they'd both decided was worth it. Now he wasn't quite so sure.

Clickety-click-click. Elizabeth Ducharme trundled out onto the deck. Today she wore a sleeveless polka-dot sundress and high-heeled mules with little matching dots over the toes. Just where did women find such things and how much time did they waste looking for them? But then he supposed he should be kinder. He had spent three hours in St. Louis looking for his suit and tie and getting them fitted.

"Is everything all right here?" Elizabeth asked. "I'm going to the market and I wanted to make sure you had everything you need."

Landon smiled up at her. Aside from being his hostess, she really had tried to make him feel welcome, almost as if she were a friend and he not just a paying customer. Southern hospitality or some such.

"I'm fine thanks. I'll just be here doing a little research."

Curiosity lit her gaze. "I thought you'd be out and about for your research. I thought that was why you came to New Madrid."

"Too true, but the heat of the day is quite unexpectedly oppressive. I believe I will sit here today to acclimatize. The levee network the Union soldiers built is not going anywhere."

She agreed and disappeared into the house, the echoes of her feminine footfall and her child's voice reaching him like reminders of the past he would never have. He was going to have to watch Vallon closely. In point of fact, he had probably erred when he chose to remain here instead of going with the two women on their explorations. But he doubted Vallon would seek her father—if it was her father—too seriously with her friend in tow, which gave him a chance to consider his options.

Francis Drake was a ruthless man, or had become that way over the years. At first he had been in accord with Landon and Gleason and Roger Decker, the original Chief of the AGS. They had been the architects of the organization when it formed with the mission of protecting American soil and research to better understand the Gift and where it came from. But Francis and a few of the others had soon chafed at the restrictions Decker had placed around them. Why not use the Gift to improve things, they'd asked at first. Then rumblings of why should we protect when we could take and they would never know. The corporations do it, why shouldn't we?

Decker had stepped hard on the sources of those rumbles. Landon had never been able to definitively show that Francis Drake had shared that view, but he had been one of the key supporters of Landon's genealogical research and the breeding program within the AGS. He'd fathered several children, and had actually gone to Europe to do research *on the ground* as it were. But over the years, his frustrations with the organization had become clearer and clearer. He'd had confrontations with Decker on a number of occasions, to the point where Drake's death had almost been a relief.

Except he wasn't dead. He was out there, and whatever he was doing, it would involve no good intentions for Vallon Drake or the AGS, he was sure of it. Francis Drake had been about the worst father he could imagine to a potent child like Vallon: strict, absent minded, and uncaring. Too bad the girl's mother hadn't lived.

So talking Vallon Drake out of seeking her father was paramount. The trouble was, he knew that was likely impossible unless she knew the truth of her situation, and that was something he could not tell her without Gleason's consent.

He looked down at the screen again:

Snow, Your name is currently being added to the most wanted roster for suspicion of treason, and your picture is being circulated to law enforcement across the country. The power of Homeland Security has turned to your pursuit. You cannot get free. To make things go easier for you and everyone at the AGS, I suggest you return to Seattle, turn yourself in, and explain your actions. Bring the girl with you and things will go easier.

As if it were true. Landon Snow would likely disappear soon after he hit Seattle, and Vallon Drake with him. He could send Vallon back to Seattle, but that likely would only lead to her demise. Running might be an option, but it failed to do what he and Vallon had sworn to do— protect their nation. He might not have difficulty finding reason to leave his duties behind, but Vallon—no, she was a true patriot. So staying here and stopping whoever was responsible for the quake, especially if it was Francis Drake, was the only option.

He just prayed he was right.

CHAPTER 16 — FRIENDS

A crevasse in the universe opened up and the stench of ozone and ether burned through Vallon as she fell. Arms and legs flailed, but there was nothing there. No dust, no stars, only eternal blackness, the stink—and the distant sound of screaming. Air burst from her lungs, blood boiled in her veins, and then her skin buckled, her body came apart, shredding into the darkness, and the pain doubled her over and her mouth opened and her voice, her mind, her essence joined the screams of the fallen.

And she was no one and nothing and....

Vallon!

The sounded echoed in the emptiness like a god's voice while the wind roared in her ears as she fell.

Vallon! *Bela Menina!*

That voice. Those words. Only one person used those words.

"Where?"

No answer, but someone had her shoulders. Her feet bumped along a hard surface as she fell. But that was impossible.

"Stop," she moaned and her shoulders dropped onto the hard surface. Her brain rattled as her head clumped to the ground, and then hands were on her face, stroking. Tears fell on her cheeks. Someone else's? Her own?

Afterburn seared through her like the worst fever ache and her skin was aflame. The red glare of sunlight came through her eyelids and the oppressive scent of muddy water filled her lungs, but couldn't fill the hollowness that bloomed inside her. Not falling. She had landed, but the great void she'd fallen through now seemed to fill her instead. She brought her forearm up to cover her eyes and winced at the pain of movement and the brightness as she opened her eyes. Every muscle and joint ached, even her eyelids, and she felt like she might disappear inside her own hollowness.

"Vallon? What's going on?" Fi, weeping, knelt beside her. "That man touched you and you fell."

Vallon pushed herself up to her elbows and stifled a groan. The strange man was nowhere to be seen, but she knew who he was now. Somehow in the nightmare of falling, she'd recognized him.

"Morgan Hoptaler," she said. "That was flipping Morgan Hoptaler."

Fi brushed tears off her cheeks, looking momentarily confused. Her eyes were red. Her cheeks streaked and blotchy. The overheated sun placed a halo around her, and the mist off the river hazed the blue of the sky. The breeze rattled in the tall grasses that straggled along what had once been the shoreline. The Camry hunkered like a blue-backed beetle in the middle of the parking lot. A truck rattled along Water Street, just inside and below the levee.

"We need to find him." Vallon scrambled her feet under her and stood, only to almost go down again until Fi caught her arm. The pain of the contact sent them both reeling back from each other and the world did a little wobble around her, but she braced her legs and ignored Fi's gasp. Where was Morgan?

"Him? Him who? What's happening, Vallon?" Fi asked, suspicion in her voice.

Vallon spun back to Fi and stumbled again. Damn it, the last thing she needed was afterburn again. She was almost as unsteady as a drunkard and her thinking would be affected that way, too. Her libido already had her wanting to loosen her clothes. Or tighten them for the friction it would cause. Damn. She yanked her thoughts back.

"That was Morgan. Didn't you recognize him? From school?"

Fi frowned and looked pretty doing it. Heck, all she needed was a wide brimmed hat to be a total Southern Belle. Good. The question distracted her.

"Morgan Hoptaler? You mean the guy who…"

That memory was no place Vallon wanted to go. She stopped Fi with her palm up. "That Morgan. The upper classman who made our lives hell." Until she'd finally slept with him, but that was after Fi was long gone, pulled out of school by her mother.

Fi's disbelief radiated off of her. "What would he be doing here? Looking like that? Why would he attack you?"

Why indeed. Given that Vallon hadn't told Fi they were on a case, it was going to be pretty hard explaining that Morgan Hoptaler had been one of the agents at the New Madrid substation. She shook her head. "I just can't figure it. He didn't seem to recognize me when he grabbed my arm." Even if he'd said her name. She shuddered and rubbed her wrist that still bore the mark of his grip. "I was coming apart and all I could hear was screaming." She glanced back at Fi. "Was I screaming?"

"Noooo. But you were moaning and thrashing around a little until I grabbed you away from him—Morgan—whoever." Then her face went still and her expression rippled as all the little points of logic fell into place. She suddenly straightened, her arms crossed over her flowered breast. "What's going on, Vallon? You don't just walk into a town and faint twice in twenty-four hours, or run into someone—a Gifted—from our past like Morgan Hoptaler."

Vallon couldn't meet her gaze. "I might faint. It might be this gawdawful heat."

"Vallon…."

She recognized the warning tone from their years together in school. The last time she'd heard it, Vallon had just fibbed about whether she'd kissed a boy that Fi liked. A boy named Morgan Hoptaler, who had made their lives hell at the same time Fi was crushing on him so hard it was painful. It had led to the one time their friendship had been at risk. They hadn't talked to each other for a week until Vallon had made a point of embarrassing herself apologizing to Fi in front of *everybody* and had not gone near Morgan again until Fi was long gone. It had not been something Vallon wanted to live through again, nor was it something she was proud of.

Telling the truth this time was going to be even less easy.

"I honestly don't know."

Fi held her hand up to stop her. "How can you say that, when afterburn is sparking so badly I can barely be near you? You've been using the power. Something's going on, Vallon, and you've dragged me into the middle of it. I think I have a right to know what 'it' is."

"But I honestly *don't* know. That's the problem." Except that there *is* a case and this isn't really a holiday at all. Just thinking about it made her brain ache as badly as her body, and the emptiness yawned inside her like a chasm she struggled not to fall into.

But Fi wasn't buying. She shook her head. "That's a problem, all right. A real problem. I'm tired of you using me and then lying." She took a deep breath. "Vallon, I know I have a lot to thank you for. You've really helped me get on my feet, but I can't stay around you anymore. You're unhealthy—to me—the way you keep expecting me to cycle you through the afterburn. It's not natural, and you're doing unnatural things. When we get home you can have your guestroom back. I'm moving out."

She crossed her arms over her chest and turned to look out over the water so that she shut Vallon out. What could she say to that? She *had* used Fi—at least a little....

"Fi, no." Vallon wanted to touch her friend's shoulder, but knew she didn't dare. She caught Fi glancing over her shoulder.

"See? You can't hide it. You've been using power."

Vallon shook her head, and the emptiness shifted like a wave inside her so she almost lost her balance. "But I haven't. You saw what happened. He touched me and it was like I was being torn apart and emptied out. If I used power at all, it was to hold myself together—and I didn't do it consciously. Or maybe it ripped power from me. I don't know." She ran her hands back through her hair and winced at the sensation of her heated fingers on hot scalp. It hurt to think. It hurt to do anything. And the hollow feeling left her insides ringing like a shell.

"You're on an AGS investigation, aren't you?"

What could she say? With both her and Landon there, it had to be pretty obvious. Vallon tried, but she couldn't quite meet Fi's pale blue gaze. My God, the woman was like a complete person at the moment, not liked the burned out street person Vallon had rescued. The cycling had done that much. "Not exactly. The AGS doesn't know we're here."

"What does 'not exactly' mean?" Fi asked, her arms crossed over her chest.

"It means we're here because something has happened, we think because of rogue agents. If the new management at the AGS knew that, they'd be likely to paint all Gifted with the same brush. We're trying to clean up a mess, Fi." Vallon shook her head. "Fi, I never thought this would be much more than a reconnaissance mission, otherwise I would never have dragged you here. I thought we *could* have fun, and I could look into something small, and that was it. Sort of combine business and pleasure."

Fi's lower jaw jutted and she looked like she was going to cry. "I thought you wanted to go on a holiday with me, but you used me as a cover. And you probably wanted me handy for power cycling, too." She held up her hand to stop Vallon's protest. "Don't tell me that didn't cross your mind, given you've already asked me to help once; and the way you're vibrating right now, you're going to ask again." She screwed up her face and a ragged breath escaped. "Sometimes—sometimes you are so much like my mother I can almost hate you."

Then she turned and marched away, back to the car, climbed into the driver's side, and drove away, leaving Vallon standing there wondering whether to run after her. Fi would get over it—she would. She'd gotten over her other mads, like the one about the little problem in Vallon's basement. It had blown over in the excitement of getting ready for this trip.

But this one felt different. Fi had been direct and clear with her disapproval of Vallon, and she hadn't been prepared to listen to Vallon's excuses. It left Vallon uncomfortable with the realization that she'd really screwed up this time. She just had to hope that she could make it up to Fi when she got back to the guesthouse. Maybe arrange that boat trip Fi was so excited about.

But given the disappointment in Fi's expression, even that might not work.

Vallon sighed and looked out over the river that had changed to a molten silver in the heating air. Evaporation shimmered above its surface and the air had gotten so full of moisture it was hard to breathe. Vallon's crisp blue blouse had wilted against her body, and she was thankful for the tan shorts that let what breeze there was reach the damp backs of her knees. She brushed off the dust from her faint. Well, she was out here, and Fi would need a chance to cool off before Vallon tried to talk things out with her. She didn't need Fi to continue her investigation. She'd dig around on her own, see what she could find, report to Landon, and maybe salvage whatever vacation there still was with Fi. She had to make that much up to her.

She scanned down the street. New Madrid Station, or what had been the station, was to her left. The town wasn't that big, and she could use the exercise, given she hadn't run for a couple of days. But first she was going to find Morgan Hoptaler, because his situation had to have something to do with what had happened at New Madrid station. The AGS wouldn't just let an agent burn out and turn into a street person. And Morgan wasn't just any agent. He'd been top of his year at school. But looking as bad as he had, and with his level of Gift, he could pose a real danger to the world.

She stopped. Was that what this was all about? Had Morgan been 'deactivated' from service and, in his crazy state, caused the quake? That would be consistent with his sign that the end of the world was at hand. But that didn't explain her certainty that her father was involved. She'd *felt* him. And inhaled his almond scent, because every Gifted had a scent, just as Xavier smelled of Cedar of Lebanon and incense, Landon smelled like faint almonds and baby fresh powder, and Fi smelled of anise and mint.

But Morgan was involved somehow. She knew it just like she knew her father was involved. Morgan was a clue, and maybe the source, and maybe he could lead her to her father.

Given Fi had dragged her away from Morgan, he had to have headed back down into town. Yesterday they'd spotted him just down Main Street, so maybe he'd be there again. She headed out, her athletic sandals slapping briskly on the pavement as she went down the levee ramp and past the handsome brick museum. The sun beat down and the levee blocked the slight breeze off the river, so she immediately started sweating.

Okay. Maybe there was a reason everyone in this town seemed to move in slow motion, but that wasn't her way. No sign of Morgan by the museum and no one walking the sidewalk down Main Street that she could see, either. Well, the man couldn't just disappear, now could he?

She kept walking, crossing Water Street that paralleled the levee and the road that ran down its top, and into the town back towards the Dixie Theatre and the little diner she'd noticed in her drive through yesterday. A low, red brick building on her left: no sign of Morgan. The theatre on her right and Randy's Diner with the open sign flashing and the scent of coffee and fried eggs wafting out through old fashioned vents in the windows. A rack of postcards just outside the door had photos of the riverboat she and Fi had seen and one actual photo of pickers in a cotton field. An actual cotton field. Okay. She was officially in the south.

Ahead was a low house signed as the Higgerson School Historical Site and Visitor's Center, and damn it, Fi should have been here, because this was what she wanted, wasn't it? A little tour around the town? But there was still no sign of Morgan, and she couldn't believe that he'd gone so far when she'd seen him hanging around this area yesterday and he'd been here today, too. She turned her back on the school site and looked around. This whole end of town might have the theatre and a few other buildings, but an awful lot of it was parking lot. He had to be here somewhere. She came even with the theatre and the diner again.

An antique bell dinged above the diner door and Vallon stepped out of the way.

"You're looking mighty lost, there. Or you still looking fer the fella you were looking for last night?"

Vallon involuntarily shivered and swung around to face the man from the Flooded Duck.

A smooth grin quirked his lips. "Or maybe I'm who you're lookin' for, pretty lady. Vallon, right?"

Oh God, no. This morning he looked just as tall and brawny and delicious as he'd looked last night, his blonde shock of hair still fell in his blue eyes, but this morning his tanned biceps were exposed under a plain white t-shirt that labored a little to cover his rock hard pecs. The afterburn from her encounter with Morgan sizzled and snapped through her core and she took a hesitant step backwards away from him, even though every part of her said grab him, push him into a corner, and have at him again. Get this feeling of insects under her skin over and done with.

But if last night had been an accident, doing it again couldn't be explained that way. She looked up at his face. "Uh, hi." Damn it, she couldn't remember his name? He'd told her, hadn't he?

Thankfully he stuck out his hand. "Toby. Toby Watts. And you're Vallon Drake."

She nodded, but didn't accept his hand. "Nice to see you again. And I am looking for someone. Did you see a homeless looking man walk past here? He was carrying a sign about the end of the world."

"You talking about Hoppy?" He looked first of all put out that she refused his hand, and then disbelieving. "The man's crazy." He edged a little closer. "I saw you walk by. You want to come in for a coffee or something?" He nodded sideways at Randy's. "They do a mighty fine breakfast."

"Thank you, no. I need to find this guy. His name is Morgan Hoptaler, if he's the man I think he is."

He worked his shoulders and scratched his fingers through that soft blonde hair, and the way his muscles worked made her mouth water. She backed up again. "Do you know where I might find him?"

"You'd really rather go find ol' Hoppy than have a coffee with me? You know it might leave me mortally wounded?" He feigned injury, then hooked his fingers sexily in the top front of jeans. "You got me kind of hot and bothered last night. I couldn't sleep all night, thinking about you."

Oh yeah, danger Vallon Drake. Big time danger if you have any intention of staying faithful to Xavier. *Except Xavier isn't here, is he? He might never be here again, and hasn't the AGS always promoted just relieving oneself as soon as possible?*

She jerked back into herself as Toby cocked a brow down at her. "We were kinda good together, weren't we? Packed a wallop between us?"

She could almost feel the concussion of his thrust between her legs. Wanted to feel it again. Damn it, she was shaking she wanted him so bad, but it wasn't going to happen. Not when she thought she'd sensed Xavier's presence out there.

"I'm flattered, but I'm afraid a coffee is out of the question. Now 'Hoppy' as you call him—where would I find him?" She thought a moment. Give the guy some hope and maybe he'd tell her more readily. Who was she kidding? She didn't want to completely cut off the possibility of getting together with Mr. Tall-blonde-and-sexy in case that brief sense of contact with Xavier was just wishful thinking. "If I find him, I might be able to get together later. Where will I find you?"

His eyes did their dilation thing and he seemed to go on alert and study her a moment, then he sagged back into his sexy slouch and grinned. Very nice. Very nice indeed, the way the sun placed highlights on his muscles and his gaze trailed up over her heated skin. She could use one of Elizabeth Ducharme's iced teas right about now. She'd pour it over her head.

"Well, now. Ol' 'Hoppy' likes to hide out in the shadows a little bit. He seems to like the Spence Building fer some reason." He nodded at the low brick horseshoe-shaped building kitty corner from the museum ."I see him around there a lot. Or else he wanders around the neighborhood just north of the levee. Don't know where he spends his nights. Probably just wherever he finds himself." He shrugged. "How about I come with you and help you look?" He cocked a brow at her and she had to swallow before she shook her head, no.

"I need to discuss some private things with him."

A sexy tilt of head and he looked down at her with the darndest pout. "You sure you don't got a thing for ol' Hoppy? Cause a man can learn to step aside."

"It's nothing of the kind." And why was she having to explain herself to this man? Afterburn that was right now crawling up and down her body like so many caressing fingers that made her want to moan and reach for Toby.

Maybe he read her expression, for he stepped into her, caught her shoulders so the afterburn seared through her as he leaned down to push her hair back and whisper in her ear. "I'll be right here waitin' for ya, babe. For the next two hours. Don't make me wait too long." Then he trailed his lips along her neck and jawline to her mouth, but didn't kiss her. He just pulled back with a grin and sauntered back inside the diner.

Holy crap. She suddenly remembered to breathe again and fought down the raging hormone fire that filled the hollow place inside her and threatened to leave her an ashy pile of nothing. It would have been so right to just follow right after him like a pet dog on a leash. He was not her type, but he oh, so was.

She jerked around and headed back to the Spence Building, trying to get Toby's scent of Irish Spring soap out of her nose. Shadows. Morgan liked shadows, like he was hiding. He smelled of fear, carried signs of the end of the world, and when he'd touched her, all she heard was screaming. His? She couldn't imagine the Morgan Hoptaler she knew ever doing any of those things. The old Morgan Hoptaler had been an overconfident asshole who'd probably had notches in his bedpost for all his conquests.

The center of the U-shaped building was a parking lot, complete with cars but no sign of Morgan. She circled around the building: more cars, garbage bins, and the antiseptic scent of old medical equipment. The place must house doctors' or dentists' offices. But still no Morgan. She sighed and studied the area. Beyond the Spence Building there was what looked like a construction company or building supply place, and a couple of low warehouse type buildings. After that it was the same low houses and sparse yards she'd driven through with Fi yesterday. And about two blocks over was the place where the New Madrid substation used to stand. Toby'd said Morgan hung out in that neighborhood—if she could trust him.

But Morgan hanging near New Madrid station made too-perfect sense. As a matter of fact, she'd just about lay money on Morgan being near the Kochtitsky House.

She started out walking, the sun beating down, the stench of oil, engine grease, and construction equipment diesel competing with the muggy fug of heated river water and mud. Her head ached. Her body throbbed, but she ran five miles a day at home, she could walk two or so blocks easily. The shade from the few trees didn't come anywhere near shading the road, so she was dripping by the time she reached King's

Highway and turned up towards the damned white and green Kochtitsky house, with its spreading lawns and graceful trees that shouldn't even exist.

Morgan had to be around here, but she wasn't setting foot on the Kochtitsky property. Go back and get Landon? But what could Landon do that she couldn't? And she sure as heck wasn't going to get Fi. She slowed and studied the scene. Cars parked here and there along the gravel sides of the road. Sun-beaten lawns. Houses that hunkered low enough they looked like they kept their heads down to avoid tornadoes passing through. Some of the houses had water stains up their sides from old floods. Nope. Like she'd thought. New Madrid was no place to raise a family.

But a couple of kids were playing with toy trucks in a brown front yard. They stopped to watch her with unfriendly expressions as she walked by, and she suddenly felt strange and foreign as if she was travelling in another country. When she smiled at them, their expression didn't change. At least little Farrah was a different kettle of fish. Now that little girl knew how to make a person feel welcome.

A flicker of movement in the otherwise still street made her stop. She had the intense sensation that someone was watching her. From one of the houses? From one of the cars? She did a casual scan, but spotted nothing—except the dusty figure of Morgan Hoptaler stepping from between two of the houses.

CHAPTER 17 — CEDAR OF LEBANON

The slick offices of Homeland Security were just that, slick. Slick looking receptionist, with long dark hair pulled back in a European-look pony tail and a business suit that bulged slightly so Jason could swear she was packing. Slick looking modern desk and waiting area, with grey leather furniture and modern steel sculptures instead of the drooping potted palm one got in Seattle P.D. offices. Unframed art on the walls of muted grays that hinted at figures disappearing in fog or rain. Not exactly a warm and fuzzy kinda place. He eyed the double glass doors beyond the receptionist. More like the kind of place you could go into but never come out of.

Jason checked his watch one more time. He really shouldn't have come. He'd just gone to Vallon's house looking to meet up with Xavier. He'd said he wouldn't come here. Hell, he'd promised himself he wouldn't, and yet somehow he'd agreed he would in his conversation with Amundson. *Come on in and tell us how you know what you know.* It sounded so simple, but what could he show them, really? Not a damn thing. All he could do is tell them about the episodes of change that he knew of. They were the ones who were going to have to determine whether they believed him. He really didn't give a damn if they did or didn't. He'd find Vallon on his own. He would.

A phone buzzed softly and Miss European-ponytail touched her headset and spoke softly. Then she stood up—tall for a woman, and model thin—and came around the desk to him. He felt ridiculously underdressed even though he was in detective standard dress slacks and tweed jacket.

"Station Chief Amundson and the others will see you now, Mr. Bryson."

Not even a mention of his detective status—as if they knew he'd walked out on the job. Maybe they did. Clint and Amundson had some old connection. He felt older and more wrinkled than he probably looked. He stood up and followed as she led him through the double glass doors and to a glass-walled boardroom with floor to ceiling windows that looked out at the million dollar view of Elliott Bay and the Olympic Mountains. Amundson sat with two men at the cherry wood table that could seat at least twenty. Two other men who looked like the brawn of the agency stood with their backs to a closed door at one end of the room. Shit, if they could afford this for a boardroom, the top office must be really something. Built to impress, no shit.

"Aah, Detective—or should I say Mr. Bryson? How nice of you to join us." Wolf Amundson's smooth voice oiled over Jason's skin. Slick, all right. Without the glass he'd probably slide right out of the room. Amundson and the two men sat with their backs to the window at the end of the room closest to the guarded door.

"Jason will do, thanks." He came around the end of the table and shook Amundson's cool hand.

"Jason, then." Amundson bared his teeth in what was supposed to be a smile, but made Jason think of wolves panting. "I'd like to introduce Dr. Sukh Sandhu. He is our chief researcher into the phenomena known as the Gift. I thought it would be worthwhile for the two of you to meet."

The South Asian man stood. He was slim, dark haired, with the lustrous doe eyes of so many of his people, but Sukh Sandhu's intense gaze was anything but deer-like. He twitched an efficient hand out to shake as if it was a tool he used in a laboratory. Like maybe Jason was a rat he planned to plant an electrode in. So maybe coming here wasn't such a good idea.

"Pleased to meet you," Jason said and took the seat at the end of the table Amundson motioned him to, then felt his skin crawl at having the two bruisers behind him out of his view. Definitely not feeling like a good idea.

"And I you," Sandhu said as he folded down into his chair again as graceful as a dancer.

Amundson folded his hands on the table and exposed his pearly whites again, but it didn't make Jason any more comfortable. The spot between his shoulder blades itched, and even when he shifted his head, he couldn't see what the two men were doing. Couldn't see them reflected in the windows, either. The light was too bright outside, and suddenly felt too bright inside, too. If Amundson had staged this to put him most on his guard, and most at a disadvantage, he couldn't have done better.

"So, Jason, we made a deal. Together we would find and return Agent Drake. In return, we would both contribute something the other wanted to the work of the other. You indicated that you wanted time alone with Agent Drake. Perhaps you can explain why."

Jason glanced from man to man. No way in hell was he telling them the truth. He wasn't sure what they knew about Vallon's little projects in the basement of her house, but he was pretty sure what she was doing there wouldn't be sanctioned by her job. He was also pretty sure they wouldn't want him knowing about it. He shrugged. "Like I said: we need to talk. I believe she might have information I need."

"And why would Agent Drake have this information?" The wolf grin seemed branded on Amundson's face.

"You know damn well why. Because of her 'talents.'" He hooked his fingers.

"Detective Bryson—I'm sorry, Jason—Agent Drake's talents, as you call them, are classified information."

Jason stood up. "If that's what this meeting is about, I'm leaving. Agent Drake told me nothing. I figured it out myself, all right? I *remember*."

He turned to leave, but a heavy hand fell on his shoulder.

Jason looked from the hand to Amundson and Sandhu, who had both remained seated. "So this's how you're going to play this, is it? Because I might help a partner, but this sure as hell isn't feeling like a partnership."

§

The sun beat down on Vallon's shoulders, and the muggy air rippled around the figure of Morgan Hoptaler as he came from between two houses and started down the street towards where the New Madrid substation used to stand. Otherwise, the street was immobilized by heat. Crows roosted somnambulant on telephone wires. A bare breeze came over the levee, but hadn't the strength to stir the leaves. Dust barely eddied along the street edges. From inside one of the houses came the shouts, squeals, and jackpot sounds of a T.V. morning game show. Even the dogs she saw in fenced backyards didn't move when she passed by.

"Morgan!" she called and hurried her pace. What was she going to do if he turned into the Kochtitsky House? Was he one of the people who lived there now? Were the other agents there, too?

"Morgan! Wait up." She started jogging, the sweat in her hair pouring down her forehead and stinging her eyes. She caught up with him before he reached the Kochtitsky property, gritted her teeth, and caught his arm, praying the filthy jacket would protect her at least a little from the blast she'd felt before.

Morgan stopped dead in his tracks. Slow as a construction crane, his head swiveled towards her.

"Morgan, it's me, Vallon. Remember? You remembered a few minutes ago, down on the levee."

His gaze skittered across her face like mice scattering from danger. No recognition. His gaze lifted from her face and looked at the houses across the street, the crows overhead. Anything but her.

"The end of the world is coming. Is coming. The end of the world is coming. Is coming."

"Morgan. Look at me. It's Vallon Drake. You remember me. You made my life hell until I slept with you at school. You were big man on campus. Everyone looked up to you."

Under the filth he still had the amazing bone structure, the thick blonde hair that had darkened with age. The dirt and the vacancy in his eyes just hid the fact that this *was* Morgan. If he hadn't actually called her by name, she might never have recognized him.

Painfully slowly his gaze worked its way back to her face again. Rested there.

"Remember, Morgan? Remember all the trouble we got into when I went ballistic when you started seeing Marcie Stewart? I broke into your room and trashed your clothes. They almost tossed me out of school, but you refused to press charges."

His eyes seemed to focus on her for a moment. His lips trembled. "V-v-v-Vallon?"

"Yes! It's me, Morgan. I came to help. To find out what happened. What happened, Morgan?"

He blinked. Blinked again, like a camera aperture opening and closing, and his face worked as he struggled to remember.

"They came." It came out clearer than she'd expected, like a drop in a clear pool that sent out waves.

"Who came, Morgan? Who? What happened here?"

His look of concentration rippled and lost form, like wave patterns meeting. The confusion seemed to bleed out into his limbs. He twitched under her hands.

"The end of the world is coming," he whispered, the whisper fading away.

He shook himself and tried to pull loose, but damn it, she wasn't going to let him go. She needed to know what had destroyed his mind.

"Morgan, why don't you come with me and I'll take you to a safe place and we can talk, okay?"

He was pulling on her hold, threatening to slide out of his jacket to get free. She ducked around him and planted her palm on his chest. "Morgan, listen to me. I'll take you someplace cool and shady. You like shady places, right?"

His transient gaze fixed for a moment. "Cool."

"Yes. We'll go someplace cool. Just come with me, okay?"

A nod that took a million years. Vallon held onto his jacket sleeve and turned him along a road that led away from the Kochtitsky House, but the feeling of someone watching didn't stop. She scanned the houses, but there didn't seem to be anyone around. Just somnambulant dogs and laundry hanging limp in the almost nonexistent breeze.

"Here," Morgan said and stopped dead in his tracks in front of a low-slung, blue-painted bungalow. It had a burned-off lawn and two garbage tins, knocked over and spreading garbage over the worn spot where a car would normally have been parked. Not exactly any spot Vallon planned on exploring.

"Not here, Morgan. We'll go to my place. It's safer. Landon Snow's there. You remember Landon. He works at the AGS, too. Just like you and me."

No sign he'd even heard her. He just kept mumbling and tugging her toward the barren front yard of the blue house.

There was something about the place when she really looked at it—almost a Kochtitsky House new-skin shininess that made her stomach feel uneasy and the little hairs on her arms stand on end. Almost as if the place didn't quite fit here, even though it had the same barren lawn, the same slow-slung, tornado-attracting tinder look as every other house around it. But the blue was different and seemed to almost glitter in the sun, like the carapace of a dung beetle. What the hell?

She stopped trying to tug Morgan away. "What is this place?"

Morgan strained towards it like a metal chip to a magnet.

"Morgan, look at me." She took a chance and caught his jaw in her fingers and turned his face towards her. "What is this place?"

His lips trembled. His face rippled with effort and a single tear ran a channel of grime down his cheek.

She looked back at the house. The place clearly meant something to him, but the place was 'off'. She -reached- and Morgan was barely a human flame beside her, no glimmer of the Gifted flame that he had been, and that was terrifying enough that she loosened her grip. What the hell has happened to him and why? Who would do this to an AGS agent? *Who could?*

Morgan ripped loose from her and headed towards the house.

"No. No. No." He shouted and clutched his head.

She went after him. "Morgan, no. It's me Vallon, remember? It's Vallon."

"Vallon, no. No. No!" He plunged like an animal trying to escape, shoved her away, and then ran toward the house. Damn it, she needed his information. She ran after him onto the property, and licorice and ozone power slammed up her legs and into her mind, tearing her away from herself. She went to her knees, her awareness knocked away into a black pit and screaming. Dammit, she knew this house was a danger. Morgan was a lure!

Earth crumbled to dust and fell away to nothing under her. The house shuddered and collapsed, its walls coming apart, the boards eaten by termites-power-something in the space of moments. Wind on her face, tearing her apart. Her flesh tearing from her hands, her hair burning around her. Power, scented cinnamon and pomegranate, tore at her and she was falling apart like an unGifted would.

An attack. This was an attack, and it had the power to take down Gifted. This had to be what had happened to Morgan. She fought back. Fought to join mind to body, and found herself face down in the rough brown grass. The air plumed around her, shimmering with change, and the house flickered and was gone, replaced by a hole in the ground, an old swimming pool, complete with scum dried on parched concrete walls. No, it was a metal-sided warehouse grown up out of the soil. No, it was… she pushed herself up to her knees and fell again. Her head filled with screaming and maybe it was her own. Morgan. Where was he? A half-seen figure slipped through the haze of Change. How could he move through this? The world was ending. It was ending for her, if she didn't get out of here. Her skin was as translucent as onionskin. Her veins and muscles showed in her hands.

It couldn't—shouldn't—be possible, but it was happening. Just-get-her-hands-under-her. Crawl-if-she-had-to. Palm-pressed-into-broken-soil-grass-already-wisped-away. Biceps-work-and-shoulders-push-up. Her face came off the lawn and the grass was gone like smoke. Lift-one-hand-and-the-next. Crawl. Crawl, damn it. The screaming in her head increased. Vertigo struck as the ground disappeared. Or did it? She clenched her eyes shut and knew she fell. She collapsed again, but her hands scrambled in grass and earth. Wasn't falling. Was-not-falling. Belly-crawled.

She was coming apart. All the little pieces of her flying off into space. An eddy, a wind that scattered her to the far ends of the earth, and she would never find herself again. Was lost. Tears fell, but never reached her cheeks. Did she have cheeks? Did she have form? What form did she take?

And then strong hands lifted her up, strong arms carried her, and suddenly hot sun and humid mud-tanged air filled the world, along with the scent of Cedar of Lebanon and incense.

That scent… it should mean something… her heart beat faster as she tried to move—had limbs to move—had not been destroyed. She opened her eyes, but there was only a dark silhouette and sun in her eyes, and yet she would know that hawk-nosed visage anywhere—or she should.

"*Bela menina*," her rescuer said and grazed her brow with his hard-soft lips.

The gesture, the voice, and the words sent her heart pounding, and she wanted to touch him, wanted to wrap herself around him and deal with the afterburn that pulsed like her blood, but….

She could not remember his name at all.

CHAPTER 18 —THE HIERARCHY OF ALL THINGS

Even carpet on the floor and a range of photographs and maps on the walls could not disguise the cold concrete walls of the project bunker. Not even though Francis Drake's office had more comforts than the rest of the installation that had been built with corporate donations and the understanding that he and his agents would reshape America more to the corporations' liking. Let them think that. Let them support his work with their billions. Soon he'd show them that the Gifted were not just tools to be used for profit. Soon the tool would rise up against the wielder. It would be an example to every other Gifted in the world. They would see and know the change had been worked, while all the peon unGifted would simply accept so drastic a change. Those with a slight gift might recognize something was different, but they wouldn't be able to make any difference.

That is, it would happen that way if his plans came together, and at the moment that did not seem to be happening.

"Explain again what happened." He paced the small room to his desk and seated himself again. Across from him, Derrick Brown—the agent he had disappeared right out from under the AGS Academy's nose last year because the kid was a talent—stood in an uncomfortable rendition of attention. The kid was average height, slim built like a runner, with chocolate skin and shaved head that showed just a hint of his natural dark curls. Francis suspected the kid had done it to look older, as he was the youngest agent on the premises. An agent for the future, which was why Francis kept him as his assistant.

"Sir. Apparently they had her. Hoptaler had led her right into the trap, just the way you thought he would. She went down like she'd been clubbed, but she was still fighting. Agent Drake seems to have unusual strength, Sir. Most agents would have been knocked out."

Francis waved his comments away. "Don't try to curry favors complimenting Vallon. Get to the point. Why isn't she here in this installation?"

If anything, Brown stiffened further, the tendons cording in his neck. A thin sheen of sweat made his dark skin shine in the fluorescent lights. "Sir, she was crawling towards safety and our men were about to retrieve her when an unknown male arrived. He's described as tall, with long dark hair, dressed in black. He drove a black suburban, stopped in front of the house, grabbed Drake, threw her in his vehicle, and drove off."

Francis closed his eyes and steepled his fingers. "And where did he take Agent Drake?"

He kept his voice mild as he opened his eyes to peer at Brown. The young agent's fear radiated off him like a cloud, and his scent of carnation and seaweed was bright in the room and not entirely pleasant.

"That's just it, Sir. By the time the retrieval team got back to the house for a vehicle, Drake and her rescuer were long gone."

Not what he wanted to hear, by a long shot. The quake, the change, the entire operation depended on getting Vallon involved. Since she was a child he'd known what he had in her—unlike most Gifted children, her nascent power had been apparent like a haze around her almost from birth. Since he'd left, he'd kept tabs on her, and her constant trouble at school and as an agent hadn't surprised him. She was greater than all of them; if anyone should rail at the constrictions of AGS work, it should be her.

"Who the hell rescued her? Her friend again? Because if it was, I suggest we take the friend, too."

Brown nodded slightly. "She *is* Gifted."

Vallon's friend, Gifted? That could be a boon. They needed the power....

"But she wasn't the one who took Drake."

Drake's gaze jerked back to Brown. "What? Who was it? Snow?" Because those were her only two allies in this godforsaken sinkhole of a town.

"A new player, according to our men. Man. Mid forties, maybe. Dark. Parker described him as foreign-looking. Something about the clothes and face. Hawk nosed and rough looking, like he'd been outside a lot of his life. Our guys searched New Madrid, but didn't find the vehicle."

Drake had to remind himself to breathe, to stifle the surge of excitement than ran like a tremor up his spine. There'd been other possible sightings before that had turned out to be nothing. They were in a different part of the country. "It could be some local boy trying to help a damsel in distress," he said.

"Could be, but I don't think so. Parker got a license plate. Vehicle was new—a rental."

"And you have checked the lessee of this vehicle?"

Brown looked uneasy. "We don't actually have the authority to do that." He met Drake's gaze.

"Yes. We do. For this." Drake picked up his phone and punched a single number. Relays clicked and transferred his call to scramble the original location. Far off, in Washington, a ring tone began to drill into Drake's ear.

"Hello." A dry, papery voice that went well with the vulturous form of its owner.

"We need some help. The lessee of a rental vehicle."

"I am not your personal investigator."

"And this does not appear to be a regular lessee." Not that Fitzsimmons would know what he really meant by that. "Whoever it is has just undone our latest effort to get the girl." He would not use her name because he never really knew how secure these calls were.

There was silence a moment. "Have you ever thought of simply walking up and arresting her? I could loan you a team if you don't have the capacity. Oh, wait, I already did."

The sarcasm sent Drake's jaw clenching. "Your team have made contact and were about to pick her up today, but someone else intervened. Then *your team* promptly lost them. The girl is now in play and we need her whereabouts. The lessee's name and address may assist us."

Silence again and then a sigh. "What is the plate number?"

Drake provided it.

"I'll call you back in five minutes, but I will have to report this to the Board."

The Board, those cretinous corporate hacks.

"Do as you wish. The girl is the last piece of the puzzle. Get her, and we can move to stage two of the project."

Stage two: wipe the government infrastructure off the face of the heartland of America—transportation systems, schools, prisons, police and fire departments, National Guard, military, everything. In this depressed economy, there was no way governments could afford to rebuild on their own. Besides, their internal expertise had long ago been outsourced. It would rip open the last niches in the American economy to private business. And the businesses poised would get rich at the cost of the taxpayer. Of course, that was what the businesses thought this was all about. He knew better, because a change as massive as he planned would have to catch the attention of the other Gifted in the world. He would have proved what they all knew—those with the Gift were the true leaders of men. Together they would rise up and assume their true place in the hierarchy of all things.

§

The tinted glass of the suburban surrounded her as the vehicle's engine ticked quietly. Everything was almost darkness except for laser-slivers of light that crisscrossed the darkness from holes in the metal siding of the shed her rescuer had driven them to. Bullet holes, it looked like, which shouldn't surprise her given the back country this was. She glanced at the driver, too aware of his electric presence. Just sitting here was like having him touch her, his hands on her skin. His musk of Cedar of Lebanon and incense almost filled her to bursting and she *should know him*, just like she should know who she was and why she was here, wherever *here* was.

She clamped her eyes shut and listened to the sound of their breathing. Heard the rustle of his clothes and knew he turned to her.

What had happened to her? She should know him, because his presence was like the beat of her heart—always there. She knew it—knew he was someone special, but his identity was lost behind a fog that seemed to eat her memories.

Finally she opened her eyes and met his gaze—dark, and with the lines radiating out like he had seen too many sunrises. Like a man of glaring sun. The desert. Yes, that was right. Blue robes pulled across his forehead and chin, orange dunes stretching into forever around him. Those eyes carried so much—hurt, pain, longing—and their expression made her want to touch him.

Her hand was on his bare forearm before she could stop herself, and the blaze of afterburn leapt like a spark from her flesh to his. The confined air in the cab seemed to crackle and pop.

"Vallon. *Bela Menina*." His voice was a low rumble that echoed through her body. "It has been too long."

Vallon. At his use of the name, she knew it was her, and was suddenly frightened that she hadn't known. She studied his face, and that frightened her more. Wanted to beg him to tell her why, but….

"Too long." She echoed and sat back against the door, putting as much distance between them as possible. Perhaps he wouldn't see her confusion, because regardless of everything she wasn't sure of, she was sure that it was him who had stayed away.

"*Bela*… after Seattle I was called…. I could not stay. I could not come back, for too many rules had been broken." He looked down at his hands that gripped the tops of his thighs as if he would stop himself from doing something he might regret. *Like touch her?*

"But I could not stay away from you—from us. I broke faith with my leaders again to come to you. To Seattle, to keep you safe. But you were not there." His gaze met hers. "And then I feel you across so many miles and I know you are in danger and so I am here." A slight European shrug and his hands loosened from his thighs and he reached for her, caught her hands even though she tried to avoid him, and then she was pulled into his chest. Strong. Arms hard around her and his mouth on hers and the fog that had seemed to fill her head parted. She pulled back from him, barely at all.

"Xavier," she whispered.

§

'*Detained for questioning.*' That was the euphemism, wasn't it? Jason slammed his palm against the room's wall—correction—the cell's wall. For the room might not have a bolted-down bed and a metal urinal attached to the wall, but the single chair and bolted-down table made the room not much more. Maybe a well-funded agency's cell. Certainly not police quality, because the air had a metal scent, not the piss and blood stink of police lockup.

He paced once more around the blank-walled room and collapsed onto the metal-framed chair. Not even graffiti on the walls. Nothing to keep the mind occupied except his anger at the confinement and his worry about Vallon. If they found her and locked her away….

The chill of fear ran fingers up his back. *He would never get Cheryl back.*

No. He shook himself and stood up to pace again. He would not let that happen. He'd found Vallon and she was his. No matter what Wolf Amundson thought. Or the foreigner. Xavier. He hadn't been around when Jason and Amundson met at the house. At least, he hadn't shown himself, and Jason hadn't had any sense he was around. Not that he'd *know* if Mr. Tall, Dark, and Mysterious was around. Hell, maybe the guy had made contact with Vallon and lit out without Jason, even though they'd agreed to work together.

Yeah, that would fit. He leaned against the cell wall and rubbed his face. His head ached. His whole body ached. Xavier de Varga and Wolf Amundson and every other fucking person out there was working for themselves, and if they could take advantage of a pathetic Seattle cop, they would. But he wasn't some simple flatfoot to be run roughshod over. He was a well-trained detective, even if he'd more or less quit, and he also had an unusual talent. At least, according to Vallon's and Xavier's reactions he did.

He walked over to the room's metal door and slammed his palm against it. Again. Again.

The cell boomed with the blows, but it couldn't be much better in the office area beyond the cell. Someone would come. He kept it up, the booms adding to his headache. So they'd try to wait him out, but he had all the time in the world, and frankly, if they wanted to piss him off, they were going at it the right way.

Soundlessly the door opened and Amundson stood there facing him, oily smooth in his too blonde, too Teutonic, too tanned way.

"You make a lot of noise, Mr. Bryson."

Again the reminder that he no longer had the police department behind him, but that might not be entirely true. He *had* walked out, but he *hadn't* handed in any formal resignation. And after all the years together, Clint would help him out if he needed it. Maybe.

"And you have no right at all to hold me." He stood toe to toe with the man. They were about the same height, and Jason had him in pure toned muscle if it came down to a fight.

Amundson shrugged. "I think you are mistaken, Mr. Bryson." The *mister* came out dripping. "You seem to have come into possession of a national security secret, and we must ascertain how, and ensure that said secret does not get disclosed any further."

Damn it, if that was all they were concerned with, he might be in trouble. He jutted his jaw and stared down Amundson. "And I've told you. I seem to have developed a talent that you don't seem to have—the talent to tell when people like Vallon make changes. I was offering to help you, but you piss me off again and the deal is off."

He held Amundson's gaze and wasn't going to back down. Finally, triumph—Amundson's gaze flickered for just a second. "Can you really do this?"

Jason narrowed his gaze. Was he being played? Amundson was the type. "You give me a chance to prove it."

"A test?" A small doubting rise of Amundson's blonde brows.

"Fine. But I don't sit in a cell while you pull the test together. I— get an office—and freedom to come and go as I please."

A small, cruel smile crossed Amundson's face and then was gone, like a wolf print lost in drifting snow. "You expect a great deal for nothing, Detective Bryson. But you may wait in an office right now. We will consider the freedom later."

We? The man was talking like the frigging King of England.

But at least he was taken from the cell to a small, empty office with a window that looked down on a Seattle side street, the harbor and the Olympic Mountains available in the reflection in the next high rise's mirrored windows. He *thunked* down in the desk chair. No phone. Nothing in the desk drawers when he slid them open. No way to call Clint for help.

Nope, that avenue was closed to him, anyway. He sighed. It wasn't good what had happened between them. He'd have to do something to heal things—after this whole thing with Vallon was over. After Cheryl was back.

He closed his eyes and thought of thick auburn hair and the warmth of her body—before the disease took her. It had been so fast, the tumor, the hope at the surgery, the horrible fight after the biopsy uncovered the aggressive form of cancer. From his warm round wife, she became a frail stick figure of a creature with Cheryl's eyes. Then a pale wraith held prisoner by white sheets, her eyes like black pits he could fall into. She'd held his hand then and smiled up at him. "You were made for me," she'd whispered. They were the last words she ever said.

"They're ready for you."

A rough voice brought him out of his reverie. Amundson's pet bruiser agent leaned on the doorframe, but the tension in his body said if Jason tried anything this guy wouldn't hesitate to use force. Jason stood and preceded his guard down the hallway, past his cell and away from the boardroom with the grand view. Into the bowels, he thought as they climbed in an elevator and the guard hit the lowest button.

It must have been an express, for the floor almost fell out from under his feet, and then suddenly the pressure was there again as they came to a halt and the door hissed open. They'd fallen far enough they must be under street level. Cold fluorescent light filled a narrow, windowless hallway with too many numbered metal doors to either side. It confirmed his suspicions. The ventilated air seemed full of whispers as if people crouched behind each of the doors, and an ammonia scent filled the air but didn't disguise the faint scent of excrement and vomit and other things that set all the little hairs on the back of his neck on end.

Jason's shoulders itched as Amundson's buddy-boy followed him.

"Strange looking place for a little experiment," he said.

A grunt and: "All the 'experiments' are done right here."

Research facility, then, but he didn't like the feeling that once you came in here, you never came out.

The long hallway ended at an unmarked metal door. He glanced back at his keeper. The man lifted his cleft chin.

"Go on in."

The door worked soundlessly and he found himself inside a large room lined on one wall with computers and with banks of cameras high on the walls. One windowed door on the other side of the room gave onto a side room that had the look of an operating theatre, and another glass door gave onto a room that held various scientific paraphernalia that you'd expect to see in a T.V. show laboratory. So laboratory, then.

In the room stood Wolf Amundson with two other men, one an emaciated grey-haired man in a white lab coat. The other man, confined to a chair by metal wrist and ankle bands, he recognized.

AGS Chief Gregor Gleason would normally tower over Amundson, but at the moment he looked diminished and tired. His grey suit was rumpled and hung on his cadaverous frame. His eyes looked like he hadn't seen a good night's sleep in days.

Jason nodded to him. "Chief Gleason. How nice to see you again." But it wasn't. For either of them.

"Detective Bryson. I'd offer to shake your hand, but it seems that is not to be." Gleason's voice was tired, and barely carried the force it once had. "But it is just Gregor, now. I have been replaced." He nodded at Amundson and didn't bother to hide his distaste.

"But if you're no longer…."

"Mr. Gleason is here to assist us in our little experiment, correct?" Amundson's glare seemed to drill into Gleason. "An agent of the United States Government is always willing to serve." He bared his teeth.

"So *Mister* Bryson has agreed to a little experiment that might be of interest to you, Gleason. Give you a sense of where we are going in the AGS. Sheldon, please."

The man in the lab coat slid forward a low bed trolley, filled with a bed of sand that was enough like the sandbox in Vallon's basement that Jason almost took a step back. He'd been in the house to feed Maggie this morning, after Amundson had left. The castle had still been in the basement, but the miniature fields of corn hadn't been there. Not even stubble, only sand. It was like someone had simply turned over the sand, and the living plant matter wasn't there anymore. He thought he'd seen movement in the windows of the castle, but he wasn't sure, and the whole damn thing had had a hazy feel to it, like the air on a hot summer morning after rain.

"What's that supposed to be for?" he asked to hide his recognition, but he felt Amundson's too heavy gaze. Had the man seen something in Jason's face?

"A workspace, let us say. Mr. Gleason will help us by creating change and you will report the change as it occurs."

He motioned Gleason to begin, but the ex-AGS chief hesitated. "This is not a circus trick, Wolf. Don't do this. The Gifted are not meant to be exposed."

Amundson's face went even colder. "The *Gifted* are not meant to be—period. But we can't seem to do anything about them, can we? We *unGifted* can't even tell what you've changed, according to you and all the reports you've suggested I read. That would seem to be a problem in the grand plan to protect the American people and the American way of life. Mr. Bryson, here, apparently offers a means to track what the Gifted are doing. Isn't that right?" He turned to Jason.

Jason nodded, but the tension between the two men was so thick you wouldn't need a very sharp knife to cut it.

Gleason's gaze met Jason's, searching. Almost like he was looking for an ally. What had happened since they last stood toe to toe in a contest of wills that Gleason had won quite handily?

"Do you know where Vallon Drake is?" Jason asked.

Something flickered in Gleason's gaze, or maybe it was Jason's imagination. But the man had been her boss. He had to know something.

Amundson looked from one man to the other. "What you are seeing, Mister Bryson, is this man's continued attempt to subvert his country. You see, we found him attempting to climb on a plane at SeaTac Airport. He has yet to explain exactly why."

"And you neglect to mention that I was not leaving the country." Gleason had straightened. "I have never done, and never would do, anything to endanger this country."

Amundson sniffed. "Then this is your chance to prove it, Gregor. Help the country develop another means to protect itself."

Against the Gifted. The words hung unspoken in the air. Jason considered. It was looking more like he'd erred by offering to help Amundson. Though he and Gleason had had their differences, the man struck him as an upright officer of the law. Stopping the Gifted hadn't been part of Jason's plans: only getting a certain Gifted to help him.

"What is it you plan to do if you can detect change without depending upon the Gifted?"

"What he *plans* to do is round up the Gifted, but keep them handy as tools to use as he sees fit. Think internment camps." Gleason shook his head bitterly. "Chief Amundson cannot believe that the Gifted of this country are on his side. He wishes you to be his tool in this."

"Then you admit that there are Gifted elsewhere!" Amundson spun to face him.

"Of course. There must be. I cannot believe that this country is unique in this."

"Then what is to stop the Gifted here from allying themselves with foreign Gifted? They are an invisible danger within the deepest fabric of our society."

"So you fear, just as there were fears of the Japanese in this country during the Second World War. But it's not the truth now any more than it was then." Gleason shook his head.

The tension in the room thickened and Jason considered his options. It would be easy enough not to show his talent, but he had little belief that Amundson would let him leave either way. How the man held Gleason was another question. Now that he looked a little more closely, Gleason's skin had a grey tinge and his gaze looked a little muzzy. Drugs?

Amundson shook his head and motioned to the sand pit. "I suggest we move on with our little experiment. Mr. Gleason will create something in the sand. You will describe what you see as you see it. We will record the session. Doctor Mendez will apply electrodes to your skull to watch the portions of your brain that work as you watch."

"That wasn't part of the deal." Even more than not wanting to be part of this, he didn't want anyone looking at how his brain worked. Not now. Not ever.

"It is a requirement of our deal, Mister Bryson. Your choice." Amundson stood by, waiting, the white-coated Dr. Mendez held a bouquet of round electrodes like eerie flowers.

"And if I choose not to?"

Amundson exposed his teeth again. It was never a true smile with him. "Well, we haven't come to that place yet, have we?"

The big man who had escorted him to this room shuffled his feet behind Jason. So there really wasn't any choice at all. Either do it by choice and potentially curry Amundson's favor, or do it anyway and likely end up like Gleason—a prisoner of the government he'd served. He'd bet there weren't even any legal documents to justify holding him. That was the problem with Homeland Security. They could basically make it up as they went along.

"I'd like to see the results myself. I'd like to know what's different about my brain."

Amundson glanced at Mendez, who nodded. "Of course. Now may we begin?"

He motioned Jason to a second chair, thankfully lacking restraints. Mendez busied himself pressing sticky electrodes onto Jason's brow and into his hair. Then he produced a syringe and turned to Gleason, whose hands Amundson's henchman had released.

"Your arm."

Gleason distaste was clear as he took off his jacket and rolled up his sleeve. "You had better give me enough that I can think clearly again, otherwise nothing is likely to happen."

So they had drugged him somehow, but that didn't seem enough to explain the grey color of Gleason's skin. Something to control the Gift? Now that would be helpful in dealing with Vallon.

"You've found something that can be used to block the Gift?" he asked.

Amundson nodded. "The AGS researched a variety of means. We just pulled the information out of hidden archives and put it into production in more reasonable quantities. It is a reasonable solution to the Gifted problem."

And could stop Vallon from doing something to him when he caught up to her. "And you're giving him the antidote."

"A small amount. You need not worry about him destroying this building. We've taken care of that danger. According to the AGS research, there are certain things that can be done to limit at Gifted's, shall we say, 'potency'?"

Jason nodded. That possibility hadn't even entered his thinking, even though he'd been in a house that was almost destroyed in just that way. And someone who could create life likely could do it, too. He would need to be very careful taking on Vallon.

Color seemed to flush and fade into Gleason's pallor. His gaze narrowed on Amundson, and a slight haze occurred around the blonde man.

"Something is happening," Jason said. Better to get on Amundson's good side. "He's doing something to you."

Amundson nodded to Jason's escort, who crossed the room to Gleason and slammed a backhand at the side of Gleason's head. His chair went sprawling backwards, Gleason's head heavily hitting the floor. Amundson was looking at Jason like he was some strange and wondrous beast. Then he jerked towards Mendez. "Anything?"

"The equipment isn't turned on yet."

"Well, turn the damn thing on!"

Mendez hurried to the equipment panel the electrodes were attached to and fiddled with switches. A series of monitors began to show scratchy lines that had to be his brain waves. He looked away, back to Gleason. The man groaned as they uprighted his chair with him in it. A bright red handprint branded the side of his skull and he blinked like he was still groggy.

Amundson grabbed his chin and turned Gleason's bleary gaze towards him. "I suggest you focus on what you've been asked to do. It seems we may have a means to track your perfidy now."

Gleason's gaze flickered to Jason. He could smell the other man's fear amid an ozone scent he'd also smelled at Vallon's. Yes, he could do this thing. *Would* do this thing and gain what he needed to deal with Vallon.

CHAPTER 19 — DOORS AND WINDOWS

"Xavier. Oh my God, Xavier!" Vallon threw her arms around him, blessing his scent of Cedar of Lebanon and incense. In the dim light strained through holes in the metal-sided shed, his strong arms tightened around her and the afterburn surged so she could have thrown off her clothes, straddle him, steering wheel at her back, and have her way with him. She rained kisses on his face, on his hands, on his lips. Then his hands caught her arms and he held her away from him, even though his dilated pupils spoke of his need.

"*Bela Menina.* My sweet Vallon. We find each other again." He raised a finger to her face, but did not touch her as he traced the shape of her cheek and chin and lips. "I have longed to see you again. It is through much travail that I get here."

"I've waited for you. Oh, God, how I've waited for you. It's felt like a dagger to my heart every day you weren't here." God, her hands were trembling. Her whole body shook with her need. She clamped her eyes shut and fought down the afterburn's greed. Xavier had taught her that. Take the pleasure in each other, and right now pleasure was just hearing his voice. Seeing his hawk face again, and being swept away in the sense of deserts and smoky Bedouin tents he always evoked in her. She opened her eyes. "What happened? I thought perhaps it was all a lie, what you said. How you held me."

My God, she sounded like some school girl with a crush. She shook herself and prepared for rebuff. "I'm sorry. I know you're busy. I shouldn't have expected anything. In fact, I'm surprised you're here at all, as busy as you are." She would not meet his gaze, instead swiped at dust on her clothes.

But a finger hooked under her chin and pulled her gaze up to him. Then his arms came around her again and formed the place she would prefer never to leave.

"*Bela*, Vallon. I wished to never leave, but there was recovery to make after the battle against Rebecca Murdoch, and then there was a matter of my performance." He looked away this time. "They were not pleased I had—met—you. They planned for me to stay away."

His eyes were so dark she could fall for eons in them. So dark as he looked back at her that a laser's glare would be as nothing, and there would be no hope of ever triangulating the nature of this man.

"I could not obey." He shook his head. "I came back to Seattle and sought you, but you were not there. I saw the policeman and he said he knew where you were or could find out and would tell me. But then I *felt* you and came myself. It has been a long journey."

He caught her hands in his and sent a pulse of power that, for a little while at least, seemed to send the searing afterburn swirling into the hollow place that had grown inside her. For a moment at least, she felt almost normal. Well, not normal, because Xavier's presence sent her pulse racing and her mind churning with all the love-hurt-anger she felt and the things she might say. He pulled her into his chest more tightly and all of them melted away. She caught his hand to kiss it, but horrible scars on his wrists stopped her. She looked up at him.

"Xavier?"

He tried to pull his hand away, but she held on and shoved his shirt sleeve farther up his arm to see. The faded remains of a series of scars on his forearms took her breath away. They had not been there before.

"What happened?"

"It is nothing. Consider them the scars of my absolution." He shook his head.

"Absolution! Xavier, it looks like you've been chained up somewhere. Like you've been tortured or forced to take drugs or—or—or something!"

"I was bled, *Bela*. Bled to keep me in place and somewhat docile."

"By your employer? Your friends?"

He loosed his arm from her grasp and cupped her cheek and smiled. "Perhaps not my friends, *Bela*, but yes, I work for them; and there are very strict rules that I break every time I come near you."

She didn't know how to react. Horror that it was her that had caused this to be done to him. Revulsion that someone would do such things, and a fury like a mother bear. She would not let them do something like this to him ever again.

But Xavier was here now. He kissed her hair, her forehead, and his lips slipped down and tasted her mouth so lightly she could have screamed. He tasted of spice and mint and coriander and she wanted more. Ran her fingers through his long hair and felt like she was home. At least for now, for something this good had never been allowed in her life for very long.

"So the others do not want you here?"

He nodded above her and kissed her hair again. "They say I have broken the most sacred of rules and told another of our existence, so now you will tell others. I do not agree with them."

"But it's true. You told me. Others know you exist because I told them before I knew I shouldn't."

He stroked her hair and pulled her into him tightly. "There are things you do not know, *Bela Menina*. They are wrong in their thinking, and you and I were meant to be together."

"For now," she said, relaxing into him, for nothing lasted forever, especially where relationships were concerned.

"For always," he whispered into her hair.

She pushed back from him. "You can't know that and you shouldn't say that. It might be nice, but it might be a lie, too."

He would not let go of her hands, damn it.

"Vallon, I speak the truth. Look at me and see it. I will pay any price for us to be together. Please do not pull back. You feel as if you would run." He held onto her hands and would not let go.

Finally she breathed again. "I'm sorry. I would never run from you. Ever." She closed her eyes a moment and felt the tingle of their mingling Gifted presences, like two brilliant flames refueling each other. The flames seemed to grow and feed off each other until the entire shed was ablaze. Surely any Gifted would see and know their whereabouts. It brought her crashing down into her predicament.

"They trapped me. Or they would have if you hadn't come along," she said into the silence that was punctuated by only their heartbeats.

"Yes. It appeared so."

She pulled free to sink back onto her side of the cab. "I don't understand what's going on." She glanced at him. "It's my father. I'm sure of it. But he doesn't have to do this. I'd go to him if he asked." She shook her head. Xavier said nothing, and when she looked at him he seemed to be studying her.

"I do not think that would be a good thing. He has hurt you badly already."

"You think? He only got himself killed. At least that's what he let me think. A kid can get over that—mostly."

"But now you learn he is alive. He chose to leave."

"He chose to leave *me*, you mean." She squeezed her eyes shut because, damn it, she would not cry. It didn't matter that he'd chosen to go. It didn't make it any different. He just hadn't been there for her—ever. Not really. It had been Landon or one of a long line of housekeepers or nannies who had dealt with the cuts and scrapes of childhood and then the easily bruised ego of a troubled teenager. She scrubbed at her face. "It doesn't matter. He was never there for me, anyway. I barely know the man. That should make it easy to go in, learn his secrets, and stop him. "

Yes, that was what she should do. She checked her watch and glanced at Xavier, not meeting his gaze. "We should get back to Elizabeth Ducharme's. Fi's probably worried by now. I really could use your help on this case."

§

To Xavier's jaded eyes, Vallon Drake was perhaps the most beautiful creature in the world. And the most damaged. Untamed and slightly wild, with her chin up and her profile stern, she tried to control the tide of her emotions; but even self-contained as she was, she could not hide the way the flames of their Gifts, as she called them, joined together so harmoniously. That was unusual, a gift. So was the fact that he could bear to be near and touch her when she burned with an afterburn so rich he had to fight his own arousal. But these people, her father, the other Gifted of this American Geological Survey, they had harmed her in so many ways. Denying her an understanding of the world as it was. Of her history, of how deeply her kind could love. Instead, love was nothing to be trusted. He saw it in her eyes and the way she turned away from him when he expressed his feelings. No, it was not possible to predict a relationship's longevity, but he had seen enough in his long life to know this one was different.

For when had any woman ever touched his heart, as she did? When had he ever simply wanted to hold a woman, a specific woman, because the world truly did go away when he did? In all the long years of his wandering to observe, to research, to report, and to remove, there had never been another.

Never one who had made him turn his back on everything he knew—not that Vallon would ever ask. After the Council Tribunal, he had been released into Leticia's none-too-gentle care and sent on a mission to North Africa. In the Mali Desert, the jihadist rebels had found one of their number had a special talent. With it, they were slowly but surely wiping the non-Islamist communities off the map, replacing them with settlements of their own people; and there had been rumblings of larger plans afoot, like an Islamist Africa and the erasure of Israel. It had been his and Leticia's task to locate the one of Gifted blood and deal with him or her.

They had found the one—a boy of only fifteen, with the hatred that could only come from one whose entire family had been wiped out like vermin by the mercenaries protecting the multinational companies that were dividing up the riches of the desert landscape that had been his family's tribal territory. The youth had hidden in a low-slung black Tuareg tent in a shadowed arroyo, when he and Leticia had transmuted into position. Then they had struck, erasing the arroyo so the tent and all its occupants had ceased to exist except the boy. He had been left to suffocate amid the sand. It had been Xavier's task to block the boy's frantic use of power to extricate himself. With his years of experience, it had been no difficulty for Xavier, but it had left a deep distaste in his mouth that Leticia had made light of.

Leticia.

For a moment regret filled him, but he had to trust she had found a way to save herself when he had tricked her into thinking he wished to quench his afterburn with her. Instead, he had used that moment of vulnerability to knock her out and restrain her, then bleed her slightly to reduce her ability to track him. Then he had left her in the desert. If she had not survived, his brother would hate him. Actually, if she had survived, he would likely hate Xavier, too.

But it had been worth it. He was here, with Vallon, even though she was gone from him in this moment, lost to her thoughts of her 'case', even though she sat beside him. He sighed and -reached- beyond the metal hut for their pursuers. Nowhere near and no Gifted, either, except for Vallon's two co-conspirators on the far side of this sad little town and the broken man who wandered up and down its streets. At least in the old country there were orange and olive groves to shade the gardens and bright blooms the women still planted. Here there was only the river and the dust that clung to skin in the humidity.

He started the engine and the vehicle purred to life, then he drove out of the shadowed shed and onto the street. Vallon sat deep in thought beside him, her occasional glance in his direction like a caress of his skin. The mingling of their flames prickled and sent his blood pounding in his temples. He clamped down on his arousal at her afterburn-flooded presence. This was serious. He might have risked the worst sanctions possible by coming back here, but he could not stay away. Not when Vallon was here and not when her case seemed to have drawn attacks directly on her. If Vallon was right and it was her father causing the attacks, somehow it did not surprise him. Not given what he knew of Francis Drake.

The SUV cruised the heat-riddled New Madrid streets with the air conditioning blasting. He guided the vehicle onto the curving street of more affluent houses on the northeast corner of town and pulled in at the house with the small discreet sign that read *Miss Elizabeth's Guest House*. When he turned off the engine, the two of them just sat there and he inhaled her scent of ashes of roses.

"Your friend, Fi, and Landon Snow are inside," he said.

She nodded and raised her gaze to his. "How do you know Landon?"

He smiled. "I know all in the AGS. I have observed for a very long time."

That brought a frown to her face. "How long? How old are you, Xavier?"

He tilted one black brow at her. "Old enough to know better, but young enough to still fall in love." He shook his head, denying the devastating consequences he would face when his people caught up to him. "But does it truly matter when we have what we have?"

He -reached- and stroked her flame, and Vallon's eyes widened. Her pupils dilated and her lips parted most deliciously. "Yes. And you can do the same for me."

He felt her presence stir and then a deft psychic caress ran through him that left him breathless and digging his fingers into his thighs to stop from reaching for her. "Enough."

He caught her grin, that she quickly masked by biting her lip.

"Quite effective, I must say."

A physical caress came his way and he blocked it. Caught her hand. "Unless you intend to have your way with me right now in full daylight in the front of this vehicle, I suggest you stop, *Bela Menina*. There are better places than this to take our pleasure."

Her eyes glittered as she met his gaze. The need ached from her as her lips parted as if to continue their repartee, but instead they drew into a line at the same time as her flame seemed to retreat from their intertwining. She nodded.

"You're right, of course." She opened her door. "Fi will be glad to see you again and Landon will be thrilled to meet you."

He followed her up to the house and inside, where she called out her arrival. Footsteps clipped along the hallway and announced a woman perched on precariously high heels dressed in a slim-fitting white-and-black dotted dress like those he had seen in the nineteen sixties. A throwback, just as he was a throwback in so many ways. Her smooth face tightened with surprise when she saw him. Behind her came a child in a frilly pink crinoline dress with two pink bows in her hair.

"Oh. So who do we have here, Ms. Drake?" the woman's blue gaze grasshoppered between them.

Vallon looked up at him. "Xavier de Varga, this is Elizabeth Ducharme, the owner of this guesthouse. The small dancer behind her is Farrah, her daughter." She bent down to the child's level. "Thank you for the loan of your doll last night. I really needed the energy the good sleep gave me."

The little girl beamed, but she looked at Xavier with a suspicion that matched her mother's.

"Who's he?" her lips curled slightly as if she disapproved.

Apparently Vallon didn't see it. She stepped in closer beside him and didn't even seem to even realize it. "He is with me. A very dear friend."

"Wellll," Elizabeth Ducharme's doubt showed in her pursed lips. "I suppose I could open another room."

Vallon looked up at him, a question in her gaze. Then she turned back to Elizabeth Ducharme as if she'd read the answer on his face. "That won't be necessary. Xavier and I will share my room."

The woman's frown deepened, but Vallon seemed not to notice.

"Where are Fi and Landon?"

Their hostess seemed to grow three inches in height and her neck muscles stood out. "Miss Drake, having an unmarried couple share a room is not acceptable behavior in this guesthouse. I have a young child here and will not have her subjected to—to—to northern morals."

Xavier stepped forward and half bowed to her. "Madam, we would never wish to upset such a gracious hostess. I will take another room if one can be available."

Elizabeth Ducharme subsided and went to do the paperwork, leaving him and Vallon to seek the others.

Fi was apparently enjoying the pool while Landon sat in the shade with his computer. Vallon led Xavier through the house to the bright glare of sunlight and the tropical blue of the pool. The woman, Fi, in a blue bikini, laid fair-skinned and somnambulant on a chaise by the pool. The small white man sat at a rattan table, intently squinting at his computer screen. He wore a suit vaguely reminiscent of British tourists along the Mediterranean coast.

"Landon. I know you always hoped to meet him, so let me introduce Xavier de Varga."

The small man jerked as if struck. He scrambled to his feet and stood there looking Xavier up and down so that for a small moment Xavier felt like an insect specimen assessed, catalogued, and compartmentalized through the little man's watery eyes. Then the moment was gone and Landon stepped forward, hand outstretched in greeting. His over-warm grip pumped Xavier's hand too hard. Too eager. As if he wanted something, but then that was gone, too, as Landon smiled.

Xavier eased his hand loose from the invasive sense of the other man's presence. It was a strange feeling this one had: not 'Gifted' as Vallon and her people called it, and yet he was not like the others. More like distant kin might have the same family nose, but none of their singing ability. That was it. He was akin, but not the same. Yet the invasive sense was there as if the cataloguing he'd sensed also considered his essence.

"Well met. Well met. I'd almost given up on ever meeting Vallon's mysterious friend." Landon grinned, but it did not suit him. This was not a man of grins and small talk. No, the man's eyes held calculations even as he turned to Vallon. "Where ever did you find him, pigeon?"

Did she see that this man might not be her friend?

"He found me." She looked back at the house, but the proprietress had disappeared in the shadows of the house. Still, Vallon lowered her voice. "There was another attack. Xavier helped me. Thank God he was there. But it tells me that they really want me. My father does. I'm thinking maybe I should let them have me."

"No." Landon's command matched Xavier's own, and Vallon looked from one to the other.

"If I didn't know better, I'd say you two were conspiring against me."

"Or perhaps what you say is a bad idea," Xavier said.

"I concur, pigeon. A very bad idea. Francis Drake, if it is Francis Drake, is not a person to be trifled with."

For a moment she just looked at them. Then she shook her head and laughed. "You think I don't know that? He's my father, for God's sake. But we've both been down here a couple of days and we know exactly nothing about what's going on *except* that it involves my father. At least this way we'd have a way inside. We could find out what's going on and then do something."

"It is a bad idea, Vallon. You should not risk yourself."

"Like you didn't risk yourself in Seattle?" Her voice had lowered, but her chin had risen and her hands had fisted at her sides. "Listen, I know you both think you're looking out for me, but I'm a big girl. I can take care of myself, and I don't appreciate being treated as if I cannot make perfectly reasonable decisions on my own. This *is* my father we're talking about."

"Pigeon, I know it has always bothered you that you lost your father, but…"

Landon never got a chance to finish. She turned on him and the quiet defiance had turned to anger. "Bothered me? *Bothered me?* I lost my father. I never even got to bury him. He was just gone. And then, after all these years, I find out he didn't die, he just left me. And I shouldn't be bothered by that? I shouldn't want to confront the man? Well I might want to do that, but I want to stop him more. So don't talk to me about this being the interest of some little girl. I'm an agent, damn it, and a good one. If this is how we stop him, then I'm doing it."

"Vallon, no. Please. Let us talk it through." Xavier tried to catch her arms, to pull her into him. The devastation he'd felt from her during the attacks was not a good thing. And the power of the quake was great. Too great for even him to stop alone.

She jerked away and stepped warily into the sunlight beside Fi.

"Vallon?" Fi stirred and stretched, her coconut-scented suntan lotion filling the air. She sat up and stretched her thin arms over her head. "What's going on? You're in my sun." The last came out a little cross.

Vallon whirled on her. "Not you, too." She looked from one to the other of them and her shoulders slumped. The ashes of roses and moist earth scent overwhelmed the space, afterburn flaring like an all-consuming force that flickered over her flesh. "You know what? Today has been a bit of a roller-coaster ride. I'm going to crash for a while."

She stalked from the patio into the shadowed house with not even a glance back, but the pulse of her presence was like a thought that would not be denied. "I do not think she will listen."

"You've that right, my new friend," Landon said. "We have to talk her out of it."

"What's going on?" Fi asked and looked past Landon, shading her eyes from the sun. She sat up on the side of the chaise, her long toes digging into the concrete, her toenails painted the same blue as her bikini, her hair floating around her face. But, beyond the well-kept and -nourished looking woman, this Fi Murdoch no longer had the wild-eyed look of the ravaged mind. Her time with Vallon had been good for her.

"Xavier? Is that really you? I thought you were dead. Vallon did, too, but she didn't want to admit it. It really broke her heart."

Xavier nodded greeting. "As you can see, I still walk with the living."

Fi raised her chin at the door where Vallon had gone. "What's her problem? She looked even worse than last time."

"Fi, what do you mean, last time?" Landon asked.

She looked away and sat on her hands. Shrugged. "Nothing really. I just helped her out the last time she had afterburn, back in Seattle."

"Helped her out how, Fi?" Landon said and sat down beside her, his white suit blazing in the afternoon sunlight.

She wouldn't meet his gaze. Inside the house Vallon was in her room, the throb of her afterburn calling to Xavier. There was only one way to truly heal afterburn, and a most pleasurable way it was. With the years you could learn to deal with the incessant ache of power taken from the earth and used, but there was only one way to truly be free of the pain.

"I think I will go check on Vallon," he said.

"Do you need someone to show you where her room is?" Fi asked.

"I will find her." He could find her any time, any place. Her presence called to him.

"I'll just bet you will." Fi's voice came from behind him, but he was already pushing into the cool shadows of the house, seeking the stairs.

The upstairs of the cool, air-conditioned house had a single, narrow hallway that reminded him of the gangways of some of the old wooden vessels he had once sailed on. Except, or course, this one did not slip and shift with waves. But like those old vessels struggling against a headwind, he battled the roiling power emanating from Vallon's room. He was an ancient mariner trapped in a storm, but caught in the need for distant treasure. And Vallon *was* the treasure.

He'd known it as soon as he'd seen her the first time. The treasure he'd been looking for, though at the time she'd been quite young. He'd watched as she grew older, and then suddenly she was a woman and events had conspired to pull him away from his duties and into her arms.

He did not regret it. How could he regret the love he'd never expected to find?

He knocked on her door. "*Bela Menina?*"

He heard her stirring, scented her presence before the door pulled open to reveal a room lit only by the sunlight that leaked in around a lowered blind. Vallon stood ashen eyed and pale faced before him, clad in only a singlet and panties, but she looked up at him as fierce as any lioness. "I'm not going to let you talk me out of it."

"Vallon, we must think of this with care. Please. Let me come in and we will do so."

She stepped aside and he entered a room that was not like Vallon at all, with its frilled curtain and flowered wallpaper. For a moment it was strange, as if two very different pictures were superimposed, and for a moment he felt unsteady. He turned back to her and the sensation passed.

"We must talk. Vallon, you know nothing of what your father has planned or of what kind of man he has become. That he wants you—we know this because he has attacked you not once, but twice."

"Three times. Four if you count the original quake," she said from where she stood by the door. The light around the blinds caught on the roundness of her breasts, the curve of her hip.

He hauled his gaze up from the delectable view to her face. Her usually guarded gaze was like a door flung wide onto her inner essence. "Three or four times, then. So he truly wants you. But for what? Do you think a man who walked away all those years ago will just walk back into your life as your father?"

Her chin came up again and she crossed her arms over her chest. "He might. You came back, didn't you?" But her lips trembled and her eyes had gone huge and moist with more insecurity than he had ever seen on her always-controlled face.

"Aah, *Cara. Bela Menina.*" He stepped up to her and caught her in his arms. "He is a fool to have ever walked away."

She stiffened and he stroked her back, kissed her forehead, ran his hands down over the velvet flesh of her arms and then down over her buttocks, and the stiffness melted a little.

"But he's my father. I need to understand why he left me." A bare whisper filled with longing, spoken into his chest.

Another kiss to her forehead and he caught her chin, lifted her face to his. "Perhaps after we catch him, you can ask him. But that is for another day. Now I think we must deal with this afterburn in the very best of ways. Do you remember?"

A single nod as her luminous gaze met his.

The very lightest of kisses was all it took. She yielded into his arms and all talk of her father faded into the half-darkness. She was his.

CHAPTER 20 — OZONE AND CEDAR

It was the laboratory's scent that most chilled Gleason to the bone: a thick mélange of scents like cinnamon and honey and grass clippings and licorice and fear. So many other scents, but most of all it was the fear. Gifted fear. There had been others here before him and it had not gone well for them.

The gleaming chrome of the equipment, the quiet hum of the computers that covered the walls with their quietly blinking lights. All made his head throb worse than the panicked hollow feeling the Homeland Security 'doctors' had left him with. His left inner arm ached where they'd bled him—bled him!—as if he were the patient of some medieval medical practice. It jarred him, given the modernity of the setting, but the Machiavellian mind of the man standing above him made it all real. Wolf Amundson had him right where he wanted him.

Gleason closed his eyes and slumped in the chair. He understood his capture and detention. He'd erred in his estimation of time before Amundson would figure out that Gleason had undermined him and sent agents to New Madrid. He'd also apparently underestimated Amundson's mining of Landon's files of AGS research, because bloodletting was one of the things Landon had theorized and tested with voluntary subjects as a means to decrease the Gifted's access to the Gift. The danger from Amundson he could understand, but now this new danger was almost more than he could fathom.

The detective had entered the room looking not at all happy, but clearly trying to hide his concern behind bravado. He was no longer the straight up, stony-eyed cop Gleason had had to pry Vallon Drake from when she'd first been arrested for the death of another agent. Now his cheeks were hollow and so was his gaze. A five o'clock shadow showed off the pallor of his skin, and his eyes kept flickering from Amundson to Gleason.

So. He recognized what was happening here. Of course, it had been made a trifle clearer when Amundson's man had struck Gleason. His head still rang, and that made it even more difficult to do what Amundson was demanding.

"Get on with it, Gleason. Or I'll turn Page loose on you. You don't want that, now do you?"

"Would it make any difference? You're already holding me in illegal detention. You really think I'm fool enough to believe you'll ever let me go?" Maybe, just maybe, the good detective wasn't fully on board. Maybe it would mean something to him that Amundson was breaking every legal rule. Through slitted eyes, he watched Bryson's gaze slip over him. He wasn't happy, at least.

Amundson's fierce grip caught Gleason's shoulder and he pushed Gleason, chair and all, back until it teetered on only two legs.

"You. Will. Do. This. Or every other agent in the AGS will be down here with you. You understand?"

It was all Gleason could do to not flounder for the floor and meet Amundson's predatory gaze. Finally he nodded. It would be interesting to see what the policeman was here for. Perhaps he could use it to his advantage. Landon had not included the complete data about the level of blood loss and the attendant loss of power. Clearly Amundson had his own research going on, but they had not fully depleted Gleason yet.

"You're sure you want to do this in front of an outsider?"

Amundson smiled and patted Bryson's shoulder even though Bryson looked repulsed. "He already knows, Gleason. Your pet project, Drake, apparently told him. Or showed him."

Gleason considered the detective. Just what *did* he know? Because he *had* reacted when Gleason had made an attempt to deal with Amundson. Had it been more than a simple coincidence? The man had been with Drake on the escapade against Rebecca Murdoch, and Gleason had seen the way Drake and Bryson had looked at each other when Drake was dealing with afterburn.

"Showed him what?" he asked, stalling for time, because if the detective could do as Amundson suggested, then he couldn't be left in

Amundson's hands any more than Gleason could afford to stay here. He used what Gift he had and -reached- down through the building's foundation to the coiling ley lines beneath Seattle. His hands shook. Sweat formed on his brow. Amundson's doctors had left him so weak, when this should be child's play.

So weak the ley line's power flowed over and around him. So hollowed out he was a straw, but had not the strength to draw on it. He had to. He gripped the tops of his thighs and held on as he forced a sip of power like breath into his lungs, but it slipped away from him almost as quickly as he drew it in. It took blood to hold the power, for some reason it was linked to that, though Landon had not yet discovered how.

"Come on, Gleason. How much effort does it take to stir a little sand for our man here?" Amundson asked.

He would part the floor, or soften it so Amundson and his man were trapped within it. Or he would if he had the Gift fully at his disposal. After his wasted attempt to do just that, this situation meant he needed to try other means. Means that the detective could not see until too late.

He -reached- and presented himself to the ley line power. Grabbed hold of the heat and let it burn through him. His nose filled with ozone and the scent of roses as he fought to hold the power within him, make it part of his starving cells. His breath rasped loudly in his ears as he wrestled the power.

Focus. There were four men beyond him in the room. He wasn't sure whether he could fine tune this enough not to hurt them all. Well, maybe that could be a lesson in itself.

The earth's power was magnetized to magnetic north and south. Apply the magnetism to the electrons of the earth under this buried room, and it could create current. He pulsed the magnet force through the damp soil and felt the tingle of current, like ants on his skin. His heart pounded. His breath wheezed in his lungs. He had to do this. It had been done in small experimental tests before. He was just bringing its application to the real world. His skin crackled with the energy he controlled and he opened his eyes. Only a few second had passed and Amundson was looking at the detective.

Gleason grabbed hold of the chair arms as he fought for the strength. He had to control this and direct the force. The air smelled of ozone and the detective frowned.

"Something—," he started.

Gleason strained and struck. Bolts of lightning crackled up through the floor, blasting Amundson back, striking the man who stood by Bryson, and crackling through the equipment so that the doctor collapsed beside it. Gleason collapsed back into his chair. Hard enough to just breathe, let alone move. One eye open. Another.

The detective had leapt up and stood frozen across the room. His gaze slowly swung from the comatose man beside him, to Amundson jerking on the floor, to the doctor, and back to Gleason. "What the hell did you do?"

"I got us the chance to get the hell out. Now get me loose and let's go." The speech took almost all of his strength. There was no way he could get out of here on his own and Amundson was already groaning. Bryson hesitated.

"Or did I read you wrong and you want to be Amundson's pet guinea pig until they can replicate whatever it is you can do?"

The detective finally nodded and sprang into action. A quick check of the man on the floor beside him. He pulled plastic cuffs out of the man's jacket pocket, grunted satisfaction, and used one length to cuff the man's hands behind him. He crossed to Amundson, fallen at the periphery of Gleason's vision, and must have repeated the action there and done something to the doctor. He came around into Gleason's view.

"Why should I trust you?"

A sheen of sweat covered the man's face and he looked unhealthy—dissolute—definitely not the imposing detective he'd dealt with before.

"Because we both have worked alongside Vallon Drake. We know she fights to do what's right and to protect this country. That's what the AGS is all about. These men are subverting the organization." God, he was so tired he just wanted to sleep for a million years, but he forced himself awake and as alert as the adrenaline surge of afterburn could keep him.

Bryson just inhaled and stuck his hands in his pockets. "Seems to me that I could just walk out of here on my own, because maybe Amundson has the right of it, given what I've just seen and what I've seen Vallon do."

Bryson's gaze met Gleason's and held. Gleason -reached- for his Gifted sight and the man really was totally unGifted. Just how he could do what he did was totally beyond comprehension. But the man was a policeman. "They are doing experiments on human subjects without consent. They are detaining people without warrant. Is that the kind of country we come from? Because it is not my America."

Something flickered in Bryson' dark gaze and for a moment the dissolute disappeared and revealed the proud man Gleason had first met in a parking lot. A short nod and Bryson snapped open Gleason's restraints and helped him up.

His legs gave and he would have fallen, except Bryson caught him. "What the hell have they done to you? Drugs?"

Gleason fought to stand on his own but finally had to sling an arm across Bryson's shoulders. Even then his knees threatened to give out and the floor was unsteady. "Drugs, yes. They also bled me."

"*Bled* you?"

Gleason nodded and experimented with a step towards the door. Nearly fell again until Bryson let him lean on him. "Let's get the hell out of here."

Bryson led to the door—thankfully unlocked—and they headed down the hall. "This is the way they brought me in. I'm assuming it'll get us out again."

The narrow hall of doors filled Gleason with misgiving. There could be so many Gifted held in the rooms beyond them. So many rooms of experimentation and torture. It had to be destroyed, but he needed to get out and recover, first. And he needed to get warning to the AGS agents. He could see Amundson rounding them all up, now.

Bryson stabbed the elevator call button when they reached it. The long ride up to Homeland Security headquarters would be their most vulnerable state. If Amundson and the others got free, they could sound the alarm and the elevator would become a trap. But the elevator dinged and Gleason pulled himself upright, staggered a little, but he had to do this.

"Just follow my lead, Bryson. I'm not officially an enemy of the state—at least not yet, I think." He pulled loose of Bryson's supporting arm and strode out of the elevator and down the hall, Bryson behind him. Brightly lit offices ranged with desks spread to either side of them. A boardroom with views out into the blessed sunshine and freedom. Agents glanced up as they passed. "So we need to have Seattle P.D. involved in the case," he said looking over at Bryson.

The detective thankfully caught on, considered a moment. "I'll call my partner. He can bring in the Chief Detective. I'm sure there'll be cooperation given the history between the Department and Homeland Security." He nodded.

"Good man. That's what we like." He clapped Bryson on the shoulder and then suddenly they were out into the lobby, where a long-haired woman guarded a central switchboard and two leather couches. He nodded in her direction and led Bryson to the bank of elevators that would take them down to street level. Stabbed the button and prayed he could stay upright long enough for the doors to open.

"Chief Gleason?"

He stiffened at the woman's voice. She was no mere receptionist, he knew, but was trained as an agent. He swung around expecting a weapon to be pointed in his direction and knowing that he had no strength left to deal with it. "Yes?"

§

Flesh against flesh, hints of it illuminated in bars of light that snuck into the room around Vallon's bedroom's blinds. A bare biceps, a naked breast. The hard line of muscled thigh, the curve of a hip, a back arched in passion. Xavier rose over her like an ancient god and Vallon moved to answer, for that was how it was meant to be after the slow removal of their clothes.

He traced a finger from her collarbone down beyond her navel, and she shivered in anticipation and rose up to meet him.

"Aah, *Bela Menina*, you rush things still."

Her pulse raced at his whisper. His lips followed his finger, dusting her flesh with light kisses, with the caress of his tongue. His palms smoothed over her flesh and left her tingling as she reached for him, stroked him. His cedar and incense musk filled the room like a sweet drug she could not get out of her head. It left her breathless and panting as he pulled her closer to him and stopped her busy hands.

"My sweet one," he breathed into her ear. "It has been too long since we pleasured each other. Too long since we have felt release into Pangea's arms. It has been painful to wait for you." Kisses strung like pearls around her throat but she suddenly couldn't breathe.

"You've waited for me?" her voice sounded strange in the suddenly cold room.

Xavier raised his head, his wonderful, shaggy, Bedouin features suddenly too intent on her. "It is against our nature, yes, but I have waited so long, for you." A slow quirk of his ever-sardonic lips and he leaned down to tongue her nipple so slowly she might go mad for the pleasure. When her breath caught, he looked back at her. "I think it was worth the wait."

His palms came up and held her face, and he raised himself and kissed her hard, dangerously deep, and demanding as his hands slipped down her breasts, her flanks, and between her thighs as he urged her open for him. As he slipped his kisses down her abdomen.

And she shivered, for she had not shown the same devotion. She had taken her pleasure with—what was his name? Toby? A stranger in a tavern parking lot, because he was available and she had felt the pain of afterburn. But she had had release before that with Fi's help. If he had truly gone these long months without anyone, she was a harlot. She felt like she might be ill, except Xavier's touch brought small sparks to her flesh, set small fires in her brain. She owed him so much, and not the least was her devotion. Only try to make it up to him. She caught his shoulders and pulled him up to her.

"It is my turn to pleasure you," she whispered. Could he smell another man on her? Would he know what she had done?

She kissed him, ran her lips, her tongue along his jaw, then pushed him down and rose above him, running skilled fingers down over his chest, tweaked his nipples and he groaned. His chest rumbled with pleasure as she spread her hair and took his nipple in her mouth. Nipped at the nubbin and then kissed it better, before stringing kisses down the dark path of hair that led down over his taut abdomen to what waited there. She took his hard length in her mouth and he groaned. Worked her tongue around him and his hands fisted in her hair as her rhythm quickened, as his muscles tightened and his hands helped her move faster. His hips arched into her.

"No!" he cried and pushed her away, dragged her by the shoulders up until she was even with him so his arms could enfold her. "That is not the way, little one. The great union requires the lesser one, no? Not that this is so much less."

He tried to roll her over, but she stopped him with a kiss. "Then let me do this another way."

She rose to her knees and straddled him, took him in her hands and slowly, ever so slowly, took him in, never taking her gaze from his face. He was like some wild thing momentarily tamed. Except it didn't tame him. Not at all. Their union brought complete awareness of the searing brilliance of his Gifted presence. It curled around her and she flared brighter. Brighter still as she began to move, as she held his gaze and could almost see inside his mind, could feel him slide inside of hers, just as he filled her body.

Slowly, because the sensation of filling and being filled brought her near to crying at the building pleasure. Faster, because she wanted more of him, deeper. Faster still because she read the arousal deep in the bright flames that flickered in his gaze, as his hands guided her hips, as he raised his torso to suckle her breast, as he thrust his hips to drive ever deeper inside her. And then he swept her over onto her back, and their faces were breathless next to each other. His gaze locked on her face, hers on him.

"You are ready, *Bela Menina*? For the great journey to begin?"

She nodded, and he placed a gentle kiss on her lips and rose above her as he moved. Slowly, the pleasure of it written on his face. Smooth flesh on flesh and the bars of light across it. Faster and deeper and his Gift opened to her. Cedar and incense-scented power flooded into her and for the first time in months she felt full, complete. Pleasure rippled through her belly. Heat flooded her body and beat back her brain. Power, huge and golden and connected to the earth so they floated outside themselves, stretched wide as the earth and became one with it as he thrust once more, more deeply, and her back arched and they cried out together.

His voice. "*Criador, a vocêeudou-lheesteamor.*"

Her voice. "Xavier, I love you."

He pulsed inside her and her insides rippled in answer. The room shimmered around them, the light bars momentarily filled with something greater than leaked sunlight, the sense of being part of everything in the world filled her up and left her feeling like crying. And then Xavier suddenly inhaled deeply, as if he had forgotten to breathe, and the world spun away from her and she was alone in a bed with a man she loved and had betrayed.

She turned her head away as Xavier settled beside her and she already missed him and the way he filled her with meaning. He would hate her when he knew what she had done. Or if not hate, he would think her nothing, a foolish child who could not even control her base urges. He would not want her around then.

"*Bela?*"

He hooked her chin with his finger and dragged her gaze over to him. She glanced away, to the light bars on the wall. Yes, she was in prison, a prison she had lived in most of her life. She knew that now, and no man could ever love her until she understood why her father hadn't.

"What is the matter?" He whispered and kissed her cheeks and tasted her betraying tears. She palmed them away and shook her head.

"It's nothing. I'm just so glad you're here. You were gone too long." She lay her head on his chest so he could not see her face, and fought to keep her breathing steady. "It's a beautiful place you bring me to, when we make love."

"We bring each other, my *Bela*. Neither can visit Pangea without the other."

The sound of his heart was so steady in her ear. The rumble of his voice a comfort she shouldn't feel.

"Tell me again, your story of what it means. Of what it's all about."

He was silent a moment as if he were considering, or as if there was something else he wanted to say. Like maybe it was the last time. Or maybe ask who was it you cheated on me with?

"You are part of the earth, *Bela Menina*. We all are, Gifted and ungifted alike. But when you use the Gift, you borrow from the great mother Pangea. So you must give back to her. She is the mother of Creation and so you must give back in Creation as well. Through the act of procreation. And so the balance is returned, no? It is when we are unbalanced because we have only taken that we feel the afterburn. You understand?"

His palm ran comforting circles on her back and down over her buttocks. The comforting heat of his Gifted presence still mixed with hers and she felt his contentment. She could purr, if so many thoughts did not beat in her head. What she had done. How her process for dealing with the afterburn with Fi fit into this whole Pangea thing. She almost asked him, but did not want to get into an argument, because she was pretty sure he wouldn't approve of her little project nor of what she'd left in her basement.

His breath slowed and his hand stilled on her hip. A long sigh escaped him and a slight snore. Asleep.

She took a chance and looked up at him and saw the weariness that the power of his intent gaze usually masked. Five o'clock shadow dulled the lower part of his face, and her cheeks stung from its sandpaper effect. As if he would smooth her down into what she should be.

But that would never happen—not when she was like this. Not when she didn't really understand who she was.

"And there really is only one way for me to get answers, Xavier," she whispered. It only made sense, really. And she could kill two birds with one stone and stop the threat of the devastating release of the New Madrid fault.

She waited for his breathing to enter another level of deep, calming breaths and then eased herself out from underneath his arm to the edge of the bed and sat there waiting. If he woke, she was just going to get a drink of water.

He didn't wake and, if anything, his slumber deepened. It had likely been a long while since he rested. For a moment she wondered how long he had toiled over whatever task his employers had set him on.

She stood up, careful not to disturb the bed, and found her clothes where they'd been discarded on the floor. She tiptoed into the bathroom and dressed quickly, then came back out into her room. Xavier slumbered, his arms thrown wide in the abandon of a child. She smiled and wished she could allow herself to feel the same. Maybe one day she could, after all this had been resolved.

She quietly let herself out of the room and eased the door shut behind her.

After she faced down her father.

CHAPTER 21 — SEA SALT AND ENDINGS

Now Vallon just needed to get out of the house without anyone else trying to stop her. She quietly left her guestroom behind and headed for the stairs, keeping to the side of the hallway where there was a lower chance of a squeaking floor board. The hallway was illuminated by late afternoon sunlight streaming through the open door of the one vacant guestroom. From downstairs came the muffled sound of voices and the clatter of pots in the kitchen. Elizabeth was fussing over dinner again. The woman just didn't get that meal time was really a non-event for Vallon. For Fi, too, though maybe Landon paid more attention to things like that.

So she needed to get downstairs and out the front door before the others were aware she was up. She kept to the side of the stairs and slowly lowered her weight onto each step. On the lower floor the voices came from down the back of the house. She turned towards the front door. Just a few more steps and she was home free.

"Let me guess. Not only did you drag me into one of your cases, you are going against everyone's advice."

Vallon froze, then turned towards Fi's chilly voice. She was curled on a chair in the living room with a dog eared paperback in hand, the light from the dining room window backlighting her so her head had a halo and she looked like a child lost in some mad aviary with all the feathers and bird prints and the canaries trilling. Her fine blonde hair fell around her face like gossamer silk and she wore a sky-blue blouse and white shorts, her legs long and tanned.

Not exactly what you expected in a door guard, but by the disapproving downward turn of her mouth, that was exactly what she was.

Vallon stepped to the living room door and forced a smile on her face. "I was just going out for some air."

"So, what? You fucked Xavier's brains out and decided to get out while the getting was good?"

Vallon did a quick scan for Farrah. A little too close to the mark, actually. "No. Like I said, I just wanted to go for a walk and think about what everyone had said."

Fi set her book down on the coffee table. "I can always tell when you're lying because you won't meet my gaze." She stood up. "Vallon, please. It's too dangerous for you to go to your father, just like it was too dangerous for me to be with my mom. Gifted people—we're like sharks or something. We eat our young." Her face was so worried as she approached, it almost cracked Vallon's resolve. But if she didn't do what she planned she would never know what had really happened.

"My dad and your mom are two different cases. Your mother was crazy."

"And your father isn't? You drag me half way across the continent to check on him, he has to be doing something flipping bad."

"I didn't force you to come."

Fi rolled her eyes. "No. You didn't force me. You offered me a holiday, a chance to have fun. Another lie, Vallon? Cause it doesn't really feel like fun yet, with you collapsing, strange men coming around that you say are long lost friends, and all this talk of your father. But then you don't really know what a friend is, do you Vallon? I'm really just a tool to you—someone to use as cover, or to help you deal with the afterburn. Like that man upstairs. Right?"

Her eyes flashed and the tendons showed in her fine neck. The last time Vallon had seen her so angry was after the episode with Morgan Hoptaler way back in the Academy. But that had been a schoolgirl fight over a boy. This was…

"I've never used you, Fi. I haven't. I wouldn't. I was trying to help you when I asked you to help with the afterburn. I was trying to offer you a holiday."

Fi shook her head in denial.

"Damn it, would you just listen without your mind already being made up?" Vallon grabbed Fi's shoulder and tried to keep her voice down.

"I asked you to help me with the afterburn because I noticed that after you did, it seemed to help to clear your mind. You weren't the confused, frightened girl-woman that came to my house. I was trying to help you get better."

Fi pulled loose. "You keep telling yourself that. Do it long enough, you might even believe it." She shook her head. "You know the truth, Vallon. We both do, and I don't want any part of it. Or you. I'm going home and I'll be moved out when you get home. *If* you get home, given the self-destructive things you're planning on doing."

She pushed past Vallon to the stairs and was half way up before she stopped and turned back. "If I was you, I'd get going, because I plan on making a lot of noise upstairs."

Then she stomped the rest of the way up the stairs and disappeared down the hallway.

Oh God, what was she doing? Was Fi right? Vallon had to fix things between them, but she had no time. She had to make Fi understand that she would never do Fi any harm. Not on purpose.

But Fi was a little bit right, too. She *had* brought Fi here for cover, and helping Fi had helped her, too. Would she have even tried what she had in her basement if she hadn't wanted to deal with her afterburn? It didn't feel good to admit it, but the answer was 'no.' God, she was such a screw-up, but that didn't stop her from doing what needed to be done.

Stepping out the front door was like stepping into a sauna. The sun placed a hundred-ton weight on her back and shoulders, and the ground reflected the heat back at her, so the humid Mississippi air seemed to sear right into her, and her shorts and her blouse immediately stuck to her. Not exactly the time of day to be out walking, but she wasn't going back inside to try to get car keys. She didn't relish the exercise, but there were really only two options. Head out towards the tavern where she'd seen the Gifted, or head to the Kochtitsky house or the one where she'd almost been trapped. Make that three options. Morgan Hoptaler. She'd thought he might be a clue and now she was sure of it. If she could find him, it was highly likely he'd lead her straight to her father, instead of waiting for her father or his men to come and get her. That would be the best scenario.

She started walking, her awareness split between the sultry heat and watching for Gifted around her. It would warn her if Xavier or Landon came looking for her—if Fi actually did as she'd threatened and raised the alarm. It was also a way to find Morgan or her father.

Around her, the sultry afternoon covered New Madrid in a somnolent haze. The air shimmered and in the silence she heard the laughter of children playing in a backyard and the rustle of feathers as a crow had a dust bath at the side of the street. Nothing else stirred, not even the leaves in the trees, as if the entire town stood so still that she'd stand out just because she moved.

She made it out of the quiet residential area and headed down Main Street. A few pickups still nosed the sidewalk so someone was about, but no old men sat on the bench outside the hardware store and there was no sign of Morgan Hoptaler. The theatre still advertised the high school play. She turned down Mill Street towards the Kochtitsky House and increased her stride. Let her get this over with. Let her see her father with her own eyes and have him tell her why.

And she was being an idiot. She shouldn't be out here doing this. Not alone. But it *was* a way to find out what was going on. They needed the intelligence, and if she was on the inside of whatever was going on, she'd be in the best place to gather it.

The white paint of the Kochtitsky house gleamed like a beacon in the dusty shadows of its trees. From around the corner, she -reached- out and felt none of the power that had so shaken her when she'd first stepped onto the property. Maybe she could just walk up the driveway and knock on the door. Hell, maybe her father would answer the door. And if she was going to take this fairy tale she was constructing to its conclusion, maybe he'd even put his arms around her.

And she was a bigger fool than even Landon might think her if she thought that was going to happen.

She drew in a breath of muddy-water scented air and crossed the street towards the unnaturally brilliant lawns of the Kochtitsky property. The place looked like a new skin graft on the worn flesh of the town. At the curb she paused and studied the house. No movement. Nothing.

From across town a laser beam of awareness found her. Xavier. Searching. [No, *Bela!* No!]

She lifted a foot and stepped down on the property. The roar of power almost deafened her as it exploded up around her. She was eaten up, blown away. Her knees gone. Her body done for. Hard concrete under her palms, her cheek. Hard concrete in her vision and a field of unnaturally brilliant grass. And then a boot filled her line of sight. Hands caught her shoulders and suddenly she was lifted up, born away. The smell of truck and old beer, and then everything went black.

§

The salt wind off of Seattle's Elliott Bay whipped down the canyon created by the downtown skyscrapers that shadowed busy Third Avenue and into Jason's face. Its opposing force made it even more difficult to support the almost dead weight of Gregor Gleason. The man hung on Jason's shoulder like a wounded soldier, his already ashen face made greyer by the building shadows. Each dragging step was like his last.

It had seemed to take most of Gleason's strength just to stay upright and face down the H.S. receptionist. The pretty woman had only asked whether he had a vehicle parked and whether he needed her to validate. Quite the job for a fully trained agent, but he supposed most new agents had to pay their dues at one time or another. But turning back to her had slowed them down and Gleason had sagged almost totally once they were in the elevator and on their way down.

Now the worst thing was the way people took a wide berth around the two of them. They weren't exactly forgettable, and moving this slowly, if Amundson and his crew came looking, they wouldn't have any difficulty finding them. Which meant they needed to get off the street—and fast.

He scanned the expensive storefronts and the hotel and restaurant entrances. They wouldn't stand out any less stepping inside one of those establishments, and trying one of the business towers would just put them right into the hands of building security. That left back alleys, which would just delay the inevitable capture and quite likely their disappearance into whatever permanent detention facility Amundson had at his disposal. Or worse.

But a taxi would be easy to track, as well. It would be one of the first things he'd check during an investigation.

Okay, smart guy—no taxi, no alley, and none of the buildings around here. What did that leave?

He fought back the little curdle of panic and kept Gleason walking. "Come on, man. We can do this."

The grey-faced man nodded, but his weight edged closer to unmanageable with every step. "Just what happened to you anyway? Why are you so weak?"

Just keep the guy awake and with him. If he went down, they were done for, because some good Samaritan would undoubtedly call 911, something Homeland Security would likely monitor.

"You saw. I just used a little of my—talent." Gleason's breath wheezed when he spoke and his words were barely above a whisper. "So you really can sense it?"

"Sure. I saw lightning come from the floor. Your doing?"

A nod and then Gleason raised his sagging head and looked at Jason from a weary grey eye. "You shouldn't be able to do what you do."

"Look who's talking."

Gleason snorted and went into a spasm of coughing that ended with Jason leaning him up against the window of a restaurant and ignoring the patrons sitting at their window-side tables.

Jason leaned in close and smelled the thin man's faint scent of spice and the deeper fever scent. Gleason's eyes were closed and sweat beaded his forehead. Definitely not a well man.

"Listen. We have to get off the street. Is there anyone you know that we can safely call?"

Gleason shook his head. "I need to call them. Warn them."

Jason thought a moment. "The agents like Vallon."

A slight nod.

It made sense, but it didn't help them in the least. A woman in red walked past, giving them a hard look, and a patron inside the restaurant was tapping on the window and waving them away. Time to get away was slipping past with each breath of car-exhaust-stained sea air he took. Unless he wanted to be confined to that little waiting room again, or worse, he was going to have to do something. He grabbed Gleason's arm again, decided.

"Come on."

The restaurant door opened with an old-fashioned ding-ding from a small silver bell hung above the entry, and the heavenly scent of rich cream sauces and fresh fish grilled in butter filled his nose. The place was a French bistro, with dark corners and tan walls covered in black-and-white iconic photos of the Eiffel Tower, Notre Dame, La Seine, the Champs Élysées. A French song crooned through the air and the low clatter of pots and pans joined with the low voices of the patrons that cut off at their entry.

"May I help you?" asked a young woman with long, straight black hair dressed in a short black turtleneck dress and black stockings, but her face said she really just wanted him gone. All the patrons were watching. Gleason groaned.

"I'm hoping you can," Jason kept his voice low. "My friend is sick, as you can see, and neither of us has a cell. Could we borrow your phone to get someone to come and pick us up?"

The girl hesitated, her attention flickering from Jason to Gleason and back. She wouldn't be forgetting them any time soon, but finally she nodded. "Just do it quickly, please. You disturb our patrons."

Jason only nodded, accepted the phone, and dialed while shielding the number. Please be there. Please. The phone line buzzed.

"Blacklock."

So just what do you say to a partner you basically told to fuck off?

"Buddy, I need your help, bad." He glanced at the girl who was too close to not hear everything he said. "I've got a friend here who's sick. Could you possibly swing past and pick us up. *He* needs a doctor, fast." Just so Clint knew it wasn't Vallon.

The line hummed empty for one moment, two, and counting.

"Shit, slick, what've you got yourself into?"

"Something involving your old friend at H.S.. We need a ride. Can you come pick us up? I'll explain more then." But not everything. Clint would think he was crazier than he already did.

Clint's long-suffering sigh came across the line. "Fine. What's your twenty?"

Jason read the name and address off the menu and then hung up. "Thank you," he said to the girl and then helped Gleason up from where he sagged in one of the restaurant chairs. At least he wasn't leaving a blood trail over the floor, but the side of his face where Amundson's man had struck him was turning a nice shade of dark blue.

"Is he going to be all right?"

"He'll be fine. It's not like the plague or anything. You got nothing to worry about." He swung Gleason's arm over his shoulder and dinged his way out into the street, then stood there waiting. Five minutes later a blessed plain brown sedan pulled up and the bulk of his red-headed ex-partner stepped out of the driver's side. Without saying a word, he helped Gleason bundle his frame into the front seat, while Jason slipped into the back. And then they were gone, the towers falling behind them, the afternoon sun glittering on the waters of Elliott Bay and gilding the space needle.

"Where you aiming for, Slick?"

A good question, given he hadn't thought of anything more than getting off the street. "Vallon's place."

In the rearview mirror he caught Clint's hardening glance. Jason held up his hand.

"Before you dump us both out on our heads, she isn't there, but it might be the last place they'll think to look for us."

"And what exactly have you done, and just how many laws am I breaking by helping you?" Clint's voice had gone cold as a Snoqualmie Pass winter night. "Shit, Slick. I've got a wife and family to think of. I don't need your shit."

"I know. I know. You think I want to cause you or Carol any trouble? You two are the closest thing to family I've got. If you can just drop us off, I won't call you again. I promise."

Clint shook his head, but kept driving. "Don't make promises you can't keep." His voice was rough with emotion. "You're going to shit, Slick, and I hate that in a partner."

But they made it over the Fremont bridge and up through the streets to the serene neighborhood where Vallon's house stood. Clint double parked in front of her house and Jason scrambled out and assisted Gleason to stand. The man teetered unsteadily, so all Jason could chance was a quick lean down to peer in to his partner. "Thanks again. I'll see you around."

Clint gave a little unconscious shake of the head. "Not if I see you first, Slick. The Captain's mighty pissed. I don't think there's any coming back." His intent blue gaze met Jason's. "Stay safe, old friend. And if not safe, at least do the right thing."

And then the window rolled up and Clint pulled away from them, like a ship pulling away from its final anchor. Or maybe Jason was the ship and Clint was his moorings. Either way, he caught Gleason's arm and helped him up and through the red door into Vallon's house. There was no one there. No Xavier. Not even Maggie.

CHAPTER 22 —RUPTURE

Vallon's house seemed to ache around Jason with the memories of what he'd done here with her: the burgundy and blue oriental carpet and furniture that had wisped away like dust in a high wind that horrible night he had almost died. When he went to get a glass of water for Gleason, the kitchen gleamed with the lust he'd felt the first time he'd come into the house and the terror he'd felt later. The scent of ashes of roses and a feeling that flicked over his skin like lightning, that he suspected might have something to do with what existed in the basement, all washed over him like a wave and, for a moment, he felt like he was drowning in a situation he was in no way equipped to deal with.

He grabbed hold of the worn grey kitchen counter to steady himself and stared out the kitchen window to the backyard. It had changed since the first time he'd been there, but it was the normal change of a homeowner. Someone had planted a flower garden. The bright blooms caught the late afternoon sunlight and seemed to nod at him. *You got what you wanted, didn't you? You've got one of them here and in your power, even if it isn't Vallon.*

He pulled back and braced himself on the counter. Maybe he could use Gregor Gleason, but it wasn't his preference. For some reason he didn't understand, it *felt* like Vallon was the only one he could ask to do what he wanted. Or maybe Vallon and Xavier. Maybe it was the fact that she had that castle downstairs and the locked doors to keep people out. Almost as if what she did was a secret from everyone, including her boss. In all the times Jason had watched Vallon's house, he'd never seen Gregor

Gleason come by. That had to mean that he probably wasn't aware of what went on here.

He carried the glass of cool water back to the living room where he'd left Gleason collapsed on the couch. The room was cool and filled with shadows because he'd left the curtains pulled the last time he was here. One burgundy chair showed a matting of white fur, showing that Maggie might not be here right now, but she had been using the chair as a place to bed down.

"Here." He handed Gleason the glass and sat down on the old trunk Vallon had as a coffee table.

The other man drank the water down, but still looked ashen. "Thanks."

"You look like you could use something stronger. I could look."

Gleason shook his head. "We can't stay here for long. Amundson will check."

"Agreed. But this is where he picked me up—or rather, where I stupidly offered my help in return for a deal. He probably won't expect me to come here." He had been a naïve idiot when he'd met Amundson. "I figure if we hadn't gotten out of there, I was going to end up as a permanent display in the Wolf Amundson memorial research lab-cum-prison. Is that about right?"

Gleason closed his eyes and leaned back on the couch, his flesh barely containing all the sharp angles of his face and shoulders. The man looked positively desiccated. "Amundson is a man on a righteous mission. I just hadn't realized how far he'd gone."

His voice was faint, as if he were either falling asleep or dying.

"So what can I do to protect us while you rest?"

Gleason managed a skeletal smile. "Too bad. You're not my type." And then his breath evened out with a deep sigh and a snuffle.

Okay. Let the man sleep. He had a few things he could do.

While Gleason slept he busied himself, using Vallon's office land line to call his contact at the airport to confirm Vallon's eventual destination, St. Louis, Missouri, and making a meal—bless Vallon for apparently being a fan of Indian food. A microwavable bag of *palak paneer* and a frozen package of butter chicken. He put the chicken in the oven, and soon the creamy scent of yoghurt and spices filled the kitchen.

He was mulling over what the heck would take Vallon to the Midwest when the cat door flapped and Maggie announced herself with a mew. She threaded her rotund little tuxedoed body through Jason's legs.

"So you missed me, did you?" He picked her up and she bumped his chin with her little pink nose. He ran his hand down her back and she purred heroically. "Let me guess. You want food."

"Mew."

"Thought so." He put her down and pulled the half-used can from the fridge. "I just want you to know that I braved life and limb to get here to feed you."

Maggie didn't particularly look like she believed him and buried her nose in her dish when he set it down for her. He turned around to find Gleason leaning in the kitchen doorway, his gaze scanning the room and coming to rest on the basement door. He limped over to it and tried the handle. Locked, of course. Jason had kept it that way.

"What're you looking for?" Jason asked.

"I'll know it when I see it."

"I'm making us something to eat."

"I can see that, too." Gleason turned back from the door. "There has to be a key around here somewhere."

"Vallon's in St. Louis, Missouri."

Gleason's eyes widened a little, as if surprised Jason could find out that much. Then he shook his head. "That wasn't her last stop. She rented a car from there, and we should, too, but first I need to help myself a little. The key?"

Tell him? Allow him to see what Vallon was doing? What would it mean to the ex-head of the AGS? On the other hand, it might give him a chance to determine whether Gregor Gleason could fill in for Vallon on Jason's little task. He fished the key out of his pocket and tossed it to Gleason.

He didn't catch it. Instead he watched Jason. "You've been in the basement, then."

Jason finally shrugged. "A couple of times. Some interesting things down there."

"Tell me."

Was that an order? Either way it got Jason's back up. "Why don't you look for yourself?"

He checked the chicken and readied the package of *paneer* for the microwave, while Gleason reclaimed the key and fumbled the door open. When Jason turned back to him, Gleason teetered in the doorway, a darkened basement below them. He hadn't left the light off.

"The light bulb must have burned out," Jason said as Gleason tried the light switch and Jason came up behind him. He claimed a light bulb from a cupboard and clattered down the stairs, wondering how the little people had survived in the pitch black. Now if he could just remember where the light bulb was. He did, and swiftly replaced the burned-out bulb.

"Try it again," he called. Light filled the basement. Everything was the same—except an empty sand pit like the one Amundson had had in his research lab stood at one side of the room. It should have held a castle.

Jason fell back a step, another, trying to understand. Then Gleason's hesitant shuffle sounded on the stair.

"Do you need a hand?"

Gleason said nothing, just slowly joined Jason on the basement floor. He scanned the room—workbench, with the pen and ink sketch of the castle that Jason had found, skins stretched almost translucent on frames in the back corner, the cracked concrete, the sand pit. His mouth drew down as his nostrils flared and he closed his eyes. Not happy, Gleason.

"What is it?"

Gleason's watery grey eyes flickered open. "You've been down here before."

Not a question, but Jason decided to treat it that way. "Sure. But it's not quite the way I left it."

As he shifted back to the sand pit, he could feel the weight of Gleason's regard. He crouched down to touch the sand, fine, white, almost soft to the touch.

"There was something here. A structure." He looked up at Gleason and saw the man waited. "It was a castle."

Gleason's eyes widened slightly and his entire body seemed to go on alert.

"Don't worry. I haven't told anyone about it. But I'm taking it from your expression that this shouldn't be here, and I probably shouldn't remember it, either."

He stood and waited for Gleason to say something, anything.

"Let me guess: spaces like this are supposed to only exist in the AGS."

Gleason's gaze flickered from him to the cracks in the floor. "Vallon Drake has never been an agent who follows the rules. Unorthodox, some would call her."

"I think I've heard the term wild card."

That brought a thin smile to Gleason's lips. "An understatement, to be sure." He sighed and crossed the floor to the cracks in the cement. "I can see why she chose this place when others wouldn't." He turned back to Jason. "Tell me, what do you see in these cracks?"

Jason crossed the floor. The air was cool, but smelled faintly like heated electrical wiring. He peered down at the pavement that had likely been broken during one of the quakes that occasionally hit Seattle. "There's concrete crumbled at the edges of the crack, and inside there's a runnel of water. Not a good sign to anyone looking at the soundness of the house's structure."

He met Gleason's gaze.

"Interesting." Gleason nodded, then closed his eyes and seemed to inhale a deep breath like someone planning on meditation, or a dive off a cliff.

His shoulders went back and his hands were spread and open over the crack as if he were trying to do something arduous, and yet nothing happened. The basement ticked around them. The slick of water glimmered and moved in the crack. The faint sour odor from the drying skins placed an unpleasant taste on the back of Jason's tongue. Then Gleason jerked and inhaled sharply again. He opened his eyes, blinked, and turned back to Jason. Smiled.

"Well. That is better."

Which didn't make a lot of sense, given nothing in the room had changed, except perhaps Gregor Gleason's color was better. He no longer looked like he'd fall over at the slightest breeze. Interesting, right back atcha, Gleason, old man. It was almost as if something about the crack in the floor had refreshed him.

He thought back to what he knew of Vallon. He'd gotten to know her over the death of an agent whose cell phone they'd found encased in a wall. He'd nearly lost his life when he followed her into the Seattle Underground. Coupled with the sandbox and the cracks in the concrete, it looked like whatever Vallon and her kind could do, it was somehow tied to the earth. Verrry interesting indeed. Was it something he could learn to do himself?

Gleason scanned the room again. "It appears Agent Drake and I must have a little discussion." He shook his head. "I wonder if Landon knows." He thought a moment, then shook his head. "Landon would know."

And the fact that the diminutive albino agent hadn't told him obviously disturbed him.

"I think we should get going, if you're able," Jason said.

"And how do you plan to do that? Amundson will have the airport watched."

Jason grinned. "Then how about we take a little drive to Portland and see about a couple of last-minute flights out of there?"

"And you have a destination in mind?" Gleason's thin lips traced the hint of a smile.

Jason started up the stairs, but his hand slid to his jacket pocket to the vial he'd palmed during the escape from the research lab. The vial of whatever it was that curtailed Gleason's powers.

"I'm thinking the Midwest, for some reason."

§

The scent of mud and standing water on the acrid tang of recycled air greeted Vallon as she resurfaced from the depths she'd been weighed down under.

Darkness and depth. The weight of the earth on her chest. Unable to move, to scream, to breathe.

Something beeped and she shuddered and came instantly awake. *Beep. Beep. Beep.* And pain stabbed her brain as if she'd been knocked down, split open, her brain tossed in a bowl. More beeping and she clamped her eyes shut against the ache of dislocation and emptiness that was her. Cold, hard surface under her back, metal under her palms. A scent she remembered from childhood: marzipan and Christmas mornings—almonds—filled her nose. She opened her eyes and a wavery whiteness filled her vision.

"She's coming around," said a voice that was vaguely familiar.

"About time. None of the others were out this long." A voice she didn't know, but didn't like for the way the 'S's hissed and coldness radiated though it.

"I thought you said they had to hit her with more than they've used on others?"

A face came into view that she didn't know. Narrow face with eyes set wide apart, so the man seemed to look in two different directions from either side of a caricaturish, protruding roman nose. He wore a white coat and a stethoscope, but she couldn't seem to move her head to see what he was doing with it. He listened to something, then took the stethoscope off his ears, then checked her pulse at her carotid; and all the time he never looked at her, never looked in her eyes.

Like she was nothing but a piece of meat—and the realization sent her even colder. She had to get out of here. She had to figure out what they had done to her. She had to stop it. She had to stop the quake. What if she'd been wrong and it wasn't her father? Who were these people? The fact she couldn't turn her head or lift her arm or even open her mouth to scream sent a part of her mind scurrying like a mouse in a wheel. Had they done something to permanently immobilize her?

The sound of screaming filled her head—the sound she'd heard when she'd touched Morgan Hoptaler and again when she'd been blasted by the weird power. Was this what the power did? Leave her trapped in her body? Was this how coma victims felt? Or quadriplegics? Panic spiraled up and up and up. Was this what she'd done to herself by not listening to Landon or Xavier?

Then another man stepped into view. She smelled his musk and knew it, knew the way his blonde hair fell in his eyes and the way his muscled chest would feel under her hands. His good ol' boy eyes twinkled a little. The guy from the bar. The guy she's fucked in the parking lot. Toby something-or-other. Oh, God. Had she really been that stupid? He was in on this?

She -reached-, but it was like slamming into a wall. She couldn't feel the earth below her at all, and maybe that was what led to the hollow feeling, because it was like she was a black hole in space that she and all creation could fall into. Was this guy Gifted? Had she missed that?

"Aah. You recognize me don't you? We had a pretty good time together, didn't we?" His knuckle trailed heat down her cheekbone and jaw, freezing her body, then bumped down over her collar bone and found her breast. She wanted to scream at the violation. It wound up and up inside her, almost strangling her. She would slam her fist into him. She would beat him to a pulp. She closed her eyes against the rage.

She closed her eyes. So she had that level of control. She couldn't afford to panic. She needed to focus on what she could do, and if she could open and close her eyes, maybe she could do other things, too. That steadied her breathing.

Someone picked up her hand. "Come on, Babe. Don't turn off on us. Hey doc, how about giving her the antidote. There're people waiting to see her."

"She'll be ready to go soon enough. I'm just making sure the dosage is right."

Dosage? They were drugging her. The realization was like a knife hanging over her. She'd known about drug research at the AGS. How else could they have come up with the inhibitor? But she hadn't given it a second thought. Something that could hold a Gifted powerless like this, and could totally block their Gift. She'd never heard of anything like it, and she couldn't imagine Landon creating something as horrible as this. So whoever it was running this little operation had the funds to have a research operation as part of it. That meant major funding.

Like government or corporations. What she'd witnessed across the Canadian border, with the creation of the Canadian Northern Gateway oil pipeline when all the media had said the public opposition would never let it happen. But now it was there and would remain there if the Gifted could just hold it in place long enough for the unGifted to accept it as their reality. So someone had obviously made the decision to do it anyway and they'd had the Gifted to do it. A little shiver ran down her back. Was this how they controlled their Gifted? Was this what the future of being Gifted was? Being held prisoner and kept immobile until the Gift was needed. Just the thought of it made her skin crawl, sent her thoughts reeling around like pinwheels.

She fought down her panicked breathing. She'd go crazy like this.

Absolutely, stark raving mad.

Like Morgan Hoptaler?

Oh, God. Was this what had happened to him and to the other New Madrid agents? Her heart pounded in her ears.

The doctor's narrow face returned to the space over her and he shoved her t-shirt sleeve up over her arm. A sharp pinprick and then he turned away again. Toby looked down at her, all tanned and boy-toy handsome. Her skin crawled at the thought she'd been with him. That she'd betrayed Xavier.

Xavier.

He'd be looking for her. She -reached- and slammed into the wall again, but something was happening. She could move her fingers a little. Could make a fist. Could lift her arm. She inhaled and jerked up to sitting and almost fell down again, but Toby caught her shoulder. She couldn't shake off his hold and it sent afterburn roaring through her.

Not this. Not now.

Shaking, she opened her eyes and fought down the desire to just grab Toby again. She sat on a metal table like you might find in a morgue, and she was so cold it was hard to move and so empty she could feel the wind inside her whistling through her bones, at the same time the afterburn was searing the flesh off her skeleton.

The room was simple. Rows of stainless steel cupboards and a counter and sink ran along one wall. Two other walls were blank concrete, the concrete rough as if this place had been built without any care of aesthetics. The fourth wall held the door. The acrid recycled air turned her stomach and her head hurt. No windows. The door that she couldn't keep her eyes off of. She might have come here on purpose, wherever here was, but the urgent need to get away beat inside with her heart. She shoved down the panic and turned to the doctor, who checked her vitals.

"Where am I?" The words came out slightly garbled around a tongue that didn't quite work yet.

"Don't you worry, you're safe." Toby answered and she could almost hear an unspoken 'little lady' in his condescending voice.

She yanked her arm loose against the heat of his hand and slid off the cold slab of table. Her legs threatened to undermine her but this time she waved off Toby's help. Far safer that way.

"I'm fine, all right? I don't want your help. And if I'm so safe, why the heck do I feel like this and why do you keep pumping stuff into my body?" She glared at the doctor.

The doctor just busied himself putting his vials away in a small fridge built into a cupboard that she hadn't noticed.

"So why am I here?"

Toby's good 'ol boy expression vanished as if it had never been. His face turned as cold as a predator. "Seems they need you. There're people waiting."

She couldn't avoid his hold on her shoulder and he pushed her towards the door. She stumbled, but righted herself and tried again to -reach-. These two might be unGifted, but there had to be Gifted here, otherwise how would they even know to target her? But instead of the bright presence of the doctor and Toby, all she got was the sensation of running head first into a wall, as if she were encased in an eggshell or something. A mental prison more like, or a cave deep in the earth.

She fought back a shudder as Toby ushered her out into a hallway lit by small overhead lights that tinted her skin blue. More concrete, with numbers painted on doors that lined the walls. She came out of number D12, painted in red. That meant something, but she needed to figure out what, and having half her senses blocked wasn't going to make that any easier.

"That's some awful shit you pumped into me."

Toby said nothing, just shoved her down the hall ahead of him, the door numbers decreasing.

"What is this place?" she tried again.

"Your new fucking home. Now shut the fuck up and just keep going."

Definitely not a good 'ol boy anymore. It made it a lot easier to resist the afterburn. She marched down the hall until it met another corridor, this one curving rapidly away in either direction. Toby turned her left and they passed another corridor spoking off to the right that had 'A' painted in blue beside it. That suggested there were only four spokes to this wheel. On the left there was only concrete until they passed a single set of large double doors. The exit?

"What's in there?" She asked and slowed as she passed.

"I told you to keep moving!" He planted his palm between her shoulder blades and pushed so she stumbled away from him down towards the next spoke in the wheel. She glanced over her shoulder. Whatever the hub of this installation was, she could actually feel it like a pressure against her skin. There was a faint crackle in the air like ozone. Power, then. A lot of it. She made a point of stumbling again and catching herself with her palm on the hub wall. Even through what she could only figure was a drug-based blockage of her Gift, she could feel the concrete hum. The vibration travelled up her arm and made her whole body ring.

She yanked her hand away and scrambled ahead before Toby could touch her again. Her hand tingled with pins and needles, but the hum had painted the back of her tongue with flavors. Pomegranate. Cinnamon. Cut grass and anise and mint and a myriad of other scents too faint to name. And one she recognized. Fi. No. That couldn't be. She stopped dead in the hall and tried to -reach- again, but came up with nothing. Whatever was there left her skin crawling, because something wasn't right. It was almost like the entire AGS was inside that wall, their Gifts somehow tangled together.

And Fi. But Fi had left town. It couldn't be so.

The corridor marked B in yellow came up and Toby motioned her down it. Same concrete, same lighting that gave the numbers on the doors a green tinge. Toby stopped her at a door numbered B4 and she wondered if this was the calm before the storm.

Toby knocked and that meant she really was going to meet someone, which meant she needed to be on her guard. She straightened and pushed her shoulders back. Regardless of how she felt and how she must look, this was why she had let herself be caught. She would deal with this and find out what she could.

A soft click said the door had automatically unlocked.

"Open it," Toby said.

She did, and a flood of almond almost took her breath away so she stopped dead in the doorway. The room that waited was an office, regimented in its decor. Table rigidly parallel to book cases that lined the rear wall, but these books weren't for show. They were stacked in neat piles out to the edges of the shelves. She recognized the style. The desktop held a single file, open, and precisely positioned in front of the desk chair. A cup of coffee, hot enough to let a curl of steam escape upwards, sat on a crystal coaster at the file's corner, evoking so many memories.

But it was the man behind the desk she couldn't take her eyes off of. Tall, square shouldered, even after so many years. His hair had gone lighter with grey, but his blue eyes still could pierce through any lie. She was going to have to be very careful. Careful most of all at the way her heart beat as fast as a small bird's in his presence. She swallowed back the conflicting emotions and stepped inside.

"I thought I'd find you here, Father," she said.

Wherever *here* was.

§

"No!" roared Xavier. He bolted upright in Vallon's bed and sought her around the floral room. Her scent of ashes of roses still lingered on his skin. The musk of their lovemaking rose off the sheets, but that was all. The room ticked around him. Her clothing was gone. The amber light of late afternoon came around the window blinds to tinge the walls bile-yellow. His stomach turned as he inhaled and -reached-.

[Vallon!]

Nothing.

The flare of the albino, Snow, came from the rear of the house downstairs. So did the flicker of the Ducharme woman and a child. No one else. He -reached- out through New Madrid, as he began pulling on his clothes. Dark shirt over his head. Black jeans up over his hips. Creator, no. Let her be out there waiting. Perhaps gone for a walk with her friend. But even as he -reached- for her, he knew his hope was unfounded. He'd felt her go, hadn't he?

Like a door closed, a light turned out.

[Vallon, *Bela*, answer, please!]

Still nothing.

He yanked on low boots and slammed out of the room. In the town, the flickering presences of people home for dinner, of people in the local diner and at the small town theatre. No 'Gifted' as his kind were known here. Gone were the sublime feelings of connection to the world and the woman he loved. Yes, loved. No man would turn his back on everything as he had for anything less. And now she was gone from him—had left his bed.

He thundered down the stairs and a white-faced Landon Snow came hurrying down the hall, his soft footfall like scurrying rats in the walls. Behind him came Elizabeth Ducharme, followed by the small girl-child.

"What's happened to her?" Snow asked, his eyes wide with almost shock and accusation. "I thought she was with you?"

"She was." He shoved the forelock of his unruly hair back over his head. "She—left, afterwards."

A small glimmer that could almost be satisfaction in Snow's gaze. "And you let her?"

Was the little man goading him that he could not hold Vallon to him, or was he actually happy that Vallon was gone? Xavier, -reached- farther out over the fields and farmhouses surrounding the town. A shoal of human light at what was a tavern. The scattered lonely fires of farm houses. Strange indeed to see so little Gifted blood amongst the people living here. That itself was an anomaly, given how prevalent the blood was now across the world's population.

He turned an angry eye back on Snow. "We—made love. We slept. She left."

"After you had dealt with the afterburn."

"Why would Vallon leave? Momma's just about got dinner ready!" piped the little girl who'd stepped up to hold her mother's hand. She was a sweet-faced little one with corn-blonde hair and large blue eyes and was dressed in a ruffled knee-length dress, while her mother wore black-and-white polka dots.

"I think they don't know, honey. Perhaps Miss Murdoch can shed some light on things. I believe I heard her and Vallon speaking together a little while ago." Elizabeth Ducharme smoothed her hair and stepped up too close for comfort. "What can I do to help?" She smiled up at him.

"But Fi's gone, too, Mommy."

"What?" Xavier, Snow, and the child's mother all turned as one and the child backed a step.

"What do you mean?" Xavier went to his knee in front of her, but the child grabbed her mother and hid behind her. Xavier stood. He should know better. His was not a visage that gave comfort to children.

"Honey, tell the man what you know." The Ducharme woman pulled her daughter in front of her.

Those wide blue eyes blinked and she turned her face to her mother's skirt. "They had a fight, I think. Fi was mad about something and she said she was going. So after Vallon left, she did. I think she took their car."

Snow checked outside the door. "Vallon's rental Camry's gone. Maybe they're together. I'll take the Prius and start looking."

But Xavier knew differently. "She's gone. Just gone." Had winked out like a candle in wind. He met Snow's pale gaze. "Check."

A brief, faraway look came over Snow's face and then he was back, his face a little paler and shaken. His Adam's apple worked in his throat.

"You see?" Xavier asked.

"But how? She cannot simply disappear. No one can."

"Apparently they can."

Xavier left them for outside and the distorted shadows of late afternoon that seemed to reflect the way he felt. Nothing was natural. Nothing was as it should be. Even the earth hummed under his feet in an unnatural manner. He stopped and let his awareness travel down into the soil, to the myriad stone ruptures that permeated the substrate of the earth's mantle far below. This area of the earth was a disaster waiting to happen if the uneasy truce of tectonic forces ever ruptured. But at the moment nothing was happening, except for the odd humming. It was almost like a chorus of voices in the soil that came from all directions and none.

Down the street a wooden swing swung idly from a tired-looking tree branch in the slight breeze. The air smelled of river mud and farm dust and the low fug of heated, standing water. Snow pattered out of the house and down the porch stairs. He really did not move like a normal man, but then what was normal amongst those who carried the blood?

"So what's really going on, do you think?" Snow came up beside Xavier.

"I think she has done what we asked her not to do." Xavier swallowed back the pain it caused. That she had lied to him. That she had left him for someone who would try to hurt her and had left behind his help. That was what hurt the most and left his breast filled with anger and sorrow.

The little man nodded. "She never did listen. Not to anybody. Not even when she was a kid." Said with satisfaction as if he were pleased that she didn't listen to Xavier, either. "Listen. I was thinking, it might be better if we look together. Join forces. Alone seems to me to be the best way to get picked off."

Xavier looked back from scanning the streets and -reached- farther into the distance. Just how far could Vallon or Fi get in the few minutes since the connection with Vallon had snapped like a rubber band and woke him?

The little man waited.

He was the antithesis of what Xavier represented—small, weak of body and eyesight and perhaps the other senses. And yet he was also kindred, all subterfuge and secret knowledge, like all their kind had to be in order to exist at all. Trust him? Snow had helped Vallon all these years, even if there was something about him that felt not quite right.

"If you do not feel safe, we can ride together, yes?"

Snow nodded and jingled his key fob. The Prius chirped at him and Xavier followed. Inside the new-car smell filled the cab. Snow pushed the button and the car slid silently out of the driveway.

"What did it feel like when she disappeared?" Landon asked.

"She was simply not there. It was—like she died." But that could not be the truth, not when after all the years of loneliness, he had finally found her. He would know if she died. A part of him would die with her.

A shiver of fear ran across Snow's face and was gone. "But she's not dead. Not yet. She knew what she was getting into. She had no death wish. She just wished to find her father."

"Yes." He felt Snow's consideration, as if the little man was trying to decide just how much Xavier knew of Vallon. Let him continue guessing. "And that is a problem on very many levels."

CHAPTER 23 —MEANING

"Come in and take a seat," Vallon's father said, and it was more an order than an invitation. "That'll be all, Watts. I can handle it from here."

Vallon glanced over her shoulder as Toby left, as if he couldn't get out of there soon enough. She swung back to her father. He was so much as she'd thought he would be and yet so—not. He didn't come around the desk to her. Didn't take her in his arms the way Xavier had when he'd found her again. And Xavier probably hated her now for what she had done.

"You look the same," she said, still standing where Toby had left her, and she could see the small frown lines deepen around his eyes just like they had when she was a child. Every part of her wanted to throw her arms around him. To demand to know why he left her behind, but emotional displays were never her father's way.

"Sit down, Vallon." He motioned at the single straight-backed chair that faced the desk. As if she was an employee come for a performance evaluation.

She sat and, as she expected, the chair was uncomfortable right down to one leg being shorter than the others so the darn thing tipped. Staged. Staged. Staged. Had her father ever had a conversation with her that wasn't? Had he ever actually touched her—given her a hug—because he wanted to? Or had they all been planned to have the best possible impact at a specific time? The hollow feeling in her gut expanded. The air smelled wrong, not just the recycled air scent and not just her father's scent of almonds, but almost like there were too many scents clashing together. It made her head hurt and worsened the hollowed-out feeling.

"It's good to see you," she tried. "I've been looking for you ever since I learned you might be alive."

His gaze barely flickered. "And you're here now and it's good to see you are well. When you did not wake, I was—concerned."

Didn't wake? "How long was I out, then?" she asked, feeling a little less steady.

"We've had you under medical care for thirty six hours. I was beginning to worry." He glanced down at the file. "I understand you dealt with Rebecca Murdoch. A good piece of work."

The sudden change of topic was a surprise, given she was still reeling from the matter-of-fact way he regarded the fact that she'd been not much more than a vegetable for thirty-six flipping hours. Her father had kept track of her. His approval wasn't something she was used to and didn't seem to fit with his attitude. Her legs felt unsteady, as if the whole world was shifting and she couldn't tell where it would end. *Get a grip, girl. You wanted to come here.*

"She threatened Seattle. She said she was going to destroy it in retribution for the death of her daughter. She had to be stopped."

"A shame, really. Rebecca Murdoch had tremendous talent, but her mind was weak. She could not take the pressure of what needed to be done." He glanced down at the file again. "But you dealt with her handily." His lips curved slightly. "You did well."

Okay. Aside from the afterburn burning up her insides and the hollow echo her thoughts seemed to have in her brain, this was about the weirdest conversation she'd ever had with anyone, let alone her father. She closed her eyes, but that didn't make things any clearer.

"You're freaking me out, a little. You never compliment me on anything." She swallowed and hefted her chin a little. "Just what is it you want, Dad? Why am I here? It's obviously not for a family reunion."

There. She'd said it, and though it hurt like a knife in her heart, she could see that this was the kind of approach her father would appreciate. No messy emotion no matter how her heart felt. A clarity of question and answer, no matter her confusion. Had she done the right thing coming here, wherever the heck this was?

His gaze appraised her and for once in her life, she didn't see the disappointment that had always edged his expression when she was a child. "You've grown up well. The Academy was what you needed."

She said nothing even though he was so wrong she could not believe it. As a child she'd always thought he knew everything. Another dream dispelled, or memory debunked. Amazing. Just keep the emotion out of it. Stay as clinical as he is until you get what you want.

"And you've done well enough in the AGS, though you aren't exactly what I would call a 'Team Player'."

So somehow he had access to all her personnel files. She chewed on that a moment. "I suppose that's one thing you taught me. You always stand on your own."

A grey brow arched slightly and there was that curve of lips again. "I suppose I did foster independence. As Gifted we must learn to think for ourselves."

The darn chair cut into her shoulder blades, almost as if it had been made specifically to do it. It teetered under her when she shifted to get comfortable, and she finally had to brace herself to keep the chair from wobbling. She smiled at his little show of power.

"Believe me, independence is the least of it. I believe there've been terms used like 'insubordinate', and 'does not play well with others,' and 'problem child.' So in the interest of independence, I'll ask my question again: What's going on, Dad? Why am I here, when you didn't even let me know you were alive for the past, what?—almost sixteen years?"

Francis Drake leaned back in his high-backed leather chair almost as if he were relieved. He considered her, then it was like he decided something. He closed the file on his desk and took a sip of coffee, the fluorescent light tinting his graying blonde hair blue. His grey gaze met hers.

"I have to say I'm pleasantly surprised. I thought bringing you in would involve dealing with an emotional child and all the messiness of a reunion. It seems I was wrong and that I underestimated you. For that I apologize. Perhaps I should have drawn you in years ago."

"Years?" She managed to keep her voice steady, when all she really wanted to do was tell him about how it had really felt. Because she *had* been a child. She'd been eleven, for God's sake. And if she were emotional, it was only because this man had abandoned her.

"Surely, you don't think an installation such as this is built overnight?"

She glanced around. The cold concrete walls, the tasteless recycled air with just the barest hint of water. It was as loveless and lifeless as her childhood home had been. She realized that now. When she came home from school that day and her house and father were gone, she hadn't really lost anything. It was always Landon who was more like her father.

"I suppose not. What I don't understand is why me and why now."

Now he did smile, ivory-white teeth exposed in a tight row that creeped her out a little. Since when did Francis Drake ever really smile?

"Because you are you—the most talented Gifted of your generation—and because the time is right."

He stood up and came around the desk to perch on its corner. "Have you ever wondered why there are people with the Gift and people without? And why all those people, with enough light to show they have some Gift, don't have enough power to use it?"

He waited for her nod, but then carried on. "It's because we're something new, Vallon. A step forward. The next step in the evolution of the Human race. A race of super beings who can interact more efficiently with the world around them. It's no longer about the use of tools, it's about the use of our minds!" He stood up and paced behind her. "And yet, these improved beings are left to hide amidst the unGifted. Or they serve the unGifted like some kind of indentured servants. Everywhere you look in the world, it's the same." He came up beside her. "Don't you see how wrong that is? For us to be seen as just another human resource to be used by governments and the multinational corporations?"

"Uh." She wasn't quite sure how to respond. "But Rebecca Murdoch said that was exactly what you and the others are doing in Southeast Asia. The tsunami caused a major disaster to so many countries, and the only way they could get aid was to sign away a lot of their sovereignty to a bunch of multinational companies." Was that what the New Madrid quake was about? She suddenly felt sick to her stomach. It was one thing to see something like that done on the other side of the world. It was another to see it done to her own country. But then, the refusal by government to let the AGS help with the Katrina devastation was another sign that something was seriously wrong.

But her father had perched on the desk edge again. He leaned down to her, his eyes glittering with excitement. "It was a sham, Vallon. A means to get the financing the Gifted needed to make things happen."

"What are you talking about? A lot of people died in that Tsunami."

"Yes. Yes. They died. But they were unGifted and they died for a purpose."

He was off pacing again, the sound of his footsteps like a metronome she remembered from her childhood. So many nights falling asleep to the same sound.

"You've been thinking about this for a long, long time."

He whirled around to her. "Yes. Yes I have. And planning. And working with the enemy to get what we needed before we take what we want."

Her mind racing, she rubbed her forehead, the soft shush of the air through the vents a comforting calm. "I'm sorry. Maybe it's the afterburn or the after effects of your little attack on me, but I'm not following. What enemy? What is it we want? And by 'we,' who do you mean?"

Francis Drake—he might be her blood relation, but, she realized now, he had never been interested in her—circled back to his chair and collapsed in it to lean forward over his desk.

"We are the Gifted, Vallon. You. Me. All our kind. Even Landon. We've allowed ourselves to be used all these years, but that's not the way it should be. We've been used by the old guard—governments and corporations—like blunt tools, when we can and should be so much more. Who are the enemy, Vallon? How about the rest of unGifted humankind. What do we want? How about our place in the world as the new dominant race."

She sat there, stunned at the epic size of his plans and trying to fathom the place the New Madrid fault played in it. But she met his gaze full on and smiled. She had to keep him talking.

"You mean someone is finally going to do what should have been done a long time ago."

His blonde brow rose a little. "I thought the AGS did a better job of indoctrination," he said softly.

Vallon kept the smile plastered on her face and managed a little laugh. "And since when have I ever really followed any AGS rules? Gleason considers me insubordinate and a wild card. The only thing that's kept me 'in the fold' is the not-so-pleasant alternative."

"Because Gifted aren't exactly allowed to retire—not like the unGifted. Gifted are watched for the rest of their lives. They are drugged to stop their use of the Gift, and in some cases worse, because they do not trust us." He shook his head bitterly. "It is not right. Was never right." His voice was tight with barely controlled anger. "I argued with Gleason and Decker. I said we should hone our power and then announce ourselves into the world as a power unto ourselves and available to the highest bidder. But they said it was suicide—that we'd be seen as the enemy or taken as test subjects into labs." He shook his head bitterly. "As if that hasn't happened already. Even here in America, Homeland Security detains us—for our own safety, they say. No, the Gifted should never have agreed to become government agents. They control us too much that way."

"Like not allowing us to practice our skills outside of the Academy or work."

He nodded. "So you've felt it as well." And his voice had gone almost soft, and for a moment his gaze fell away from hers.

She nodded. "And fought against it." She cocked her head. "Maybe we've been on the same side all these years, Father. Maybe you shouldn't have left me behind."

His hands fidgeted with the file on his desk. Then he looked up at her and smiled something that might have been real. "But look what you've become, Vallon. A daughter any man would be proud of."

Her breath left her chest. He was proud of her? He actually cared?

"Why did you leave me? How could you do it? I've torn myself up asking that question." She almost couldn't breathe waiting for his answer.

"It was the right thing to do."

She opened her eyes, not believing what she heard. "How could abandoning your child be right?"

"The life I've led had no place for a child in it. Not any child."

Not good enough. She was not going to let him off that easy. Not when he hadn't even said he loved her. Had he loved her? "But you still made a choice to leave me."

"I did. Yes. I knew Landon would be there for you."

Nothing about it being better for her. Nothing to show he cared. He said it so matter-of-factly she fell back in her chair deflated. "He wasn't my father."

"No. But sometimes upbringing means more than blood. Landon did a good job. You are here."

"You mean you expected me to come to you at some point?" How did she feel? Elated that he'd awaited her arrival, or angry that he'd thought her so predictable.

"Don't most adopted children seek out their natural parent at some point?"

All the hopes she'd allowed herself to feel were lost in his chill grey gaze. She was no more than a foundling to him, or a pigeon that had come home to roost. Was that why Landon had called her that all these years? Was Landon complicit in her abandonment? Her stomach rolled over and she thought she might be sick, but somehow she formed her lips into a smile.

"I hate being predictable."

"As do I, daughter. As do I."

And it was wonderful to hear him call her that, but she couldn't let herself believe there was any feeling behind it. She leaned forward to place her hands on his desk.

"So you brought me here because you need my help?" Get straight to the point. Be as ruthless as he was. Play the game as he would, but win it herself, even though a part of her felt like a puppy that couldn't help wagging its tail. Because he was her *father,* damn it. And he wanted her with him after all these years.

Finally he bowed his head. "Correct. I did not foresee it when I left, but you are the answer to a prayer."

He did need her. Heat flooded her cheeks and she had to work to hide her grin. "Then what do you need? Tell me your plans."

She could go along for a while, at least. Learn what she could of his plans and then diffuse the harm it would do. Or perhaps she could help her father see a different path, where Gifted and unGifted coexisted as equals.

He stood up and his regard seemed to sift through her essence. She -reached- towards him, but again hit the grey wall of resistance that kept her confined to her body. The fact that he hadn't counteracted whatever drug they'd used on her suddenly did not bode well.

"I think we'd better get you fixed up. Let's take a little tour." As if he'd read her mind.

Vallon scrambled to her feet and followed him to the door. Toby waited there, an expectant look on his too-handsome face.

"We're headed to central," her father said.

Toby nodded and left them, striding down to the curved hall and disappearing around its curve.

"So what exactly is this place? Where is it?" She strode beside her father and couldn't help the little thrill it gave her. She matched him stride for stride as they followed after Toby.

Her father smiled. "Consider it a gift from the corporations. We needed a place to work and they had the funds. After Southeast Asia there was no difficulty getting patrons. Even governments."

Vallon thought about that. "The Federal Government funds you?"

A hard smile curved her father's lips as they turned back the way she'd come along the curved hallway. They turned up the hallway marked D. "Actually, yes. Along with a couple of other foreign powers. Not overtly, of course, but there are a number of large corporations who are contracted to provide most of the security services for the American government and a number of others. They contract with us, and the governments don't really want to know how the private security forces get things done. Plausible deniability, I believe it is called."

She thought about what she knew of Homeland Security and what had happened at the AGS since H.S. had taken it over. They'd subcontracted things out there, too. So the private companies were gaining access to all the AGS research and running their own, too. They saw the value of the Gifted's abilities. She wondered who would be the big losers in the battle for control of that power. Somehow the chances of the Gifted coming out on top seemed pretty small, no matter what her father planned.

"So where are we?" At least figure out where they were. Do her job as an agent.

Her father stopped her at a doorway. "Where we have always been: at New Madrid. We've always seen it as a lynchpin to our plan. The heartland of America, and sitting on top one of the most destructive forces on the continent, second only to the Yellowstone volcanic system. But if Yellowstone exploded, it would damage the atmosphere. We don't want the devastation that would cause. A quake, however, will not."

How nice of him to care about the atmosphere. Thank God for small mercies.

He opened the door and stepped inside to a boardroom. Or maybe it was a war room. The concrete walls were covered in maps that showed the bootheel of Missouri and New Madrid and what was known of the main fault lines. One map showed the 1812 New Madrid quake and the levels of damage ranging out from the epicenter. There'd been hundreds of aftershocks after the main quake, and some had barely been smaller than the massive 8.1 of the main quake.

Actually, now that she looked at it, the room was more like a shrine to the quake. An overflowing bookshelf carried volumes marked with the stamp of the US Geological Survey.

"Everything ever written about the New Madrid Fault is in this room. We wanted to know what we were working with."

She glanced up at her father. He was still taller than her by a good three inches—not quite Xavier's height, but maybe her attraction to Xavier was because he shared her father's stature and was almost as inaccessible. She shivered.

"So show me what you're planning."

Her father nodded over his shoulder. "Best if you understand, I suppose."

He supposed? He supposed!?

But he motioned her up beside a map. "The main New Madrid Quake had its epicenter here." He motioned to Northeastern Arkansas and up through New Madrid on a Northeast line. "But it was felt in Boston and Colorado. A total of 50,000 square miles were affected strongly, compared to the 1906 San Francisco earthquake that was felt over 6,200 square miles. A different level of magnitude entirely."

"And you've learned how to replicate it."

He glanced up at her from the map, and this time he truly did smile; and his teeth showed feral yellow and far sharper than she remembered, so she braced herself for his answer.

"I've done better," he said. "I've learned how to increase it a thousand fold."

§

The river ran as dark as Xavier's thoughts, as deep as sorrow, and as muddy as the confusion he felt over Vallon. She had left, abandoned him in her bed, after promising that she would not. She had left him to seek out someone who would hurt her. He clamped his hands into fists at his frustration. The night wind brought dampness and fragrant hints of growing things like the scent of the dark places under Vallon's hair. He'd carried her with him always in his heart, but had tried to lock those feelings away and do his job.

But some things erode a mental lock swifter than others. Though he'd kept confidences and been an obedient agent of the Council for long years, meeting Vallon Drake, speaking with her, inhaling her scent, and touching her skin had been acid to his resolve. He loved her and so he had given up everything: his post, his past, his connections to everything that had been a constant in his life, and now he had lost her.

He chuckled at the irony. She chose her father over him.

"What is it? Can you sense her?" the strange one, Snow, asked.

Xavier held up a hand to silence him and -reached- into the dawn.

Across the water, the lands of the Kentucky Bend blended farmland with stands of trees that had grown on the soil that the mighty river pushed up like the back of some serpent rising from the water. The trees glowed in his other sight, birds and small animals were bright sparks amid the coals, even though the river placed a heavy weight across his sight. Behind him, New Madrid slumbered, the small, guttering flames of the populace a frustrating sign of life, but not the life he both wanted and needed. There was no bright, sizzling flare of Vallon, her essence like a brilliant bonfire and fireworks explosions combined. There was barely any sign of Gift at all, and that was strange in itself. Over generations, the blood of his people had spread through the world's population like precious droplets lost. There should be something here, more than the poor half-crazed fool they'd found during their first search of the town.

He yanked back into himself and shook his head. His head was muzzy with fatigue, or was that sorrow that weighted his limbs and mind? "There is nothing. No sign. No scent in New Madrid."

The little man seemed to glow beside him, his pale suit, hair, and skin catching the moonlight.

"There's no way that she could have been taken out of the town by the time we started looking, and she was still in New Madrid when we both felt her taken."

"When she ended, you mean." There, he had said it, because it *had* felt like the way a person's flame just stopped when they died.

Snow just shook his head. "She'd not dead."

"You think I don't know that? She is here. Out there somewhere, and I seem to not be able to do anything about it." He tore himself away from the torture of the view of the town and back to the river. At least there was a serenity in the smooth coil of water. With his houseboat, he and Vallon could float serenely down to the Gulf and across the ocean to wherever they chose to go. That was what he had intended to propose to her. To leave this life of toil and rest with him as he had never rested before. With her he could have rested and found new life again. A reason to live beyond duty. "By all of Creation, why can't I find her?"

Snow stayed silent a moment, peering with Xavier out over the river. "We—the AGS. We were working on ways to block the Gift." He spoke quietly so his voice was like part of the hissing shush of the water on the shore.

"What? You have done what?" He grabbed the little man's shoulders. Wanted to shake him, for that was the only answer. Something like this. Like the things the Council would do to contain one of his people who disobeyed the edicts.

Like himself.

If these people had come up with something as well, it could not be good. "Tell me!"

The small man's eyes had widened at Xavier's outburst, but then his face smoothed into something Xavier could not trust. Something about Landon Snow spoke of so many layers of secrets that perhaps even Snow no longer knew his way through them.

He shrugged off Xavier's grip and brushed the folds out of his suit shoulders. "The AGS had to have ways of dealing with Gifted who would not abide by the rules. If we found someone with the talent to do what we do and they would not join us, well then, we couldn't very well leave them in society to change things as they saw fit, now could we? We were forced to take them into custody and find ways to 'contain' them for the country's safety."

It made his stomach queasy, just thinking of what they must have done. All of the Council's agents went through a period of questioning every few years. That involved subjecting oneself to the most unpleasant removal of one's power. It also served as a powerful reminder of what would happen if the agent disobeyed his masters.

"And, pray, what does containment involve?"

Snow's pale gaze flickered like ice in the moonlight. "There are drugs. We experimented with blood loss. A few other things."

Bile soured Xavier's throat. "You are a pitiless people." But then so, it seemed, were his. He rubbed his forearm.

Snow met his gaze and a soft smile coated his lips. "And what are yours, to be so secretive all these years while we are out here struggling?"

The question caught him off guard. "How…?"

Snow's painted-on smile broadened and became real. "How could you not exist? An emissary does not work alone, but I've known your existence for years. I've researched the family trees of all the Gifted we have. I think I may have even located some of the families you come from, de Varga. Like yours. Portuguese, if I'm not mistaken. Your ancestor studied at the great Cartographer's School at Sagre. It makes me wonder whether that was really a cartographer's school at all."

"An interesting question. I have no answer for you. I am no historian." Xavier turned back from the river to avoid showing his shock. Did all these people know this? If so, he must warn his people. These 'Gifted' were an unruly, upstart people, with none of the discipline of history to warn them of the consequences of their actions. "Vallon must be here, somewhere. By now they could have taken her very far away." He -reached- again, out over the flattened landscape that had once been a great forest of floodplain oak and cypress and pine, and now was parched fields—in a new form of desertification. Change caused by unGifted might not be as swift, but could be just as deep and devastating.

But the unGifted could react to major devastation caused by those with the Gift. They could rear back and destroy those who caused the devastation. It had happened before. It could happen again.

Something glittered in the darkened landscape and he froze and -reached- farther.

[Vallon?]

A Gifted came through Sikeston, the last major town north of New Madrid, but the bright flame was wrong. No ashes of roses to lead him on. Not her friend, anise-and-mint scented Fi Murdoch, either, though he and Snow surmised she had left out of pique and would return. This Gifted reeked of spice markets and wet earth and was coming closer, travelling the highway southward. They could just pass through, or they could turn away before New Madrid, like he had sensed one other had done about twelve hours into their search.

He stood there waiting, tracking the Gifted as they passed the last main turnoff to the next small town Northeastward, East Prairie. He pulled partially back to Snow.

"Someone comes in our direction down the main highway, I think. Someone perhaps you know?"

The little man got the telltale distant look in his eye, then he jerked back and shook his head. "Gleason. That can't be good. He wouldn't leave Amundson unwatched. It has to mean things have gone badly at the AGS."

"And what does that mean?"

Snow wouldn't meet his gaze and looked away eastward as the first rays of the sun found their way over the horizon. The blood red on Snow's features wasn't pretty, painting bleak age lines in stark relief and giving him the mask of something dead and incredibly hungry. A huge sigh escaped him and finally he shook himself and turned back to Xavier. Shadows hid the ravenous light Xavier had seen in his gaze so that Xavier almost doubted what he'd seen.

"It means that the Gifted have lost all control of the AGS. It means we may be running for our lives. It means I need to get to a computer." He started towards the Prius. "You can drop me at the house and then go meet them at the overpass into town."

Xavier shook his head and turned northward again, because something bothered him. He -reached- again, towards the town of East Prairie, but there was nothing there except the flickering low light of unGifted. All of his internal alarms, honed by years of tracking unsanctioned acts of power, jangled in his head. "You will greet them. There is something I must check."

Because suddenly that lone presence he had felt in the midst of the darkness of unGifted took on other significance. Especially now, when it apparently had disappeared.

CHAPTER 24 – INCANDESCENT

Vallon looked from the map on the table and back to her father. He stood like a predatory statue caught half in one of the spotlights that illuminated key parts of the war room, and reminded her far too much of Amundson. Yes, her father was much like the man who had stalked and eventually taken over the AGS. A little shiver ran through her and the too-scented cool air made her skin gooseflesh. No, maybe it wasn't just the cool air. There was something about this place, beyond the maps and stacks of paper and old tomes published by the Geological Survey. Something was wrong. Almost like whispers in the air.

She managed to pull herself back to her surroundings. She looked back at the map. "This is *Gild the Lily,* isn't it."

His expression sharpened. "Where did you hear that expression?"

"In a dream, actually. But Landon said it was a code for doing something bigger. Something that would put the Gifted higher up the food chain, shall we say."

"Snow." He shook his head, but his expression said he was hiding something. "He never could keep his mouth shut."

"He thought you were dead." And she had never known Landon Snow to give the full goods on anything. What had he left out? She looked back at the map again. "Bigger than the original New Madrid quake. Is that advisable? I mean, the level of devastation… the lost lives… the infrastructure destroyed. Are you sure you want to leave America in such a state? We'd be ripe for foreign takeover."

"Are you suggesting I haven't thought this through?" And a veil had come over his gaze, as if he doubted her support again.

"No! No, not at all. Just trying to understand your choices." Because something bigger than the original New Madrid—who knew what it could do? "Do you know what it will do? The whole central part of North America could come unzipped. It could create another super volcano like Yellowstone."

His lips tightened across his teeth. "*We* control what will happen, Vallon. That is part of being Gifted. It is also the part I need your help with."

"My help? Let me see if I've got this straight. You want me to make sure something *really* terrible doesn't happen." He nodded and she steeled herself. "I can do that."

"That's my girl." He wrapped an arm around her shoulder and suddenly he was the father she'd always dreamed he would be, smiling down at her, happy with her because she'd pleased him. She could almost believe in him when he was this way. Almost wanted to do more to please him.

She let him lead her out the door and found Toby waiting, clearly unGifted, in the glow of her father. He barely looked at Vallon, but gave a nod to her father.

"Good." He smiled down at her, his big hand large on her shoulder, and he actually squeezed her against him and he felt warm and smelled of marzipan and Christmas mornings. "Things are ready for you."

He led her down the curved hallway again, telling her about his plans for the future: how the landscape would be rebuilt into a Garden of Eden, how the Gifted would take their place in the world, and the face of the nation would be replaced—the government changed to one led by Gifted instead of the corporate lobby groups who currently corrupted the democratic process. She held her tongue from pointing out that he was talking about a dictatorship born out of the deaths of millions and that he was leaving America vulnerable to outside actions. A weakened America would be a prime target for aggression. It would destabilize the world order. She had to fight the shivering.

They reached the door that led into the core of the installation. Her father waved at a camera over the door and the door clicked and swung open onto another concrete wall, but released a puff of scent-filled air that would have sent her stumbling to her knees if not for her father's hold on her.

"It's like that the first time," he said. "Too much at once."

She blinked up at him and tried to make sense of the horrific, overwhelming sensations that came through her regular senses: sweat and whirring, iron-blood and pain, cut hay and cinnamon and painful whispers. Anise and mint and so much more she could not sort out from under the miasma of fear. "What is this place?" she managed to choke out.

"Our main installation," her father said and half led, half dragged her inside.

Every cell of her body wanted to turn and run, but she had to do this. She inhaled the muddy air and hauled herself upright. She would do this. She would. She had to find out just how he was doing this.

The concrete wall ended just over their heads, leaving many feet between it and the high steel girders of the ceiling. A maze? A trap? There were still no windows, and the feeling of smothering increased even though this was the largest space she'd been in. It took a moment for her to comprehend that the wall only stopped people from directly stepping into a single large room. Then they stepped past the wall.

A huge machine crouched in the center of the room like a carnival Octopus ride. Computers ranged around the room. White-coated men and women moved silently around the space and the place was hushed, almost as if she saw it through a window, except for the low whir and whispers that seemed to penetrate her flesh and bones. And there were beds. Ranks upon ranks of them ranged around the octopus contraption, all filled with men and women, some dressed in jeans and western shirts. An older woman wore a flowered dress. Nearest to her lay a young girl in shorts and a t-shirt, who must be no more than fifteen—the age when most Gifted began to realize their power.

"You must be wondering what all this is," her father said. He led her forward, his grip firmer on her arm.

She looked up at him, but she knew. The configuration of the people was too similar to what Rebecca Murdoch had done with the Gifted street people of Seattle. She had stolen their power from them like a leech drinks blood, a Gifted version of a succubus. As she studied it, the octopus installation reconfigured into eight dragonfly desks, all joined together so monstrously that her stomach churned. Around them spread a moat of what must be the largest map pit in creation. This was the AGS gone wrong. For the moment, at least, all the desks hung empty.

"Years ago we realized that it was possible for one Gifted to add their power to another. It's why the AGS prefers to send agents out in teams, but that doesn't begin to get at the power potential of Gifted working together."

He led her into the room towards the ranks of beds and their unmoving occupants. So many. "These are local people, aren't they? The local Gifted. I knew New Madrid was strange for having so few people with even a partial Gift."

Her father turned his proud smile on her again and her skin crawled.

"Right you are. We harvested the partially Gifted to augment our power."

Harvested. She tasted bile and had to fight the urge to retch. All these people like cotton bolls or stalks of corn taken from those parched fields. They wended their way through the comatose figures now. IV lines ran from poles above the beds, amber fluid dripping down tubes that ran down to needles taped into their arms. Weird wire mesh caps covered the tops of their heads.

"How long have they been here?" Then she held up her hand. "At least since before the first quake, right? That's over a week." At least. It would have taken a while to collect all the Gifted and partially Gifted from the area and do it in a manner that would stop the unGifted from noticing it. Her gaze caught on a thatch of red hair and the curve of a nose that looked familiar.

"Drew? Drew Libernaum?" She pulled away from her father and trailed between the beds to look down at the red-haired man.

"It is." She swung back to her father and almost stumbled from the surge of adrenaline. "What's he doing here? He's an AGS agent."

Her father calmly met her gaze and then glanced down at the comatose man. Drew was one of those uncommon redheads that did not have alabaster skin. Instead, a smattering of freckles crossed sun-golden nose and cheekbones. His eyes were closed, but not enough to completely cover the whites of his rolled back eyes. The wire mesh on his head half hid in his hair and cut across his golden forehead like a macabre crown.

"Does it bother you to see him here?"

Careful Vallon. "I'm just surprised, is all. That he'd agree to be here."

She felt his study like a heat on her skin. Behind him stood Toby, like a silent guard. "Your Mr. Libernaum was assigned to New Madrid. We could not very well leave him to call in the cavalry—not that it would have made any difference. We brought all three AGS agents in. Their talents might as well be put to some use."

Three agents. Her gaze skittered across the crowned bodies. If Morgan Hoptaler had been one of the agents, then he had been brought in here. The fact he was wandering New Madrid as a burned-out husk of himself did not bode well for the people lying in this room. She swallowed. "I suppose that makes sense. How long do you plan on keeping them here?"

She let herself be drawn away from Drew's side and on towards the odd, crouching bouquet of dragonfly desks. The multi-headed metal creature turned her stomach.

"Not much longer," he said. "We're almost ready to go."

The reek of heated metal filled her nose and she studied the mutant dragonfly configuration. "So you use the sleepers' power to fuel the agents in the desks. Is that why I'm here? To fill one of the desks?"

If it was, she wasn't sure she could actually make herself climb into one of the seats.

The sharp jab into her neck sent her reeling sideways. Ice flooded through her veins and sent her knees sagging. She half turned towards her father, but he wasn't there. Instead it was Toby, with his boyish good looks stepping back with an empty syringe in his hand. Her father stood beyond him, his expression bland. She had her answer.

"Why? I would have helped…" she asked, her voice disembodied, her lips barely managing the words as the ability to breathe was stolen from her. The afterburn from the attack that had brought her here incandesced like phosphorus. Her knees gave, but she could barely feel it as she sagged against one of the occupied beds, fighting for breath. She was strangling, dying.

Toby grabbed her arm to stop her fall, but his touch was worse than a scald. She tried to bat him away, but her hands were gross flippers she couldn't control. Her legs jellied under her and she started to fall, to the floor, down a long tunnel.

"I thought I would give you a chance to prove yourself. One as powerful as you could be an important asset to our cause. But you never were a good liar, Vallon. Not as a child. Not now."

The words followed her into the darkness.

§

Jason jerked upright once more and rolled down the car window so the wind blew cool in his face. Better than the sullen air inside. That and the hum of the car engine on this apparently unendingly straight highway was enough to put Jason at the dangerous edge of sleep. It had captured his companion. In the barely-there first light of early morning that placed gangrene-colored streaks on the horizon, Gregor Gleason slumped against the passenger window like a man already dead. His chest rose and fell so slowly, you could think he wasn't breathing. His skin was truly the color of ash and sagged around his lips and neck, so his large bald head could have been melting.

He'd more or less acted like he was almost dead, too.

"Not quite the in-your-face head of the AGS anymore, are you, bud?"

Gleason's gaze flickered open and went once to Jason, then out the window to the flattened landscape still caught in darkness. Stunted fields of corn stretched as far as he could see on either side of the highway, beyond the darkened truck stops that only boded ill for the economy of this part of the country. Gleason groaned and sat up—or maybe it was the seat that groaned.

"Where are we?"

His strength had gradually faded into an old man's voice, complete with tremor, that just didn't fit with the man who had gone toe-to-toe with Jason and won only a few months ago. Just what the hell had they done to Gleason, anyway? Could blood loss cause such a complete change? But Jason had changed a lot since then, too. Hell, he was probably a wanted man, now.

"Getting close to New Madrid. It should be the next exit." He motioned to a paper cup of coffee in the cup holder. "I bought it for you at the last gas station. Thought caffeine might help keep us going. It's probably cold by now."

"And I suppose you used a credit card to pay for the gas." Gleason's voice was stronger now. He'd straightened in his seat and was studying the landscape.

"Nope. Cash. We left enough of a trail at the airport and renting the car." Because Amundson would be coming for them, there was no question about that.

The dawn progressed, and they got closer to Vallon, the new sun sending apricot streamers into the fading sky. A lone bird flew overhead—an egret or something awkward looking—towards a band of trees that turned green in the sunlight. The wind smelled of dust and murky water that made him think of darkness and almost dying in the Seattle tunnels. He shivered as the sun lifted over the horizon and light fell on the flattened landscape like a hammer.

"Whoa." He fumbled for sunglasses and pulled down the visor as a road sign advertised *New Madrid Next Exit*.

He pointed the car into the off ramp and up and over the highway, where a small blue Prius was parked at the New Madrid end of the overpass. A figure slid out of the open door. Short. Incandescent white in the morning sunlight.

"Stop the car," Gleason commanded as he leaned forward.

"Who is it?" Jason asked.

"Landon Snow. Another agent."

Landon Snow. Jason remembered him wheeling Vallon for a visit when both Jason and Vallon were in the hospital, but the pain drugs had kept Jason mostly out of it. He pulled over and shut off the car and the little man approached and peered in Jason's window. He barely glanced at Jason.

"Thank God you're here. They've got Vallon. We're pretty sure it's Drake. We've been searching the area for the past day and a half but no luck in finding her."

"Damn," Gleason said. He shoved open his door and clambered out, still moving like an ancient. Jason scrambled to join them, his tired joints popping after the long drive.

Snow's gaze widened at the ex AGS Chief. "What happened to you?"

"Amundson. When he realized you and Vallon were gone, he hauled me in." The big man shrugged. "I'll recover. The sleep has helped." He nodded at Jason. "He got me out."

Jason stuck out his hand. "Jason Bryson, Seattle P.D.—probably ex." It kinda hurt to say it. "You're Landon Snow. Vallon spoke of you."

"Ah, yes. The policeman who—ah—helped her." The little man looked him up and down before sharing an almost effete, moist hand. Not surprising given he wore a suit like fucking Colonel Saunders. But Vallon had obviously confided their relationship to him. Still, there were calculations in the little man's eyes, the kind you saw in suspect's gazes. Nope, he wasn't going to trust this one as far as he could throw him. The only surprise was that Vallon did.

"So what's the plan?" Jason asked. "And who's Drake?" Because it couldn't be a coincidence that Drake was also Vallon's last name.

Landon just turned to Gleason. "Vallon became convinced that her father was alive and that he was responsible for what has happened in New Madrid. We tried to dissuade her, but she just up and went."

"We?" Gleason and Jason both spoke in unison.

"Xavier de Varga—the foreigner Vallon spoke of meeting in Seattle. He showed up here and the two of them picked up where they left off, but even he cannot find her now. It's like she has never been here. The whole town is like no Gifted has ever stepped foot in the place." He shook his head in an odd wooden movement like a ventriloquist's dummy. "It is the strangest thing I have ever seen."

De Varga was here. Jason almost felt weak. Just how had the man gone from the vague hint that Vallon had gone east to beating Jason here?

"You're sure de Varga isn't the one responsible for Vallon's disappearance?" He wouldn't put it past him. The man was a menace, at least to Jason's plans.

Snow did that little head waggle again. "He was with me all night searching. I don't think he is the kind to feign emotions, and he was quite distraught."

"Yeah? So why isn't he here?" The little guy might be smart, but he wasn't a trained investigator. "In an awful lot of crimes you need to look close to home for the perpetrator."

Snow's gaze went cool and calculating. "I appreciate that there may be *challenges* between you and Mr. de Varga, but I can assure you he was not involved in her disappearance. Or I do not believe so. There have been several attacks on Agent Drake since she arrived in New Madrid."

"Of what sort?" Gleason asked.

Snow described scenarios that would have sounded farfetched with details about earthquakes and blasts up out of the earth, if he hadn't seen the weird shit he *had* seen since he'd met Vallon. He found Snow watching him.

"You seem quite comfortable with the odd events Agent Drake becomes involved in, Officer Bryson."

Jason shrugged, but weighed what he should disclose. "I saw some strange things when I helped Vallon in Seattle."

"He's an anomaly of some sort, Landon. He's unGifted, but he knows things. He remembers change," Gleason said.

Snow's gaze had turned from general calculation to downright interest. "Now that is a talent, indeed."

So much for playing his cards close to his chest. Jason shrugged uneasily. "Just lucky, I guess. It doesn't seem to exactly have a lot of uses."

"Except Amundson had him."

Snow closed his pale blue eyes and suddenly he was just a diminutive little man in a cut down version of a larger man's suit. "That is not good. It's good you got free and brought him to me."

"Whoa, there." Jason held up his hands. "I came to find Vallon, not be someone else's guinea pig. So I'll ask again, what's the game plan and is it always this fucking hot here?"

Because the sun had risen and burned away all the cool night air, leaving behind a heating furnace that just reflected hotter off of the road. The highway he'd driven down was a line of heat haze that got lost in a distance that looked like just more of the same. Small copses of trees looked half-dead and grimed with dust. Dust rose in small wind funnels over the dry fields. In a place like this you could wish for one of Seattle's winter rain storms. He wished he still had some of the poor excuse for coffee he'd bought earlier.

"If you will follow me, we can get out of the heat at our guest house. De Varga will likely meet us there. He said he had to check something out, but would be back soon."

So Snow climbed in his Prius—somehow the car suited him, built low to the ground and not quite normal. Jason and Gleason returned to their rental.

"I take it you've worked with him a long time," Jason asked, trying to keep his voice casual.

"From the beginning. He was there at the start of the AGS. Why do you ask?" Gleason gazed out at the decrepit little town they passed through. The place looked like it was on virtual life support—at least at this end of town.

"Just wondering if I should trust him." He grinned over at the big man. "Of course, that begs the question of whether I trust you."

"We worked together to get away from Amundson."

He had Gleason's attention now. The big man looked at him, his hoary brows twitching like they had a life of their own. So he wasn't real happy with Jason's line of questioning. Good. Put the guy on notice.

"Yeah, but that was to both our advantage. I'm just not sure we both want the same thing for Vallon." Actually he was totally sure they didn't, because he could be pretty sure these guys wouldn't approve of his proposition for Vallon any more than she would. It was all going to be in the way he asked it and what he could do to convince her she had no choice.

Gleason considered that for a moment. "I think it's safe to say that neither Landon nor I want her held by her father. He wasn't good for her when she was a child. I can't imagine he'd have her best interests at heart now. Francis Drake was always a man who wanted what he wanted and would do anything to get it." He sighed and looked almost as exhausted as he had in Seattle. "He's had so many years to advance his agenda, apparently right under the noses of the AGS. He had to have had a lot of help to do that, and I doubt the 'help' is exactly our friends."

"You really didn't know he was alive?" Jason asked as they followed the Prius into a nicer neighborhood of low-slung ranchers hunkered down under the sun's weight.

Gleason shook his head. "I hoped he was dead. He and the others." He studied his big old hands. "I was a fool. I should have followed up and checked at the time. It took the Seattle debacle to prove they've been hiding out all these years."

A two-story house loomed down the block and Snow pulled into the driveway. Jason pulled up to the curb. The house baked in the morning sunlight, but a porch along the front of the house, its rails festooned with overflowing geraniums, offered blessed shade. The low hum of an air conditioner beckoned and a whiff of chlorine hinted a pool might be in the offing. In the driveway sat a large black suburban. It had to be de Varga's vehicle.

Even if the man was here to help, Jason didn't have to like it.

CHAPTER 25 – LIKE SLIPPERY SILK

The rain pounded at the window sills of the brown ranch-style house, and fractured the afternoon light so the room seemed filled with liquid flowing down the walls. Six-year-old Vallon knelt in the middle of the grey living room carpet, a towel pressed hard into the plush pile, praying it would sop up the cherry soda she'd accidently spilled, and listening for sounds from down the hall. If she could just get this cleaned up before her father left his office, he would never have to know.

She pulled up the towel and the rich red of the soda clung to the carpet fibers.

"No..." The small moan escaped her and she ran for the kitchen, poured some water into a glass and ran back to the carpet. Maybe she could dilute it and then sop up the water. She carefully poured the water over the spot and the bright red faded, but spread farther into the grey tufts.

"No. No. No!" Pressed the towel down, hard, but the towel was sopping wet now and dripping pink liquid onto the carpet. She juggled it back to the kitchen, and claimed the other dishtowel, but when she returned to the living room, a clear trail of pink spots showed where she'd been. She crawled along her back trail, scrubbing the worst of the spots away, but the big spot sat waiting, taunting her.

"Please. Please. Please." She pressed the towel down onto the mark, folded the towel, and then pressed again. Again.

It was looking better. It was going to be okay. She sat back on her heels and considered. If only it had the chance to dry he might not notice, but wet like this he definitely would. She glanced wistfully at the coffee table. He'd notice if she moved it. He hated if she left her things on the floor, but maybe she could leave something there to cover it until the spot was dry. She grabbed Rusty, the red stuffed cat Landon had won for her at the carnival that had set up in the Safeway parking lot. Landon was a neat guy, so different than anyone she'd ever met. He took her places her father was always too busy to go, and he really talked and listened to her, like she was special.

"You'll fix it, won't you, Rusty? All you gotta do is stay here and guard this spot until the carpet's dry. Okay?"

Rusty didn't say anything, just looked at her from his amber marble eyes, his plastic whiskers bristling around a black plastic nose. But he had the cutest smile and cute round ears and a long tail that curled just perfectly around her neck when she put him on her shoulder. She ran her fingers through his soft plush fur and settled him on the carpet.

Then she crept down the hall to her room. Maybe Daddy wouldn't see her and she could say she'd been in her room all afternoon, instead of going into the kitchen for a drink and then doing exactly the thing Daddy said never to do and taking her drink into the living room. She swallowed and slowed as she neared the open door to his office. Daddy was talking. He must be on the phone. When he talked on the phone he usually sat with his feet up on his desk, facing the door. He would see her.

She huddled there, not sure what to do. Too wet to go outside. She didn't dare be found in the living room, and her bedroom was so close, but might as well be all the way down by the ocean—too far to walk.

"I'm telling you, everything's fine. I don't care if there's been strange men seen around." Daddy didn't sound happy. As a matter of fact he sounded angry, and an angry Daddy was always better off avoided. When he was angry, she always tried to stay in her room unless Landon came to get her, like he often did.

"I'm telling you, Gild the Lily is going just fine. She's growing up strong and obedient, just like she's supposed to. They aren't going to put two and two together. Too much time has passed."

Silence again and his feet thumped on the floor. Another sign she should be in her room, and that he was unhappy. Daddy yelled when he wasn't happy. Sometimes he slapped her and sometimes that felt better than all the times he ignored her. Maybe she should just walk past like nothing was wrong. Yes, that was what she'd do. She's be extra brave and just walk past the door and into her room like nothing was wrong at all.

She stood up.

"Landon, why all the questions? Nothing's going to happen. It's all going just the way you planned. Now relax and let's get on with things. All right?" He paused and Vallon took a deep breath and stepped past the doorframe, glanced into the room and waved and then ran to her room and closed the door as softly as she could behind her. Leaned up against it and tried to stop the shaking.

That was where he found her fifteen minutes later and dragged her back to the living room where Rusty's red fur dye had run all into the sopping carpet.

Vallon jerked awake with the distant memory of furious words, of an unbeatable hold on her arms, and the terrifying feeling of being unable to run, to talk, to move as her father had held her so tight as he yelled at her and shook her. She remembered it now. Remembered being sent to her room with no dinner and no breakfast the next morning until Landon showed up at recess at school with a perfectly folded brown paper bag with a tuna fish sandwich and homemade peanut butter cookies and a bright red apple for her. Far better than her father ever packed for her. Daddy usually put baloney and mustard together even though she'd told him she didn't like mustard.

God, it was all so long ago. A lifetime ago and she'd been so small and felt so vulnerable, eavesdropping on her father as he talked about *Gild the Lily*. So she had heard the phrase before it came up in her dreams in Seattle. This must be where it came from.

She tried to rub the sleep out of her eyes, but nothing happened. Her hand didn't move. Tried to roll sideways and that didn't happen, either.

"She's coming out of it," someone said and her eyes flashed open.

That she could do. She looked up at something off-white and indistinct that soon came into focus as concrete and girders. Something large and metal-colored filled the edge of her vision, but she couldn't turn her head to see what. A weight like a crown of thorns rest on her head. What was happening? Was she paralyzed? She -reached- and this time the barrier that had stopped her before was gone. The world around her exploded into a conflagration of brilliant flames, and suddenly it all came back to her. She knew where she was. That horrible room. That horrible place run by the horrible man who was her father.

She could have screamed except just breathing took all her energy.

Something stirred lower down by where her body should be and then Francis Drake stepped into her field of vision.

"Hello, Vallon. I'm glad to see you're with us. Sometimes the drugs don't sit well in a body."

A body? Was that all she was to him? A body?

Stop it. Just stop it. You knew you were nothing to him. You knew. You've always known. That's how he could leave you.

Breathing came a little bit harder as she tried to hide her hatred. Her heart beat faster and she wanted to scream. Wanted to hit him for all of the pain he'd caused her growing up alone in that house with him. And now she understood she'd known about *Gild the Lily* all her life. Her father had always been plotting to leave her.

"You probably want to know what we're doing to you." He smiled down at her, and it wasn't a good smile. Had never been a real smile. It was a smile because social conventions required it. "You see, daughter, we need the Gifted for power. You, I can't trust to implement our plans. You've tried too hard to stop them already. But there is one thing you bring that no one else here has, and that is your power. You have a talent, one that gets even your friend Landon excited, and I intend to harness it. So here is the way things work."

He leaned over her so she gagged on his almond scent and glared up at him. "You will feel a tug and be forced out of your body as if you had -reached-. You will obey and you will allow the Agents controlling your power to do what needs to be done." His hand smoothed her hair off her forehead and he leaned in closer. "Now here is the part you must listen closely to. We know about your power and so we will monitor you closely. You have been injected with a curare derivative that paralyzes your nervous system. This tube provides a bare minimum of antidote to allow you to breathe. Should you misbehave, we can easily stop the flow, like this."

He pulled the tube into her view and rolled the drip closed. Almost immediately it became harder to breathe. Then her chest stopped moving and she smothered. Oxygen depleted in her veins. Sparks formed in her vision. Her limbs tingled. Her field of view darkened and she needed air. By all creation, she needed air!

Her last sight as she started to black out was her father's fingers moving. Suddenly oxygen flooded in. The soft sound of her breathing was the most blessed sound in the world. She glared up at him. She would find him and kill him. She would. And not just for her. For all the other Gifted trapped here. For all the people who would die in the cataclysm to come. She thought of little Farrah Ducharme and her comforting doll. Children like that would be the victims, just like her father had victimized her. She would *not* let that happen.

But her father leaned in close enough she could see the spittle on his teeth. "Do we understand each other, Vallon? No tricks. We can pull the plug on you easily enough, but you might think we can't afford to kill you. That would be true. So try anything and we will stop the drug flow to some of the people in this room. You will be responsible for their deaths. Blink if you understand me."

She blinked and hated herself. Hated the view of the ceiling, his face, and hated him more as he disappeared from her bedside.

She'd been a fool to come here, just as Xavier and Landon had counseled. But her memory suggested Landon was somehow involved. It just didn't make sense, but maybe it did. Landon had never been above using cheap, reverse-psychology tricks on her to get what he wanted. Just what had been said in that long ago conversation when he'd revealed the meaning of *Gild the Lily*?

The memory slipped from her grasp like a newly caught fish. She'd almost have it one moment, and then the next it had slipped away again. Something about *Gild the Lily* and Landon knew. But the conversation hadn't been about power and destroying the American infrastructure. She almost had the conversation regarding *Gild the Lily* in her grasp when the scent of ozone and the purr of machinery said that something was happening. The peripherally-seen stanchion swung more firmly into view, lifting higher until she could see the bottom of one of the heads of the medusa dragonfly desk. She closed her eyes.

A surge of power ripped her up from her body and she flailed mentally, even though it was not much different than her own seeking. But that had been under her control. She fought against the pressure that shoved her, disembodied, above the room. Below her the beds and bodies spread out in concentric circles from the map pit and the central machine. The map showed continental United States, with the machine centered above what could only be the New Madrid fault, and the air filled with the ozone and ether-scent of the Gift in use.

The air vibrated with the cinnamon, apple, blackberry, winter ice, cut hay, old socks, wet earth scents of the Gifted around her. And so many more. Frantic. Buzzing. They didn't know what was happening, only that it was. Only that they were prisoners and someone had ripped them free from the only safe place in the world—their bodies.

[*Stay calm,*] she sent. [*I will help you.*] She just needed to figure out how.

A whiff of anise and mint floated past and the scent was one she knew too well.

[*Fi!?*]

A panicked presence. Fear as large as life.

[*Fi, no. It's me.*] She tried to catch the flickering presence of her friend, who was trapped somewhere below. How she came to be here wasn't clear: probably her father's men catching the last Gifted they could find, and Fi unfortunate enough to stop for gas before she escaped from a friend who had used her. All Vallon's conviction that it had been for Fi's own good had been a lie, just as her father's belief that the Gifted could do a better job running the world was a lie. People were too flawed. Either way they'd screw it up, just like she'd messed everything up with Fi.

The anise and mint stopped its frantic hummingbird flight and slipped against her as fine as silk.

[*Vallon?*] Slow, cautious.

[*Me.*]

A flood of relief that wasn't Vallon's. Fear slowly replaced by hope.

The ozone scent increased in the room and frantic stirring of the trapped Gifted presences became a vortex. And then Fi ripped away and they shot like lasers down through the map and into the rough sediments that made up the New Madrid fault.

§

As Xavier vibrated back into existence the earth and air felt heated around him. He stepped naked from the earth at the back of an abandoned New Madrid home next to the cache of clothes he had left behind, before returning to the Guesthouse to meet with Gleason and Landon. He quickly donned his dark jeans and shirt. Too hot by far for this humid climate, but it was what he always wore and he was not about to change now. He had endured worse. He would likely endure far worse in the future. He crossed to the gate and let himself out, swiftly striding down the road towards the rendezvous at the guesthouse. At least he had news now. Something to go on.

He was one of the few of his kind who had reclaimed the power to use the old way of transiting through the earth's ley lines, but that didn't mean he hadn't placed himself in danger by using the process to get what he needed. The Council would know he was gone by now and Leticia would be out for his blood. They would know he was refusing to answer their calls through the ley lines, and they would use the disturbance of his transit in the ley lines to track him. But to find Vallon he had risked it, and he would do so again if necessary.

Twenty minutes of walking and his hair and clothes were damp from the humidity and heat. He climbed the stairs to the Ducharme guesthouse and already knew what he would find. He did not wait for the doorbell to be answered, but simply entered. Elizabeth Ducharme and her child were in the kitchen. Male voices and the tinkling of ice cubes came from the oddly decorated living room, and three faces looked up at him. Two, he knew, and he crossed to the newcomer.

"I am Xavier de Varga, and you are the chief of Vallon Drake." He offered his hand.

The bald-headed man unfolded his legs to stand and look Xavier eye-to-eye, but his aura and the shadows in the man's eyes showed deep depletion almost as if....

"They have bled you." Xavier recoiled from the memory of the experience.

"Gregor Gleason." The tall, desiccated man said as he held out his hand. He held the Gift, but so small an amount in Xavier's world it would barely be counted. "And it was two days ago. It's getting better."

Xavier inclined his head in greeting, then turned to the other newcomer in the room and pasted an amiable smile on his lips. "Bryson. What took you so long?"

The good detective's face colored. "I could ask you the same. Just how did you figure out where she was?"

Xavier looked away to the chirping canaries. He hated to see anything wild kept in a cage. It was unnatural and led to early death. Living with the rules of the Council all these years, he could understand the long-standing nature of dying. It was something none of these men ever would—except perhaps the albino.

"Vallon and I connect on many levels. There was a moment when I felt her presence. I followed, and so I am here before you."

His explanation clearly didn't satisfy the detective, and that was too bad for him. The other two, though, considered him with suspicion. "Before you ask questions, perhaps I should tell you what I have found.

"When Snow and I noticed your approach to New Madrid, it put me in mind of another Gifted I sensed when Vallon first disappeared. That one did not come to New Madrid, so I discounted it, but then I thought there are no Gifted left in this county or surrounding areas. It made me question who was this Gifted I had sensed. So I travelled north to where I had felt him or her. They were not there, gone—disappeared like Vallon, and yet—there was a feeling like lightning in the air and yet I could not put my finger on it."

He closed his eyes, remembering: a feeling like silk slippery across the skin, the smell of almonds, mint, and spices like a north African market, bright flashes in his optic centers like fireworks or streetlight reflected in Vallon's dark gaze. When he opened his eyes the men were all looking at him.

"It was very powerful, this feeling of things happening. The earth itself vibrated, but I could not sense from where. I thought perhaps together we might determine the source through, how do you call it? Triangulation?"

The small white man and Gleason looked at each other. As if rehearsed, they stood up together.

"Hold on a minute, here. Just what are you talking about—lightning in the air. What does that mean?" the detective asked.

"We do not have time to explain." He caught the wrists of Gleason and Snow and felt the little man's attempt to slide inside Xavier's mind. A simple block kept him out, but it was a surprise to find the little man could do it, given he had no talent to speak of. An anomaly the Council would be interested in, no doubt.

"I will show you what I felt. I suggest we each physically go to different points: one on the highway. One near the river. I will return to the north where I sensed that other. Then we will each -reach- for a certain sensation I will show you. Together we can triangulate our Vallon's position, no?"

He sent the image flowing into them and felt them stagger at his presence. When he released their wrists, both men took a step back. Fear and respect mixed on Gleason's face. Snow's gaze held only further calculation.

"And just what the hell am I supposed to do?" demanded the detective.

Xavier shook his head. "What you think will help. Perhaps have a vehicle handy and come when called." He glanced at Gleason and Snow, then tossed his vehicle keys to Bryson. "I have no need of it."

Xavier swung on his heel and strode out the door and upstairs to the room he had shared with Vallon. He stripped off his clothes and was gone, following the ley lines towards her again.

He hoped.

CHAPTER 26 —A WRENCH OF EARTH AND ROSES

The power dragged Vallon down through flood plains mud, heavy with rich silt that sifted through her essence. The voices of the other Gifted prisoners rustled in terrified whispers around her. Her essence rippled loose like baker's flour and she could be blown away on the wind. Down through the layers pressed solid as rock, her presence, and the others, strained painfully through the sediment. Moans like the wind. The scent of fear mixed with their identifying mélange. Dragged lower, inexorably, towards the broken layers of earth and stone and the rich gleam of ley lines deep below the earth's surface. If they got there, they would start the quake.

If they needed her power to make it work, she had to get away.

She strained to get loose, but her sifted parts would not obey. The flow of power was like a net and she a billion minnows caught in its grasp, mixed with the billion-trillion particles of the other trapped Gifted. They were held, twisting and inert as power poured from them, feeding the agents on the desks.

She felt them, like a school of salmon might feel the presence of the killer whales. Something predatory and circling, herding them down, controlling their passage, and she had no will to stop it, to dart away and escape, to do anything but flow with all the billion other fishes the way she was told.

No. She would not. She was *Vallon*, not some mindless salmon running. She had never followed orders without agreeing with them. She had training. She had fought Rebecca Murdoch and *won*!

She pulled inwards and stopped. The fleeing presences of the others crashed into her, dragging her with them. *Become one.* As one, she would be herself and be strong. *Build up a barrier. Don't let them do this.* How had she stopped Rebecca Murdoch when she was trapped before? Somewhere far away, heat formed on her forehead. The wire crown resisted her resistance.

"Vallon," her father's voice split her attention: back to her body while her essence still ripped through the substrate of broken rock and shale.

"Vallon, you try anything more and this is what happens."

Through the multitude's whispers and moans flared a terrified scream that grew stronger, more frantic, and then weakened and was gone.

"That was your friend Drew. Next will be your friend Fi. Yes, we know who she is. Think carefully before you try anything."

Then he was gone, leaving her shocked and falling apart like a sand castle in the desk agents' wind. She flowed.

But she had to do something. Slowly, like sediments congealing, she dragged her essence back together again. She became *one* amongst the crashing kaleidoscope of the frantic many. If she could not simply pull loose without risking the others, then she would have to find another way.

The ozone burned. Lightning crackled across her thoughts and, around her, other sparks and candles filled the darkness like fireflies as their captors fed from them.

They were deep now, flowing through the innumerable cracks in the stone. That was the difficulty with New Madrid. Unlike the fault lines along the west coast that allowed, if not predictable, then at least comprehensible movement of the tectonic plates, here the mishmash of fractures left an uneasy peace of broken stone that, if disturbed, could set off a chain reaction up and down the fault that no one could predict.

A sudden cold darkness spread below them. Water. Shifting, but slow. They skimmed its broad surface and were herded lower, down to the golden, rose-scented reaches of ley lines flowing like fiery veins through the earth's crust. The scent of licorice almost burned out her senses. She stopped, and the maelstrom of others stopped around her. Power pulsed like lightning as her father's people siphoned power up from the flowing ley lines. They sent it surging out through the churning mass of broken Gifted, heat, burning. It sent their myriad pieces spreading like molecules, out through the stone, spreading their heat, their fear like a furnace, the stone heating, turning white hot and steaming.

Steam.

The underground lake lay cold, dark, and echoing with the sound of eyeless creatures creeping and living out their lives with no sight of the sun. It was no longer cold. Instead, its creatures stirred uncomfortably. Vapors stirred across its surface. Steam rose into the cracks of cold stone, and in turn the voids in the stone spread further. The rock groaned, and suddenly she understood.

This was how they would do it. This was how the somnolent New Madrid fault would be woken to devastate America from within. The stone of New Madrid did not come in solid sheets of granite. Instead it came in shattered layers, and all those fissures provided a place for steam to destabilize everything. The quake would run up and down the Mississippi River Valley. It would send out shock waves large enough to set off other weakened faults in the northeast, and would travel outward farther and farther. With more steam, it was possible the shock waves could even reach the west coast and set off the San Andreas and other Pacific faults.

The whole country could be in ruins. And who, then, would come to the aid of a country that had been the source of aid for the rest of the world?

The magnitude of the consequences left her hanging in the depths, as the pulse and push of the agents stole power from her, cycled it through the ley lines, and poured power out into her, into the others. The heat rose and, on her bed, her bones ached. Her fever rose. A bead of sweat ran down her brow and along her nose.

She had to do something, but would not risk Fi. Not after what Fi had done for her, and not after all that Fi had been through. She'd grown strong enough to stand up to Vallon. Even though Vallon told herself that the cycling had actually *helped* Fi, Vallon knew that her motives for involving Fi in everything had really been selfish. And she had gotten Fi into this situation, lost along with the rest of the nation unless Vallon could come up with something.

The earth rumbled around her and the steam seared her through. Stone and earth shifted and ground against stone in an uneasy awakening, and she thought of the ancient stories of Krakens waking. The stink of mud and heated stone were so pungent she thought she might never smell anything else again. Each tiny crack and fissure swelled with darkened steam, and the rock groaned and shifted and shifted again, each tiny movement enlarging the next. The fall of a single grain of sand would lead to the devastation of the United States.

Something had to be done, and she could think of only one option.

If Fi was just seen as another of the Gifted and not monitored. *If* she could find Fi. *If* she could convince her to help one more time. Maybe there was something they could do. The earth's groans turned to rumbles, and suddenly the sediment collapsed around her.

The earth lurched. The steam-filled fissures exploded outwards from the searing steam and then collapsed inward. New cracks formed. Sand and water formed hot mud and shoved upwards. The earth lurched again. She tried to rip loose, but her father's agents kept her tethered like a goose. They dragged on the ley line and fed on her to channel the power outward, to destabilize everything.

[*Fi!*]

No one would hear in the maelstrom of falling stone and shifting water and mud. The sundering of stone was like bone breaking.

[*Fi!*]

A whiff of anise and mint. [*Vallon?*] A whisper distant and yet close, her essence dispersed over many miles of earth.

[*Let me help you.*] Fi's anise scent increased. [*You have to pull yourself back together. Don't let them spread you so far.*] Fi was a ghost so ephemeral no one would see her at all, her molecules so spread she was lost in the space between them. [*Like this.*]

She showed Fi how to fight back the fear, to stop letting her father's men send her floundering through the soil, adding to the already growing quake. Grab the pressure building in the stone. Use it to force herself back together, a diamond of will, even as New Madrid shook.

Vallon -reached- and split her awareness, felt houses sway, heard their timber crack and rumble. A fire started at the diner across from the Bijou Theatre and people tumbled out of their houses and stores and into the streets. Pressure sent sand and water upwards, to explode through the fields in dirty geysers.

Cracks spread through the fields. Roads split, one side of the concrete falling into a sinkhole, another part rising. The stands of trees rippled, their tops like waves in water, and flocks of birds darkened the sky, silent and whirling, crows dancing with sparrows, hawks with egrets. Then they wheeled and headed southward, seeking safety. It would not help them. The fracturing fault followed.

She came back to herself, caught in her father's web. Fi swirled around her, not complete, but her anise and mint so much stronger.

[*Fi, you have to help. They have me guarded. If I try anything, they'll kill you. But I don't think you're guarded. You need to turn the power against them.*] Please let her understand. Please let her try.

The quake spread outward in great concentric waves. St. Louis rocked; its huge Gateway Arch swayed. Another jolt and the foundations of One Metropolitan Square, St. Louis's tallest building, crumbled. The tower leaned, leaned farther, and slid towards the ground. The famous archway split and smashed into the Mississippi River, the resultant wave washing away the vehicles and people who had fled to safety along the water.

[*How? I don't know how. I'm not you, Vallon.*]

[*You went to school. You remember how.*]

A sensation of fear spiked the mint scent.

[*Like this.*] Vallon enveloped Fi. Allowed her father's people to force the ley line's power into her, used their force against them to send her pouring outward, but chose her own path. [*Where are we? Do you know where we are?*]

[*Sort of. It was dark and wet. There was water. We went underground.*]

Underground? That made no sense. How could her father ever plan to survive the quake in an underground installation? He must have safeguards. Or the supreme confidence that he and his people could fix anything that went wrong with the Gift. That sounded like her father. But it didn't mean he'd be prepared for something more.

Like attack.

[*Show me.*]

Fi's contact withdrew, but there was something different about it. Something like grit covered her friend's usually soft exterior. The whirling presence that was Fi used the pressure to flee up through the stone, up through soft earth and soil and the pale white ever-searching roots of growing things to the base of a huge, basin-shaped concrete structure and beyond, up into sunshine.

Trees in all directions. And water. The power of her father's people ripped her out of the air and back down into earth. Her father's voice rose. "That's one too many, Vallon."

[*Fi!*] she screamed with her mind.

But Fi wasn't there. Instead, the earth fractured around Vallon. The darkness roared and she was thrown out into the earth on the edge of a shockwave. She was heat and anger, shredding through the uneasy soil, destroying millennia-old equilibrium, sending rock shifting, rolling, breaking the North American plate apart into fissures that threatened to allow magma to explode upwards. Steam and poisoned gases reached the surface. Cities fell. Towns were mowed under when the land rolled like a wave. Outward, westward, towards the mountains. Northwestward towards Yellowstone. What was her father doing? Release the Yellowstone mega volcano, and who knew if anyone had the power to stop it from causing another ice age.

She fought to free herself, but it was no use. Her father's people focused on *her*. She had failed. Had failed in so many ways. Had caused Drew's death. And Fi's, and was going to help cause the deaths of so many more.

A sharp jolt of her body sent her eyelids flashing open, her awareness torn: smothering darkness of stone and water; a grey-white ceiling, and wildly swinging octopus stanchion. She fought the weird overlay of perception. The force still thrust her through the heated soil outward, spread ever thinner in ever expanding circles until she felt like a membrane about to burst. Outwards, while cities fell and foundations crumbled. People screamed and the flare of their life forces failed. The entire United States crumbled, and she helped cause it.

Another wrench brought her back to the swinging octopus stanchion, a dragonfly desk coming into view. A man worked franticly over the console she knew was there. The stench of heated wiring curdled her nostrils. Something. Shouting, the sound of footsteps running.

Another wrench and the desk swung dangerously lower. Overhead, a maze of cracks cut through the ceiling.

"You!" her father's face cut off the view. "What are you doing?"

She couldn't deny it was her, even though it wasn't. Was he going to cut off her breathing?

The room wrenched again, and the ceiling shuddered and so did her bed. Her father stumbled away and her useless hand fell off the bedside. Another wrench and she might fall, too.

Her father scrambled back to her. He leaned in so close his almond scent smothered the burning-wire scent in the air.

"What. Are. You. Doing?" he said through clenched teeth. A vein pulsed in his temple. Another pulsed in his jaw, and his left hand encircled her throat, denying her precious air.

She wanted to hit him, slam her fist into the side of his head and come up swinging for all the times he'd never been there for her. For all the years abandoned. Instead she was here, in his grip, and could do nothing. He could kill her as easily as snuffing out a flame.

Another wrench and jolting that ran up her spine, like driving too fast over a pot-holed road.

"This place is supposed to be stable. It was built to withstand anything but a direct bomb hit." Her father's hiss filled her ears as she strangled. As everything slid away from his almond-scented nearness. Her vision darkened and sparks frothed his face as she slipped through the scent of mud and hot earth and into darkness, where there was no air, only the distant blue glimmer of the farthest star.

§

The quake hit as Xavier plumed up through the soil at the southeast of the small town of East Prairie, Missouri, a town of proud Midwesterners he'd visited as he'd come seeking Vallon. Dappled shadows and hot sun hit his skin and he stumbled and went to his knees as the earth wrenched around him. The lightning scent of ozone and ether hung so thick he kept waiting for thunder, but this was no electrical storm, this was power. Screaming came from the distance, dogs barking, and the sound of sirens. The scent of smoke tinged the air.

Naked, he up-righted himself in the stand of trees. He stood in the forest of Ten Mile Lake, a landlocked vestige of the great forests that had once covered this landscape. Now it stood like the last buffalo on the verge of the town and on the edge of extinction. His skin tingled from the transition from energy to living being; everything not of his blood was left behind in the guesthouse room he shared with Vallon because it could not make the transition into the pure energy flow that he travelled to get here.

Withered brown grass crumbled under his feet. Twisted oak, poplar, slippery elm, and others he did not recognize twisted around him as they thrust up out of parched earth that was no longer so firm. The air was still. The leaves barely quivered. Then the earth wrenched again and he went to his knees; the stench of apples and cut grass and roses and mint hit him so powerfully it almost blinded him. He groaned and hauled himself up, pressed against an oak trunk, its bark rough against his skin. His breath came in short, sharp gasps as he tried to understand what was happening. The voyage through the earth always cost him greatly, but this was no weakness born of that travel. This was earthquake.

And the powerful ashes of roses and incense scents said Vallon was involved.

Wherever she was. He held onto the tree and -reached- out into the landscape. The powerful wrenching wave of destruction dissipated away westward, leaving an uncanny silence. No birds sang. No insects chirped, and then slowly, slowly as his blood started to move in his veins again, a chirrup, the slow hum of a cicada's song. A sparrow fluttered down into the trees and sang. Then another.

Warm earth lay under his feet—too warm to be natural. The ley lines throbbed beneath him, so he no longer thought of the importance of triangulation. She was there—he turned southeastward in the direction that the waves of destruction had come from. The epicenter of destruction. The epicenter of his heart.

[*Vallon*,] he called, but there was no answer, no sign of anyone with the Gift to do what was being done to the landscape. That was a concern. Someone had learned how to remain hidden while causing this mayhem. Usually the work of someone of this power was immediately evident to all of the blood across the world. The Council would want to know of anything that could block a fully trained operative from sensing the presence of the power-wielder when they were this close. In contrast, Gleason's presence shone like a star in the darkness that was the Missouri countryside. Snow's oddly flavored baby powder scent permeated the landscape in the other direction, where his presence flared. Yes, between them and himself, they could triangulate Vallon's presence easily, but he no longer needed their help.

The building swell of more pending earthquake violence and a sense of fear-frustration-rage radiated up off the earth. He -reached- down seeking ashes of roses and found a confusing mélange of scents like stepping into a spice house. He pulled back for a moment and then instantly surged back down again. She was there, where the center was, and he would go there, but first he -reached- through the landscape.

The small sparks of animal and insect and bird, all moving to get away from the quake's wrath, the huddled family groups of humans at tinder-pile remains of farmhouses. Barns collapsed on cows and horses, the animals screaming their pain. With each wave of quake, the country was being transformed into a war zone. Nothing would be left. The country highways had split when the earth broke apart and the sections slipped past each other. No one could drive where he sought.

There. Trees. Water. The sparks of owl and egret and squirrel. A few unGifted. Otherwise the place was blank. Unnaturally so. Like the area around New Madrid was devoid of Gifted, only more so—a perfect blank upon the landscape. Vallon was there.

He -reached- again and found Gleason and Snow. [There.] It wasn't good to show them this means of communication—another thing he would have to account to the Council for—but he had to let them know where she was, in case he was not successful bringing her out. They might not be able to get there with roads as they were at the moment, but with the detective's help, they might be able to bring in the local authorities. Anything higher up the line of command was more likely to be in collusion with Vallon's father.

He left them startled and clamoring for answers. Hopefully before they could fathom that their communication, and his form of travel, were really just extensions of his ability to -reach-.The little albino was too clearly a man who would think things through, given enough data.

The earth groaned and he felt it bulge under him. The stink of ozone and ether soured the air, and all the birds that had roosted took flight again in a cacophonous maelstrom of chirps and cries, and whirred up into the sky in a dark cloud that wheeled away southward.

"Fly, but fear follows on your heels," he whispered after them.

The earth wrenched again. Trees whipped around him and fell. A sound like a train wailed towards him and the earth broke apart. Pressure built beneath him and exploded upwards. He had to get out of here. He stumbled back. Shattered trees sent wooden daggers through the air. One caught in his right shoulder. Another his left hip, deep and agonizing. He -reached- and caught the power of the ley line, dragged its heated glow into himself, and his flesh frothed. He held still through the pain and increased the vibration of the molecules of his body. Faster, and they spread farther apart. He merged with the ley line just as the pressure underneath him exploded upwards in a huge geyser of sand and mud. His last image of Ten Mile Lake forest was the trees thrown outwards, hot water and earth boiling up thirty feet into the air.

Then he was a white froth boiling through his mother's, Pangea's, veins. Her rose scent was almost painfully beautiful as it surrounded him. Perhaps that was what attracted him to Vallon; her ashes of roses scent was so similar.

He followed the webbed veins of the earth back towards the blankness on the landscape. The east side of the coiling river. Trees, water. Not a farm, then. He remembered the maps of the New Madrid area.

Big Oak Tree State Park. It had to be. He came up into old lowland bog, now parched under the late afternoon sun. Sunlight through leaf-shadows dappled his skin as it formed. A dragonfly whizzed past his nose. Mosquitoes and midges buzzed in the cooler shadows. Here and there, small runnels of water trickled through channels towards the lake he knew stood at the center of the forested area. It was one of the last true remains of the ancient hardwood forest that had been almost completely logged off for farmland. Of course, that logging caused more flooding, and so the government had built levees and water channels that had diverted the water from places like this park, so it probably barely represented anything of the forest that had been here before. Still, some of the trees around him were huge and must have lived through the decimation of their brethren.

The air ached with a heavy pressure. He stood silent: listening, scenting the air, and using his other senses to try to find what was there. The mélange of scents reached him and then blew away, almost as if they were leaving on the wind. This place had the odd stillness you could only find in the center of a storm, and yet….

He stepped carefully through the forest, blood trickling down his shoulder and hip. His trip through the earth would only take his body, and so the guilty wood daggers had been left behind. The flesh would heal eventually, as it always did. Pity he was no healer.

Anise and mint flared his nostrils as he stepped up onto one of the boardwalks, built to encourage visitors to stay off the sensitive forest floor and to give them dry footing when the rains and floods came. He stepped up, careful there was no one around. The last thing he needed was to be arrested for his nakedness. There would be no way to explain it to these people.

The scent was familiar and he inhaled it deep into his lungs. A dreadlocked spitfire, thin limbed and wild, who had led him on a merry chase with Vallon. Fiona Murdoch.

He -reached- for her and came up against blankness, like a man running into a metal door. Damnation and creation, what was that?

[*Fiona*] he called.

He felt, no, heard, no, smelled-felt-heard her awareness suddenly fix on him. No communication, only her excitement like a bird fluttering its wings, trying to break free of its cage. But damnation, he could not find her, it was like she was everywhere and nowhere at all.

A wind suddenly gusted through the trees. The earth groaned and the ground began to bounce and buckle, the slats of the boardwalk bounding like accordion keys in the hands of a Lisbon street player. He leapt back onto the forest floor and the contact helped him. Fiona was trying to do something. A quake. But she had no focus and not much power that he could sense. He decided to help her, -reached- for her presence, and acted as a conduit to the ley line.

Let her do what she would do. The woman was Vallon's friend. Helping her would help Vallon.

Then the earth exploded under him, wrenching violently and throwing him into the air, slamming him into a tree. He collapsed at its base, his legs buckled, his ribs broken. Then he heard the groan, felt the roots tear loose, and looked up in time to see the trees falling towards him.

§

The first thing Jason noticed was the canaries go silent. He paced the ridiculously decorated living room —*I mean, just who wanted to live in a room like this?* He could positively develop a bird allergy with all the feathers, not to mention the incessant trilling of the stupid little birds. The warm glow of late afternoon came through the dining room window and lightened the cool shadows as he marched up and down between the feather-patterned couch and chair. He checked his watch again as he turned for another lap. From the rear of the house came the sound of the Ducharme woman's voice and the higher-pitched answer of her kid.

He checked his watch again. Damn it, where were they? Gleason and Snow had headed out in their rental cars and de Varga had gone who-knows-where, who-knew-how, leaving Jason here. He shouldn't have agreed to act as home base in this venture. He'd let them get away from him, and if they didn't come back, he'd have nothing.

"Fuck."

The birds went silent.

Okay. Maybe he should swear a little more often. He glanced at the cage, just as the birds suddenly took wing, throwing themselves at the bars of their cage, screeching wildly.

"Holy crap!" He fell back a step. "Hey! Hey, Ms. Ducharme! Something's the matter with your birds," he called.

The *clickety-clack* of her heels came from the kitchen. Then the house heaved. Actually heaved like a large woman's bosom, and Jason stumbled against the couch. The bird cage teetered. Vases, filled with peacock feathers, toppled from the fireplace mantle and smashed on the carpet. The Ducharme woman screamed. Wood groaned and a huge crack zigzagged across the exterior wall. Jason scrambled to his feet, but the house hadn't quit moving. Instead it began to buck and shudder like a dog trying to get rid of a fly.

The bird cage fell and the bird's suddenly fluttered around in panicked dives. The living room window cracked with a sound like a bell and then exploded inward. Only the gauzy curtains stopped a shower of glass covering him.

A quake. It took a moment to register. Quakes came in Seattle, but not here. He thought. He'd lived through the Seattle quake of 2001 and seen the destruction of some of Seattle's heritage buildings. But the shaking of that quake was nothing like this.

The whole house heaved again and his first responder training finally kicked in.

He dove for the hallway where the Ducharme woman and her daughter shrieked. They'd fallen in a heap and huddled together.

"What's happening? What's happening?" The little girl sobbed into her mother's shoulder. The house's floor began canting to one side, the rear of the house rising. From the kitchen came a pop and whoosh, and suddenly flames burst into the hallway. The reek of gas filled the hall.

"Come on! The whole place is going up."

He grabbed the Ducharme woman's arm and heaved her up, but she yelped.

"My ankle. I've done something to it."

He looked down at her idiot shoes and swung her up into his arms. "Hold onto my belt," he ordered the little girl. She did, and he stumbled down the hall and prayed the front door would open.

The front room's exterior wall now had an open crack that allowed in daylight. The canary cage had toppled and the canaries were long gone; the furniture had slid forward into a jumble in the corner. He passed it by. The house canted further and the front door had buckled. He tried the knob; it turned, but the door wouldn't budge. He set the Ducharme woman down, grabbed the door, and heaved. Nothing.

A sound like a train coming filled the living room. The house shuddered so badly he had to use the wall for balance. There was no hope in hell he was going to get that door open. That left the broken living room window.

"Come on," he shouted over the roar and the popping sound of timber shattering. He hefted the Ducharme woman again. Her flesh was cold. She stank of fear. Her eyes were round and staring. The little girl clung to his side like a limpet shell. He kept his back against the wall for balance and teetered into the living room. The furniture had driven into the bird cage and its weight had crushed the cage. But the heap of furniture was like a shoal of driftwood, shifting and moving together as the rear of the house lifted. What the hell was going on? He set the Ducharme woman down.

"You're going to have to climb over the couch and chair. Then I'll hand your daughter to you."

She looked at him with huge desperate eyes. "I—I don't think I can."

He looked her up and down. She teetered on one leg like a turquoise flamingo, her perfect hair now a tangle around her shoulders.

"Listen, I could climb up there and help you up, but I won't be able to help you as much if I do. I'll lift you as far as I can, but you are going to have to do the rest. We can't stay here. It's too dangerous."

As if to emphasize his point, the house suddenly tipped forward as though a giant car jack had just ratcheted up the rear.

She still hesitated.

"If we don't go now, the whole house is likely to tip and we'll be trapped. Now move." There was no time for cajoling. He grabbed her, half tossed her onto the heap of furniture. Above them, the dining room table had caught one half of its length on the half wall that separated living from dining area. If the table came loose like it was probably going to, it would slam into the furniture and crush whoever was standing here. He had to get them moving. The Ducharme woman scrambled feebly over the couch and two chairs, the multiple tables, now crushed into kindling. Finally she reached the curtains and tried to delicately part them.

"Just pull them down!" He shouted. Behind him the table groaned as its loose end began to tip towards him and the little girl. Farrah. That was her name.

He bent down to her. "Honey, I need you to be really brave and crawl up over the furniture like your momma. Can you do that?"

She nodded, so he picked her up and pushed her as far as he could up the heaped furniture. She was a natural, scrambling up beside her mother and yanking the curtain down so it flopped over the glass-filled window sill.

"Good girl! Now you jump down and help your momma!"

The table side screeched against the wall. He leapt up onto the sofa and scrambled over the chairs and table. Felt the house tilt further, and the wind of the table's drive down towards him. Grabbed the Ducharme woman and threw them both out the broken window at Farrah's feet.

He was up and running away from the house, the woman in his arms, herding the little girl before him. The entire front of the house was sinking into the ground, while the land behind the house was rising. The huge black SUV that de Varga had driven was sitting in the driveway, threatening to slide down into whatever hole the house was falling in. He headed for the car, praying the doors were open.

They were. There were no keys, but years of working with crooks developed certain skills. He reached under the ignition and ripped out the wires, hauled his jackknife from his pocket—a long-time essential piece of cop equipment—and bared the wires, spliced them together, and the SUV roared into life. He tromped the gas and the SUV blasted up the now-tilted driveway and went airborne before slamming onto the road.

The huge hole forming under the Ducharme house had already taken the bungalow next to it. A wave of water cascaded out through the window they'd escaped through. The pool had obviously burst. Maybe it had put out the fire, judging by the gouts of smoke coming from the rear of the house. Telephone wires were down along the street. Groups of people stood in front of collapsed heaps that had once been houses. The ground shuddered and shook, huge waves making the ground undulate like a liquid. Jason drove like a drunkard, barely escaping some of the parked cars jitterbugging at the curb.

He drove as fast as he dared through the neighborhood. Behind them, a huge piece of land lifted like a new cliff where the Ducharme house and the ball diamonds behind it had been. The train roar of the earth's transformation masked the little girl's sobbing as he headed towards the highway. When he got there, he pulled over onto an open stretch of road and fished in his pocket. Across the fields, huge geysers of mud and sand erupted, each new explosion shuddering the car and sending Farrah burrowing deeper into her mother's arms. Elizabeth Ducharme sat white-faced and inert beside him like something carved.

He pulled out his phone and tried Gleason's number. Let it ring and ring, swearing at the man at the other end, at the way the ground kept shifting. A car careened too fast onto the highway, heading north behind him, but another wrench of the earth sent the vehicle off into the ditch beside the road in a cloud of dust. Fools. You couldn't drive away from a quake this size. Not at that speed. The best you could do was get to a place where you might survive. It looked like the entire state was shaking. He climbed out of the car, the phone still at his ear, the tone drilling into his head, the earth shuddering under him so he almost fell. If was a miracle he'd been able to drive this far.

People emerged from the car in the ditch. They stumbled up onto the road and stated walking.

"What the hell do you want?" The voice was scratchy and distant as if Gregor Gleason was countries away.

"The quake. It isn't natural, is it?"

Silence a moment. "Bryson. How did you know?"

Jason clung to the suburban door as another set of waves ran across the landscape like someone had dropped a rock in a pool. A huge crack had formed in the field closest to him and an irrigation line stretched, twisted, and broke with a high-pitched *ping* and then geysered water up into the sky. "Just a hunch. You find Vallon?"

A pause, then: "Yeah. Northeast. The epicenter. Near a place called Big Oak State Park. She's there somewhere."

The line clicked to silence and Jason stuffed the phone in his pocket and climbed back in the car. It wasn't smart to keep driving, but he needed to get to Vallon. "We need to get to Big Oak State Park. You know where that is?"

"Why? Is it safe there?" The Ducharme woman's blue eyes turned towards him, barely seeing him through the shock plastered on her face.

Jason shrugged and put the SUV in gear. "Safe as anywhere at this moment." He looked over his shoulder at New Madrid. A new plateau stood in the woman's neighborhood. Across what remained of the town's rooftops, pillars of smoke rose. A siren wailed weakly, finally heard as the earth silenced.

The SUV's engine sounded suddenly too loud.

"Is—Is it over?" She sat up in her seat. The geysers had died in the fields, leaving masses of wet mud on the parched ground.

"For the moment, anyway. With quakes, there're usually aftershocks." He remembered that, at least, now that he was thinking again. "Listen, I'm heading after Vallon. She's someplace called Big Oak State Park. You can climb out here and head into town, or you can come with me. Your choice."

She seemed to steady when he looked at her. She looked at the little blonde girl she held and took a deep breath, swallowed. "Our house and everything in it is gone. We'll stay with you for now."

Jason shrugged, then looked at Farrah. "How is she?"

"Farrah, honey? Are you all right?" She tried to tilt the little girl's head up to her, but Farrah protested and pressed herself harder into her mother's breast.

That didn't look good. At all. "Maybe you should stay here."

The woman shook her head. "You don't know where Big Oak Park is. Besides, the people back there are just going to be as numb as I feel. At least you're doing something. I feel like as long as I can keep moving I'm alive. Maybe I'll eventually feel that way, too."

She met his gaze and her name finally came to him. "Okay, Elizabeth. Which way are we headed?"

She pointed him north along the highway, and they reached a town called East Prairie in about forty minutes. They had to stop part way for another round of shaking and ground-warping tremblers, and had to make their way off road around the span of the highway exit that had collapsed on the highway. On a side road to the town, people stood outside of vehicle pileups. A lone ambulance, its red light still turning, lay on its side in a ditch while people stood staring.

The town itself, when they reached its borders, didn't look very much like anything anymore.

"My God!" Elizabeth Ducharme breathed. "It looks like something out of those old war photos of Japan after the end of the war."

"Hiroshima. Yes." It was mind numbing, really. He'd seen what the quake did in Seattle. Had even seen photos of the great San Francisco quake, but it was nothing like this. This was total devastation. Nothing remained but chewed up foundations and stacks of kindling that had once been houses.

"Tornados might do something like this," she said, but there was no inflection in her voice. Instead it had gotten full of air and space like a balloon about to pop, and he realized she'd had just about all she and her daughter could take.

He slowed the SUV. "You know, maybe it's not such a good idea, you coming with me. Maybe you should stay here where there're people who can help you."

"Here?" Her gaze seemed to bounce off the scene out the window. "I grew up here, you know. I just moved to New Madrid because I thought being closer to the river might bring more tourists. All my people are in East Prairie, but everything's gone, now."

Christ, she was turning into a zombie before his eyes. The shock was eating her up from the inside. There was no way he could care for her and the child and look for Vallon.

"How's your leg?"

"My leg?" She looked down at it now. Somewhere in their escape she'd lost her shoes. Her feet looked small and delicate on the truck floorboards, but her left leg had swollen around the ankle and was swiftly turning the color of the rainbow. He'd been right not to leave her to walk back into New Madrid.

"I think you need a doctor. Is there a hospital here?"

"A clinic. Nearest hospital is twenty miles from here." Again in that vague voice that said her mind was roaming far away.

He looked back at the road. A dust-covered couple were trudging toward the town and he rolled up beside them. "I've got an injured woman here. Where should I take her?"

The man, about thirty-five, was dressed in jeans and a faded Garth Brooks t-shirt and had a bloody cut over his eye. The woman, who looked slightly younger, cradled what looked like a broken hand against her chest.

"That'd be the clinic, if the damn thing's still standing. Given not much is, I'm not holding out a lotta hope." The man wiped his exhaustion-etched face. "We could show ya'll where it is in exchange fer a ride."

Jason almost drove away. The need to find Vallon and the others was like a pain in his gut, but all his years of training and work just couldn't be pushed away. He *helped* people. He always had, until his little obsession with Vallon. Yeah, he could admit it.

He hooked a thumb at the back doors of the SUV. "Hop in."

They clambered in and the woman slumped on the seat, pain radiating off her face.

"What happened to you two?" Jason asked to make conversation.

"I was in the barn with the dog, fixing some irrigation pipes. Rachelle, here, was in the house, but then the dog yipped and ran off, and when the ground shook, the whole place came down. I crawled inside and found her. She was okay, but her hand was pinned under the fridge. I didn't think I'd get her loose, but I grabbed the jack from the truck and did."

He leaned back and peered bleary-eyed out the window. "We walked into town. Take this left coming up."

So they crept into the remains of what had been East Prairie, struggling over rubble when they had to, adding a few extra patients along the way, and going so slowly Jason wanted to scream or just climb out and run.

The clinic, when they reached it, was a low slung stucco building painted a bright yellow that seemed to radiate in the sun. One corner of the building looked like it had slumped, but otherwise, miraculously, it seemed intact. Jason pulled through the crowds of people bringing injured to the site and finally stopped mid street. He helped the others out of the vehicle and half-carried Elizabeth Ducharme towards the building. Outside, a woman in a medical smock stood with a clipboard, stopping everyone who tried to get into the building. Rows of folks sat slumped on the crumbled-to-dust pavement of what had once been a parking lot.

"Name?" she intoned.

"This's Elizabeth Ducharme of New Madrid. I think she might have broken her leg."

She eyed him over her clipboard. "You do, do you?" Then she turned that doubt on Elizabeth and frowned. "Lizzy? That you?"

"Bets?" Elizabeth straightened slightly. "Bets, this is Mr. Bryson. He was a guest at my house." She blinked. "It's not there anymore, Bets. It fell in a hole." Her voice filled with disbelief and awe. "This is Bets Cramer. We went to school together."

Bets still didn't look at Jason any more kindly. "Listen, Lizzy. I'm sorry, but I can't do anything but ask you to wait your turn. We got people coming in who are real bad. Yer just going t' have ta take a seat like the others." She hefted her chin at the ground. Then she turned back to Jason. "That your SUV I see out there? 'Cause we sure could use another ambulance to bring in the injured. The one ambulance we had hasn't come back in."

"We saw it out on the road. It was in a ditch," Jason said as he frantically thought about what he needed to do. "Tell you what, I've got a piece of business to do, but as soon as I'm done, I'll come back and help."

He felt Elizabeth's and Bet's gazes on him. Farrah's was like a weight as he got Elizabeth settled on the ground, then backed away.

"She means a lot to you," Elizabeth Ducharme said, though her face was pale with pain. "Even though she was with that other man, that foreigner."

Jason tried to hide the way he stiffened. "I'll be back in no time, just you wait and see." He smiled down at the little girl. "You take care of your mom, okay?"

The kid nodded and he quickly turned away and strode between the walking wounded back to the SUV, hating himself. It went against everything he believed to leave without helping, but he needed Vallon or one of her kind to get Cheryl back, and he wasn't taking a chance of losing them.

The engine roared as he backed up through the crowd and pulled a map out of the vehicle's glove box. Big Oak State Park lay about fifteen minutes out of town in normal conditions. He drove as fast as he could through the blocks and blocks of razed townscape. Another quake roared through and splinted the buildings further. The SUV bounced like a bronco and he slid into a fallen telephone pole and backed out of the mess carefully. Thankfully, the heavy-duty bumper was barely dented. He sent a thank you to de Varga for renting a decent vehicle, as he dropped the vehicle in drive again and plunged on through the roar and the trembling landscape. People tried to stop him. They tried to wave him down. By the time he got to the town limits—*Thank you for visiting East Prairie. Please come again,* said the sign—it felt like a part of him had died from the number of times he'd just had to turn his head away and drive.

His hand felt for the vial in his pocket. The precious serum he had stolen from Amundson's laboratory was still there, after everything. Vallon first, and then he'd be back.

He could almost make himself believe it.

CHAPTER 27 —THE SCENT OF MINT AND ROSES

Vallon sank through blackness and stars and came up shaking, into the sound of concrete tearing and the overpowering taste of licorice-anise and mint coating her mouth and nostrils. She moaned and tried to move, but it was like invisible shackles held her in place.

In place.

Her eyes flashed open. Her father. He had tried to kill her. Maybe he thought he had to try to stop what was happening to his bunker. The room wrenched around her and she was tossed on her cot. The whine of the octopus desks ran loud in her ears, the concrete groaned, and people yelled. The cot shuddered under her like a barely tame horse and she could-not-move, damn it!

The flow of power ran like lightning over her skin so the little hairs on her arms stood on end. They still worked the power. The netting on her head burned into her skin as they drew on her. The stench of heated earth and water was almost overpowering. What had been tiny fissures in the New Madrid fault had been wrenched apart, and through her connection to the earth's ley lines she felt the gaps grow. The massive quake her father had planned had become self-sustaining, spreading out and out and out from this epicenter.

Through her molecules spread through the soil, she sensed the ghost town devastation of New Madrid, saw the landscape of Missouri boiling as the net on her head yanked her back into the earth. Power rushed through her, dragging her down into the depths, down to the ley lines. Sucking more power from her, when what she wanted to do was fight. She just wasn't about to have more Gifted deaths on her hands.

They dragged power from her and cycled it into the flow of the ley line, drew power up from it and cycled it through her again and into their control. Sent more heat into the crumbling bedrock. Didn't they see what they were doing? Didn't they feel the way the magma was encroaching from down below? They really would end up with another Yellowstone.

[*Fi?*] She called. Whatever Fi was doing, it was too little. [*You have to do more.*]

Fi had been so Gifted in school, but her mother's use had stolen that talent from her and left only fear of the Gift. Fear Vallon had disregarded. She felt sick at what she'd done.

A huge wrench snapped her back into her body. The bunker rattled. A huge piece of concrete crumbled in the narrow piece of ceiling she looked up at. Her metal cot bounced and danced on the floor. Another wrench—sideways this time—and the cot toppled, spilling her onto the shuddering concrete in a heap because she was not strapped to the bed. A sharp pain ripped her arm. Concrete dust rained down on her. Around her the other cots jumped and jerked like milling animals. The octopus desk whirred and hummed, but the stench of burning wires said its delicate motors where working too hard to keep position over the map.

The huge room shuddered, and waves ran across the floor. Over the roar of what was happening, her father's voice rose, demanding action from the desk riders. Demanding they make it stop. She lifted her head to try to see him.

She lifted her head.

And suddenly realized she could feel her legs and arms, could move them slightly though they were sluggish as worms. The IV in her arm had pulled loose. A small pool of clear liquid was growing on the floor from the dislodged needle, and she was no longer dragged down into the earth by her father's agents.

The cot's fall had freed her of the IV and dislodged the net on her head, though it still rested against her temple. Which meant she could fight back, now.

She -reached- for Fi and almost couldn't find her candle-bright presence in the too bright congregation of the Gifted in the room. But the rich scent of anise and mint told her where Fi was. [*I'm free.*]

Vallon felt her friend's exhaustion.

[*You did good. I'll take over now.*]

And she did, -reaching- out into the soil beyond the bunker.

Whoever had built it had been wise. The entire thing had been constructed like a pontoon boat that could float in the muddy soil, immune to the shock waves they caused through their endeavors. Well, that wasn't going to happen.

Fi had done well. She'd somehow reflected the quake shock waves back into the epicenter, had helped sustain them through the thick mud and sand soil, and had focused them on the bunker to cause the shaking within. Vallon could do better than that.

She closed her eyes and focused on the soupy soil outside. All her years of practice in her basement had to be good for something. She grabbed hold and forced the sand and earth together, geysered the moisture out until it became stone. She couldn't hold it for long, but she could do it long enough. She threw more heat into the stones below and the fissures grew, the stone shook.

The massive power of the quake no longer missed the bunker. Instead, the solid stone outside it send the shock waves directly into the concrete. She'd turned the quake back on its maker.

The entire room wrenched and twisted, throwing her across the concrete to slam against another cot. Around her, cots toppled. The octopus motors screamed and the stench of burning wiring overtook the scent of lightning.

She fumbled weakly to her knees and ripped the net off of the head of the Gifted on the cot, tore the needle out of an arm. Afterburn left her weak and shaking. The Gifted wore the clothes of a farmer and probably didn't understand what was going on. She pushed herself up and her legs almost gave under her, but she placed herself into his field of vision.

"You'll be able to move in a few minutes. Just stay calm." His wild-eyed look was anything but calm, but his gaze at least met hers with understanding. "When you can move, help the others."

Fi. She had to find Fi and free her. And the others.

The quake shook the bunker like a dog with a rat. With a roar, a spreading net of cracks ran through the ceiling and down the walls. She tried to stand, but the shock waves kept throwing her down. The octopus stanchions wavered and swung wildly.

"You!"

Her father's roar came from behind her and she turned and almost fell as another shock wave threw everything sideways again. She came up against another cot. Her father picked his way through the Gifted towards her. From her left, Toby came to his aid, a gun in his hand.

She backed up. Even if she could get away from them, she couldn't leave Fi or the other Gifted. She turned and ran, scuttling through the cots, searching for Fi. Dust and concrete chunks rained down around her. The room jerked and sent her sprawling against one of the cots. She tore the net off the person's head, the needle out of their arm. At least she could stop her father's plans. Tear enough Gifted out of the web and they couldn't sustain the quake. She hoped.

"Vallon, stop! You don't understand."

She whirled to her father, still a few cots away, his pursuit slowed by the vibrations that made it hard to stand and harder to walk. "I understand perfectly. You're a monster."

She ripped the needle out of another arm, the net off another head. The Gifted woman groaned and looked at her with terrified brown eyes.

"Toby, get her!"

The beach-boy blonde raised his gun. Vallon backed up and half fell over another cot. She stumbled up, but a violent shake sent her to her knees again. The gunfire roared in the already thunderous noise of the quake, but the jumping floor sent his shot wild.

"No!" her father roared. "No guns. We need her!"

She scrambled up and ran again, tearing out the needles wherever she dared. A wave through the concrete sent the cots undulating. More dust and larger chunks of concrete slammed into the floor and into the trapped Gifted. A large piece barely missed her and slammed into the temple of the man she'd just freed from the needle. He had to be dead, judging by the shape of his head.

The octopus desks swung wildly, the stink of heated wiring filling the room. Another jerk and three of the desks collided in midair. Two of the desk riders were thrown the twenty feet to the floor where they lay still; the third was caught in the wreckage, screaming. That had to stop the focus of the others on the quake. Surely it would be ending.

A set of hands grabbed her from behind. She twisted away from Toby, but he grabbed her arm, twisted it behind her. She slammed her heel onto his instep, swung around, and drove the heel of her hand into his nose. She felt cartilage break and move. He went down like she had clubbed him, his nose mashed out of place, his eyes furious.

"Bitch!" He raised the gun and she dove out of the way. Heard/felt a wind over her head, a huge crash, and her father's yells cut off.

Shaking, she looked up from where she'd fallen. Two more of the octopus desks must have hit. One hung dead in the air, its rider collapsed over the side, the second desk had been thrown loose of its stanchion. It must have passed right over her head before it struck down and mowed across the sea of beds. Her father was gone, in its path.

Gone.

She stood and almost fell again, grief and anger warring inside. Toby was nowhere to be seen. The cavernous room shuddered around her and one corner of the concrete roof came thundering down, allowing a river of dark water mud and shattered stone to cascade in.

These people would die unless she got them out of here. Her father's people were gone, no more white coats moving along the computer consoles. The three remaining octopus desks had slammed to the floor and their riders limped towards an open doorway. Escape. They all had a way out if she could just get them up and moving.

Moving methodically through the sea of beds, she kept pulling out needles, pulling off headdresses, though she probably didn't need to worry about the netting now that the desks were inert. Behind her she sensed movement, so the people were stirring, but Fi. Where was she? Had she missed her friend? Had Fi been one of the unfortunates caught by the octopus stanchion that had come loose and gone flying?

She turned around. Water and mud rolled over her leaden feet and up to her ankles. More of the mud poured into the map pit around the remains of the octopus desk. The lights overhead flickered and dimmed, then steadied. The way the water was carving a larger hole out of the wall, there wasn't much time left.

[*Fi?*] She -reached- and the room filled with the myriad glows of the Gifted. Some wandered blankly around the room. Others were helping remove the needles from other Gifted's arms. Were dragging them away from the flooding mud.

She had to do something to stop the flood—to give these people a chance to get free, and to have a chance of finding Fi. It was just so hard to move. Every part of her throbbed with afterburn and the need to sleep forever, but that was not to be.

Closing her eyes, she -reached- for the pouring mud. Reached- for the power in the ley lines below and almost moaned as their power poured into her. Her bones quaked, her flesh trembled like mud in a rainstorm. Everything was coming undone, and the quake had gone far enough that it wasn't going to stop on its own. It was spreading out across the American landscape. Soon it would reach Yellowstone. When it did, there was too much chance it would unleash the devastation that slept there. She had to stop it before then, but first….

She hauled herself back to the bunker. She could do nothing for all the people out there until she'd dealt with what was within the bunker. Get them free. At least give them a chance. Then she could try to stop the quake before it became unstoppable. First try to stop the flooding.

The flooding water and mud came from something up above, not from the general soil that she'd already hardened. If she could just rebuild the concrete, or place stone between the bunker and the flooding water, then she could find Fi.

"Vallon!"

Her name rang across the room and she spun around.

§

The little Prius rattled and protested as it careened along the remains of a two-lane county highway. It was one of those quiet moments between the successive waves of quakes. The geysers that had dotted the landscape had subsided into circles of damp mud and sand on the drought-riddled corn and cotton and soy fields. The heaps of kindling that had once been farmhouses and barns stood out like beaver dam heaps in the midst of the pond of landscape. Nothing moved except the beetle of Landon's little car and a lone crow, circling far above. At least he thought it could be a crow. Could be a vulture, for all he knew.

The air blew hot and electric through the open car window, parching the sweat off his skin as he pressed the ridiculous little car over the crumbling concrete that had once been pavement. The car might be good for the environment, but its road clearance was definitely not made for the uneven terrain he was driving. The quake had just about obliterated what his maps had said was a main local highway. But then the quakes had taken down the trees along the road, too, snapping their trunks close to the ground or upturning their roots.

The power had been amazing. All the little hairs on his body still stood on end, and whatever Francis Drake was doing, it was still brewing far below. He might not be able to work with the power, but that didn't stop him from feeling its presence, and right now he felt like all his nerve endings were rubbed raw and bloody.

The message from the foreigner de Varga had come not too long ago, blasting into his brain like lightning. He'd almost driven off the road before he slammed on the brakes and steadied his breathing. Vallon was northeast. That had been the message. He'd already felt the direction of the quake and knew they could triangulate without problem, but de Varga had made that unnecessary. Of course, the fact he could communicate that way had sent Landon's mind whirring. Could all Gifted do that if they were trained? The AGS had never even explored *that* possibility. Something to think about. Hold onto how it had ripped through him, and do some research.

At the least it suggested he was going to have to be very careful, because it might be a sign that de Varga could read his intentions.

Ahead, across the landscape, a large mass of trees seemed to sway in a stiff wind. Quake or aftershock, it had to be; because the light wind through the car window was the product of his speed. The field that separated him from the trees undulated like the surface of a not-quite-calm sea, the ripples expanding towards him. He stepped on the gas and made it to a turnoff just as the movement hit. The road leapt under the Prius and groaned, almost throwing the little car off the road. He slammed on the brakes and slewed around. Thrown-up crumbled pavement pinged against the car and pelted him through the open window. He covered his face—too late—a cut on his brow trickled blood down his face. Bright red drops speckled his white suit.

The shaking stopped. Definitely not like the first quake that had gone on and on and on for what seemed like forever. The first five aftershocks had been almost as powerful as the quake. When he -reached- he could still feel that power travelling through the landscape, distant now, but still powerful as it wreaked its damage over the country. Whatever Francis Drake was doing, it was damned effective; but knowing the man, he shouldn't be surprised. Drake had always been single-minded in his pursuit of what he believed in. But that he would attempt to virtually destroy the United States—that was the surprise. Landon had always figured Drake would try to use his power to create Change, but not devastation. Drake had never been a man who would want to deal with healing the aftermath.

On the other hand, the devastation would allow rebuilding in Drake's vision. He might even have figured out a way to make people remember how he helped them so he could become their savior.

The image of Francis Drake, the man who had abandoned everything, including Vallon, suddenly being seen as a caring savior almost made Landon drive off the road into a toppled sign. *Big Oak State Park*, it said. Beyond, what looked like a thousand-acre wood shifted and moved, a false wind sending branches swaying, leaves whispering, boughs squeaking against one another.

The road led in between the trees, straight towards where he could see a few vehicles in a parking lot. He eased the car forward and the earth jerked and bounced under him, the rush of mint and anise so powerful he sneezed.

Not Vallon, but familiar. Not Gleason, either, though one of the vehicles up ahead looked suspiciously like Vallon's rental Camry and another like the big SUV de Varga had driven. Which meant that the detective was here, too. So another Gifted caused the quake that left the earth unsteady under the trees and set them swaying.

He pulled in beside the other two vehicles and climbed out. A water tower had crashed over part of the parking lot and crushed a rusted pickup. Any occupant would be dead, there was no question.

The trembling underfoot vibrated up his legs so his joints felt like they'd come loose. There was no sign of any of them. He'd been too slow. But a rickety-looking boardwalk ran into the woods. It seemed likely that they'd gone that way, so he followed.

Huge trees overhung the path, some with girths that suggested centuries of life, and yet the forest hung eerily silent. If this was what the entire forest had been like when the settlers first came here, he could understand the need to cut the trees down. Their presence weighed on him, or maybe it was just the heaviness of the air that felt like a storm brewing, even though the sky was clear. The powerful stench of ozone and ether made his eyes water.

He had not smelled it so powerfully since the last battle in Seattle. Then he realized who the mint and anise belonged to. Fi Murdoch, Vallon's friend. The woman was the cause of the disturbance under him. He stopped. But Fi had left.

The lightning scent spiked and the air crackled painfully around him so his body hair stood on end. The boggy soil to either side of the boardwalk began to bubble and seethe and the boards made pinging sounds under his feet as the nails gave way to undulating movement. Then the earth groaned and the trees swayed and added the groan of stressed wood so the forest sounded like it was dying. Maybe it was. The boardwalk bounced violently and threw him off. He landed in the bog on his hands and knees, cold water bubbling up through the vibrating soil so it covered his hands, his shoes, the fronts of his white trousers where he'd landed. He picked himself up and his little patent moccasins sank deeper into the vibrating soil. He grabbed a tree trunk for balance, then lunged for another.

A crack overhead and he leapt to the side as a huge oak limb crashed down. He looked down at his feet. He'd lost one shoe in his lunge.

Damnation, he was not a field agent—was not made for this kind of arduous venture. He was the brains, the mind, meant to plan the actions of the others. Well, that wasn't going to happen unless he found Vallon, was it?

He released the tree he clung to and stumbled his way beside the boardwalk. The air was thick with the mint and anise scent of Fi Murdoch, but then the pungent odor of roses rose from the earth and the ground lurched under him and threw him down. In the forest he heard the crash of giants—trees coming down. The leaves ripped from trees, branches crashed down over his head and shoulders as he struggled to run, following the boardwalk.

"Gleason!" He yelled. "Bryson!" The detective might have no power himself, but he was brawnier at least. At times like this, strength of body was worth something.

But his cries were lost in the sound of a locomotive engine that ran through the ground. Something had changed underfoot. The gentle bubbling of the soil had become ripples and cracks as if stone shoved tree roots up through the flesh of the earth. Stone that seemed to spark with lightning where it shone grey-white in the forest shadows. Unnatural rock—changed. Rock that would magnify the impact of the quake's shocks. As if to prove a point, it threw him down again. He landed in a heap; his leg twisted under him and a horrible pain radiated up his leg from his knee.

He couldn't breathe. Had to wait for the initial shock of pain to subside a little. But he couldn't stay here. The trees dropped branches like bombs. The earth split underneath them and trunks groaned and tore apart, spraying needles of wood around them. He needed to get out from under the trees.

For a moment he considered heading back to the Prius, but Vallon-scent of roses egged him on. He hauled himself to his feet and a grunt of pain escaped him. Not good. Not good at all. The ground shimmied softly. Time to get going. He pushed off towards another tree and stumbled, wove, fell, and struggled up again.

The stench of lightning and ozone was almost more than he could bear. It was so unfair that he did not even have the Gift to save himself. But he would not cry. He was stronger than that—was stronger than all of them, in his own way. He had always controlled his emotions, had not let them see his envy, or the way that envy had slowly grown roots and limbs as he planned.

It looked like the trees parted ahead. If he was going to find the others anywhere, it was likely to be here, but when he -reached- to confirm it, they were not there.

He came out of the trees where the boardwalk was torn off of a platform like the body of a tapeworm yanked loose of its head. The platform apparently had deep teeth dug in that held it in place. He half-limped, half-hopped to the platform edge and pulled himself up, then stopped. His legs crumpled under him.

The platform was an ordinary wooden viewing platform, set in the middle of a large, half-dried pond. Low brush filled most of the wetlands, but eastward, stunted trees revealed a larger opening. It had to be a lake or something.

Another tremor rippled through the forest and the platform rumbled under him, but he was too tired to move. The pain in his knee seemed to suck the strength right out of him. He rolled up his pant leg and saw the problem. It was a wonder he'd been able to walk on it at all, the way the kneecap was pointed to the outside of his leg, which just went to prove he was stronger than he'd thought. Now he just had to prove it.

He gripped the offending patella and closed his eyes, held his breath, and jerked the bone sideways. The scream escaped him before he could stop it. Now he really was crying, but he stumbled up and towards the center of the platform, because that was where the dried-out viewing platform was different. The sunlight beat down on a large section of the wood that had swung up and away to reveal a dimly lit set of concrete steps that led down into the vibrating earth.

Sounds, like concrete groaning and coming apart, or maybe voices shouting, came from the darkness. He -reached- and the flare of Gifted reached him. The scent of roses and incense said Vallon was there. His pigeon. Ignoring the pain and using a wall for balance, he started down.

From below came the unmistakable sound of gunfire.

CHAPTER 28 —LAVENDER AND ROSES

The voice Vallon knew and yearned to hear. She spun around, searching, just as the room shook again and the overhead lights flickered once more and died. Darkness flooded in like the water and mud. So dark she couldn't see her hands in front of her face. Everything was roaring—water, groaning concrete, the tortured earth. The air filled with the stench of swampy water and the ozone-mélange of power. She had to find Fi and get her out of here, but it had sounded like Xavier.

She -reached- and the room flared to life with the myriad forms of those imprisoned here, and near the door the most brilliant flare of the man she loved.

"Here! I'm here!" But he was already threading through the tangle of cots and octopus stanchion towards her. With him came two others: one a Gifted she knew with a taste-scent like old earth and spice. Gleason? What the heck was the chief doing here?

The question went double when she read the dim flame that followed after them. He might not be Gifted, but she knew him—and he shouldn't be here, either: Detective Jason Bryson. Something else was going on beyond the obvious plot of her father.

The earth groaned and lurched as emergency lights flickered on and filled the installation with an eerie red glow. She fell against an unoccupied cot and suddenly the cold mud and water flooded up to her knees in a wave. She spun. More of the corner of the room had given way. A growing waterfall of mud sluiced into the room and was already threatening the

Gifted trapped on the cots in that part of the room. She caught sight of a flicker she knew too well. Fi was there.

Xavier would have to wait. She struggled through the muck, yanking needles as she went and praying it would be enough for the Gifted to help themselves. The waterfall of muck had already engulfed those cots closest to the corner, drowning the Gifted trapped under the torrent. Fi, though, was just beyond that deadly area. The force of the mud had shoved her cot into others to form a logjam of comatose Gifted. The best Vallon could hope for was that the shifting cots had ripped needles and head nets loose, but it still didn't look like anyone was moving.

Around the wreck of the Octopus and the rogue map pit, she waded into the shifting sea of cots, making sure as she went that the needles were freed. There she was. Far too close to the deadly flow of mud. Vallon ripped at the cots, tore her hands on sharp metal.

[*Vallon!*]

[*Help me. We have to get them out. Get Fi out.*]

And then warm, strong arms came around her, his scent of Cedar of Lebanon and incense so powerful she could have collapsed in his arms and wept.

"Xavier." She cupped her filthy palm on his cheek and kissed him. "Fi's there. We have to help them."

Gleason and Bryson were doing just that, getting the other Gifted started out the door that was hidden behind the half wall.

Xavier nodded. "Or perhaps I stop the flow."

She nodded and turned back to her task, yanking the needles out of arms as she felt the tingle and spark of power behind her. The mud deluge slowed. The roar diminished, even though the floor wrenched again.

"Bitch!" The voice came out of the dimness from by the map pit.

Vallon swung around. Toby. Somehow he'd survived the fall of the stanchion. He was filthy, mud glowing red over his face and body, but he still held a gun. She froze.

"He a friend of yours?" He motioned to Xavier, who also faced him.

Not knowing what else to do, she nodded.

The double gunshot happened so fast she couldn't believe it. Xavier staggered and went down and Vallon screamed. She leapt for Xavier and hauled him up out of the mud. He groaned and looked up at her with pain-darkened midnight eyes.

"So. *Bela Menina*. It comes to this."

"No! You will not die! You will not!"

She ripped power up out of the earth and poured it into Xavier. His back arched, his dark eyes closed, and for a moment she thought she'd killed him. But no. He breathed. And the man who had done this to him should. Not. Be.

Power burned in her hands and she twisted it, grabbed at the concrete under Toby, and twisted elements so it was no longer there.

Toby stumbled and fell. Suddenly was up to his knees, sinking up to his hips, and mud yanked him down in a whirlpool.

"No!" he screamed, but then the mud took him and his gun and pulled him under.

The room diminished to the sound of Xavier's breathing. Yes. He still breathed, each bubbling exhalation like a blessing. He had to live, but she had to get him out of here to safety. To a doctor. But Fi. With Xavier's collapse, the mud had resumed its cascade into the room, and now the whirlpool was sucking Gifted-laden cots towards it.

Then hands were on her shoulders.

"Drake! Look at me! We have to get out of here. The whole place is coming down."

She looked up into the exhausted face of Gregor Gleason. "How did you get here?"

A slight smile rimed his thin lips. "Flew, mostly. And followed you. But that's another story."

She tried to get Xavier up, but his unconscious body was too heavy.

"Here. Let us help you." And then suddenly there were two. Gleason and Jason hefting Xavier between them. She stood.

"Get him out of here," she said and looked around at the cots now floating in the mud. Fi was still there. Somehow still trapped in the needle's power. "I'm getting the others."

She didn't want to leave Xavier. One last stroke of his face, one last kiss on his lips, and a prayer. "Please let him live." Then she was gone out into the red-tinged mud, yanking cots away from the whirlpool, helping people up who then helped others. There was no time to make sure Gleason and Jason got Xavier out of here. She had to trust. Kept going and finally reached Fi, almost last.

Her eyes were closed and she wasn't conscious. Probably she'd used all her strength just causing the quake that hit the installation. Afterburn radiated off of her and she looked like a tossed doll the way she lolled on the cot, one arm outstretched, the needle somehow tethering her in a spot where the mud poured down, mud splatter covered her face and fine hair, the sundress she wore.

Vallon ripped her free of the needle and dragged the cot away from the whirlpool. The other Gifted were helping each other across the flooded room. The mud was almost hip high, and even the emergency lights had begun to flicker.

A groan brought Vallon back to the cot's side. Fi's eyes flickered open.

"Vallon?"

"Right here, sweetie." She stroked the mud off Fi's face, and Fi struggled up to sitting.

"Oh, my God." Fi took in the destruction. "Did I do that?"

Vallon pulled her into a hug. "Not all, but you gave it a good start. You did good, Fi. Really good. But we need to get out of here. Do you think you can walk?"

With a nod, Fi slipped her feet into the mud and stood. She almost fell, until Vallon caught her, fighting the afterburn's pain while she half led, half carried Fi towards the door and the other Gifted. By the time they reached the door, Fi was walking on her own. The other Gifted were still making their way down the dimly-lit curved hallway.

Vallon stopped. The roar of the mud inundation continued; the quake had momentarily stopped. Maybe, just maybe, the crumbled tectonic structures underneath New Madrid had found a new equilibrium. Maybe. She -reached-.

Not equilibrium. Deep in the earth, the huge lake her father had used to cause the quake still bubbled and boiled, but now it wasn't the Gifted using the ley line's heat to do so. The earth had fractured, allowing magma closer to the surface. Close enough it was superheating the water towards another series of quakes that would likely be even worse than those that had already wreaked destruction. And when the fissures weakened further and the water was gone, it would leave the perfect geological structures for the magma to continue rising through the weakened earth's crust. It might not form a volcano, but it *would* create something too akin to Yellowstone, and pose a danger not just to continental United States, but a danger to life on earth, if it ever did erupt as a super volcano.

With a sharp intake of breath, she pulled back to Fi. "You have to go."

She pushed Fi along the curving hallway. "Go with them. Make sure they make it out and make sure Gleason and the others take care of Xavier."

"You're staying here?" Fi's voice quavered.

"There's no time for me to get out of here. I have to do something now. Go, so I don't have to worry about you." She shoved Fi down the hall again, then couldn't wait any longer to see if Fi obeyed. Vallon turned back into the red light and ozone stench of the installation room, already -reaching-.

The shock waves of the earlier quake had rushed away north, south, east, and westward. The bustling metropolises of New York, Boston, and Atlanta had been devastated. Buildings had come down. Hundreds of thousands injured, dying, their candle flames of light flickering and going out. Closer in, the quake's destruction had flattened the entire cities of Lexington, Birmingham. The grand arches of St. Louis were gone, that city's only saving grace the fact that the city buildings were lower.

But westward, the quake's waves rolled over Minnesota, smashing the Twin Cities, entering the Dakotas, and the border of Montana and Wyoming neared. The Yellowstone caldera simmered, its fault lines already trembling at the power of what was coming. Precursor quakes rumbling.

In the chill, dank air, she sank down on the top of a desk that had lodged near the door and focused on what had to be done. She had stopped a volcano before. Now she had the quake to address and the simmering mess beneath where she sat, not to mention the shattered underpinnings of the entire Midwest landscape. Such was the destruction her father wrought.

It made her feel sick to her stomach. She shivered and her cold hands trembled as she held onto the desk, while the room rumbled again and twisted sideways, almost throwing her into the mud flooding into the room. If she stopped the quake first, the explosion below would be more difficult to stop. If she focused here, there was no way she would be able to stop the Yellowstone eruption. And this time she had to do it herself. She had no Fi, no Landon, to help her.

She drove her awareness deep into the soil. The lightning stench of power flooded her and tingled her skin. So much power that she felt like a gnat on a charging bull, and she had to do something. *Think, Vallon, think.*

The ley lines sizzled and fed power into the landscape. Power roared westward on the edge of the great quake wave. Destruction on two levels—the quake and the change—combining to cause devastation, and the destruction brewing below her almost as if it turned the power back on the quake's maker.

Perhaps there was a way she could do that, too. Turn the power of one into a weapon against the other.

She drove her presence far out over the landscape to the preceding line of the quake. The landscape rippled as if it came unmoored. Forest became plains, became mountains, became death valleys. Behind it the quake destroyed what remained, leaving a jumbled landscape of geological features still caught in change that shifted and twitched between what had been, what was, and what could be. Rivers ran dry. A great lake appeared until the changed ripped away a natural dam and inundated everything downriver from it. No one could live through that. The landscape would die.

She -reached- for the power, and tried to inhale it. It was power she and the other Gifted had drawn from the ley lines and that her father's agents had crafted. The air stank of roses and mint and ashes and grass and coriander and cinnamon and anise and too many other scents to name. The quake was bad, but with the change like hounds at its head, there was no telling what impact it would have on Yellowstone. Power flooded in, the heat crisping her skin, the lightning and ether making her lightheaded. It filled her up until she might burst, she was spread so thin.

She had to do something with the power—drain it off again, because right now it was as uncontrolled as a fire hose without handlers. She turned back to New Madrid. Use the power to heal the fractured fault lines. She poured the lightning into the substrate, brought fractured stone together, and used the power to heal it. Gravel into stone. Stone into geological platform. Knitted fault lines together so that New Madrid would never shift and grind the way it had in the 1800s.

She fell back into herself into darkness. The emergency lights had gone out and that couldn't mean anything good. Her skin still itched with power and sparks played across her skin, even though the weakness of afterburn waited like a specter just beyond. The mud covered her calves where her legs dangled over the desk edge. Even with the whirlpool hole in the center of the room, the mud level had grown. She had to get done and get out of here soon, or she wouldn't be getting out at all. But getting done was more important. Already the magma pressure from below was eating at the healed surface fractures. The lowlands of Missouri and Arkansas were rising.

Another deep breath and she drove back into the earth. The quake, now only a massive upheaval of earth, still travelled westward.

She drew on the power that fueled it. It tasted of ashes of roses and she knew it was her scent. She had caused this, by letting her power be used. Now she would end it. She drew the power into herself and cycled it outwards, diffusing it across the landscape. Heated earth caused updrafts that caught against cooler heights. Snow fell on mountains. Rain fell below, drenching the drought-stricken prairies.

The quake lessened, but still not enough. She sent power flaring out through the ley lines, out under the Atlantic.

The quake became the barest ripple, and surely the Yellowstone caldera could withstand it.

[*Watch it!*] she flared out at the AGS agents on the desk in Seattle and Los Angeles. Felt their shocked awareness of her touch before she yanked away. They would have to find a way to deal, because the magma pressure under New Madrid had grown. The earth's always heated mantle had heated more, so the huge underground lake boiled like one of Landon's pasta pots on the stove. The steam placed scalding pressure on the stone she'd healed.

There was no way to remove the magma's heat: it had the heat of the entire earth's core fueling it. That meant she had to do something else. She drew the stone closed over the magma vent and drew out the heat that ran through the stone. Her skin burned at the effort. She had to spend the heat somewhere else. Had to channel it off.

The rose-scented ley lines were her best hope, but everyone near her flowed from east to west. The battered western states didn't need more power running through them. Something glimmered far below. Blue tinged and lavender-scented. A different kind of flow. Power, but power she hadn't felt before. Huge channels of power wound through the earth's flesh travelling in the other direction, like veins travelling back to the earth's heart.

She yanked back and shivered. Wasn't it Xavier who had described the earth as the great mother? What did he know that she didn't? Would he live to tell her? She closed her eyes against the image of his pale features and the vivid stains on his chest from Toby's gun. He had to live. She couldn't lose him. Surely no god would make her lose him, too.

Swallowing back pain, she -reached- again. Far down beneath the rushing rose-scented lines that traced beneath the earth's surface like capillaries, she touched the blue; and the reek of lavender power tore through her, tore her away eastward, out under the ocean. Cool here. Far cooler, though the line ran hot with the earth's power. Perhaps it was that the ocean's weight kept the earth's crust thinner, the waters carrying the heat away.

She poured heat that way, cooling the lake and the rock beneath it. Underwater volcanoes erupted. Fallen islands rose through the water, saw daylight after a thousand-thousand years of being inundated, and then something stopped her, as if the earth itself rejected her attempts to pour more heat into the water. From so far away that at first she thought it was just the ocean murmurs, she heard a wild chorus of many voices yelling.

[*Stop! You must stop!*]

Something stung her like a bee and she yanked back into her body, still too full of the power to be safe, shaking and exhausted, but still listening. Nothing sounded in her head. Only the roar of the mud still falling, otherwise all was silence. The shaking was only the tremors running through her body. The floor was steady. Surely the voice had been her imagination, for who would be out there to urge her to stop what she was doing?

None of the other AGS agents would even have been aware of the deep blue ley lines. No one she knew had ever spoken of them, not even Landon. And not Xavier.

She had to get out of here to him, but she needed to heal the destruction left by the quake. A certain little girl in New Madrid deserved her home back, deserved the chance to live a normal life with her family. The thunder of more concrete falling and the sudden wash of chill mud across the desktop decided her. It left her chilled and feverish and said that her chances of getting out were diminishing with every minute. She would heal the destruction when she saw sunlight again. She slid off the desk and immediately fell up to her neck. Her legs refused to work. She clung to the desk, the cold mud flowing over her, and managed to pull herself around the desk until she was closer to the exit. At least she hoped so. In the darkness she wasn't so sure anymore.

Holding on with one hand, she groped through the darkness and found something square that she couldn't shake loose. She grabbed hold and then released the desk, pulled herself up to the thing she couldn't see, and caught a glimmer of red to one side. It hurt to turn her head. Her vision swam vertiginously, but then firmed.

An emergency exit sign. The power might have gone out in the room, but the exit signs apparently still worked. That meant she must be clinging to one of the banks of computers. Cautiously, she pulled her legs underneath her and tried again. The mud pushed her towards the door. If she could just get her legs working, she stood a chance of finding her way out of here.

She tried putting her weight on them and staggered. Released the computer and lost her balance again, went down, but the mud oozed her along with it towards the exit. By the time she reached the door, she had her legs under her and, filthy and sodden, stumbled out the door.

The curved corridor was a darkened tunnel, a river of mud flowing down its length. She used the curved wall to hold herself upright and staggered on, into the darkness. Somewhere ahead would be a tunnel that Xavier and the others had taken to get in. Somewhere ahead she would find him.

She -reached-, and a sudden tremor almost sent her to her knees. She hauled herself upright, pressing her face against the concrete wall. She couldn't find him. She couldn't find Landon or Fi or Gleason, either. Had something happened? Had a roof come down and killed them all? Fear bubbled up in her chest and she fought back tears. Tears weren't going to help her get out of here. Someone had to be able to stop anyone who might pick up her father's work. It had cost too much, too many lives, to let it go further.

A dim red light came into view through the darkness ahead. Another exit sign, and the most blessed thing she'd seen in a long time. She followed it into a side tunnel, but she hadn't gone far when the mud rose up to her knees, her thighs, and she back-pedaled to the central corridor before it got any deeper. Something had happened in that tunnel. If it had been clear before, for the others, it wasn't any longer. Something had breached the walls.

The fact she might be trapped wasn't something she could contemplate. She struck off down the curved tunnel again, praying that another exit sign would come into view. The stench of sour mud and rot made her eyes water. She dragged her fingers along the rough concrete, praying she hadn't been a fool to seek another exit. Every moment she ventured farther meant that the way behind her became less passable. Had she consigned herself to drowning in this mud hole?

Maybe it would be fitting. There would be no family to miss her. Her father had never wanted her and Xavier was dying. And stupid, morbid thoughts like that were not her way. She had always lived her life to make her own way, to be dependent upon nothing and no one.

Her fingers slipped off the wall into a void and she almost fell. Another opening, another spoke tunnel, but there was no red exit sign beaming hope. So maybe she had trapped herself, but she was not going to give up hope. She struck out into the deeper darkness, the mud rising around her calves. But maybe the air was fresher here, as if the mud had not filled this area yet. A few more slogging strides and the level of mud began to recede. A few more strides and her bare feet—just when had she lost her shoes?—slipped on only the barest sheen of mud on the cold floor. She hurried along, her fingers crossing metal plated doors, small windows set in them so she wondered if there were people trapped beyond them. But there were no calls, no one pounding on the walls. Perhaps it was where the Gifted had been held until they were needed.

A shudder ran through the walls and the concrete groaned. Dust and debris peppered her shoulders and filtered down, filling the darkness with dust. A low boom came from somewhere behind her and a rush, like wind on water.

She froze, sneezed from the dust, and turned. A rush of wind shoved her sodden hair off her shoulders. Wind? The stench of something fetid and dead filled the tunnel. Old mud and decay and moving towards her. The tunnel walls began to vibrate and hum, the tune rising to a horrible pitch. Something came.

She swung around and ran, sliding on the floor. Tripping and falling. The vibration in the walls grew and made it almost impossible to run. She bounced from wall to wall and suddenly realized she wasn't in darkness anymore. Ahead, a phosphorescent green arrow glowed on the wall pointing upwards into darkness.

Her feet slid through mud as she tried to stop. She grabbed hold of a ladder rung and clung to it, realizing mud flowed around her ankles again and was rising fast. Mud. The hole in the installation room had probably given way. The entire installation was filling with mud and she *would* drown if she couldn't find her way out.

She grabbed the ladder rung and hiked herself up using adrenaline for power, scrambled up the wall until she perched on the lowest rung and listened to the rapid flow of the mud while her heart pounded.

There was only one way to go, and that was up. To go back in the mud was to be swept away for good. Blindly she climbed up the rungs into a narrow shaft. Up towards sunshine and air, she could only hope.

Then her head drove hard into the ceiling and she stopped dead.

§

When the lights went out, Landon was cautiously following the well-lit tunnel into the bowels of the earth. At least that was what it had felt like. Now he had the strangest impression of being trapped in a birthing canal, and all the walls pressed in around him so he could not seem to get enough air to breathe. He clung to the wall, fighting the fear that roped his limbs and that seemed to steal all the strength right out of him.

He was not afraid. He hadn't been afraid when he'd come down into the tunnel and had discovered the place where two bodies had lain half encased in a wall. A Gifted had come this way, and when he opened himself he tasted cedar and incense. The dark one—Xavier. So he'd kept on coming, figuring Vallon's dark foreigner would deal with any danger.

Until the lights went out. He fought back the seeds of panic, would not let them grow. He was stronger than this. He might not be an agent, but he had a brain. He could think his way through any situation. He could.

The trouble was that the very air he breathed held too much power and too much scent. It was like a kaleidoscope, so overpowering no human brain could make sense of it and his faculties overloaded trying. He shook himself and pushed away from the wall. Something was horribly wrong here, and yet threaded through everything was the scent of ashes of roses that spoke of Vallon. And as he shoved through the miasma of power, Vallon's presence only grew until it was like she became the walls, the earth, the air he breathed, in a show of power so incredible he could barely believe it was his pigeon.

His Vallon, for truly he'd raised the girl every bit as much as Francis Drake had.

Gild the Lily, indeed. Whatever Francis Drake had done to the girl had truly brought her far beyond anything he'd thought possible. The upper end of the upper end of his population curve, surely.

The walls trembled around him and a swell of concussion rushed through the confined space and shoved clean air out to be replaced by fetid. The entire tunnel shuddered and then went quiet, and a sound like wind came towards him. He pressed back against a wall and the wind sound changed to the sound of rapid footfall and voices. Red lights flickered to life, and half-seen figures in white coats and armed figures rushed past for the exit Landon had left behind. So something was happening or had happened.

When the sound of running died away, he kept going, creeping ever deeper until the tunnel he'd followed met a curving tunnel filled with the sound of something moving. The floor reflected red in the emergency light and he stepped up to his ankles in mud. More gun shots came from his left, but distant, and he struck out at once, wishing he had some weapon. Anything would be better than having nothing in his hands.

The vibration in the tunnel increased and so did the mud. A huge crash and the squeal of tearing metal that spoke of something massive having met its end, and then suddenly figures came out of the darkness. Tall, three abreast, and more massed behind, and there was no doorway to duck into, no place to hide.

He -reached- and the flare of Gifted filled the tunnel. Gleason. The foreigner, and the detective with his strange-colored, unGifted light. But the foreigner's light wasn't right. He stepped up to meet them, and Gleason and the detective almost stumbled into him.

"Snow?" Gleason rumbled. "What the hell?"

"I came as fast as I could, but apparently I've missed all the fun."

"Not much fun," grunted Bryson. "Vallon's friend, here, has been shot and there's a whole boatload of people we need to get out."

Landon took in the haggard look of de Varga. In the blood-stained light, he barely looked alive. Not good at all. He looked back at Gleason. "Where's Vallon?"

"Trying to find her friend," Gleason said, and hefted the injured man's arm over his shoulder

"Fi?"

The detective nodded as the tunnel lurched around them. Somewhere in the crowd behind them a woman screamed. "Can we get moving? There's no saying how long this place is going to stand. The whole damned ceiling in that room could come down."

"This way," Landon turned and led them back the way he'd come. If Vallon was behind them, then he darned well had to get the foreigner out and to safety. He had to heal him, and by the look of him, that wasn't going to be any simple matter.

The tunnel leapt and shuddered and the reek of mud and decay built behind them. De Varga came to at one point, but the rigors of the run for the exit tunnel sent him out again. They had to keep moving, the crowd of Gifted pressing behind them, the air taking on the stench of roses so powerful it was almost gagging, the floor and ceiling shuddering around them; and then suddenly a frame of sunlight hung above them.

Blessed blue sky and sunlight beckoned as he scrambled up the steep stairs and spilled out onto the platform. He stumbled out of the way as Gleason and Bryson hauled the dead weight of Xavier de Varga out and to the side, and then waves of filthy men and women climbed out, blinking as if they hadn't seen the sunlight in years.

A hot wind ran through the trees, sending leaves rattling; the platform swayed and a sound like a cannon came from a distance away, followed by the rushing sound of water. From the tunnel, a cloud of dust and fine spray erupted with a rumble. The platform shook and shuddered and canted sideways so that the concrete stairs groaned, moaned, and then the screeching sound of metal tearing filled the forest clearing.

The platform canted further and Landon clung to the wooden railing as the concrete stairwell lifted up and tore itself sideways. Suddenly the platform came loose and crashed back down onto the forest floor. Landon rushed to the stairwell, but where previously the stairs had led into the darkness of the tunnel, now they ended in mud and a sucking vortex as the muddy pond was sucked into the underground complex.

His legs gave under him and he sat, staring down. The entrance was gone and Vallon was still down there.

CHAPTER 29 — A PRAYER FOR THE HEAVENS

The roar, and the fetid odor of mud, filled the tunnel. There was no question it flowed faster now, filling the space below in a swiftly flowing wall of mud and debris as she fumbled to understand what blocked her. She had hooked one elbow through a ladder rung and tried to secure her slippery feet as she fumbled blindly above her.

Cold metal. Circular shape, but smooth, without any catch she could feel to make it open. An escape hatch, though, she was certain. All she had to do was figure out how to get it open. Then her searching fingers found a small, square pad along the wall almost in front of her face. She touched it and a small light came on, illuminating the pale orange face of a numbered keypad. A lock, and she needed a code to get out. If she'd worked here, she undoubtedly would have it memorized.

"No," she groaned and looked below her. The reflected light on the swiftly rising mud below said she didn't have long. Certainly not long enough to try all the combinations a ten button pad would allow for. She punched in her father's birthday—who knows, it might work. A red flight flashed its denial. There was no way this would work—not when she didn't even know how many numbers were in the combination.

The touch of mud on her bare feet sent her searching for an opening clasp. There had to be something. There had to be a way out of here. *Think!*

She closed her eyes and stilled her breath, ignoring the way the mud lifted over her ankles and made the metal rung almost too slippery to stand on. Once before she had gone through a locked door. That had been a wooden door. This was metal. It should be easier.

She closed her eyes and reached out into the metal. Yes, there were the clasps, broad spokes of metal that held the cap closed above her. Get rid of the spokes and the hatch should open.

Her hands shook as she tried to steady herself within the small tunnel. The mud was up over her knees now and the force of the current tugged downward. If she fell, she would not get back here.

The metal spokes had to be her focus, a place to spend some of the lavender energy that burned in her veins. She sent it flaring into the metal and almost fell when the walls and the rung became almost too hot to touch. She narrowed her focus, and surely to goodness the metal must be hot enough. If she could just get enough purchase, she should be able to push the hatch open.

The mud was almost up to her waist until she lifted herself up and grabbed the top rung with both hands. She pressed her shoulders and neck against the metal and shoved. Nothing moved. Her breath sounded like sobbing in the dwindling space she had left. Again.

She strained against the hatch and something moved. Her feet slipped on the lower rung and she barely caught herself before the mud took her. Shivering, she hauled herself up again. Pressed once more, and sent a bolt of energy into the door.

It exploded upwards and a draught of fresh air blew into her face. She hung there, staring into the sweetest blue, like a lover's eye. The sky. The sun. The world.

She forced herself up the last five rungs and fell out onto muddy barrens that surrounded an unnaturally circular lake that, even as she watched, had its water level receding.

§

They found her that way, sitting in the silent, empty lakebed, her muddy clothes and hair baked dry so when they came to her, she cracked as she looked up into their expectant faces. She just needed a moment to catch her breath, to believe she was here and safe. And there, coming over the lip of the lakeshore, was Gleason, deathly grey and cadaverous as always. There was Landon, small, and somehow still pristine, though he was barefoot and his white suit was filthy. And there was Jason, his gaze still watchful and hungry as ever, so she had to look away.

No Xavier.

"Did he die, then?" She couldn't find the strength to cry, because there was still so much to do for Farrah and all the others affected by the quake. Buildings down. Entire towns gone. The mixed-up landscape of what had once been the Great Plains.

"No. But we need to get him to a doctor right away. We only stopped when Landon said you were here."

She glanced up at him. "I guess I should thank you. And Fi? Did she make it out?"

Gleason nodded. "Your little friend seems to have come into her own. She's organizing things to get the Gifted out of here and back to civilization. It's going to take some time, because phones and such aren't working."

She took that in. At least she'd made it out. Fi had done a lot, getting Francis Drake's attention long enough for Vallon to get free and take over the attack. It was Fi who had made ending the quake possible. Heck, Fi had made a lot more than that possible, and had filled a hole in Vallon's life she hadn't even realized existed.

She looked out across the drying base of the lake, at the fish flopping in the sunlight and the egrets circling overhead. Change needed to be done before she could get on with her life. Xavier would understand. He was all about the duty.

"You better get going with Xavier, then. Get him help. I've still got things to do to set things right." She looked up over her shoulder. "I'll be okay. I'll meet you at Elizabeth Ducharme's place."

Jason looked like he was going protest, but a glance from Landon made him shrug and turn.

She -reached- into the earth and barely heard their retreating footsteps as she loosed the lavender-scented power she held. So much power it could burn her out, but she had to chance it. For Farrah's sake. To give a chance to all the other Farrah's across the broken country. She reached across the landscape and did her best sculpting, resurrected the towns, the cities and villages, the forests and drained wetlands, smoothing the destructive vagaries of Change until the great plains again lost themselves in the folded foothills of Wyoming, and the cities of New York and Lexington and Birmingham and all the others stood as if the Change and the quake had never been.

Last of all she rebuilt the town of New Madrid, placed Elizabeth Ducharme in her kitchen, and charming Farrah, so much like Vallon had once been—innocent and full of possibilities—helping her bake cookies. Yes, things would be good for them still. And the lake in front of her, whatever it was, would be filled with water and silver fish that drew herons and kingfisher and boys with fishing rods with their fathers.

When she opened her eyes, she lay beside the perfectly circular lake that must reflect the secret, destroyed installation that had once been under its surface. The grave of her father—or the man who had never been a father to her except in name. The sky had turned azure and a faint dusting of stars had found their way into the eastern sky, like a prayer for the heavens that would come later that night. It had been a long time since she looked up at the sky. Yes, her predecessors had used the stars to measure the earth, but for years now, her vision had been tied to the ground. To her father. He had bound her here somehow, because she had wanted him so badly she had forgotten to reach higher.

She -reached- and the flare of Gifted came from nearby. Amongst them was the familiar taste of anise and mint that could only be Fi, her BFF, her sister, even though for a while Vallon had forgotten and had tried to use Fi as only a tool, just as her father had tried to use her. The shame was almost too much to handle.

Further she -reached-, because she had to know. Gleason's crackling flare came though the distance. A town not far away. She realized, now, that he had always been on her side, a warrior protector. With him was the low simmering flame she knew was Landon, her friend and mentor, and yet the heart of him locked forever away. And there, powerful in the gathering darkness, pulsed the flame she would always know. Xavier lived. He would live in her heart always.

She sank into his power, sank into him, and felt his awareness and his afterburn flare, then pass away into slumber. Her body burned with promise of him, but she followed him there into the darkness of rest just as she would always follow him anywhere.

Sleep now. She had no need of the man she had called father.

When she woke she would climb the banks of the lake. She would grieve the lost and then reclaim the people who were truly her family.

To Read the exciting first chapters of *Aftermath*, book 3 in the American Geological Survey Series, *turn the page.*

ABOUT THE AUTHOR

Author of the unique Cartographer Universe series, Karen L. Abrahamson writes poetry, short fiction, and fantasy, romance and mystery novels, as well as non-fiction for newspapers and magazines. In her words, "a bad day of writing is still better than the best day working for a living."

A born wanderer, she currently lives in the Metro Vancouver area of Canada with two Bengal cats who channel James Dean's attitude. When she isn't writing she can be found with a camera and backpack in fabulous locations around the world.

To learn more about her, visit her website at www.karenlabrahamson.com

To find more of her writing, visit www.twistedrootpublishing.com.

To read more of Vallon Drake and the American Geological Survey,
turn the page for the first chapter of *Aftermath*,
Book three in the saga of Vallon Drake and the AGS.
Coming in January 2014

AFTERMATH

Chapter 1 – The Scent of Home

The rear of the red brick building hunched silently amongst its playing fields and the tall cedars and spruce that spread a rolling carpet across the hilly countryside. Though the wind carried the dampness of the nearby ocean, here a mélange of scent as rich as any spice market reached Vallon Drake's nose. Cedar, yes, but also the cut grass-coriander-warmed honey-bicycle grease-cinnamon-licorice-baked bread and oh-so-many more scents of the Gifted faculty and students at the American Geological Society Academy. She knew it was the academy even though she didn't know how she got there. It sat in Redmond, Washington and she was—where was she?

The question passed through her and was gone because something was wrong. Not only was there no sound of the wind in the trees, but, like a gaping wound in a beautiful woman's cheek, fear ached through the looming brick building, dark as licorice but dense and metallic like copper. She recognized it too well, and the Academy with its Gifted children should not have that scent.

Had never made all the hairs of her body stand on end the way they did now. All the years she had attended after the disappearance of her father and she might have been a problem child for the academy faculty, but she'd never been afraid. Even through the student hazing, the younger students never oozed the stink she smelled.

The rear door to the dormitories opened easily and she stepped inside and stopped. Usually the dorms were the bustling center of student society—seniors preying on the freshmen, boy-meets-girl drama, the melt-downs of academic pressure. Now the air ached with unnatural quiet. Nothing moved. No one ran for a late class.

"Hello?" she called just slighter louder than her normal voice.

No response. The beige-painted corridor and common room ached around her and the silence said she would find the same emptiness in the five floors overhead, or else she had lost all sense of hearing. Something was clearly wrong because it was almost impossible to find a time when no one was in the dorms. She closed her eyes and -reached-

out through the brick walls to the school itself.

A blast of fear scent her stumbling back against the wall. What the hell?

Many Gifted, their flaming presence burst into the air and she turned, following her sense of them. The gymnasium, crowded with students and faculty, their flames milling and mingling. And there was Smith, the mustachioed and ginger-haired-now-grey haired headmaster whom, she was sure, had turned grey because of her. Other faculty she recognized. And students from the youngest with their barely visible flame of incipient Gift, to seniors who showed the same kind of steady flame about them as the faculty did. Everyone was there. And a small cadre of those who had no Gift at all.

Clearly something wasn't right. The fear was palpable and laid a thick copper-blood and bile taste on her tongue. This was early September when the faculty expected to inject as much academic knowledge into their student's brains as possible before refocusing their attention on the truly important work of the academy: training the next generation of Gifted to save the American landscape from foreign and domestic acts of terrorism that might redraw it.

She hurried to the gymnasium, following the empty linoleum-floored halls, pushing through the doors. When she entered the stench of fear almost took her legs out from under her, but no one turned in her direction, not even when she staggered back against the wall. All their attention focused on the man with the microphone standing at the exit door that led to the parking lot next to the playing field outside.

He was tall and brawny with hair the color of sand and features that seemed to have been eroded of everything memorable and human except the danger he posed. Like the gun he carried. Large. Modern. Automatic. Anyone tried anything and a strafe of fire could take down everyone. Doubly so when she spotted similar weapons held by similar men placed strategically around the room.

The faculty had been herded to one side of the room. Ginger-haired Headmaster Smith stood in front of them arguing with another of the armed men. Then the man suddenly hefted his weapon and shot Headmaster Smith in the leg. He went down in a spray of blood and the faculty surged towards the children. The students children tried to run, but the men with the guns blocked them. All in silence.

Vallon stood over Headmaster Smith as he clutched his leg. Mrs. Church, the school's first aid attendant rushed to tie a tourniquet above the oozing wound. Their mouths moved, clearly talking, but there was no sound. Nothing. None of the screams she saw in the eyes of the people around her. None of the terror in the children's gaping mouths.

What the hell was going on, on so many levels? She knelt beside Smith and went to help him sit up, but her hand passed right through his shoulder like cold mist. She stumbled back on her bum, but then realized Smith had stopped yelling. He searched around him as if he'd somehow sensed her. His lips mouthed 'Vallon'. She scrambled up and stood over him and wasn't sure what to do. A dream? A nightmare? Something truly happening? She reached her hand out for him again. There were her long fingers, the torn cuticles around her finger nails. But she swiped through Smith's outstretched hand even as he tried to close his fingers. She tried again and placed her palm against his and his scent of hickory and old socks suddenly poured in her senses. His flame beat around her and was swiftly joined by pain and fear. Not for him, for his charges.

His mouth moved as if he was speaking to her, his gaze blindly passing over her. Beyond him, the armed men had herded the children towards the exit, even as the senior class tried to keep the younger children protected. Tears on faces. Stumbling and fear so great it was like a giant weight on her chest.

What the hell was happening here? The armed men were too practiced, too methodical as if they were used to taking orders. This wasn't some random attack on a private school. These men were soldiers and they were here for a purpose and that purpose had to do with the AGS school.

When the children were pushed outside, she abandoned Smith and ran across the floor and outside to see. Trucks: ten of them. Panel trucks with signs like Piggly Wiggly, and Cheetos and best Bagel and Ice Cream World. The men slid one of the panel trucks open and began shoving children inside, standing room only. Then they rolled the rear door down and locked it and she could imagine the sounds of the screaming, the small fists on the metal, but then the truck started up and left its place in line, to be replaced by another. And another. And another.

And she could do nothing. She was in New Madrid recovering, and yet she was here.

She fell back inside to where the faculty stood at gunpoint, Smith on the ground in front of them, his hand placed palm up on his lap as if he truly believed he'd felt her presence. She'd always thought of Smith as a bit of curmudgeon with little humor and far less imagination. Totally wrong, apparently. She knelt down beside him and placed her palm against his and felt again the flare of heated hickory. His gaze searched again, but he finally quit looking. Just gazing ahead, weary resignation in his eyes.

She looked back at the guns. The children were gone now and there were only the teachers and too many men with too many guns.

[Who?] she sent knowing it was highly unlikely he could hear her when she couldn't hear him.

Then he seemed to look directly at her and his lips formed a word she recognized.

Amundson.

That was when the men started firing.

§

The dark wood stair railing had the unnaturally smooth feel of plastic under Vallon's hand as she came unsteadily down the stairs to the meeting in Elizabeth Ducharme's living room. Had she really seen what she'd seen, or was it a dream? A dream with all the nightmarish aspects of foretelling that she would never accept as possible. Yes, she might have the Gift, but foretelling dreams was nothing more than fairytales.

Still... She swallowed. The disturbing images seemed on continuous replay in her head and coupled with the plastic feel of the house and thick tang of ozone and lightning on the air-conditioned air, nothing felt right and she really thought she might be sick.

Sure, the ozone and ether and the plastic feeling of the house were the normal results of the power that had undone the devastation of the New Madrid quake. The whole town probably felt that way. Actually, given the wide swath of quake destruction, it was likely that she'd experience this finger-nails-on-blackboard feeling of Change just about anywhere in the American Midwest. The afterburn and the too vivid images of the AGS Academy made it feel like her head might explode at any moment.

She clung to the railing and walked cautiously to the main floor of the house that had previously been destroyed by the quake. But now it stood right where it should be and Elizabeth Ducharme and her daughter, Farrah, were safely back home none the wiser that their world had been destroyed one minute and restored the next. Such was the power of the Gift.

The living room was filled with a pleasant mix of scents—old spice, anise and mint, baby's breath and the powerfully attractive scent of incense and cedar of Lebanon. At least it would be attractive if not for the fear-stink that clung to her nostrils and tainted everything. She held onto the doorframe to the room decorated liberally with feathers and bird-flocked wallpaper and took a deep breath, because everyone was waiting for her— they just didn't know about the information she was bringing. The canaries in the huge cage by the front window set off a flurry of singing as she limped to Xavier's side. The whole place was like a flipping aviary.

Gregor Gleason, the ex-Chief of the ultra-secret American Geological Survey, the organization that was supposed to keep America safe from just the kind of attack that had occurred here at New Madrid, sat his cadaverous frame uneasily on one of Elizabeth Ducharme's uncomfortable looking straight-backed chairs drawn in from the dining room area at the back of the room. His skin was still slightly grey from his time in captivity, when Homeland Security had decided that he was an enemy of the state. Beside him, on one end of the bird-feather patterned couch, perched Landon Snow. Her fastidious, diminutive mentor plucked at the pleats of his trousers, but he looked up as she entered. His strange, blue-pink eyes almost seemed to glow the way the light caught them through the gauzy living room curtains. To Landon's right sat Fi Murdoch, Vallon's best friend, her blonde pixy cut hair scrubbed clean of the mud she'd been covered in last time Vallon had seen her at the quake site. Beside her sat Jason Bryson, the tall, café au lait-skinned, Seattle Police Detective who had for some reason followed her here just like he'd been following her around in Seattle. It made her just a tad uncomfortable.

All her comrades. All had helped deal with the New Madrid quake, but it was the last person in the room who held her gaze. She knelt beside the feather-print Queen Anne chair and the tall, dark and mysterious man who sat there. Her lover, Xavier de Vargas. His ragged dark hair hung over his collar and his forehead and his skin was pulled tight across his hawkish features that always reminded her of Bedouins in long blue robes crossing a distant desert. But now his normally olive-toned skin was sallow and his hands made white-knuckled fists on his thighs.

"Xavier." She leaned in and chanced a kiss on his lips even though her afterburn raged as soon as she saw him. There was only one way to deal with the pain of having used the power and a most pleasurable way, at that, but this was not the time. When their lips touched she received the familiar sense of connection to this man who was everything in the world, but this was a wounded Xavier. She could see it in the slight wince as he moved and in the intensity of his black eyes and in the dark streaks that ran through his flaming essence when she -reached- to see him. "Shouldn't you be in bed?"

A single left-right of his head. "Snow has patched me up for the moment. I will do until I can get further medical attention." He frowned. "*Bela Menina*, are things well with you?"

Such a charming accent. "Always. With you."

But she swung back to Landon and the others. "Shouldn't he be in a hospital?"

Landon gave his usual slight shrug and smoothed the tip of a very pink tongue over his almost translucent lips. "With a bullet lodged in the chest, I should think so, but our mysterious friend does not seem so inclined. I can do the surgery myself, but I need the proper supplies."

Xavier had been shot in the battle to stop an earthquake that would have destroyed America as a free country. Vallon's rogue-agent father had learned how to harness the power of Gifted to unzip the fault lines along New Madrid and would have destroyed everything from Colorado to New York.

Tell them about her vision/dream/fortelling? She wasn't sure how to begin. "How do we get the equipment?"

She reached for Xavier's hand, but then stopped herself. In his condition, the last thing he needed was to have to fend off the afterburn that must be radiating off of her. Xavier, too, simmered with his own use of power, but in his condition, dealing with the afterburn was far less a priority.

"Well, Pigeon, we could look for a surgical dealership and purchase the instruments, but I suggest that moving your friend and ourselves out of here might be the first order of business."

Gleason was nodding. "He's right. Amundson's gone nuts over the Gifted. I'd still be his prisoner if Detective Bryson hadn't gotten us both out. He'll be gunning for us now, and though we tried to cover our tracks, there's no question he'll be coming after us. It's only a matter of time before he finds this little hide out."

She looked back at Xavier, calculating. Chief of Homeland Security in Seattle, Amundson on the warpath could never be good and it jived with the horror she'd lived in her vision/astral travel whatever. The man was a menace. But Xavier didn't look able to travel anywhere.

"Where are you suggesting we go?" She stood up protectively behind Xavier's chair.

Landon looked around the room and then down at his hands again. "I can't think of too many safe places right now, but I do know of one. It's in the desert outside of Las Vegas. A little anomaly I discovered a number of years back. Off the map you might say and completely safe, especially from people like Amundson." He glanced at Jason and nodded. "No offence intended."

Jason shrugged. "None taken." He was the only unGifted in the room.

Gleason shook his bald head. "I won't be going. Amundson has got to be stopped. If I know him at all, after losing me he'll be arresting every other Gifted he knows of. Given what he did to me, I hate to think what he could do to the others. I sent word to scatter before I left, but I doubt everyone was able to get out—not with their families." He hefted himself out of the chair. "I'm headed for Washington. Homeland Security head, Fitzsimmons, might be a power-hungry fool in some ways, but he's not stupid. If I can show him that Amundson is out of control and actually weakening the country, then maybe he'll remove him and put things back they way they were. Besides, he needs us to deal with the rogue Gifted who caused the quake. The destruction of their installation won't have got them all."

There was a pause of disbelief in the room, and Vallon felt her skin crawl. If her father was still alive he had to be stopped, and she was the one to do it, but Gleason shook his head.

"I've got to do something, and running and hiding is not my thing. I'm a bureaucrat and I know how to get things done. Washington is my job."

And what was hers? Vallon's fingertips brushed the edge of Xavier's shoulders from where they rested on his chair back, but she should be going with Gleason if he was taking on her father.

"So we're just going to allow Amundson to drive us out of Seattle?" Jason asked with a frown that placed a deep V across his forehead. "That doesn't seem right to me. And what about the other people he's hurting? Are we just going to let him do it? Round up the Gifted in Seattle and do whatever he wants to them?"

All eyes shifted to Jason.

"Why should you care, Detective Bryson? You aren't one of us?" Landon asked.

"I'd say like hell I'm not." He shrugged. "I might not have the Gift, but I happen to have a little talent to know when your Gift is being used and he wants that. I'd prefer to have my life back." His gaze flickered around the room and landed on Vallon. "I'm prepared to go back to Seattle and try to stop him from there, but I can't do it alone. Heck, can't one of you just wipe him out?"

Vallon met Landon's gaze. It said Jason might have a point, but if her father was out there....

She swallowed and took a deep breath, because at this point if they didn't stop Amundson's destruction of the Gifted there'd be no one left to stop the rogues. "I think Jason's right. There are too many innocent's potentially going to be hurt by what he's doing."

Tell them about what she'd seen? But she didn't know if it was true. Given all she'd been through in the past few days, it *could* simply be dream product of a very overwhelmed mind. It could.

But Amundson did need to be dealt with, because he could potentially lead a crusade that could destroy everything the Gifted had built in the United States. It could lead to a pogrom worse than the medieval witch hunts that had burned so many innocents. If the Chief was going to Washington and Landon was taking Xavier to the safety of his hideout to heal, then that left her to check on what Amundson was doing and stopping him if need be.

"I'll go. I have to get Maggie anyway. I can't depend on neighbors to feed her forever. Amundson might use her as a hostage." She managed a grin. Maggie, her flirty, opinionated, black and white cat was a problem child, but had been the only constant in her life for the past five years. The little vixen might treat anything Vallon did with disdain, but she was Vallon's cat and she didn't leave her little buddy behind.

"*Bela Menina*, rethink this idea, please." Xavier reached up and caught her hand, pulled it onto his shoulder and the touch of his warm dry fingers, and the throb of power up through his shoulder washed over her like a heady perfume of cedar. The afterburn flared, but he somehow controlled it as their essences merged. It became a slow, banked throb of desire that was fixated on him. He wanted her. He wanted her with him where he could keep her safe.

With the deepest of reluctance she slipped her hand free and came around in front of him. "Jason's right, Xavier. What if Gleason can't do what we need in Washington? Then someone has to be on the ground to act. Next to you, I'm the best one to do it. Besides, they won't expect me to come waltzing back to Seattle. Not right into the center of the fire, so to speak." She looked at the others. "Am I right?"

Landon thought a minute, his gaze making small leaps from her to Xavier, assessing. Finally he gave a small nod and that was something because Landon had the quickest mind she'd ever seen. Sometimes it almost seemed like he could read the future—or maybe it was just that he set people in motion so the future unfolded as he planned. It was an ability she wished she had. She'd create a place where she and Xavier could be alone to explore the bounds of their love for the rest of their lives. But apparently that wasn't about to happen now. She turned back to Xavier.

"It makes sense, Xavier. And I won't be able to help Landon with your surgery. I'd just be standing around going crazy with worry until it's all over."

Xavier's fathomless gaze seemed to drink her in. Then his hand came up and he ran a knuckle down the side of her face with an intimacy that sent shock waves running through her. Everyone in the room had to see the flames erupt out of her head. The way the afterburn's lust burst forth for just a moment.

"You—you're not supposed to do that." At least not in front of the others where she couldn't just jump his bones.

His hard mouth quirked in a wicked grin. "You are intent on going to Seattle with a handsome man. I wished to remind you of me."

And he had. The memory of that sensuous burst seemed to reverberate inside her and was distinctly connected to his incense and cedar of Lebanon scent.

"As if I needed reminding." But she turned back to the others as Fi uncurled her feet from under her.

"What about me? Do I go with you? I've got a job to get back to, Vallon." She pressed her hands between her knees and looked up at Vallon with those huge blue eyes that had always managed to get Vallon to do whatever she needed—until she disappeared as a child.

"I don't believe that's possible, Fi." Gleason's deep voice rumbled in the room. "Seattle is too dangerous for any Gifted and Amundson knows you are one of us. It is especially dangerous for a Gifted without full training. You'd have very little protection from him. No, I've given it some thought: Landon will need to focus on helping Xavier into hiding. That is dangerous work. Vallon and Detective Bryson go into their own dangers. I think the best course of action is for you to come with me to Washington."

She frowned. "But my job…."

"Fi. You should go with him. Really." If what Gleason said was true, then those children really were in serious danger. She had to tell. "I think… I think it has already started—Amundson's round up." All eyes centered on her and she steadied herself on Xavier's chair and told them about her dream-vision.

"The thing is, it wasn't a dream. Not really. Not the way Headmaster Smith could sense me and not the way he told me something I couldn't have known myself. If what I saw was right, then the entire school faculty is dead and all those children are in Amundson's hands. Capturing you, Fi, would just give him even more of a hold over us. I'm going to Seattle to check whether it really happened and, if it did, to find and free those kids."

"And so, young lady, you will come with me," Gleason said to Fi with finality. "Accept it. You cannot go back to your job as long as Amundson is looking. That leaves going into hiding with Landon or travelling with me. I think Landon will be busy enough as it is without also caring for you."

Her friend's frown had turned into an out and out scowl, but she finally nodded. Vallon gave her a hug. "Honey—Fi—you've made the right decision."

Fi glared up at her. "For you, maybe. So you don't have to have me around."

Vallon held FI away from her and looked her in the eyes. If you believe that, you're no longer the smart woman I know you are."

Finally, Fi's quirky smile came to life. She sighed." All right. You win again."

Vallon grabbed her in another hug, ignoring the uncomfortable flare of afterburn at the touch of another. "Fi, we will always be best friends and I will always need you around—and not for cycling. What you did saved us all. We—I—will always remember that. You're a hero."

Fi's pale features brightened visibly. "Really?"

"Absolutely. Without what you did, none of this would be here now." She waved her hand around the room at the ridiculous aviary-inspired room and the wafting scent of fresh cookies that came in from the kitchen at the back of the house. Farrah Ducharme's happy chatter was the background sound to their discussion.

Vallon looked at Chief Gleason. "So it's settled. You go to Washington with Fi, Landon takes care of Xavier and I go to Seattle to free those children and hopefully stop Amundson. Afterwards we'll deal with what's left of the rogue Gifted."

The others nodded. All except Xavier. His looked at her out of desert-night dark eyes and she inhaled his heady scent of incense and cedar of Lebanon. These people were what passed for family and Xavier most of all. They had come together here after their whole world had fallen apart. She leaned in to places a soft kiss on Xavier's lips.

Now they were making the decision to once more tear themselves apart.

Look for Aftermath coming in 2014.

FANTASY, ROMANCE AND HIGH ADVENTURE FROM TWISTED ROOT PUBLISHING

If you enjoyed this book, you might enjoy other titles from the Cartographer Universe available from Twisted Root Publishing in your local bookstore or wherever e-books are sold.

www.twistedrootpublishing.com

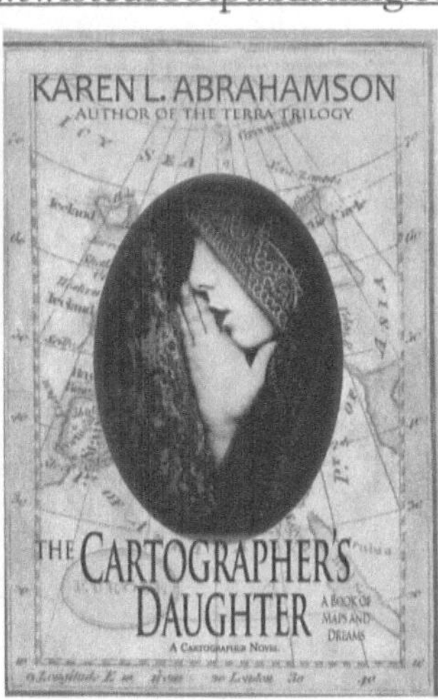